PRAISE FOR *THE TRIALS OF ADELINE TURNER*

"A perfectly paced rom-com that consistently places you right at the scene; the summer reading escape I didn't know I needed."
    —Emily Belden, author of *Hot Mess* and *Husband Material*

"*The Trials of Adeline Turner* is a fast-paced tale of dating in your thirties and learning to trust your inner voice. Brimming with wit, banter, romance, and heart, it has all the ingredients of the perfect beach read. I was charmed!"
    —Lindsay Cameron, award-winning author of *BIGLAW* and *Just One Look*

"The verdict is in, and Angela Terry's *The Trials of Adeline Turner* is a must-read! Readers will root for Adeline, and enjoy Terry's sparkling writing style, which creates the feeling of catching up with an old friend who has quite the story to tell. This novel has it all—but my favorite part? The ending which had me smiling from ear to ear, completely satisfied, albeit sad to leave the world of Adeline behind."
    —Ashley R. King, author of *Painting the Lines* (Ace of Hearts Book 1)

The Trials of Adeline Turner

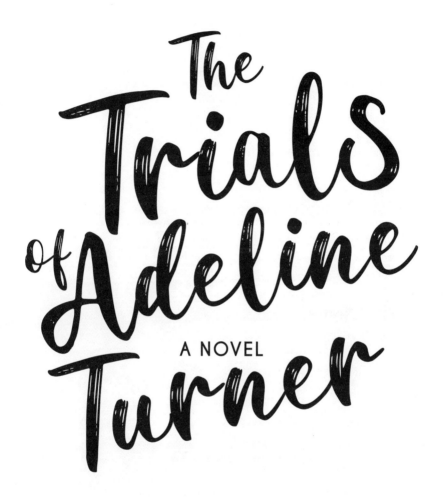

The Trials of Adeline Turner

A NOVEL

ANGELA TERRY

GIRL FRIDAY BOOKS

 GIRL FRIDAY BOOKS

Published by Girl Friday Books™, Seattle

Produced by Girl Friday Productions
www.girlfridayproductions.com

Design: Rachel Marek
Production editorial: Laura Dailey
Project management: Katherine Richards

Cover image credits: © Nataliia Semeshchuk/Shutterstock and © Andrey_Kuzmin/Shutterstock

ISBN (paperback): 978-1-7363243-7-0
ISBN (e-book): 978-1-954854-00-0

Library of Congress Control Number: 2021906018

First edition

For my parents,
Catherine and Richard Terry

CHAPTER ONE

Brad Summers was beautiful. There were no two ways about it. He had hazel eyes and the longest eyelashes I had ever seen on a boy. His thick, wavy hair was coppery brown, and when the sun shone on it, glimmers of light bounced back. And his smile. *Sigh* . . . It was the broadest, friendliest, but almost-shy-at-times smile, and my whole world revolved around seeing it. At age sixteen he was already six feet two and had the most perfect long, lean limbs and athletic body. My stomach flipped at the mere sight of him. Everything was perfect . . . except for the fact that he didn't know I existed.

Now, you may be wondering, Why is a thirty-three-year-old woman daydreaming about a sixteen-year-old boy named Brad? Well, because I was once a fifteen-year-old girl in love with him. Let me clarify. Not just love, but I *lovvvved* him with all the intensity of my innocent, teenage-girl heart.

When my family moved into our small neighborhood outside Appleton, Wisconsin, my ten-year-old self immediately noticed the boy who lived down the street. He was always nice, sometimes shy, but pretty much definitely not interested in me.

I understood. I was a frizzy-haired, bookish kid with glasses and a slight weight problem. By junior high, I had realized the sad importance of looks if one wanted to attract the opposite sex, and so I tried to lose my baby fat and made an effort. My love grew, but still nothing. In high school, Brad started dating a cheerleader who, by the way, I personally thought looked a bit like me, but obviously must've been much "cooler," since she got Brad and I didn't. However, it didn't last long, so I was able to keep my fantasies of becoming Brad's girlfriend alive.

Then, in my sophomore year, his family did the cruelest thing—they decided to move. Not just from the neighborhood, but to a different state. Not even a bordering state, but several states away, to California.

When I heard the crushing news, I knew this was my last chance, so I summoned the courage to ask him to the Spring Dance. Yes, I, bookish, quiet Adeline Turner, knocked on the door at 25 Ashbury Drive and asked for Brad. True, once his mother went to get him, I wanted to run away, but my knees were shaking too much. When he came to the door, he was still wearing what he'd worn to school that day, a plain gray T-shirt and faded Levi's.

"Hey, Addie," he said. "Um, what's up?"

Noting the confusion in his eyes, I swallowed and said—as coolly as I could muster—"Hey, Brad, I was just wondering if you wanted to go to the Spring Dance with me?" Before he could respond, I rushed on with my defense. "You know, since we've been neighbors for so long and now you're moving, I thought it might be nice as a last get-together." As if we had ever "gotten together" before.

He blinked a couple of times and then looked at me for what felt like a million years, but was probably only for a second, while I sweated it out on his front step. Then he beamed that beatific smile and said, "Yeah. That'd be fun." He stepped aside. "Do you want to come in?"

Feeling ready to pass out, I shook my head. "Thanks, but I better get home. Geometry test tomorrow." I shrugged non-chalantly, all the while bouncing on my toes, giving away my excitement. "We'll figure out details later?"

"Sure, okay. Then I guess I'll talk to you later."

"Yes, later. Bye!" I said, then quickly turned around to happy-dance home.

I think he was caught off guard, but being the nice guy he was and probably not wanting to hurt my feelings, he said yes. Brad said *yes!*

We shared a limo with two other couples who were Brad's friends. As soon as we stepped into the streamer-draped and balloon-filled gymnasium, Brad's friend Todd pointed to the bleachers and said, "Hey, there's Steve and Shannon." Off we trooped to the bleachers, where we unfortunately spent most of the evening. *So, this is what the cool kids do: they sit on the side-lines,* I remember thinking.

Other than one girl smuggling her parents' vodka in a hair-spray bottle, there was no sneaking out for beers or obvious debauchery. Brad's friends monopolized him and ignored me, though Brad was sweet and would check in to ask if I was okay. I understood this would be his last night out with his high school friends and I was the interloper. Once I realized the night wasn't going to be the passionate, declaring-our-love-till-our-dying-day experience I had hoped for, I settled on at least being in his pres-ence. But whenever a slow song came on, I felt a little pang in my heart and stared longingly at the sea of swaying spaghetti-strap dresses and ill-fitting blazers.

When the last song of the night was announced, some of the other couples in our group migrated to the dance floor, and Brad asked me, "Do you want to dance?" and my stomach did a little flip-flop as I nodded.

On the dance floor, I tentatively placed my hands on Brad's shoulders, he rested his hands lightly on my waist, and we shuffled awkwardly to Edwin McCain's "I'll Be" while avoiding eye contact, and I tried to burn into memory what I thought was the greatest moment of my life.

Since I lived closest to the school, I was the first to be dropped off at home. I assumed that Brad would stay in the limo until his stop. Instead, to my great surprise and delight, he said, "I'll get out here and walk home."

As the limo took off, I expected Brad to simply say he had a nice time and then head home. But no! He walked me to my front door. Standing at my doorstep, he kept shifting his weight awkwardly from one foot to the other, his hands shoved in his pockets, and his eyes gazing at me intently.

"So, Addie . . . ," he started, and then leaned toward me. My whole being froze and I felt goose bumps on my arms, and not from the chilly night air. Even with my lack of experience, I knew what was coming. Brad was going to kiss me! Maybe all this neighborly friendliness had just been an act, or maybe he had a change of heart during the dance. But I didn't care—I was about to be kissed by the boy of my dreams. When Brad's face was mere millimeters from mine, I closed my eyes.

Just as our lips were about to touch, the front door flew open, and my dad was standing there sounding a little out of breath as he said, "Addie, are you coming in?"

Startled, we jumped apart, and I shot a furious look at my dad. When I turned back toward Brad, he was already halfway across the front lawn, running backward, stumbling, his eyes wide open in fright.

"Um, see you at school!" he called out, and then turned around and ran home.

My heart crushed, I turned toward my father with eyes that silently asked, *Why did you take this from me?* before stomping up to my room.

I know now that it was because my father loved me and waited up for me to come home safely, and I imagine he couldn't quite bring himself to see his daughter kissed by a boy just yet. But at the time, none of that mattered. All I knew was that the moment was gone forever, and then Brad moved away.

You're probably thinking, if that's the worst thing that happened to you as a teenager, you've led a charmed life. Yes, it's been okay. I certainly wasn't popular in school, but I also wasn't quite a nerd. I didn't really have anything going for me to even bring that sort of attention, positive or negative, to myself. I flew under the radar as far as high school went and was still waiting for life to happen.

And please don't think I'm still pining away and saving myself for this one guy eighteen years later. That's certainly not the case. But let's just say, it made an impression.

After high school, and a handful of dates my junior and senior years that never resulted in relationships, I headed to college and fell in love "for real." My senior year, I met Tim, a fellow English major who I thought was wonderful, and stayed with him for the first few years after graduation. Tim and I both dreamed of becoming writers. During college, I even managed to write a novel about a young girl who had been abandoned by her mother. But as the rejections poured in during my senior year, I realized that I was the only person interested in reading my book. I shelved that dream and channeled my energy into something practical and applied to law schools, following in my father's career footsteps. *Lawyers do a lot of reading and writing, and it will pay the bills. You can always write in your spare time,* I naively consoled myself.

So I went off to law school in New York. Tim moved in with me and got a job at a coffee bar so he could focus on writing the next great American novel. But even after I had graduated and was hired as an associate in the corporate department by the prestigious Chicago law firm Gilchrist & Jenkins, Tim was still working in a coffee bar (albeit a different one), and I had yet to read, or even see evidence of, his manuscript. I secretly felt that Tim's dream had changed—he wanted me to support him while he spent his days reading and making coffee. But after footing my share of the bills and more, I felt taken advantage of and broke it off. Luckily for him, there was a pretty cashier waiting in the wings; so although broke, he certainly wasn't heartbroken.

Once I got settled in Chicago, I dated around a bit until I became quite serious with a new boyfriend, Gary, an accountant. But Gary had no desire to marry. Again, I think another secret motive was afoot. He simply had no desire to marry *me*. Even though I wasn't pressing for it, there is something a bit depressing about spending years with someone who is just biding time with you, waiting for "the one." I figured if I was ever going to meet my one, I should break up with this guy and did.

Unfortunately, though, I still haven't met "the one."

It's fine, I guess. I do want romance, but I'm just so darn busy. I'm still at the same law firm that hired me out of school. With more money in my pocket, I swapped the thick glasses for LASIK, so now the world can see my blue-green eyes. Every month, I visit an expensive salon to keep my unruly brown (or *caramel*, according to my stylist, who applies the color to my roots to keep the premature grays at bay) hair in shape, and I joined an expensive gym to keep the rest of me in shape. If my high school classmates could see me now, they'd be shocked.

From the outside, I look like the epitome of the smart, sophisticated career woman. But on the inside, I'm still that awkward, bookish kid waiting for someone to find out what a fraud I am.

I'm not telling you this to elicit sympathy, since I'm obviously doing pretty well. But let's face it—it would be nice to share this life with someone I love, and I'm still waiting.

CHAPTER TWO

*K*nock, knock, Adeline," interrupts my friend and fellow colleague Nora as she steps into my office. "So are you getting excited yet?" she asks. Tall, stunning, and blond, she could be Charlize Theron's long-lost younger sister. If Nora hadn't been so friendly to me on my first day, I probably would've been intimidated by her. Right now, she has a huge smile on her face. After spending the last few hours carefully drafting the terms of a financing agreement, I'm happy for any distraction, especially one that has Nora this enthusiastic.

"Excited? Excited for what?" I ask.

She gives me a good-natured sigh complete with an eye roll and begins rifling through some scattered mail on my desk. She finds what she's looking for and waves it at me. "Uh, Monterey?"

In her hand is a brochure for the 2016 Corporate Counsel Conference and Retreat. Not-so-exciting sounding, I know. But depending on where they are held, in this case California, they can be pretty fun.

"Oh yes!" I grab the brochure from her and start flipping through it. "I could use some spa treatments, and I think I read something about wine tasting."

"Yeah, the hotel looks great. I'm thinking of signing up for golf. Should we be a pair?" Nora asks in all seriousness. Bless her.

"Uh, no." I emphatically shake my head. "How 'bout I just meet you at the bar afterward?" Although I've played golf before, I do so badly, and given that the primary purpose of these conferences is networking, I wouldn't want anyone to equate my legal skills with my putting ones.

"Fine. Spinning at six?" Nora asks over her shoulder as she turns on her heel to leave.

"Yep, see you then."

"What's that about spinning?" Roger says as he saunters into my office carrying a large file. Oh, sorry. I mean, *Roger Hamilton III, Esq.*, according to his business cards. This, of course, lets you know there were probably two beady-eyed, creepy Rogers before him. My heart sinks a bit.

"Nora and I are going to the gym after work." *Ugh. Why did I say that?* Especially since Roger belongs to the same gym, right across the street from our office.

"Maybe I'll join you guys," he responds to what was *not* an invitation.

Nora spins around to look at me with her back to Roger, rolls her eyes again, and then turns toward the door. "Okay, guys. I'm outta here." She avoids Roger's leering eyes on her way out.

I think Roger likes me a bit. He definitely likes Nora a lot, but she's out of his league.

At age thirty-five, either stress or genetics are causing him to lose what once might've been a nice head of brown hair, and sitting at a desk all day surviving on takeout isn't doing his waistline any favors. The guy probably just needs a girlfriend to pull him together. But Roger is also pretty much a bigheaded, chauvinistic jerk who lets everyone else know what sort of dirt they are beneath his feet. So he's not really a big hit with the ladies, or with most of his colleagues either, for that matter.

The only good thing about him is that he pulls me onto a lot of projects. This is his one saving grace in my eyes because at a law firm, the more billable hours you have, the more secure your position and future with the firm.

"What can I do for you?" I ask.

"So," Roger says, dropping the file onto my desk, "I'm swamped with this AGU financial deal, and Dennis needs someone to do a quick review of these license agreements for Moonstruck Animation. Can you take a look?"

"Sure." I eye the stack of papers. "When does he need it by?"

"Tomorrow before five. He just wants an initial review. So don't spend too much time on it. Flag any issues and write up a memo with your findings and suggestions."

The file before me is at least eight inches thick!

"'Don't spend too much time on it,' huh?" I give him a skeptical smile.

Roger stares back at me blankly, not getting the joke—or more likely, not really caring. So I change tactics. "Okay. No problem." I smile politely.

Once he's out of my office, I look at the file again and sigh. But I've looked at quite a few of these types of agreements, so anything unusual should jump out at me, right? At least this is the pep talk I give myself.

Unfortunately, it was unusual. The reason it was so large was due to corporate acquisitions, name changes, and attachments and addendums that required further research on my part rather than just a quick review of terms, as Roger led me to believe. I end up working on it the rest of the morning and all afternoon until it's time to leave for the gym. Although I had planned on taking the file home with me, I somehow miraculously managed to get through most of it. Thus, my load is significantly lightened, and if I can get to the office at seven tomorrow morning, I can finish it. This is, of course, barring any unforeseen crises, also par for the course in my job.

* * *

Hmm, maybe I should go back to the office and finish that memo tonight, I think as I pack my gym bag after spin class. My phone rings, interrupting this thought.

"Hey, Bridget," I answer. "What's up?"

"Hey, you!" my closest friend says. "I just got out of work and was wondering if you wanted to go for a drink. I had a crazy day and *seriously* need to go out."

"Um, okay. But I'm leaving the gym right now, and I *seriously* need to take a shower. Do you want to meet me at my place? I'll tell the doorman to give you a key."

"Sure. But hurry up 'cause I need a drink, *now!*"

"Okay, okay." I laugh. "See you soon."

Guess that answers the question of whether to head back to work tonight. Instead, I rush home, let the doorman know to give Bridget my extra key, and jump into the shower. Although I'd like to wash my hair, there's simply no time for my regular blow-drying and straightening routine. I'll just wear it in a loose knot and suggest a dark bar.

I hear a noise as I'm coming out of the bathroom. "Bridget?"

"Yeah?" She appears in my bedroom with a glass and an open bottle of chardonnay that I had in the fridge. I raise an eyebrow at her.

"Oh." She holds up the bottle. "Hope you don't mind, but I couldn't wait. Today was insane!" She raises her arms above her head, glass and bottle still in hand.

I laugh at her dramatic expression. "No problem. Give me two secs to get dressed." Towel-clad, I head into my closet to select an outfit. "Should we do the Boarding House tonight?" I call out.

"Sounds good." I hear the clinking of glass as Bridget pours herself a glass of wine and begins, "Now let me tell you what happened today."

Bridget and I were roommates in college and have been inseparable ever since. I went to college close to home, but Bridget is originally from New York and came to Wisconsin just "for a change." Given that she moved straight back to Manhattan after graduating, I guess the small-town Wisconsin setting wasn't quite her scene. Since at that point I was ready for my own change, I applied to law school in New York, and we kept up our close friendship, if not our roommate relationship.

So how did we both end up in Chicago? Even though I loved New York, I knew that if I accepted a job at a firm there, I'd be in the office a hundred hours a week and would never have time to enjoy the city. So, I set my sights on Chicago, figuring that even though I would still put in long hours, being the Midwest, people would be more laid-back in some respects and I would only be working maybe seventy hours on my worst weeks. A year later, desperate to put some distance between herself and a hideous breakup and begin anew, Bridget transferred to her advertising firm's Chicago branch. And lucky me, she's still here today—my favorite partner in crime.

As I get dressed, Bridget complains about her day and clients who wanted major last-minute changes to a brochure that was scheduled to go to the printer that afternoon and couldn't understand why they couldn't change the text, design, and images right before it went. Bridget, by the way, is an art director—and looks it. Medium-length dark blond hair cut on an angle and funky-looking glasses frame her face. It's not surprising she went into design, since she has such a flair for the visual whether it's in fashion, interior design, or what she creates in advertising. This evening her clothes are tight and black, but usually she has on some eclectic printed blouse or sweater that I yearn to borrow. If I wore some of the things Bridget wears to the office, my clients wouldn't take me seriously. But if Bridget wore my clothes, people would assume she's a stiff with no creative insight.

I throw on a pair of slim dark jeans, a sleeveless silk blouse, and some sling-back sandals. True, it's still more Addie-looking than Bridget-looking, but this is a weeknight, after all. I apply my lip gloss, and we head out into the June night.

Even though it's only a Wednesday, the Boarding House, a popular wine bar, is buzzing. The tables are all packed, so we head straight to the bar, where the usual tall, dark, and toxic bachelors are milling around. As we approach, they give Bridget an appreciative once-over. I'm next. Then two guys, looking as if they stepped out of a Hugo Boss ad, make room for us. They're both attractive and (*yes!*) offer to buy us drinks. Since Bridget already vented back at my place, it's now flirting time. When Eric, the tall, blond, and strong-chiseled-features one asks what I do for a living, I reply matter-of-factly, "I'm a fashion buyer."

Okay, yes, I lied. I read some magazine article where the same woman flirted with men in different bars, and whenever they asked what she did for a living, she gave a different profession to gauge the men's reactions. Which profession bombed the most? That's right, the attorney. (I think that when most people learn you're a lawyer, you're immediately labeled as argumentative and boring all in one go.) So I've settled on fashion in these situations because, after all, I do buy clothes for myself. Oh yeah, and my bar age is twenty-eight, not thirty-three. All in the name of research, of course.

Bridget and I take off a little past midnight, but not before we give the guys our numbers. No one-night stands here, though. My life isn't a *Sex and the City* episode where single thirtysomethings go out every night (despite their demanding full-time careers) and hot sex is guaranteed. Demanding full-time career, yes. Scores of men, no.

* * *

When my alarm goes off at six, I curse that last "one for the road" drink I got talked into. Five hours of sleep. *Argh.* But I really need to make sure I finish typing up Roger's memo before the day gets too busy.

Although I live only a couple of El stops from my office, I decide to be a bit extravagant this morning and hail a cab, but not before hitting up the Starbucks across the street. Usually, when I see someone carrying a venti-sized coffee, I think, *Who needs twenty ounces of coffee? It's not a Slurpee.* Today, though, I put my scoffing aside and order a venti cappuccino with an extra shot for good measure.

When I check my email in the cab, I already have one from Roger asking what my status is on the licenses. Considering I have until five o'clock tonight and I've never been late on an assignment, this is a classic Roger micromanagement power move. I type back, Finished my review yesterday and will finish my memo by later today, and then take a gulp of my supersized coffee.

* * *

Like yesterday, I work through lunch and have a salad at my desk. In the afternoon, Nora comes by and tries to persuade me to go to a six o'clock spin class, but I tell her to ask me again at four. I finish my memo and work on some new assignments that magically appeared on my desk because, for some reason, the busier I am, the more work comes my way. The law of attraction, I suppose. I do manage to make it to class with Nora, but afterward I head back to work until ten to finish up another project. Unfortunately, this is how most of my days are—rinse and repeat.

When I get home, I feel my phone buzz with a text. I pull it out of my purse and see a message from Bridget: Still up? As I'm about to text back, I notice a missed text from—*oh my god*—tall, chiseled-featured Eric from the bar!

> Great meeting you last night. Would you be
> up for a drink this week?

My heart does a little skip. I'm amazed that he texted the next day, since most guys I meet wait a couple of days, or never make contact at all. It's too late to text him back tonight, so I'll wait until tomorrow. But with this sudden burst of energy, I call Bridget.

"Did you just get in?" she asks.

"Yeah. It was a long day."

"You poor thing," she says sympathetically. "But I guess that's why you get paid the big bucks."

"Yeah, 'the big bucks,'" I repeat in a worn-out monotone, then perk up. "Hey, guess what!"

"Hmm . . ."

"Eric texted!" No recognition on her end. "The guy from last night."

"Really?! What did he say?"

"Just that it was great meeting me and would like to meet up for a drink this week."

"Nice! He was cute."

"Yeah. But I'm gonna have to blow my cover as a fashionista and tell him what I do for a living."

"And at some point your age," Bridget says with a laugh. "Don't forget that."

"Oh yeah, that too. Hmm . . . But maybe not if I can get him to meet me at another dark bar or somewhere with flattering lighting . . ."

"Whatever. You're gorgeous and he won't care." She pauses. "Ooh, I wonder if his friend is going to call me? I could use a hot meal. And a hot guy actually." Now she's off on her own musing.

"Well, Bridge, I'm exhausted. Mind if I cut this short to go to bed?"

"Sure thing. Sweet dreams of the Eric kind," she says gleefully.

I chuckle. "Night, Bridge."

* * *

As I walk into the bar, I feel my palms begin to sweat as I scan the room. And when I spot Eric sitting at the bar alone, I become a lot more nervous because I think he might have gotten even hotter since Wednesday. *Wow!* I had texted Eric back this morning, saying that I'd love to meet for a drink, and he suggested tonight, and I figured, why not? So I'd worked through lunch to ensure I could make it out of the office in time for our date. But now I wish I had taken a little more care in getting dressed this morning, or had had time to go home and change, and immediately start smoothing down the creases on the front of my pants.

When Eric spots me, he smiles and waves me over. I smile and wave back and walk over to the empty stool beside him.

"Hi," I say, approaching him.

"Hey there." Eric stands and gives me a big hug while I make a mental note that he smells as good as he looks.

We have two cocktails at the bar, and I find he's also really easy to talk to and is even nicer than I remembered. Although maybe that's not saying much, since we met at a loud bar where we were forced to converse by shouting. When he tells me he's a broker, I come clean and mention that I'm an attorney.

"Sorry about that. I was a little buzzed and having fun." I shrug and take a sip of my drink.

Eric laughs. "Actually, that's a relief because I'm not the most fashionable dude." This warms my heart a little. "And besides, now that I know you're into a little role-playing . . ." He trails off with a wicked smile.

"Ha ha. Very funny." But I feel a slight blush rising on my cheeks. "Besides, role-playing is reserved exclusively for the tenth date."

He raises an eyebrow and clinks his cocktail glass against mine, grinning. "Then I hope there's a tenth date."

Right now, so do I.

And, okay, I didn't fess up to the age thing. If it ever comes up—like when we fill out our marriage certificate or something—then I'll come clean. But really, I figure he probably doesn't even remember or care.

The bar happens to be next to a pretty swank restaurant, so we end up grabbing some dinner. When it starts getting late, we reluctantly call it a night. Though we share a cab back to my place, it's not what you think. Remember how I said my life isn't quite a *Sex and the City* episode? Turns out, Eric lives right near me, and when we exit the cab, I get a light kiss on the lips (not bad) outside my building and a promise to go out again. After an enjoyable date filled with good food, alcohol, and great company, it's hard to let the night end, but I'm confident there will be a next time, and I can wait. I thank him again, wish him goodnight, and go inside and text Bridget: He's wonderful.

CHAPTER THREE

*A*re you all packed for tomorrow?" Roger asks, leaning against my office doorway.

As a result of having worked on the license agreements for Moonstruck a few weeks earlier, I have somehow gotten roped into more work for that client. So before heading to the conference in Monterey, Roger and I are flying to Los Angeles, where Dennis, the head of our corporate department in Chicago, and Mark, a young partner from our San Francisco office, will join us to meet with the client and discuss possible acquisitions of 3D technology and animation companies.

"Not yet. I've been swamped," I say while I finish typing an email. "What about you?"

He laughs. "Of course!" And then walks off.

Yes, of course he is. I'm not really crazy about the prospect of spending a four-hour plane ride next to Roger, but that's what happens when his secretary books the flight. Mine knows better.

After work, I rush home, do laundry, pack, pay a few bills, and fit in a phone call with Eric. We've been on a handful of dates, and even though we're taking it slow, the fact that he seems understanding of my lack of work-life balance is promising. The timing of my trip isn't great, but I'll be gone less than a week, and I would think that our fledgling romance can withstand the distance for a few days.

Even though I'll be with clients most of the time, I do pack a couple of fun clothing items because one can always be hopeful. I was planning to wear something comfortable on the flight, but now that I'll be sitting next to you-know-who, I set aside something more business casual: slim-fitted black pants (I always wear black pants on a plane because you never know what you might spill—something I learned the hard way), a lightweight sweater (crewneck because Creepy Roger), and my go-to block-heeled pumps. Heels on a plane? I know, but I'm five feet five, and with heels I can be five feet seven or even five feet eight. (I read somewhere that people usually assume the tallest person in a room to be the leader, and since then I've become obsessed with wearing some sort of heels at work.)

I was also originally planning to sleep on the plane, but now I pack some files to read during the flight. Since Roger is a partner—something I hope to make this year—I'll feel like too much of a slacker if I curl up in my seat trying to catch some zzz's. By midnight, I'm miraculously done with everything—and ready for a vacation.

* * *

Since I'll be gone for almost a week and had to bring a full lineup of suits, business casual, and sportswear, I have to go through the whole ordeal of checking luggage. After handing my suitcase to the airline clerk and receiving my luggage tag, I smile, say thank you, and turn around while readjusting my tote bag on my shoulder. As I do, I run smack into a blue shirt.

"Ow, sorry," I say apologetically. "I should really look where I'm going."

"No problem." A deep male voice laughs as he places his hands on my elbows, obviously trying to stop me from running him over. "Are you okay?"

As I'm standing there rubbing the tip of my nose, something about his voice strikes a chord inside me and I look up.

Whoa! This man is beautiful, and his smile is even more so, and I stumble a little as I take a small step back.

"Yeah, thanks. Sorry again for my clumsiness!" I answer laughingly, embarrassed.

"No problem."

He releases my elbows, and I move aside as he goes up to the check-in counter.

Away from the line, I recombobulate myself, pulling my tote back onto my shoulder. I'm a little shaky, though, and feel a flush spreading across my chest. I sneak a look at the back of the man I just bumped into. Very tall and fit-looking with a gorgeous head of hair. The most perfect shade of chestnut, it's thick and a little wavy and flops in all the right directions. He's running his hand through it as he waits for the airline clerk. He's looking around now. *Mmm . . . what nice, strong-looking shoulders. Oh wait, he's looking at me! Probably because I'm staring at him. Oops!* I give a half smile, and just as I turn around to head to security, the clerk says, "Thank you, Mr. Summers," and I freeze.

I know this man!

My flush escapes my crewneck to my cheeks, and I'm freaking out—not so much that I know him, but at my reaction. Am I sweating? One half of me wants to get the hell out of here, but the other half, the deer in the headlights, is rooted to the spot. Even if I wanted to run, my legs are like Jell-O and I'm too shaken to even try to take a step.

The blue shirt appears in front of me again. "Hi," Brad says.

Brad Summers, my unrequited high school crush, is standing in front of me eighteen years later.

I look up and smile. "Hi again," I stutter, trying to act as coolly as possible. *Impossible.*

"Do we know each other?" He smiles tentatively. "You look so familiar." The way he says it is friendly but a bit cautious. From anyone else it would sound like a bad pickup line, and I can tell he's trying not to make it sound like a pickup line because it's true—I do know him.

"Umm, I'm not sure," I say, giving myself a second to mentally catch my breath, and then extend my hand. "Adeline Turner."

He takes it and there's a pause. Then his face lights up with recognition and a huge smile. "Hey, I do know you! We used to be neighbors!" He puts his free hand on the other side of mine that he's shaking, then lets go and points to himself. "Brad Summers? You probably don't remember me."

Don't remember you? Is this man insane? He was my first crush—my *only* crush during those formative years. Though I can barely speak, I have enough wits about me to sneak a peek at his wedding finger. Nothing!

"Of course, *Brad!*" I laugh. The charade's over. "You moved away during high school to, um . . ." Look at me playing it cool now. "California, right?"

"Yeah, that's right." His smile grows wider. "Wow, I thought you looked familiar, but I couldn't place you. And then I was worried you were going to think I was some creep hitting on you in the airport." He cringes and then laughs.

This would be my chance to say somewhat flirtatiously, "Well, that wouldn't be a bad thing. You look great!" Wait, I said that aloud. *Who am I right now?*

Is that a slight blush on his part? He runs his hand through his hair again and looks down, smiling, then looks back up at me. "Yeah, you do too."

I can't even handle this. I'm going to burst. Need to get on solid ground. "So, um, where are you flying to?" I ask.

"Los Angeles. What about you?"

Now this is too much. "Me too! Do you live in Chicago?"

"Uh, no. Actually, I'm flying home. I had some business here. What about you?"

"I'm also flying to LA, but for business. I live here in Chicago now." I pause and then realize, "Hey, we must be on the same flight."

"At twelve forty-five?"

Darn it! It was already too perfect.

"Oh," I say, a little deflated. "I'm on the eleven thirty. That's too bad. We could've caught up by the gate."

He looks at his watch. "Well, it's still early for your flight. Would you like to grab some coffee or something? It'd be fun to catch up."

I look into those hazel eyes I spent so many nights dreaming about as a girl and say, "I'd love that. There's a Starbucks right after security."

"Okay. Let's go."

I am in a surreal, dreamy haze as we catch up in the security line and have to focus on asking intelligible questions like, "So, wow, you still live in California? What do you do out there?" all while surreptitiously noting the changes and new lines on his face, a more polished demeanor than the boy from Wisconsin that I remembered, and much more handsome. When I hand my boarding pass and ID to the security guard, I want to shout, *Do you know what momentous thing is happening right now?* But I think better of it.

When we reach the Starbucks, we order our coffee, and Brad kindly says, "Here, let me get this. It's nice to see an old friend." The fifteen-year-old girl inside me swoons. If he considers his plain former neighbor an old friend, who am I to argue?

We sit down at a table and begin firing off more questions. Would you believe that my beloved Brad is, of all things, a real estate attorney? Who would have guessed? Especially since, let's be honest, most attorneys are pretty bland personality-wise. But Brad is nothing like that. He's funny and charming, and his eyes sparkle when he laughs. I'm dying to ask him, *And why aren't you married?* but we stay on nonromantic conversation points, such as where we went to school, why we decided to become attorneys, and what our chosen career would be if we could do anything and not worry about finances. (He'd renovate houses full-time, and I'd be a writer, and yes, we both would travel.) Throughout the conversation, I simply bask in the warmth of his smile and the full focus of his attention. At some point, though, I glance at my watch and realize I need to get to my gate *now*.

"Shoot. I better go if I want to catch my flight," I say with definite disappointment in my voice.

He in turn looks at his watch. "Oh yeah, you better get a move on."

We both stand up at the same time. "Yes, well, it was really great running into you. Have a good flight," I say.

"Yeah. You too."

I'm about to reach out to shake his hand, but then I figure, what the hell? He did say earlier I was an old friend, right? So I lean in and give him a hug. A hug that lingers a little too long. But as I feel the warmth of his skin rising and catch a delicious scent of cologne/aftershave, I don't want to let go, ever.

When I reluctantly pull away, Brad looks slightly flustered. Maybe the hug was a little inappropriate. Oh well, I have my getaway, since they've probably started boarding my flight.

"Okay, bye," I say, spinning away and starting to make my way to the gate.

Then I hear Brad's voice behind me, "Hey, Addie!"

I stop and turn around, and he catches up to me. "When you're in LA, will you have any free time?"

"Maybe. It depends on what happens at the meeting . . . um, you know how it is."

"Well, here's my card. Give me a call if you have any time off and want to get together. I can show you around."

"Thanks! That would be fun." My heart dances in my chest as I take the card. Just then a boarding announcement for my flight comes on the loudspeakers. "Okay, I really better go now. I'll call you."

I practically run to my gate, and yes, they're on final boarding. I find my seat, and Roger, of course, is already there.

"Hey, Adeline. I didn't see you out there. I was getting worried you weren't going to make it." Funny. Because sitting there checking his BlackBerry, he doesn't look worried; in fact, he doesn't even look up at me.

"Sorry. I ran into an old friend and we started catching up and time just flew." I crawl over Roger, since he is in the aisle seat and I have the window and god forbid that he should think of getting up and courteously letting me by. I cram my bag under the seat in front of me and buckle up.

Roger looks at me and grimaces distastefully. "You look like you ran here! You're all red."

"Yes, well, I practically did," I say, settling back into my seat. I know I'm flushed, but not from the run. I never would've guessed Brad would have the same effect on me now as he did so many years ago. I mean, when you're younger, your hormones are out of control and you're boy crazy. Never in my adult life have I had that knock-your-socks-off, tongue-tied, weak-in-the-knees reaction to a guy. Most of my encounters tend to be more of the Eric kind. Meet a guy who you find physically attractive, strike up a conversation, get to know each other a little better, and *then* start to feel somewhat excited about him. The will-he-call dance is always a bit nerve racking, and the first official date, like a big-time dinner or something, will cause some butterflies of nervousness here and there. But nothing close to what I just experienced having coffee with Brad.

And I have his card! He wants to show me around LA! He said to call him! And you know what? I will. I will make free time. Roger and work be damned. Since I have his card and he doesn't have mine, the ball is in my court.

"Looks like we're taking off on time," Roger says, stating the obvious as the plane starts to move.

"Yup, seems like it. Guess I'll get some work done."

I pull a folder out of my tote, turn away from Roger, and pretend to read. But honestly, how can I read boring files now? I'm just so happy! I want to sit here and recall every bit of my conversation with Brad, everything he said, the way he looked, and the warm glow in my heart when he smiled at me. If I had a journal with me (and I was fifteen), I'd write down every little detail of our encounter. How I wish it was Nora sitting beside me rather than Roger.

I have *got* to call Bridget as soon as I get to the hotel.

CHAPTER FOUR

The next thing I know, we're landing. I open my eyes and see Roger typing on his BlackBerry. I shift in my seat.

"That was some nap," Roger says, his eyes still glued to his email.

"Yeah, I didn't realize I was so tired," I say. Must've been caused by the adrenaline crash after being reunited with my long-lost crush.

But, oops, falling asleep in front of a partner isn't the best start to an important business trip. Pulling myself together, I sit up straight and intently focus on gathering my loose papers back into their file folder, taking my time so that I don't have to meet Roger's eye.

* * *

After the usual airport rigmarole, we finally arrive at the hotel and check in to our separate rooms. As soon as my hotel room door shuts behind me, I pull out my phone and text Bridget: Oh. My. God! You'll. Never. Believe. What. Happened. To. Me!

My phone rings, and I answer to Bridget whispering loudly, *"Whhhaaat?"*

"The boy of my dreams is now the man of my dreams!" I flop backward onto the bed. Oh dear, even I kind of cringe when I say that aloud.

"O-kay," she says slowly, confused. "Elaborate, please."

"Bridget, I ran into Brad Summers at the airport! The guy I had a crush on all through junior high and high school!"

"What?! Tell me everything!"

I fill her in on my unrequited crush, my bravery in asking Brad to the Spring Dance, the kiss that never happened, and how he moved away and I never saw him again until today.

"So what's he like now?" she says.

"He's perfect. Absolutely perfect. I thought he had already achieved perfection back then, but guess what? He's even better-looking now!" I've totally reverted to my dramatic teenage self.

"Wow!"

"And not only that . . ." I pause. "He's the nicest guy. And an attorney!"

"No way! So what's his story, then? Married?" she asks cautiously.

"No sign of a wedding ring! And I didn't ask. I just don't want to know. Well, I want to know, but you know," I say, making a note to do a social media search after this call.

"Hmm . . . could be divorced or something. How did you guys leave it? Any possibility of seeing him again?"

"I think *yes*, but this is where I need your help."

"Auntie Bridget to the rescue." I can feel her smile through the phone.

"Exactly. Now, when I had to catch my flight, we both stood up, and I wasn't sure what to do. I know the normal and polite thing would've been to shake his hand and say how nice it was running into him and give him my card and if he's ever in Chicago, blah, blah, blah, and goodbye."

"Yes, that's what normal people do. So what did *you* do?"

"I hugged him."

"Uh-huh. And then . . . ?"

"Uh, well, then I continued hugging him for several inappropriate seconds."

She laughs. "I'm sure it was fine. It's not like you started making out with him. And then?"

"Then I took off."

"You didn't give him your card?"

"No. *But* when I started walking away, he called out and caught up to me. He asked if I was going to have any free time in LA, and I said, you know, how it all depends on meetings, whatever. So then he gave me his card and said, well, if you have some downtime, give me a call and I can show you around or something."

"Or something . . . ," Bridget says naughtily.

"Yeah, yeah. If I'm so lucky, right?"

"What do you mean if you're so lucky? Trust me—if you want a guy, you won't have a problem," Bridget says, giving my ego a little boost. But Brad knew me way back when—in the awkward years; hopefully, this second impression can wipe out those earlier memories.

"So when are you going to call him?" Bridget asks.

"I'm not sure." I frown. "It really does depend on my client meetings. But either way, I'll call him. But here's where I need your help." I pause. "Do you think it's weird that he didn't give me his number right away? I mean, it was almost like an afterthought, don't you think?"

"Well, sweetie, you didn't even have the presence of mind to give him your card at all, and yet you claim he's the man of your dreams. I really wouldn't let it worry you. He was probably just too caught up in the moment, blinded by the beautiful creature in front of him."

"Okay, okay. In other words, I'm being neurotic and overanalytical."

"That you are." I hear her rustle some papers on her desk. "Sorry, Addie, but I better get going. If I'm going to get out at a reasonable hour tonight, I have to get some work done."

"Sure thing. Thanks for listening."

"Anytime. Talk to you later."

I hang up thinking how crazy I get sometimes. If someone gives you their card, you call them.

While I was on the phone with Bridget, I got a text from Eric.

> Hi Adeline, you're probably in LA now and
> I just wanted to wish you a good trip. Can't
> wait till you get back.

That's sweet of him. We haven't even had sex yet, although if the long goodbye kiss after our last date was any indication, then it's definitely coming. To be polite, I type back a quick Thank you. Same here. with a smiley face. But unfortunately, Eric has been upstaged, and I'm not sure he can recover. My BlackBerry rings with Roger's number interrupting my thoughts. *Already?*

"Hello," I answer.

"Adeline," he says, "I got emails from both Mark and Dennis saying something came up this afternoon, so now neither of them will be here until late tonight. But they want to get together with us at seven tomorrow morning and review everything before the meeting at nine."

"Okay. Sounds good." Actually, it sounds awful, but what can I do? I unpack my laptop while he's talking and set it up on the desk.

"So I think we should grab dinner together and go over our notes for the meeting," he says, not asking.

"Sure thing. When should we meet?"

"Let's say six at the hotel restaurant. I have some work I want to get done now, and I'm sure you do as well." *Ugh.* A clear dig at my unintended nap.

"Okay. See you then," I say cheerfully, to let him know his snark can't ruffle my feathers.

Six o'clock is still a while away, and I can probably get something done before then. Of course, the second I open my laptop, I can't help but check out the website of the law firm where Brad works. Ah, look, there he is—as handsome as ever! How am I ever going to get any work done today? I gaze lovingly (okay, lustfully) at his picture and read his work profile. I do a quick social media search, but the only account he seems to have is LinkedIn, which has the same information as his firm profile.

This is crazy. I need to stop mooning like a love-struck teenager and focus. I'm an adult with work responsibilities right now that I've been blowing off for the last several hours. This is not how a future partner of Gilchrist should be acting. Also, I am new to this team and need to make a good impression at the meeting. I reluctantly close the website and get down to work.

* * *

Despite my best efforts, however, my mind keeps wandering back to Brad. The perfect hair. The perfect smile. Those perfect eyes. Even I'm making myself gag. But, oh, his perfect physique, which I could only get a hint of under his clothes.

These thoughts keep coming back to me even during dinner with Roger. I try to focus between bites of my Caesar salad, but it certainly isn't easy.

"Earth to Adeline . . ."

"Mmm, what's that?" I turn to Roger, my fork just kind of hanging in the air.

"You're really out of it. Are you feeling well?" He eyes me warily.

"Oh, sorry. Yes, I'm fine. Just a little tired, I guess." I put the fork in my mouth. There's nothing on it.

"How can you be tired? You slept the whole way here."

"Oh, so I did." I give a small laugh.

He rolls his eyes. "I see we aren't going to get a lot done tonight."

"Don't worry. I'm fine." Roger is in his full seniority mode of I'm-partner-to-your-lowly-associate-status, and so I force myself to focus. "I have my laptop with me, so we can go to the business center after this and go over the presentation."

"Adeline," he says in a condescending tone, although I can never be sure if it's just his normal way of speaking. "This presentation contains pretty sensitive material. Haven't you heard of the attorney-client privilege?" Okay, yes, definitely condescending. "I reserved a conference room. We'll head over after dinner."

Three hours in a conference room reviewing the presentation with Roger makes me forget about Brad. As we carefully cover each slide, Roger tells me not to worry because I will not have to speak during the meeting and just need to click the arrows to change the slides. This is one of those moments where I simply nod and use all my strength not to slap the patronizing smirk off his face. I highly doubt the firm flew me out here for the sole purpose of pressing a button on a laptop. I'm a seventh-year associate, for god's sake. *I'm* almost a partner myself. *But whatever, Roger.*

I just need to stay coolheaded, because hopefully in six months, I, too, will be partner, and he'll have nothing to lord over me. So I just give him my usual reply, "Okay." An *okay* with a thousand different meanings behind it.

CHAPTER FIVE

At Moonstruck's offices in downtown LA, we present our preliminary due diligence analysis on three companies that offer the 3D animation technology Moonstruck is interested in acquiring for its studios. During the presentation, when the client asks us why we included Imogen, a company that has famously turned down other offers, Roger simply says, "We wanted to present you with the best three technology companies in this area. And frankly, any company can be bought at the right price."

I can see the general counsel's eyes narrow a bit, and I know what he's thinking: *I pay you how much an hour for* that?

"It's not just about the money for Imogen. It's about their CEO," I say, jumping in. "He doesn't just want to sell the software or his company and move on to the next thing. What he wants is to *work* with another company that can help give his current software the best platform and to create even better technology together. So, the right type of deal *is* possible without having to beat prior offer amounts."

Moonstruck's CEO nods. "I'm listening."

While Roger focused on the narrow checklist of due diligence items, finances, potential liabilities, IP ownership, and so on, I had a paralegal pull for me every article and interview for each company's CEO and CTO, to glean some insight into each of their motivations and mindsets. As I talk, I can feel Roger's eyes boring through me, but I don't care because I can tell the client and the other partners are impressed.

When we're leaving the offices, Dennis leans over to me and says, "Great job, Adeline." Despite Roger's "assurances" that I wouldn't have a speaking role, my extra research and speaking up kept our client for another day.

* * *

Back in my hotel room, still riding the high from this morning's meeting, and having my afternoon free, I decide it's the perfect time to contact Brad. I pull out his card and type what I hope is a nonchalant email.

> Hi Brad,
>
> It was so good seeing you at the airport yesterday. I'm finished with my client meeting and have some free time this afternoon. I know this is last minute, but I was wondering if you had any time to meet up today?
>
> Best,
> Adeline

I hit Send and cross my fingers.
Two minutes later my BlackBerry pings.

Hi Addie,

So good to hear from you. I'm tied up this afternoon and tonight. Any chance you're free tomorrow? I have to look at some real estate in Malibu tomorrow afternoon, and it's a scenic drive.

I have to stop myself from typing back: *Yes, I'm free tomorrow, and Friday, Saturday, Sunday, and every day of the week for the rest of my life, you gorgeous man.*

Then I remember, and my earlier high comes crashing down—tomorrow is Thursday, and I'm flying to Monterey for the conference a day early. I sigh. It was too good to be true.

I'm about to type back my regrets, but my memory flashes back to that night eighteen years ago on my front porch—Brad's face so close to mine, the moment before my dad opened the door—and my fingers freeze over the keyboard. Am I really going to choose a flight with Roger over time with Brad?

I type back, my hands shaking a little. Tomorrow works. What time?

We agree that Brad will pick me up at three tomorrow afternoon. It's a date.

After solidifying plans with Brad, I immediately email my secretary to change my flight and then call Roger. Roger sounds a bit peeved, but informs me that he will return the rental car to the airport and that I'm on my own getting myself up north. I can feel the chivalry oozing down the telephone line, but this is a small price to pay for an afternoon with gorgeous Brad. Now the question is, What to wear?

I lay out all the clothes I have with me on the bed and call my lifeline. Thankfully, she answers.

"Addie!" Exactly the excited response I hoped for.

"Okay. So I'm driving up to Malibu with Brad tomorrow to check out a house, and then we're going out to dinner. What do I wear?"

"Whoa, whoa, whoa! You're going to Malibu with Brad?" I can hear Bridget go into full-alert mode. "To look at a house? Are you moving in together? What happened since the airport?!"

Remember those friends you had in high school who you would talk to every day on the phone about every minute detail of your life? Even though you had spent the entire day in school together, there was still so much to analyze about it—who you liked and what you were going to wear the next day to get his attention? Yes? No? For me it's a no. I didn't really have friends like that, and I was way too embarrassed to ever admit who I liked to anyone. My relationship with Bridget is what I imagine those friendships back then would have been like, and so I'm all the more grateful to have her in my life now.

After I recount my email exchange with Brad and the details of the trip to her, she gets down to the business of wardrobe.

"Okay, so you're going to be on a long car ride during daylight hours. That rules out most of your lawyer wear. You'll need something that's casual enough for daytime but will still be sexy enough for night. Hmm . . . how are your legs looking?"

"I've got a good Jergens glow going on."

"Well then, have you got any short skirts? But not businessy ones!"

I inventory my clothes on the bed, an array of business casual, two suits, workout clothes, and a couple of tasteful black dresses for dinners, which I considered my "fun" clothes while packing. None of it is appropriate. "I have this camel-colored skirt. It's above the knee?" I offer weakly.

"Not great, but it's a start. What tops have you got? I'm thinking something fitted and that shows off that cleavage of yours."

She's right about that—I do have breasts with a capital B, or in my case C.

"Let's see." I scan the possibilities. "I have a fitted white blouse that I brought to go under a suit. I also have a V-neck white T-shirt, where if I stretch in certain directions there may be some 'accidental' midriff baring."

"How much?"

"Not Britney Spears much. Just an accidental peek."

"You do know that all these options sound dismal. The blouse is out, and the T-shirt sounds iffy." She sighs. "Anything sleeveless?"

"You've already got me baring my legs and cleavage, and possibly even midriff. You want me to go sleeveless as well? Isn't it better to leave something to the imagination?"

"No," she replies firmly. "You have one night. There's no time to leave anything to the imagination. In fact, if I were you, I would just show up naked and get that part out of the way."

"*Come on.* Seriously. I need help here." I feel my cheeks go hot at her mention of "naked" and thoughts of Brad. A girl can dream.

Bridget and I settle on the camel skirt, white T-shirt, my black cashmere cardigan (even though it's June, I've noticed it gets chilly in the evening), and wedge-heeled espadrilles (it was decided that proper heels did not seem "casual" enough for an afternoon drive). To pull the look together, she recommended that I wear my chunky orange-and-gold statement necklace. After our call, I set the outfit aside in the closet while I try to focus on work for the next several hours before having to get dressed again for dinner.

* * *

Moonstruck's general counsel, Scott Schulman, invited our team to his house tonight for drinks and dinner. Although we typically entertain clients with dinners, sporting events, or something else to make their stay in Chicago pleasant, I had yet to be "entertained" at a client's house, not to mention one that was in the hills of Los Angeles. The house, or I should say mansion, is spectacular. It's a Mediterranean masterpiece tucked into the hills with sweeping views. And by drinks and dinner, I mean a catered affair with waitstaff. No kidding.

While sipping cocktails on the deck with the warm evening air enveloping us, I quip to Roger, "I could get used to this."

"Pfft. Who wants to live in California?" he sneers and loudly swirls the ice around in his drink.

I'm not sure if he's joking or serious. Probably the latter, but I can never tell with him. So I say a noncommittal, "Yeah, who wants to live in California?" Then I excuse myself to freshen my mojito at the bar, all the while thinking, *I want to live in California. That's who!*

The best part of the dinner, though, is that it distracts me from thinking too much about tomorrow and my impending date with Brad.

* * *

In the morning, I'm wide-awake at seven. Since I have no office to rush to and am not being picked up until three, I take advantage of the situation to get in a morning workout.

Running to nowhere on the hotel gym's treadmill, I start daydreaming happily about my upcoming date. But is it really a date? In fact, I don't even know if he's single. I look at my reflection in the gym's mirror and get worried. Of course, right at this moment a musclehead walks in, catches my look in the mirror, and proceeds to eye me up and down. I quickly shift my gaze to the treadmill monitor. Presumably, the musclehead sees a decent-looking brunette. Brad, though, knew me during those awkward years, and he did recognize me at the airport, which means I still must look somewhat like I did when I knew him. True, I recognized him as well, but that was easy. Hot then, and still hot now.

Back in my room, as I shampoo my hair in the shower, I try to scrub away any such negative thoughts that once again Brad wouldn't notice the charming, enticing creature I am. Of course, if I don't totally buy it, then why should he? After my shower, I do a quick email check and determine that there have been no been fires at the office today. Great, because I have other serious business at hand—I need to try on the getup Bridget and I decided on yesterday.

Standing in front of the mirror in the Bridget-approved ensemble, I have to say that it's not bad. But it's not great either. The white T-shirt and camel skirt are drab, and with the black cardigan and "statement" orange necklace, the only statement I seem to be making is that every day is Halloween. Granted, I packed for work and a conference, but *this* is the best I could come up with?

There's only one solution—I need to go shopping. This is a new Addie Turner for Brad Summers, so I need new clothes. Never mind that he hasn't seen my wardrobe for the last eighteen years. This is a necessary psychological boost.

I call an Uber, and minutes later I am deposited in front of a humongous shopping center. Since I don't have time to explore each and every store, I head straight to the Bloomingdale's in view. I zip straight up to the women's apparel floor. I must look determined because within seconds of stepping off the escalator, a saleswoman approaches me.

"Hello! I'm Candy. Is there anything I can help you with today?"

"YES!" I practically grab her. "I need a dress. It's for a date *today*. Something casual enough to wear during the day, but sexy enough to wear out to dinner."

"I have just the thing. Follow me." Candy crooks her finger, beckoning me to follow, which I dutifully do.

I follow her to a section that is all dresses. All very short, all very fitted. She pulls out a tiny one-shoulder-strapped white (*Uh-oh? Is that Lycra?*) dress. I swear I've seen dinner napkins that have more fabric than this dress.

"Let's try this. What's your size?" she says.

Let's not. "Um, I'm thinking a little less tight, but still sexy," I explain, as politely as I can. "And maybe not so short. I have to wear it on a long car ride." I shake my head as if I'm sad to see the white dress return to the rack.

"Okay. What do you think of these over here?" She points to some other dresses, all short, many of them shiny or beaded, and most of which are better suited to a seventeen-year-old gazelle than myself. *Do grown women wear these things?* Trying not to say what I think, I look around frantically. I spot a sign for Alice + Olivia, a brand I recognize, and there in the distance, I think I see it—the perfect dress.

"Actually, I think I'm going to browse around over there." I gesture to that section. I make a beeline over to the dress (with Candy at my heels), grab one in my size, and head to the dressing room.

* * *

In my hotel room mirror, I strike a pose and admire my outfit. The comment I made to Bridget about my wanting to leave something to the imagination is now probably betrayed by my choice of outfit—a crimson-red sundress with spaghetti straps and a deep V neckline. It's made of soft jersey that hugs my hips, yet is flowy closer to the hemline, which ends right above my knees. True, it's red and a bit revealing, but at least it's not all skintight. I also found a perfect, delicate gold bracelet and small hoop earrings in the accessories department. Suddenly, my strappy espadrilles look better by simple association.

As for my hair, Bridget suggested I keep it down. "You have such gorgeous hair. Go for the bedroom look and let him get lost in those waves." But as I'm second-guessing myself today, I am also second-guessing Bridget, even though so far her track record is great despite the business casual, Halloween-inspired debacle decided on yesterday (but, poor woman, she didn't have much to work with). With such a sultry dress, I think wearing my hair down might be too much, so I put it up in a casual knot. By two forty-five, I'm more than ready to go, so I head down to the lobby a little early.

I sit there, crossing and uncrossing my legs, jiggling my feet, and obsessively checking my phone, but I still jump when it rings at three o'clock on the dot.

"Hello?"

"Hi, Addie. It's Brad." No mistaking that warm, deep voice. "I'm just pulling into the parking lot. Are you ready?"

"Yes, I'm all dressed and waiting in the lobby." Okay, that sounded dumb. Why wouldn't I be dressed? *Pull it together!*

"Great. Should I park the car?"

"No, no. I'll just meet you outside in front."

"Okay. See you soon."

As I hit End Call on my phone, I notice my hand is shaking a bit and my heart is hammering in my chest. *Wow.* I haven't been this nervous about a date since the day I asked Brad to the Spring Dance. Although I want to be all confident and sexy when I see him, I look at myself in the lobby mirror and see insecurity reflecting back at me. I look away and decide on a fake-it-till-you-make-it course of action.

I walk through the hotel doors into the sunny afternoon. Not wanting Brad's first glimpse to be of me squinting with my hand over my eyes, I grab my sunglasses out of my bag and put them on. They offer me a barrier to catch my cool, and just in time, because Brad is pulling up to the entrance in a silver convertible BMW.

As he parks, a broad smile spreads across his face as he recognizes me, and waves. "Hi!"

"Hi!" I smile back and wave as I walk toward the car. A valet appears and opens the door for me, and I slide into the charcoal-gray leather seat.

We do a bit of an awkward half hug in the car (because apparently I'm now a "hugger"). When he pulls back, he leans far back against his door as though eager to get a good look at me. "Wow! You look great!"

His compliment dissolves my earlier nervousness. "Yeah, well, you don't look too bad yourself," I say, smiling. And he doesn't. He is wearing dark jeans with that vintage worn-in look and a white button-down shirt. I notice a black sports jacket in the back, and it makes me curious where we're going for dinner. Even though his look would fit right in in an urban setting, Brad's natural tan and chestnut highlights are clear evidence of his healthy Californian lifestyle. Not to mention, the twinkle in those hazel eyes.

"Shall we go?" he asks as another car pulls up behind us.

"Sure." I'm ready to get this show on the road.

CHAPTER SIX

*A*s we drive off, I comment, "This is a beautiful car."

"Thanks. I was actually kind of worried about bringing it, since it's a convertible and all. I was afraid you'd think I'm having some kind of midlife crisis."

I laugh. "Well, it is a convertible. But then, it is LA." I mock-ponder. "Also, a midlife-crisis car has to be a red speedster or some other obnoxious color. This is very nice."

"Phew! That's a relief. I didn't want you going back to Wisconsin and telling everyone how LA I've gotten."

"Hardly. Besides, I never see anyone from there anyway, except my dad."

"I always liked your dad. We didn't talk much, but when I mowed your lawn, he always paid me more than what I asked. And back then that was reason enough to like someone."

"Yeah, sounds like my dad. He's a good man, *and* he really hates mowing the lawn."

Brad laughs. "And how is your dad doing?"

"He's good. Still practicing estate law and still in the same house in Wisconsin," I say, and make a mental note that I'm overdue for a visit up north. "And what's up with your parents?" I ask.

Brad tells me how his folks are semiretired and thinking about moving into a smaller house. This is probably the time to explain more about my family life. Brad didn't ask about my mother because there's nothing to ask. She left us when I was twelve years old, not long after we moved into our new house and neighborhood. Whereas my dad is quiet, my mother was the life of the party. She was very beautiful and expressive, a painter. Although I have my mother's eyes and Brazilian coloring, it's clear I have my dad's Celtic personality, since I've always been shy and studious. As a child I tried to bond with her creative side by sharing my stories with her. I would timidly hand them to her as she sat in her studio, and she would stop what she was working on and read them aloud, afterward praising my talents and telling me I was going to be a great writer. I still have some stories that she illustrated for me buried in my old bedroom closet at my dad's house.

My mother also had dreams, and one day she acted on those dreams and took a painting retreat, leaving my dad and me on our own for a month. But the day she was supposed to return, I came home from school and found my dad ashen-faced and deflated, waiting for me at the kitchen table. I remember the cold feeling that came over me, knowing my world was about to change. My dad looked up at me with watery blue eyes and said, "Your mother isn't coming home. She was offered a job teaching art at the retreat, and she is going to stay."

"For how long?" I asked carefully.

He stared at me, unable to speak, but his sad gaze said it all. She didn't just leave us for a month—she had left us for good.

What mother leaves her daughter to *teach art*? As an adult, I realize there was probably more to the story, but I've never broached it with my dad because to this day the pain is still too raw. *I was twelve, for cripes sake!* But my dad did his best to make up for it. Instead of my mother, he drove me to the mall to buy my first bra. When I got my period for the first time, he bought me every kind of sanitary product on the shelves (there was even an adult diaper in the mix). I was mortified and embarrassed, and never loved and appreciated my one remaining parent so fiercely. Over the years my mother has tried to reach out to me and still sends me birthday cards, and my dad gently encourages me to contact her, but I can't. Although at some point I *may* forgive her for leaving me, I don't think I can ever forgive her for leaving my dad.

Anyway, that's why Brad doesn't ask about my mother. It was a scandal in our small neighborhood where people stayed married forever. Though I knew all our neighbors were whispering about us, they were too polite to ever bring it up in front of me. A week after she left, Brad came over to mow our lawn. When he was finished, he came to our front door as usual and rang the bell. Normally my dad would answer and pay him while I stayed hidden in my room or my latest spying spot, but that day he was out running errands that single fatherhood warranted, so I answered the door.

"My dad's not here," I mumbled. The pain of my mother's leaving was still too fresh and numbed any nervousness around my crush. "I'll let him know you finished the lawn."

"Okay." Brad nodded, looking hot and tired.

He stood there for an awkward second.

Right when I was about to close the door, he said, "Hey, Addie? Matt and I were going to play a game of HORSE at his house if you want to come over."

Even though this was my crush asking me to do something with him, I was so devastated that all I could do was shake my head. "Thank you, but I . . . I can't today."

Brad paused. "Okay. Well, if you ever want to hang out with us . . . um, just call me. Or just come over."

I nodded and said, "Okay," before closing the door in his concerned face. Other than the odd hello in the neighborhood or acknowledgment at school, we didn't really speak again until I came over to ask him to the Spring Dance.

"How did your meeting go yesterday?" Brad asks, dispelling my gloomy thoughts.

"It was good." I'd love to brag some about my role at the meeting, but that would require details that would be too confidential. So instead, I fill him in on the dinner at the client's house. And while he makes all the appropriate head nods, I remember that he is a real estate attorney in LA and is probably familiar with such obscene properties, so I decide to change the subject.

"So what's this real estate you're checking out today? A nice little beach house slash mansion on the water for yourself?" I tease.

"Sorta. It's kind of a business thing that I'm checking out for someone."

"Attorney-client privileged stuff? Or can you tell me?"

"I'd love to tell you about it, but I guess I should keep it hush-hush." He glances over at me. "Hey, are you still okay with the top down?"

It's my first time in a convertible, and I'm feeling a little buffeted from the wind, but cruising down the Malibu highway with my high school crush makes me feel like I'm in a romantic movie. "Yes. I love it!" I lean my head back, grinning and taking in the perfect blue sky.

Brad laughs again. "I'm glad you like it, but I guess I didn't consider how hard it would be to talk. We should probably save our voices for the agent and dinner. How about some music?"

"Sounds good." It's true. Though the windshield offers some protection, as we've picked up speed I feel like I've been shouting over the highway noise. We settle on some nonoffensive adult alternative rock station, and I shift my focus to enjoying the beautiful panorama flashing by us.

The deep-blue ocean waves are crashing calmly on the shoreline, the sun is shining, and a light breeze keeps the heat of the day at bay. The jaw-dropping beauty all around us makes me want to pinch myself. And I can't wait to see this house. Maybe it's a celebrity's home?

However, when we drive up, my excitement quickly fizzles into a disappointed *oh*. It looks like a little, one-story white box with a garage. Definitely not a celebrity's house.

Brad is very quiet as he parks the car. When he turns the engine off, he gives me a small smile. "Thank you so much for doing this with me."

"No problem! I love looking at houses. I'm addicted to HGTV and *House Hunters*." I undo my seat belt. "I'm curious to see the inside." Even though the outside isn't much to look at.

An overly effusive real estate agent greets us at the front door. After our hellos, Brad immediately introduces me as a colleague, with no further explanations of my presence. Since I'm unsure about what Brad's intentions with the place are, I stay mum but smile brightly at the agent to dispel any potential unease or questions. Plus, I'm finding it hard not to stare. With his blond hair, gleaming white teeth, bright aqua-blue eyes, and I'm presuming hairless chest (the first two buttons of his shirt are undone), the agent resembles a real-life Malibu Ken doll.

We follow Malibu Ken through the small front hallway into the main room. *Oh my gosh*—I was wrong. This place is not boring at all. In front of us are floor-to-ceiling windows with breathtaking views of the beach and ocean. The entire main floor is open concept with a contemporary kitchen that faces the dining area and great room. And what a great room it is, with sleek furniture and a fireplace in the middle of the room that you can see on both sides. I can't stop gawking. If I had the money, I'd buy this place in a heartbeat.

During the tour, Brad asks lots of questions about the house, the owners, neighbors, schools, heating and cooling systems, and so on. As the agent enthusiastically answers each question, Brad simply nods in response and silently surveys each room. From everything the agent says, the house sounds like the perfect family home. But since I'm not privy to Brad's business here, I don't know if this is a good or bad thing. The deepening crease between his eyebrows and the way he stuffs his hands in his front pockets, gaze focused downward, while the agent speaks could mean that he's disappointed with the place. Or maybe this is all part of a negotiation tactic.

Afterward, I give Brad and the agent a chance to talk privately and head outside to the deck to admire the ocean. As I gaze out at the sparkling ocean on this glorious day, I can't help but wonder what it'd be like to live out here.

Brad interrupts this reverie with a quick, "Ready to go?"

"Oh." I turn around. "Sure." Back in the house, I shake the realtor's hand, thank him, and head out to the car.

As soon as we drive off, I ask, "Now where to?"

Keeping his eyes on the road, he says, "It's still early for dinner, so I was thinking we could grab a coffee or maybe a pre-dinner drink? Or go for a walk by the water? I saw you admiring the ocean."

"The ocean walk sounds great. I don't get to see much of it in Chicago."

"True, the lake is nice but not quite the same, huh?"

"Just different." I smile. "So, where are we going to dinner?"

"I made reservations nearby at an amazing sushi place," he says, then adds a little nervously, "Wait. Do you like sushi? Maybe I should've asked first—"

I put a hand on his arm. "I love sushi."

"Great. Then you'll love this place."

He turns on the radio again and focuses on the road. Something about this gesture stops me from responding. The frown between his eyebrows is still there, and I assume he's thinking something about the house and decide to give him some mental space. I turn toward the ocean on my side of the car and just try to enjoy the view, and not worry about our lack of conversation until we pull off the highway.

"Here we are." Brad parks and shuts off the engine. Before I can open my door, he rushes out to open it for me, perhaps to make up for the quiet ride. Even from the car, the waves sound wonderful, and as I take in Brad's concerned expression, I hope they're loud enough to drown out the silence between us.

When we reach the sand, I take off my shoes, which is a tricky balancing act. Brad holds my hand to steady me. "It's beautiful here," I comment. "Is your place on the water?"

"No, but very close. I try to get down to the beach to run every day. Why be inside the gym when you live near this?"

"It's obviously working for you." I give him a little smile, which he returns with a mischievous twinkle in his eye. Maybe his troubled look in the car was just because he was focusing on the drive.

"And whatever you're doing in Chicago seems to be working for you." He lets go of my hand and puts his arm around my shoulders. *Whoa! Now this is progress.*

"Thanks." I lean into him, and we stroll along the shore in silence.

Am I crazy, though, or is his mind still somewhere else? Maybe he simply enjoys the silence? Maybe this is comfortable for him? Maybe I'm a freak for wanting to fill up every minute with conversation? We never really spoke as teenagers, so maybe this is what he's always like. Besides, we still have dinner tonight. He'll have to talk then, right?

* * *

After Brad and I have ordered, and I've had a chance to soak in the airy atmosphere of the restaurant, with its bleached-wood interior and spectacular view of the ocean, I take a couple sips of my sauvignon blanc, and finally say, "You seem a bit quiet. Are you okay?"

"Really?" He gives me an apologetic look. "Oh, I'm sorry, Addie. I'm really happy to be here with you. I guess I'm a little stressed out these days."

"That's okay. Work stuff?"

He runs his hand agitatedly through his hair, looks around the restaurant, and then looks back at me. "Yes, work stuff."

Just as I release my hand on my wine glass, he covers it with his, leaving us holding hands across the table. His arm around my shoulders at the beach, no wedding ring, no mention of a partner—all evidence confirms that this dinner is officially a date.

"I was blown away when I saw you at the airport," he says, "and I knew I had to take this opportunity to see you again. But life's a little crazy right now."

"Anything you want to talk about?" I give what I hope is a sympathetic smile. "Is it something with that house? A deal gone bad?"

"Ugh," he groans. "That house. That's the last thing I want to talk about." And he is saved from having to say more by our waiter who serves us our first plate of sushi and asks if I would like a top-off of my wine. Yes, please.

Brad picks up his chopsticks, and with that tries to shake off his depressive mood. "Forget work, I want to hear more about you." He expertly balances a piece of tuna roll. "So whatever happened to your dreams of writing?"

I maneuver my chopsticks much less expertly than Brad. The glass of wine is the first "food" I've had in me since my complimentary continental breakfast, and it's hitting me hard. "What happens with all dreams, I suppose. I would still like to write, but I also like the security of a job. I guess that makes me boring." I leave out the part about my repeatedly rejected novel from college.

"No. You're definitely not boring."

"Thank you." Though, at the moment I feel I am, because I'm not quite sure what to say to recover our earlier mood when he picked me up at the hotel.

All during dinner when Brad looks at me, I feel a cloud of sadness behind his eyes that I'm not sure how to respond to. I don't really know him well enough to know what topics would distract him, and we already covered the basics at the airport and during the car ride. My earlier insecurities start to return, and I wonder if he's thinking better of this "catching up" dinner. When we both decide to skip dessert, I can only assume that I've proven to be a lame date and that we won't be catching up again anytime in the near future. So much for our "big reunion."

Brad drives me back to the hotel after dinner. Given our disappointing date, I'm shocked when he asks if I'd like to get a nightcap at the hotel bar.

"Sure," I reply. *But why bother?*

We sit up at the bar, which is sparsely populated. I continue with the wine, while Brad settles on a vodka tonic. And then another. Not that I'm exactly a teetotaler, but I can't help but comment, "Whoa, there. You'd better watch yourself with the hard stuff. You don't want to ruin that beautiful car."

"No worries. This is all I'm having." He clinks his second glass with mine. "To old friends." We each take a sip. "And besides, this is a hotel, so I can always find a bed here."

True—though I'm not sure whether he is intimating that it may be mine. Feeling emboldened, I put down my drink, look him straight in the eye, and say what I've been thinking this whole time since the airport. "So how is it that you're not married?"

He smiles, takes another sip, and volleys, "I could ask you the same question."

"Well, as for me, I'm not ready yet." No need to get into my work-too-much-no-time-to-date spiel. "So, what's your story? Is there something terribly wrong with you?"

"Yes." He pauses and looks at me very seriously. "I have seven toes on my left foot. It frightens off the ladies." Then I see the corners of his mouth twitch, fighting back a smile.

"You do not." I playfully hit him, and as I giggle I almost fall off my chair. Brad reaches his arms around my waist to steady me. His hands send heat shooting through my body, I can smell the faint scent of his cologne, and his face is just inches from mine; with the memory of our unfinished night urging me on, I lean forward and kiss him.

The second my lips touch his, I'm about to swoon off my chair, not from drunkenness, but from desire. The feeling is electric, and the fifteen-year-old in me is shouting, *Oh my god, this is really happening!* I can tell I've surprised him, because he remains motionless on first contact. But then his grip tightens on my waist, and I feel his lips opening up to mine, deepening the kiss, escalating it from chaste to urgent, and I know he is feeling every overpowering feeling that I am right now.

He's the first to pull away, and whispers, "We shouldn't be doing this here."

"Then let's go to my room," I whisper back.

He nods, his eyes dark and intense, as he pulls out his wallet and throws some twenties on the bar. "Let's go."

In the elevator, we can't keep our hands off each other until we reach my floor and the elevator doors open. I lead the way and he follows. As I'm sliding my keycard into the door, Brad wraps his arms around me from behind and starts kissing my neck. I'm about to melt into the floor because it feels so amazing. When I get the door open, he picks me up like a bride crossing the threshold, carries me inside, and kicks the door closed behind us.

"Brad!" I exclaim in shock as he throws me on the bed and pulls off his shirt. He takes off my dress in one expert move, and I'm so turned on that I begin undoing his belt and pants. He's still not saying anything, and the intensity in his eyes makes my hands tremble as I tear off his clothes. But god, he's so sexy, and I love the way he looks at me as he lowers himself on top of me and we start kissing like two long-lost, sex-starved lovers. We move together, and I feel shivers ripple across my skin. Drunk or sober, this is the best sex of my life.

* * *

"That was incredible!" Brad says, lying back on the pillow. I lay my head on his shoulder and wrap my leg and arm around him as he puts his arms around me. "Amazing."

"I know." I start laughing. He turns his face to mine, kisses my forehead, and then pulls me in tighter.

All the discomfort of the day has washed away with, let me say it again, *THE BEST SEX OF MY LIFE.* In this blissed-out state, I suddenly feel the effects of the alcohol and begin to doze off with my head on his chest and his arms securely around me.

CHAPTER SEVEN

When I wake up, I'm alone in the king-sized bed. I glance blearily at the digital clock: 5:47 a.m. Did I just dream that I had the best sex of my life? Somehow that does seem more plausible. I sit up and whisper, "Brad?"

"Yes?" answers a quiet voice from across the room. As my eyes adjust, I can make him out sitting on a chair, pants on, legs spread apart, elbows resting on his knees, and his forehead buried in his hands.

"Are you okay?" I ask. I become suddenly aware that I'm naked and quickly gather the sheets around me.

"Yes." It's not convincing. He lifts his head and looks at me. "I should go." He starts to shift in the chair as if to get up.

"No, no. You don't need to go. Why would you go?" At my age I've had the average number of one-night stands (well, let's just say I can count them on one hand), where yes, the guy has had to leave immediately afterward. But this is Brad. We knew each other growing up. We just spent an entire day together. I just experienced one of my greatest sexual highs with him. He can't go.

"Is something wrong?" Feeling my own head begin to pound, I ask, "Would you like an aspirin?"

Even though the room is dark, I can feel his sad eyes on me. He reminds me of the way he looked in high school, very boyish and unsure. What could have happened while I was sleeping?

"Addie, I'm sorry. I'm so sorry." He buries his head in his hands again.

Now he's scaring me. I get out of bed, making sure the sheet is wrapped around me. "I don't understand. Why are you sorry?" I walk over to him and perch on the arm of the chair. I put my hand on his shoulder and shake him. "Hey? Brad, you have to tell me what's wrong."

Silence.

"Brad!" Still nothing. "What's wrong?" I grab his face with both my hands so he'll look me in the eyes. His are bloodshot and watery.

"You're going to hate me."

Oh no! My stomach sinks.

"I have to tell you something," he begins.

Oh god. I brace myself.

"I lied to you at the bar. I'm so sorry."

My stomach sinks further, and I'm suddenly feeling very cold. "What do you mean? Lied about what?"

He gives me a tormented look. "I'm still married."

Once the words are out, they are a knife to my heart. *I'm. Still. Married.* And what does he mean by *still*?

Suddenly I feel nauseous.

I should jump up and start calling him names. I should kick him out. I should threaten to tell his poor wife what a sleazebag he is for sleeping with another woman.

But I can't move. Because Brad is not a sleazebag, right? He can't be. He is my dream crush.

"Addie, I'm so, so sorry." Then the words start spilling out. "We're getting a divorce. It's been terrible for so long. But this divorce has been just as terrible and she doesn't want it and I don't want to lose my daughter." His jaw tightens, and his eyes begin to water as he blinks quickly. "I'm so sorry. I should leave."

He has a daughter? Oh god.

He's right—he should leave—but instead, I look at him again, searching his eyes, and say, "You have a daughter?"

He nods.

"Why did you lie to me?"

He shrugs slightly. "Why does anyone lie? Because I like you. Because I wanted you. Because you were the first person I've wanted since I can even remember."

This is worse than my father opening the door before our first kiss could happen. A hundred thousand times worse. In my teenage bedroom, I had daydreamed about Brad saying these words to me, but this was not how it was supposed to happen. Maybe my father knew what he was doing back then and tried to save me. My beautiful Brad is nothing but a liar. Everything is shattered.

"Addie?" he pleads, brushing my hair back from my face. "I am so sorry."

I feel sick. I remove myself from the chair and walk over to the edge of the bed and sit down. The room is spinning and feels claustrophobic. Now I rest my forehead in my hands as I press my palms into it, trying to stop the pounding. I need some space to think.

"You need to leave—now," I say.

"Can I explain?"

I shake my head. I can't handle explanations right now. The pounding in my head is getting worse, and I'm exhausted. I stand up and head to bathroom to get some water and something to stop the growing pain in my head.

"Please, Brad. I need to be alone." I close the bathroom door behind me.

I drop the sheet and put on one of the huge hotel bathrobes that's hanging on the door. Turning on the sink faucet, I let the water run and watch two big, fat tears drop into the basin. I brace my palms against the counter, holding myself up, and let myself cry quietly for a couple of minutes, hoping the water drowns out the sound. Sure he's gone, I splash some cold water on my puffy face and carefully open the bathroom door.

I take in the bed in its disarrayed state and, knowing why it's in such a state, can't get back into it. I look over to the chair where Brad dropped his bombshell.

"Brad?" I jump. "I thought you left." His eyes bore into me, and I want to hide back in the bathroom, but I'm frozen in my spot.

"I know. But I couldn't." He stands up. "I just really need to talk to you. Please let me buy you breakfast and explain."

"I don't need you buying me breakfast. I just need you to go." Also, I still have enough vanity that I don't want him seeing me like this. *Go already!*

"Please, Addie." His voice cracks, and his strong shoulders sag with what looks like the weight of the world. Am I really going to feel sorry for him?

Unfortunately, yes.

I let out a sigh. "Fine. But I need to order some coffee first and take a shower."

"Okay. I'll go downstairs and wait in the lobby until you're ready."

I nod my thanks, and once he is gone, I quickly call room service and then get in the shower.

What am I doing? This is way too emotionally draining for what I thought was going to be a typical business trip. But if I don't hear the whole story, it will drive me insane. And because it will drive me insane, it will drive Bridget insane because I'll be obsessing about it all the time, and I can't do that to my best friend. So, really, hearing him out is good for everyone's mental health.

When I come out of the shower, room service has arrived. A few sips of black coffee give me instant—if temporary—strength. I throw on the skirt and T-shirt I was originally going to wear yesterday and blow out my hair, as if pulling it straight is some sort of penance, wondering all the while what Brad's story is going to be. Once my hair is dry, my makeup is on, and my coffee cup is empty, I need to make a call before feeling brave enough to head downstairs.

Bridget answers on the first ring. "Hey! I've been waiting for this call. How was the big date?"

"He's married," I blurt out.

"Married?! *Oh no!* When did you find out?"

I take a deep breath. "After sex."

There is a beat of silence on her end, then, "What?! Slow down, I think we're missing a bunch of steps in between."

"I can't talk long, he's still here."

"He's there?!" I can hear the shock and sense the disapproval.

"Well, he's downstairs in the lobby. We're going to have breakfast." I swallow.

"Why?"

"He wants to explain. Do I let him?"

"What's to explain? He's married and he cheated."

"I know. He said the marriage was terrible and they're in the middle of a divorce."

"Sounds like a familiar story." Her voice drips with cynicism. "You buy it?"

"I don't know." I'm exhausted. "So do I listen?"

"Did you ask why he slept with you?"

"Yes. He said because he liked me." I can hear Bridget harrumphing. "He said because I was the first person he's wanted since he could remember." I play with the handle on my empty coffee cup. "So do I hear him out?"

Pause. "I guess it can't hurt. But, Addie?"

"Yes."

"Be careful. Okay?"

"K."

And with Bridget's grudging blessing, I head downstairs.

I immediately spot Brad waiting for me on one of the lobby sofas. His clothes are a bit rumpled, and stubble shades his chin. But sitting there reading a paper, forgive me God, he still looks so sexy. *Remember, Addie, he's a cad.*

"Ready?" I say brusquely.

He jumps a little. "Yes." And with that, he quickly folds the paper and stands up.

"So, should we just eat here?" I ask, trying to tamp down the competing desires of wanting to reach out and slap him and gently touch the stubble on his cheek.

"I was hoping we could drive someplace."

"Well, it can't be far because I have a flight today to Monterey and I need to pack before then." I fold my arms and start tapping my foot nervously. I just want to hear his story, not dillydally about where to eat.

"What time do you need to be there?"

"At the airport by two or so."

"I meant Monterey."

"It doesn't matter. It's a conference trip." I shrug.

"Why don't I take you?"

"What? To the airport?"

"No. To Monterey."

I look at him, not totally comprehending. "You want to drive me to Monterey? I'm not that familiar with California geography, but isn't it really far? Like several hundred miles?"

"It's a long drive, but it's a long story." We stare at each other for a beat.

This, I did not expect. I don't think I can handle spending a day in a car with a man who just broke my heart. Okay, I realize it was a one-night stand, and therefore, we're not talking heartbreak in the classic sense. But something was definitely broken.

"But I already have a plane ticket," I say, though not as firmly as I wanted.

"I'll reimburse you."

"That's stupid."

"Please." He stands there in his rumpled clothes, his eyes pleading. Damn it. Despite my better judgment, I can feel myself wanting to give in.

"It's a Friday," I challenge. "How are you taking off of work?" Good, the ever-practical Adeline Turner returns.

"That's for me to worry about."

"And what about your wife? Don't you need to let her know you'll be driving the woman you slept with last night across the state?"

"Again, that's something for me to deal with," he says evenly, his jaw visibly tightening.

Spoken like a true cad, I think. But then I look at him. Look at him really hard. My Brad. Could he really be a sleazebag? I know what it looks like on paper, but as I stand here, I can't help but think that maybe he's telling the truth. Finally my resolve breaks and I give in.

"Okay," I say, shaking my head. "Listen, I'm going to go pack and check out. Don't worry about the plane ticket." I hold up my hand to stop him from interrupting. "If you're going to drive me all the way to Monterey, you'll probably want a change of clothes. Maybe you should go home and change first." I gesture to his day-old outfit.

"I don't mind."

"If I'm going to be in the car next to you for that long, *I'd* prefer that you had a change of clothes."

"You're not going to change your mind?" He looks at me carefully.

"No. I'll be here." I wave him off. "Just go home and call me when you get back. I should be ready in an hour."

When I return to my room, I call my secretary and ask her to cancel my flight, telling her I'm driving up with a potential client. So I now have to enter "business development" on my time sheet to explain the next six hours or so of my life. I also email Roger to inform him of my new ETA. And because life must go on even when one's heart is broken, I quickly check and respond to other work emails before packing.

I'm tempted to call Bridget for another assessment of my situation, and I'm sure she's waiting for an update. But I've already made my decision to drive up with Brad, and Bridget would surely try to talk me out of this insanity. Since nothing about the last twenty-four hours has been rational, I'm not ready to heed any rational advice.

But as I'm standing outside with my bags, watching Brad's car pull up to the hotel, I'm dreading my decision.

"Ready to go?" he asks. I note he's freshly shaved and his hair is still slightly damp.

"Guess so," I answer warily while he places my bags in the trunk.

When I get in the car, I'm surprised to notice two Starbucks coffees sitting in the cupholders.

"Is one of those for me?" I say.

"Yes. I got you a grande skim latte since I remember you ordered that at the airport. I got a regular coffee, but I haven't had any yet if you'd prefer that? Or we could just dump it all and get you something else?" he says, rambling and nervously meeting my eyes.

"Thanks." I'm not sure how I feel about the fact that he remembers my drink and how I drank it. Maybe he's just particularly observant. But then again, I'm not sure how I feel about anything at the moment.

On the way out of the city, we drive in silence. Brad looks horribly stressed—his eyes on the road, one hand on the wheel, the other visibly shaky and intermittently reaching for his coffee. He's not the only one.

After ten minutes of driving, we're finally on the freeway and I can't take it anymore.

"Okay, Brad, start talking."

CHAPTER EIGHT

Despite my pounding heart, I keep my eyes on Brad for a good two minutes, silently willing him to offer me the explanation he owes me. Finally, he speaks.

"I met Kathryn at a party during my first year of law school at UCLA. She was an undergrad, just starting her sophomore year there. Encouraged by her friends, she came up and kissed me. My college girlfriend and I had just broken up that summer, and she had just moved to New York. I wouldn't say I was on the rebound, but Kathryn was the first girl I'd met since the breakup. We ended up talking the whole night, and I asked for her number. The next day, I called her and we went out to dinner at a Mexican restaurant. She was sweet, funny, and outgoing, and we got along so well that the next thing I knew, I had another girlfriend."

I find myself holding my breath, imagining all the ways Brad was first attracted to Kathryn, and feel a small secret pang of jealousy at his words.

He continues, "Unfortunately, the getting along didn't always last." He tells me how, for the next three years during law school, they had a rocky relationship, and when I ask why, he says carefully, "She can be a lot."

"What do you mean?"

"Her emotions. She's up, she's down." He explains how there would be days where she would hate him one minute, instigating a fight, and then the next minute passionately declare her love. "And granted, we met when she was nineteen and I was twenty-two, and in the early days I wrote off a lot of her dramatic behavior to age. Also, she was an art major to my law degree, and so I figured it was the way her right brain worked compared to my more left brain."

I try to take all this in. Though I personally didn't experience those types of relationships, I witnessed many of them in my dorm. But I don't remember any of those couples making it down the aisle. I interject, "But you married her."

Brad casts a somber look at me and says, "It's not that simple."

By the end of law school, Brad was tired of the reality TV show–level theatrics in their relationship. The last straw was during his final semester of school, when he finally realized she had been stealing from him. While they were dating, he had noticed cash missing from his wallet from time to time; but then she took his credit card and maxed it out on a Nordstrom shopping spree. When he confronted her, she said their cards must have gotten mixed up and that she thought it was hers. The first time, he believed her. But then it happened again, and again. Each time she would give him a tearful apology but had no means to pay him back. He had already secured a job after graduation at a prominent law firm in Los Angeles and figured he could eventually pay off the debt, but he decided that he needed to break up with her for good.

"Kathryn was graduating, I was graduating. I thought this would be a natural time to end things before the next stages of our lives."

Kathryn did not take the breakup lightly. She would pound and scream on his apartment door at all hours of the day. She would stalk him at the library and make a scene. She would call incessantly, leaving tearful messages apologizing and begging him to take her back. Since Brad needed to focus on studying for the bar exam that summer, he got back together with her simply to keep the peace.

During that time, she went grocery shopping for him, did his laundry, cleaned his apartment, and did everything she could so that he could focus solely on studying. This was the sweet and thoughtful Kathryn he had fallen for, and he figured this was her way of making up for everything.

After the exam, they planned a post-bar trip to Asia before he started his new job in September. His friends who had witnessed their tumultuous relationship tried to talk Brad out of it. But he hadn't listened to them before, and after Kathryn's devotion the past two months, he thought that she really had changed and matured.

"Turned out my friends were right and I was wrong," he says, sighing.

The moment they stepped off the plane, Kathryn's temper returned and they fought the entire trip. Finally, on the last leg of the trip on a beach in Bali, he broke up with her again, and when they returned to the States, Brad resolved to keep the relationship ended. This time, though, there was a complication—Kathryn was pregnant.

"I don't know how she got pregnant," Brad says.

Although I'd been trying to suspend judgment while he was talking, I can't help myself on this one. I arch one of my eyebrows and look at him pointedly. "You don't know how she got pregnant?" *Geez, it's not rocket science, Brad.*

"She told me she was on the pill," he explains.

Right. And with her history of erratic behavior, you believed her? At this point in the story, I commiserate with his friends' frustration, and don't really trust myself to speak without saying something judgmental. So, I hold my tongue and let him continue uninterrupted.

"She cried and said she was thinking of getting an abortion. She told me that her parents would freak out and disown her if they found out she'd gotten pregnant right after college, and what was she going to do alone in LA with no real job and a baby? So I promised to support her in whatever decision she made, and that if she wanted to keep the baby, I'd help provide for them."

She debated her options for another month, concluding that she didn't want to be a single mother and that the only way she would keep the baby would be if he married her. He was scared and still didn't trust her, but as more time went by, he also couldn't bear the thought of never knowing his child. He told himself that motherhood would bring out the thoughtful, sweet Kathryn he remembered when they first started dating and that he still caught glimpses of from time to time. With all that in mind, he married her at city hall.

Even though Brad was working, he couldn't afford childcare those first few years. He had to first pay off his own school loans, as well as the credit card debt Kathryn had amassed, and provide for the three of them. And since Kathryn's degree had been in art and she had only interned at a couple of small galleries, any entry-level job wouldn't cover childcare either, so they decided she'd be a full-time mother until preschool.

"But it was okay," he says. "Because when I saw my daughter, Ivy, for the first time, I decided I would do anything for her."

Unfortunately, to relieve the boredom of being a stay-at-home mom, Kathryn returned to her compulsive spending.

When Ivy was old enough for preschool, Brad asked Kathryn to get a part-time job to help pay off the Damocles' sword of debt hanging over them. He also hoped a job would give her more purpose and distract her from spending money they didn't have. And while she said she went on some gallery interviews but that they didn't want to hire someone her age with no experience, Brad suspected she never applied to any jobs.

"Ultimately, even though we agreed on marriage and raising Ivy together, and her working afterward, she resents me as if I've taken something from her rather than tried to support her. And it seems the more I try to fix things, the angrier she is," he says. Some weeks she would give him the silent treatment while she stayed in bed all day and left Brad responsible for getting Ivy to school or events; other times he wouldn't even be able to get ahold of Kathryn all day. He knew she was prone to depression, and Brad regularly suggested that she talk to someone and even offered to research therapists. But these suggestions only made her angrier, so much so that Kathryn would threaten to leave him and take Ivy away forever. A few times, she even threatened to take her own life. In those instances, Brad would back off, but it scared him enough that he started seeing a therapist.

"My therapist suspects that she suffers from borderline personality disorder," he says.

"Oh my god," I interrupt. "That sounds serious. If that's the case, should she even be around your daughter? Wouldn't you be granted full custody?"

"She loves Ivy and is a good mother when she's not depressed. And when she's in one of her moods, then she's mostly just disengaged. It's *me* she directs her anger and mood swings toward." He pauses. "Even though I can't stand the thought of being separated from Ivy, I also can't bear thinking of her growing up in such an unhappy family. So I broached the subject of divorce."

To Brad's surprise, Kathryn begged him to stay with her and promised to change. She said that more than a job, she just needed time to herself. At this point he was making more money at the law firm, and so, to give Kathryn some relief from motherhood, he hired a nanny to help with Ivy after school. Things got better. They stopped fighting, but they also stopped trying to maintain any facade of a marriage. They simply led separate lives, except when it came to Ivy.

"You hear stories about people who fall in love, get married, have kids, and live happily ever after," he says wistfully.

"I wouldn't know," I say a little bitterly, thinking of my parents.

"Oh, I'm sorry, Addie! I wasn't thinking. I guess I'm too lost in my pity party."

I wave it away. I don't want to feel sorry for myself either, and I'm still waiting for Brad to get to his divorce. "Don't worry about it. Continue."

"Though we weren't fighting, the peace still felt too tenuous and I constantly felt like I was walking on eggshells. Finally I had to admit that we were never meant to be and no amount of work would fix that." Brad pauses and takes a deep breath. "So I filed for divorce and joint custody of Ivy. Kathryn, though, is fighting it and demanding sole custody. She's threatening to take Ivy permanently away from me, and I don't know what to do." His voice cracks slightly. "Ivy is starting second grade, and she is so adorable, Addie. I love her so much. I would do anything for her."

I'm stumped into silence. What can I possibly say? That everything will work out for the best? I don't believe that Ivy will come out of this situation unscathed, no matter how much he wants to protect her. Since I can't console him, I selfishly ask, "So with all of this going on, why did you sleep with me?"

"I couldn't not." He blinks a couple times and swallows. "I know that makes me sound terrible. After seeing you at the airport, I couldn't stop thinking of you. I had the hugest crush on you in high school. But you were so quiet and smart, and I didn't know how to talk to you."

"You . . . you . . . ," I start, feeling a bit dizzy. "You're kidding!" I flash back to that adolescent invitation to play HORSE and inwardly kick myself for never having taken him up on the offer.

Brad shakes his head and continues, "I couldn't believe it when you asked me to a dance right before I moved. I wondered why at the time but figured it was simply because we were leaving. I actually had a date already when I said yes. So right after you left, I had to call the girl to tell her. She was *not* happy with me." He cringes at the memory. "I knew it was wrong, but it was also my last chance. Maybe that's what I was doing again? I haven't seen you since the night of the dance, however many years ago that was, and I knew I couldn't let you get away again."

He turns his eyes away from the road for a second to look at me, and I detect the sadness in them. I can't believe that all that time I was pining for him, he was doing the same one street over. *Why, why, why, universe?*

Since I'm still incapable of responding, Brad goes on: "I remember you sitting in your house in the window, reading books I didn't even hear about until college. I remember how you were always pushing your glasses up to see better. I remember how you always wore your hair in a ponytail, and I only saw it down a couple of times when you were at home, getting the mail in your pajamas, and I couldn't believe how beautiful you were."

I finally find my voice. "I've thought of you many times too. You were my first crush. You never forget that."

Neither of us says anything for a couple of minutes. My imagination conjures up an alternative universe where Brad and I got together in high school, and what would have been.

"But then we moved," Brad says, and the thought of what could have been disappears.

His family moved. Even if we had dated, we wouldn't have stayed together. There is no alternate reality where we would have ended up together. From the way he described his situation, my guess is that his divorce is going to drag on indefinitely. His sweet words that moments ago filled my heart to bursting, now only break it as I realize our night was merely a drunken one-night stand.

"So, I guess that's it, then," I say. "Thank you for telling me everything. I'm sorry you're going through this, and I appreciate you giving me the full story."

"Thank you for listening. I just felt like you deserved to hear the truth after last night. I should've told you when we drove to Malibu. And I was going to, but then I chickened out. And then at the bar when you asked me why I wasn't married, that was my opening, and I avoided the question." He sighs sadly. "But now you know everything. More than you probably wanted to know." He tries to laugh a little.

I put my hand on his shoulder and offer a half-hearted smile. "Hey, what doesn't kill us makes us stronger," I say, and softly pat his shoulder.

"So they say." But he doesn't sound convinced.

CHAPTER NINE

fter Brad's story, we both need a change of subject, and our conversation becomes more like it was at the airport. Although nothing between us is resolved, we're in a strangely relaxed mood as we cover a wide range of topics: current news stories, my life, his life, pets, vacations, movies, pancakes, what is that woman in the car next to us doing, we can't believe we both watch *Survivor*, why is California a desert. We can't stop talking.

The closer we get to Monterey, the sadder I become. The signs with their decreasing mileage are a reminder that our time together is rapidly ticking down. When we turn off at our exit and Siri navigates us the remaining few miles to the hotel, I say, "What are you going to do now? You shouldn't drive back. You must be exhausted."

"Yeah. I think I might drive part of the way back and then find a motel."

"You should probably take a break, though. Maybe we could have dinner someplace? It's about that time," I say tentatively, even though I have dinner plans with Nora tonight. But I know in my heart that this is probably the last time I'll see him, and I'm not ready to say goodbye.

"That sounds like a great idea."

I realize I've been holding my breath and silently exhale.

We navigate our way downtown until the hotel comes into view. I was excited that it was near the water, and I'm sure the views from the rooms are gorgeous, but now it looms in front of me, ready to pop our bubble of intimacy in the car.

Brad parks and helps me carry my luggage into the lobby. As I'm about to walk up to the reservations desk, I hear a big, booming voice calling my name. "Adeline! You made it!"

I look over, and there in the lobby is Scott Schulman, general counsel for Moonstruck Animation, standing with Mark and Dennis. *Oh god. Already?* I'm not quite prepared to mix business with pleasure. But I put on my happy face and walk over.

"Hi! It was a long drive, but I made it." I shake Scott's hand.

I nod at Mark and Dennis. "Hello, hello." Mark is looking quizzically over my shoulder. My nerves are pretty frayed at the moment, and I can feel the heat starting to rise in my cheeks.

"Brad? Is that you?" Mark says. "I didn't know you were going to be at this thing."

"Hi, Mark. Good to see you." Brad approaches the group and shakes Mark's hand. Then he turns to Scott. "Hi, Scott. It's always a pleasure."

Now Mark is looking even more curiously at Brad, as am I.

Scott, not noticing anything unusual, says, "Brad! How are you?" He shakes Brad's hand and heartily claps him on the back. "I see you guys know the best real estate attorney in LA."

I guess we do. Except for Dennis, who holds his hand out. "Dennis Sullivan."

Brad shakes it. "Nice to meet you, Dennis. Brad Summers, Levenfield."

Mark says, "Oh yes. Sorry. Dennis, Brad and I went to law school together at UCLA." He turns to Brad. "Dennis is the head of corporate in our Chicago office."

That answers the Mark and Brad question for me, but what about Brad and Scott? Before I can ask, Mark turns to me. "So how do you two know each other?"

I'm too tired right now to engage in these introductions, and I falter. "How do we know each other?" I repeat the question so I can carefully form my answer.

Fortunately, Brad swoops in and answers. "We grew up down the street from each other and kept in touch."

Scott guffaws. "And you both became lawyers. Ha! Must be something in the water there."

I don't know Mark that well, but I can anticipate what his next question is going to be, which would be why we arrived together. But luckily, Scott saves the day.

"So are you playing any golf this weekend?"

Oh god. Please, Brad, don't say you're not staying. Don't say you just drove me up. I concentrate heavily on these thoughts, hoping to reach him telepathically.

"No. I can't stay for the entire conference. I wasn't sure I was going to make it, but then I had some time today and tomorrow, so I thought it'd be good to come up and at least catch part of it." The lie flows smoothly. "Unfortunately, I have to drive back tomorrow night."

I don't know how much longer I can stand here politely because my brain is about to explode, so I force myself to interrupt the niceties and small talk.

"It's good seeing you all," I say, "but I have to excuse myself to check in."

"Of course," Scott says. "We're just heading to the bar to get a drink before dinner. Why don't you join us after you've had a chance to settle in?"

The client is asking little ole me, who is up for partnership soon, if I would like to join him for a drink. With Mark's and Dennis's eyes on me, there is only one answer.

"Thank you." I force a smile. "That sounds great." *It doesn't.*

"What about you, Brad? How 'bout a drink?" Scott asks.

"Sure. I still have to check in too, so I'll see you in a few?"

Brad and I walk back to the reservations desk together. Why does this feel like the walk of shame?

"So, I guess I'm getting a room here," Brad says.

"Guess so. Who knew it was such a small world?"

After checking in, I wait for Brad to make his reservation. Luckily, they still had a room available, though it's one of the suites. Brad jokes, "This is definitely an upgrade from whatever roadside motel I was planning on finding tonight."

I shake my head and start carrying my bags toward the elevator.

Once the doors close, Brad says, "So what do you want to do tonight? It looks like it might be hard to have a quiet dinner."

"I guess we should just play it by ear," I say a little sadly. "I mean, if those guys ask me to have dinner with them, I kind of have to."

"I understand. I do a lot of real estate work for Moonstruck, so I can't blow off a client either."

Oh! So that's *how he knows Scott.*

Before I can ask more, the elevator doors open. I'm the first to exit, as I am in one of the lowly, standard guest rooms.

"Guess I'll see you down there," I say.

"Yep. Guess so." He gives me a grim smile.

I make my way to my room alone with a heavy heart. I wish I had time to call Bridget or at least some time to mull things over, but I have to get back to reality. No matter how much I want to lock myself away for the next couple of hours—or days—I have to be "on." So I take a two-minute shower, change into my business-casual uniform—dark gray slacks, a black cashmere sweater, black sling-back heels, and a simple silver necklace and earrings—and try to energize myself for an evening of schmoozing.

When I make my way downstairs, I see that Brad has beaten me to the bar and is chatting with Scott. I also spot the usual suspects—Dennis, Mark, and Roger—with drinks in hand standing nearby. I decide that entering their circle might be the easier way to start the evening.

"Welcome, Adeline," Roger says stiffly. It's a chilly but expected reception since I did blow him off yesterday.

"What are you drinking?" Mark asks.

Although I would like something strong and on the rocks, I think it's best to leave the hard stuff for later. Like when I'm alone in my room wondering what the hell happened tonight. "A glass of chardonnay sounds nice."

Mark turns around and catches the bartender's attention. "A chardonnay, please."

Although I know Dennis and Roger from my office, I don't really know Mark all that well, because he's based in our San Francisco office. Conversation all around is a little stiff, and Roger still seems upset with me. We mostly talk about their flight and which panels we're thinking of attending tomorrow. Blah, blah, blah. I'm inwardly rolling my eyes—could this conversation be any more boring?—and using all my willpower not to glance in Brad's direction.

Before I know it, I've downed my glass of wine. That gives me an excuse to make my escape. "If you'll excuse me, I'm going to get a glass of water."

I walk over to a different section of the bar. While I'm waiting for the bartender, I sit down on one of the dark wooden stools and look over to where I last saw Brad. He is still sitting at the other end of the bar, engrossed in conversation with Scott. I give up any last lingering hope of having dinner with him, and try to console myself that it is probably for the best in these circumstances.

I'm wondering where Nora is, so I take out my BlackBerry.

"Hey, now. None of that. It's the weekend," Mark says, sitting down next to me. He orders another vodka tonic for himself.

"Ha ha. So it is." I slide the BlackBerry back into my purse.

"Sorry I didn't have a chance to say this before, but great work on the presentation. You really impressed Scott."

"Thank you!" Finally, I start to relax. "Roger and I worked really hard on putting it together."

"Yes, well, it showed. You definitely did your research. On the down low, it looks like they're going to proceed with this acquisition. In which case, there'll be a lot of work over the next several months."

"That's great." More work—or, more precisely, more billable hours—is a good thing. Except when it's not. I am barely holding a life outside of work as it is.

"How funny that you know Brad," Mark says, abruptly changing the subject.

And we're off! So much for relaxing. "Yes." I flag down the bartender to order another chardonnay, leaving my water untouched in front of me.

"So I guess you know Kathryn too." Good lord, my glass of wine cannot get here fast enough.

"Actually, no. I haven't had the chance to meet her." I take a sip of water to hide my discomfort.

Mark gives a low whistle. "Phew! Count yourself lucky, then. She's a piece of work, that one."

Oh! I almost splutter on my sip of water. Mark must be one of those law school friends Brad told me about, *and* I can't believe he's sharing this with me when we don't really know each other. "What do you mean?"

Mark looks surprised for a second, then shrugs. "What I mean is, she's crazy. In law school we all called her Psycho-Kath. In fact, I still call her that. The woman hooked her claws into him and won't let go. She's turned his life into a living hell. He sees it but doesn't know how to get out of it, and therefore avoids the situation by working all the time." He shakes his head. "I hear they're finally splitting up, though. Thank god! But we'll see."

"Wow. I had no idea." My chardonnay has appeared, and I sip at it innocently, hoping he will divulge more.

"She's very beautiful." My stomach tightens a little at this knowledge, and the old insecurities come knocking. "But very hard. Very cold person."

Interesting. From Brad's description, I would have pegged her as damaged and emotional, albeit manipulative. I'm about to casually ask for more details, but we're interrupted by Roger, who informs us that it is time for their dinner reservation. He apologizes to me, "I'm sorry, Adeline. I thought you were arriving later, so I only made reservations for four."

Yeah, right, Roger. I've worked with him long enough to know he intentionally excluded me from this dinner, the chauvinistic jerk.

"That's okay," I say, trying to hide my relief. "Nora and I planned on getting dinner later with some of her friends." At least that was the original, albeit tentative, plan.

"Are you sure? We could probably add one more," Mark says.

Maybe Mark is just being polite, but I should probably play along. "Thanks. Let me just confirm with Nora if we're still on." I walk out to the lobby and check my BlackBerry. There are a couple of messages from Nora asking what time I'm arriving, whether we're still on for dinner, and who is this potential client I am driving up with. Someone get me out of this hell.

I decide the best thing to do is to call her. "Nora! I'm here at the bar. Where are you?"

"In my room. Are you still on for dinner?"

"Yes, of course. What time?"

"I'm meeting Olivia and Elaine from Smithson Harvey in fifteen minutes in the lobby and then heading to the hotel restaurant. Didn't you see my email?"

"Yes, sorry, I just saw it, which is why I'm calling. Is there any chance you can come down now? I'm trying to get out of dinner with Roger and the crew," I whisper and explain that I already got roped into drinks.

"Yikes! That sounds awful. I'm on my way. See you at the bar."

With excuse in hand, I return to the bar and offer Mark and Roger my regrets. Roger, sporting a cocky grin, looks pleased.

Although I don't have to sit through dinner with them, I do have to sit through dinner in the same restaurant as them—two tables away. I try to keep my eyes averted, but Nora doesn't make it easy.

She nods in the direction of their table. "So what's going on over there?"

"Clients," I tell her.

"I recognize Scott, but who's the other guy?" Shockingly, Roger *was* able to add a fifth to the reservation.

"Brad Summers. He does real estate work for Moonstruck."

"He's hot."

I laugh my first real laugh of the night, though it's bitter. "I suppose he is."

"He keeps looking at you." Nora gives me a pointed look. "Why aren't you returning the favor?"

No matter how old we are or where we are in life, women are always nosy about each other's love lives. Nora is my friend, but she is also my colleague. I've always tried to provide enough details about my dating life to entertain her, but not enough to expose myself to someone whose respect I need.

"We know each other. We're old friends from Wisconsin. That's who I drove up with today."

"Oh!" Nora's eyes widen.

"We're just friends. He's married."

"I see," she says. She takes a sip of her wine and arches her eyebrow. "Not to make you uncomfortable, but my friends don't look at me like that."

Luckily, Nora's friends arrive and start trading law school stories, as well as law firm horror stories, but it takes all my strength to focus on our conversation. When I hear laughter emanating from the guys' table, I think I can make out Brad's laugh over the others and I can't help but sneak a peek. He is perfectly at ease, smiling and laughing at some story Scott is telling, and then our eyes meet for a nanosecond and an electric shock goes through me and I have to look away.

Thankfully, we finish our dinner before they do. In fact, I notice another bottle of red being poured at their table and figure they are probably in for a long night of trading war stories. If I were at the top of my professional game this evening, I'd go over there to say good night. But I can't bring myself to do it. I just want to get to my room and into my anonymous hotel bed.

Of course, once I'm in bed all I can think about is Brad. I replay the day's events over in my head. I wish I could call Bridget, but it's late in Chicago. Sleep proves elusive.

Around midnight, my phone rings. When the caller ID shows it's Brad, my heart leaps.

"Hello," I answer.

"Hey, Addie. It's me."

"Hey. What's up?" Besides *everything*.

"I'm sorry we weren't able to have dinner tonight."

"Me too."

"Um . . . ," he stammers. "I hope this doesn't sound like a come-on, but I have a lovely view from my room."

"I'm sure you do." I laugh. "And yes, it does sound like a come-on."

"So . . . would you like to see the view?" he ventures tentatively. "And this is not a line. I just want to say goodbye in person. I'm leaving first thing in the morning."

"Oh." I am tempted. Really, really tempted. But Nora already caught us looking at each other across the room, and the way the evening has been going, I'm sure to run into someone I know in the hall or elevator, and I don't want to be "caught" going to or from Brad's suite. All of this is messy, and it's time to return to real life now. "I'd really like to, but I think it's best we just say goodbye on the phone," though each word hurts to say.

"Oh, I see." He pauses. "So, I guess this is it, then. I just want to say again how sorry I am for everything."

"I know. Thank you." After the car trip, I've softened. "Sometimes life is complicated."

"That it is," he says quietly.

Since there's nothing left to say really, I say with regret, "Good night, Brad."

"Good night, Addie."

I hit End Call and carefully lay the phone next to me. Even though my head tells me I made the right decision, I toss and turn all night as my heart wonders if it was the right choice.

* * *

I spend the rest of the weekend avoiding contact with everyone. Although Nora and I had planned to schedule some spa treatments, I instead feign interest in attending various panels. The last thing I want to do is be alone with my thoughts. The second to last thing I want to do is talk to anyone. Therefore, I spend an entire day attending workshops with sexy names like "Tax Strategies for Corporate Acquisitions," "New Developments in Securitization," and "Advanced Venture Capital." Nora looks at me like I have lost my mind. But it solves both my problems and gives the impression that I'm some sort of gunner rather than the victim of unfortunate romantic circumstances.

All weekend I count the hours until I am safely back in Chicago and swear I am never returning to California. I remember Hollywood's motto, "The land of broken dreams," and decide that it applies aptly to the entire state.

CHAPTER TEN

A giant rain cloud follows me all the way home from Monterey to Chicago. When my flight lands at O'Hare, all I want to do is jump into a cab and return to the safety of my Gold Coast condominium. Eric sent me several texts offering to pick me up from the airport, but I'm too emotionally and mentally drained from the last few days to want to see him. But after I kept texting back that I would prefer to take a cab from the airport rather than put him out, I could sense his radar going off. So, not able to handle more drama, it just seemed easier to text back, If you insist, then that would be nice.

I head over to the baggage claim at O'Hare and spot Eric standing at my carousel—a grinning, golden-haired knight in shining armor ready to help me with my bags and whisk me home. My stomach tightens at the sight of his kind, happy face, and I silently chastise myself for being swept up by the fantasy of my high school crush. When Eric sees me, he smiles and waves. I force a smile and cheerful wave in return.

When I reach him, we hug and I'm glad he's so much taller than I am, because it gives me an excuse to avoid too much eye contact. He helps me collect my suitcase and carries all my bags to his awaiting chariot, not letting me lift a finger. "You've had a long trip. Let me get these."

In the car, he asks me about California. I try to come up with something entertaining to tell him, but I have nothing.

"The scenery was nice, but overall it was a pretty boring trip. I just spent the whole time working or going to presentations."

I turn the conversation back to him. While he talks, I look out the window at the drab suburban landscape. It's dark outside, and the streets are black and slick. Eventually, I make out the Chicago skyline coming into view. I know that the skyscrapers' tiny flickering lights are workers burning the midnight oil, and I'm glad that, starting tomorrow morning, I will be back sitting in my own high-rise office, focusing on something other than Brad or Eric.

When we pull up to my place, Eric miraculously finds street parking in front of my building, which never happens, and I am now thoroughly convinced that the universe is using me as its whipping girl. Eric insists on carrying my luggage up to my condo. When we enter my building, the doorman eyes Eric and gives me a knowing look. I try to shoot him one back that conveys, *Mind your own business*, but not too much because he is my gateway to my deliveries, dry cleaning, and HOA gossip.

As soon as we walk through my front door, still holding my bags, Eric asks, "Where would you like these? In the bedroom?"

"Oh no! That's okay. You can just drop them there." I point to a spot in my tiny entrance hall.

"Are you sure? It's no problem."

"No, really. This is fine." *Just put down the luggage.*

He sets them down, and there's an awkward moment as we both stand in the hallway. So I begin, "Thanks again for the ride."

"Of course. Happy to do it."

Another awkward moment as I think of how to say goodbye.

"So, what do you want to do now?" Eric asks.

"I'm really beat after this trip. So I'd love to just take a shower and go to sleep."

Eric grins. "You know, I could probably help you with that." He puts his arms around me and moves in for a kiss.

Oh god, this is happening. I move my head away and say, "Oh my gosh, I'm sorry. I didn't have time to brush my teeth."

He looks a little offended, which fair enough—he should be. I'm being a jerk because I can't handle any romantic overtures in my current headspace.

To make it up to him, I say, "You know what? I'm actually really hungry. I haven't eaten since breakfast. Can I take you out to dinner? You know, to thank you for picking me up."

I can tell by his expression that he had a different idea of how I could thank him. But he backs off and says, "Dinner would be great. I should've asked you if you were hungry. Sorry about that."

"There's a great Italian place down the street."

"Let's do it."

I breathe an inward sigh of relief and grab my purse. I can't get out the door fast enough.

"Don't you want to freshen up at all?" he says.

"Oh?" The brushing my teeth comment comes back to me. "Um, yeah . . . just give me a minute, if you don't mind." I go into the bathroom where I brush my teeth and wash my hands, making a show of freshening up, so he can hear the water running. But mostly, I just stare at my tired face in the mirror and wonder what's wrong with me. There's a good-looking, gainfully employed man sitting in my living room. One that a few days ago I thought had romantic potential. But then some cheating blast from the past blows in—*who is in no position to have a relationship with me*—and now threatens this fledgling romance? My jaw tightens, and I pull my shoulders back as I take one last look at myself in the mirror. I am going to be on my best date behavior tonight at dinner, and I'm going to kiss Eric good night. I might not be ready for more right now, but if Eric is the guy he seems to be, then that should be okay.

Over wine and pasta, I'm at my best—listening to Eric's stories, asking lots of questions, laughing at his jokes—all despite the gaping hole in my chest where my heart should be. When I try paying the bill, Eric takes it and says, "Let me get this one." And with a wink he says, "You can get the next one. What do you think about that?"

"I think that sounds great." And I sort of hope I mean it.

He walks me home, and we do kiss good night in front of my building. As it happens, I press my lips hard against Eric's to block out any thoughts of my weekend, but it only makes me feel worse.

* * *

At ten o'clock the next morning, we have a team meeting regarding Moonstruck Animation. They were impressed with our presentation and want to go ahead and begin formal due diligence for an acquisition of Imogen Software. That means I am going to be even more swamped than usual for the next month (or, more likely, several months). Circumstances being what they are at the moment, I do not mind the idea of immersing myself in a big project, especially one that is so high profile.

Although, I must admit that work is not at the forefront of my mind this Monday morning. The entire day is really a waiting game until I can meet Bridget tonight. I've been saving up my story until I can see her face to face, with a strong drink in hand.

At six forty-five, I shut down my computer and walk over to the wine bar we agreed on. Since it's only Monday, there are a few empty tables, and I grab one by the window. As soon as I sit down, I receive a text from Bridget that she is going to be a few minutes late. I text her back, No worries. Sitting by window. See you soon. I order a glass of cabernet sauvignon and wait.

Through the large plate-glass windows, I watch commuters and other worker bees leaving their offices and walking down the sidewalk. Some hurrying past, probably to catch the train. Others walking in pairs or groups, strolling and laughing, in no hurry to go home. Twentysomethings dressed in suits or business casual, probably heading to or from a happy hour. I love people watching and making up backstories of whatever characters walk by. I've always been more of an observer than a participator and tend to live in my own head sometimes, which is why I probably liked to write stories so much when I was younger. But once I started working at Gilchrist & Jenkins, I lost a lot of my free time (and motivation) to write a new book. Also, the pile of rejection letters stuffed in a shoebox in my closet indicates that I probably chose the right career path. And I'm okay with this, I guess.

Before I can feel too sorry for myself, a flurry of activity and apologies in the form of Bridget interrupts my thoughts.

"Addie! Oh my god, I'm so sorry to keep you waiting. I had this last-minute proof I needed to send out, and the file wasn't loading properly . . ." She rambles on.

I wave my hand as if batting her excuses away. "Don't worry about it. I know how it is. Let's just get you a drink."

The server comes over to take Bridget's order. Not wasting any time, Bridget says, "I'll have what she's having."

When the server leaves, Bridget turns to me and says, "Are you sure you don't want something stronger? Seems like you had a hell of a weekend."

I lower my forehead into my hands and shake my head. "You don't even want to know."

I go over every excruciating detail of my night with Brad, the car ride up to Monterey, and our arrival at the conference, including the few details that Mark shared about "Psycho-Kath." Bridget listens carefully, asking few questions, just letting me get it all out. Two glasses of wine later, I'm finished and wait for her verdict. She's definitely going to chastise me—something along the lines of, *What a cheating prick! Why did you even get in the car with him?! You need to forget him.*

Instead, Bridget surprises me with, "You must've really had a connection for him to take that risk with you."

I almost knock over my third glass of wine. "What? What do you mean?"

"Well, no disrespect to the sisterhood, *but* . . . from what you just told me, his wife sounds legitimately crazy. And if she found out he did anything like that, surely she would use it against him in the divorce. Maybe rightly so. But also probably psychotically so. For him to take that risk, and the consequences that might ensue, he must've felt very strongly about you."

"I didn't think of that." I pause. "But what does it matter, since he's in LA and it doesn't look like he's going to be getting out of his marriage anytime soon?"

"You don't know that. I mean, he filed for divorce and clearly"—she gestures to me with her glass—"he's moved on."

This is the last thing I expected to hear from Bridget, whose strong moral compass and sleazebag detector usually keep her out of trouble.

"Okay. True, but I don't want to get my hopes up." I sigh. Also, it feels a bit icky to wish the end of someone's marriage, no matter how bad. "But, Bridge, it was incredible when I was with him. I don't remember the last time I felt like that. Maybe it was just pure lust, but I don't know." I look her in the eye. "Do you remember the last time you had butterflies?"

Bridget sips her wine thoughtfully before answering. "Not for a while. Or at least not in the last few years. I often wonder if I'll feel that way again. But maybe it just doesn't happen as much as we get older?"

"Yeah." I nod. "Maybe that's why it was so incredible. But also why it's such a letdown. I know I need to let it go. And it's not like I had him, so there's nothing really to let go of. But I just keep dwelling on it."

"You know what's worse than dating in your twenties?"

"What's that?"

She makes a face. "Dating in your thirties."

I laugh, again almost knocking my glass over and saving it from a near miss.

"It's true," she says, waving her now unsteady hand in the air to emphasize her point. "In your twenties, everything is fresh and new, and you can easily walk away from a relationship, confident that another one is out there. In your thirties, though, all the mistakes of your twenties come back to haunt you. Everyone has baggage. And if you don't have any baggage, then that means you probably haven't lived much."

"I don't have any baggage," I mumble, looking down into my glass.

Bridget lets out a hearty guffaw. "*You!* Who are you kidding? You have so much baggage."

"What?! I don't talk to any of my exes. None of them have scarred me."

Bridget softens her tone. "You grew up in a single-parent household. You have no contact with your mother, who left you and is out there living her life. You're this perfectionist in everything. Except you have these lackluster relationships when you know you deserve way better. I'm sure ten minutes with a therapist would sort this out, but you're too stubborn to see your own patterns."

I'm not really in the mood to be psychoanalyzed and am grateful when the server interrupts our little session by arriving with our food.

When he leaves, Bridget puts her hand on mine and gives it a little squeeze. "I'm sorry, sweetie. I know you really like him. And you never know . . ." She trails off in a hopeful tone.

"True," I say, ready to stop talking about Brad. "So what about you? What's going on?"

Bridget must have sensed my unease, because she launches into a hilarious description of her date with Eric's friend, which didn't sound all that pleasant. So then I tell her about Eric, and how he picked me up from the airport and our dinner together.

Bridget seems impressed. "Wow, he's way less of a dud than my guy. Good going, lady. You're swimming in men these days."

"Thanks. But I don't know. After everything with Brad, I'm just not feeling it now with Eric."

"I wouldn't break it off. Sounds like you're just in a funk. Give it some time."

"But wouldn't that be pursuing one of those lackluster relationships I'm so prone to?" I throw back at her. But I know she's right. Eric is the better choice—the only choice, really.

"Touché, but no. He sounds like a keeper. And that would be another example of you cutting off your nose to spite your face."

I laugh. "I'm not sure that's the correct expression for it. But yes, yes. I hear what you're saying."

She crinkles her nose. "Throwing the baby out with the bathwater?"

"No. Try again."

"Don't look a gift horse in the mouth?" she ventures.

I laugh harder. "Thank you, Dr. Bridget, but I think I can take it from here."

That night I hit the pillow hard and fall into a dreamless sleep. When my alarm goes off at six thirty, I hit snooze despite a night of solid sleep. I close my eyes again and think about everything.

It was only one night, but *seriously*, it might as well have been a yearlong relationship given how depressed I've been. And even though Bridget was trying to give me some hope last night, I have to face the facts. Brad has not attempted to contact me since the conference, nor have I attempted to contact him. Even though he came clean and confessed his story to me, in the cold, hard light of day (or early dawn in my case) our meeting was nothing more than a one-night stand gone wrong.

I scold myself for being so silly and resolve not to think about him again.

CHAPTER ELEVEN

For the next month, I'm swamped with the Moonstruck and Imogen deal, currently dubbed "Project X." My days are filled with the same routine of work, working out, and Eric, in that order. I let both work and the gym take precedence over the poor guy, but Eric claims he's just as busy with work as I am, and so we've agreed to take things slow.

On a nondescript Friday morning, I receive an email from Dennis, the head partner on Project X, asking me to meet him in his office at 1:00 p.m. regarding an important matter. For the last month, everything on Project X has been an "important matter." So I don't give it much thought. I figure that he's probably going to give me a new laundry list of assignments. I've been billing like crazy lately and am thankful to have such a big project keeping me busy. Although I've been working with Roger, ever since the LA trip he has chilled toward me, so I've been taking most of my direction from Dennis and from Mark in the San Francisco office.

When I enter Dennis's office with a notebook and pen in hand, he is talking on the phone. I give him a *Is this a good time?*

look and he waves me in. I sit down in one of the chairs across from his desk, trying not to look like I'm eavesdropping on his conversation, which I'm really not, as it's not that interesting sounding on his end.

"Yes, yes. That's right," he says into the phone.

I look idly around the room, admiring the photographs of his family behind his desk, the framed diplomas on the wall, some abstract oil paintings, until my eyes rest on the floor-to-ceiling windows and their view. Dennis's office is on the east side of the building, facing Lake Michigan, which is a glittering sapphire blue on this clear day. I remember how Brad made a comment that Lake Michigan was no Pacific Ocean. *But whatever, Brad, what do you know? I would trade Lake Michigan for the Pacific Ocean any day of the week if it meant I was far away from you.* Also, how dare he, a fellow Midwesterner, speak disparagingly of the Great Lakes? What a jerk. California totally ruined the guy.

Dennis finishes up his phone call. "Okay, talk to you soon. Bye." And click.

I turn my attention back to his desk and see him scribbling a note on a legal pad. When he's done, he puts down his pen, folds his hands on the desk, and leans forward. "So, Adeline," he says, looking at me intently. "How are you today?"

"I'm fine, thank you." I try to stifle a laugh at this nicety. He sees me every day and until now has yet to ask me how I am. "And you?"

"Very good." Then he gets down to business. "I wanted to meet with you to let you know that we've been very impressed with your work on Project X. You've worked hard and shown a lot of initiative on this deal."

"Thank you." I feel like a child being singled out as the top student in class. Praise for hard work is pretty scarce in this office. The only way you typically know you're doing a good job is more assignments.

"Have you been happy working on Project X?"

"Oh yes. I've really enjoyed the exposure to different aspects of this deal, such as the IP and real estate. It's been very interesting."

"You've also been getting a lot of compliments on your work from the client."

"That's great. Thank you." *Really? That is interesting.*

"Yes, I've never heard Scott speak so highly about an associate before."

"I'm happy to hear that." Even though I'm lapping up the compliments, I highly doubt that Dennis called me in here just to say what a great job I'm doing. When is this meeting really going to get started?

"Therefore, we were wondering if you'd be willing to transfer to the San Francisco office?"

Hold on. What?

But before I can say anything, Dennis continues, "Scott Schulman has requested that you work exclusively on this deal. He was very impressed with your knowledge at our meeting and the work you've been doing for them. Since Imogen Software is located in Silicon Valley, rather than flying you out every other week, it would be easier if you were closer to the action. Plus, once the deal goes through, they're planning to build a new facility and offices out there, and there will be a lot of ongoing work with them."

My mouth suddenly feels dry, because apparently my jaw has been hanging open. Fortunately, I still have the power of speech. "Is this a permanent thing? Or just temporary?"

"It's up to you. If you want to move out there for a year, and then decide you hate it, we can always reevaluate," Dennis says casually, but the look in his eyes is serious. He continues, "The firm has a great relocation package. You don't have to do anything. The movers will pack everything for you, and the firm would find you housing. HR can give you all the details on that."

"When would you want me out there?"

"In a few weeks, ideally."

"O-kay," I say slowly.

"You don't have to give me an answer now. Think it over this weekend and let me know Monday." He pauses and then says, "Do you have any questions?"

I have a million questions, but I can't seem to think of one to ask.

I shake my head. "No. I can't think of anything right now."

"Okay. Mull it over. I'll have HR send you the relocation packet." Dennis drums his fingers on his desk. "This is a great opportunity. It's also a *great* compliment."

"Yes. I recognize that." I stand up. "Thank you. I'll let you know."

I walk back to my office in a daze, my head swimming with what-ifs. Once inside, I close my office door and flop down onto my Aeron chair.

I've been to San Francisco before as a tourist and for work, so it's not like I'd be moving someplace sight unseen. I liked it well enough. But what about my life here? Which forces me to ask the existential question, What is my life here? My father lives four hours away, by car. My only "friends" here are my work colleagues, like Nora. And Bridget. I'd be really sad to move away from Bridget. But that's it? I have only two friends in Chicago? There's my "relationship" with Eric, but who am I kidding? Almost two months into dating and we still haven't slept together or declared any sort of relationship, so I suspect he's probably dating other people. Then there's my condo. I love my place, but I also chose it primarily for its proximity to work. I'm sure I can find something similar in San Francisco.

They say the unexamined life is not worth living. After examining my own, I'm not sure that I'm much of a fan of it myself. I don't even have a pet that would be disrupted by this move. Maybe this is a good opportunity—*for me to get a life.*

But I like it here. I'm comfortable. I have my routines. Navigating a new city could be exhausting. I remember the move from New York to Chicago. Just finding a new hair salon was pretty traumatizing.

What if I were to stay? Would it interfere with my work on Project X? Would I sour a good client relationship when I'm "thisclose" to partner? Would I piss off Dennis? We're in the business of client service. Shouldn't I be showing my dedication? If my lack of a bustling social life here is any indication, my only real dedication is to my job. Do I want to screw up the one thing I really have going for me?

I was planning on heading to the gym after work, but this is an emergency and I need to call in the big guns. Or, as I just realized, my only true friend in the city. I text Bridget.

> The firm wants me to move to San Francisco within a month. I have until Monday to make a decision. I don't know what to do??? Can you meet for drinks tonight?

Within minutes I receive a reply.

> What???!!!! OMG! Of course. What time?

I type back:

> Whenever you get off work, just call me
> and we'll figure it out.

A few minutes later, I receive an email from HR with the relocation package attached. How am I expected to get any work done today?

I decide to call my dad.

"Hey, Dad! You'll never believe this." I tell him the whole story.

"That sounds like a great opportunity, honey!" The pride in his voice is unmistakable.

"So do you think I should take it?"

"Of course! This is a great move for your career."

"But I'd be really far away . . . ," I start to say. Wouldn't he miss me?

"Yes. But you've been far away before and we both survived." He says it kindly, but also a little patronizingly. I feel embarrassed at my sentimentality. But coming from stoic stock, my dad has never been much for expressing his emotions, so I tamp down my own. "Besides," he continues, "it might be a good thing for you to visit your mom."

The hair on my arms bristles. My mother is currently living in Berkeley, California, uncomfortably close to San Francisco. "I know, Dad. But I can't think about that now," I say sharply. I never like thinking about it.

My dad takes the hint and we change topics. Before we hang up, I promise to visit this weekend. I had planned on working, but maybe a little road trip home will help me make up my mind.

* * *

"I'm honored. But I guess it's also practical, since I've done so much work for them, and I could probably do better work being out there. So it would still be like my old job, but less of it, if that makes sense?" Or at least that's how I describe it to Bridget over dinner and drinks.

"That sounds fabulous! All that hard work and those all-nighters paid off," says Bridget. "The only thing is that I'm completely selfish and don't want you to move because I'll miss you horribly."

"Same here." I frown. "Frankly, I don't really want to go. I know it's a huge honor and everything, but I'm just really settled here. And moving's such a pain."

"True. Moving sucks, and I understand being settled and feeling comfortable. But, and I say this in the kindest possible way, in your case *settled* means 'stagnant.'"

"Hey!" I sit up straight and try to look offended, even though I know she's totally right.

"Sure, you're kicking ass at work, but what about your personal life? I mean, you haven't had any serious relationships since law school. Which is, what, five years? Seven years?"

"I'm seeing Eric."

Bridget rolls her eyes. "And I repeat, you haven't had any serious relationships since law school."

"What about Gary? I dated him after law school."

"Gary sucked. I hated Gary, so he doesn't count."

"Your point?"

"And the only people you hang out with besides me are your lawyer friends." She does air quotes around the word *friends*.

"I work a lot. That's just the business."

"Really?"

"Yes. And I only hang out with other lawyers cause they 'get it,'" I say, mimicking her air quotes. "As opposed to my other friends."

Everything Bridget is saying is true, and I'd come to the same conclusion earlier this afternoon. But it's one thing for me to recognize that my life is pretty sad and quite another to know that someone else thinks the same thing.

Bridget leans back in her chair and slowly spins her wine glass on the table. "You know, personally, I would jump at this opportunity. I love you and will be super sad for you to move, but now's the time to make this type of leap. Your move is paid for, and you luckily"—she raises her eyebrows at the word *luckily* to drive her point home—"do not have any other responsibilities or ties here. If you hate it, you can always move back."

She's right. I know she's right.

"I know. I've been thinking the same thing. It was just so out of the blue that I haven't had a chance to process it all yet. But yeah, I think it's time to shake things up." I raise my glass. "To a new city and adventure!"

"And to having your good friend Bridget come out and visit!" She raises her glass and clinks it with mine.

* * *

I wake up early Saturday morning and throw a few things in an overnight bag. Unfortunately, I also pack my computer bag, because at the moment the law and Project X never sleep. But otherwise, I'm looking forward to the four-hour drive to my dad's, and to being alone with my thoughts.

Even though we are only a state away, I haven't been up to Wisconsin for several months, and now that I may be moving, the landscape takes on new significance. I will miss the transition as Chicago sprawls into the suburbs all the way past the state line and through Milwaukee. Beyond Milwaukee, the scenery is a collage of old barns, cornfields, and dairy cows, and I begin to feel nostalgic as I get closer to home.

My dad still lives in the same house I grew up in, the same one my mother left us in. Our close neighbors rallied around us, bringing us casseroles and offering kindnesses, their greatest kindness being not asking me about the details. At the time I was devastated, but looking back now, I can smile at some of the divorcées and widows who gathered around my dad, and I can see past their kind motives. My dad never dated, though—or at least not that I knew of, and I don't want to ask—and so he never remarried. Maybe we are both bad at relationships? Or maybe, sharing a personality, we pick the wrong people? When I see that therapist (never) Bridget keeps urging (and teasing) me to see, I should ask about this.

I'm relieved when I pull into the driveway, more than ready to shake off these morose thoughts.

My dad comes out to greet me with Winston, his trusty bull-dog, waddling behind him.

"Addie! Welcome home." He gives me a quick hug.

"Hi, Dad! Thank you."

"How was your drive?"

"It was fine. The usual. A lot of traffic until Milwaukee and then it cleared up."

I open the back door of my car and pull out my bags.

"Let me get those." My dad takes them from me while I lock the car and then follow him up the path to the house. I take the opportunity to look around the yard for any cosmetic changes since the last time I visited, but everything looks like its same tidy self.

We chitchat about the weather, and my dad carries my bags upstairs to my old bedroom.

"Are you hungry?" he asks.

"Starving."

I forgo my usual healthy eating mentality and ask to head to my old favorite burger joint that has the most delicious custard shakes. That's right: not milkshakes, but custard shakes. Dietary devils they are, but I'm craving some comfort food, and my old hometown isn't exactly a mecca for healthy options.

We hop in his car and head straight to the retro-looking burger shack. After placing our orders inside, we carry our trays out to the patio. My dad gives me just enough time to unwrap my cheeseburger from its wax paper and take my first bite, before starting in.

"So how's work? Have you thought more about San Francisco?" He takes a bite of his own burger.

"Yeah. Even though I dread the physical move itself—unpacking, figuring out what to do with my place, navigating a new city, etcetera—I think it's a great opportunity."

"Good. I agree with you. This could be a big career move."

"Sure, but I was also thinking about the adventure part—being in a new city and all."

"When are you up for partner again?"

"Next year." I steal one of my dad's fries. "Well, actually, end of this year. They usually announce it around Christmas."

"Then there's your answer."

"Hmm?" I'm still nibbling on the fry, kind of wishing I'd ordered some too.

"If the client is so impressed with you that they want you to move closer to their offices and work more directly with them, then that's your ticket to partnership. If you don't move, and this is the client you've been primarily working with, then that could really jeopardize your position with the firm. They want to solidify that relationship. And who knows? Maybe you could eventually go in-house with them if you decide you want to get out of firm life."

Did I mention that my father is a lawyer? Whereas my reasons for moving are because if anything I am too focused on my career, it doesn't seem to faze my dad, who has been working almost every day for the last thirty-six years. Although I secretly think he would like grandchildren to dote on, he rarely asks about my dating life, and I prefer it that way. Instead, our major discussions focus on my career, and I think he is proud of me and glad that I'm financially independent. Thankfully, he doesn't seem to notice that his daughter may also be a bit boring.

When we get home, we decide to take Winston for a walk around the neighborhood. During our walk, I take in the suburban-style homes with their large front lawns and mature trees. Some of the neighbors are out doing yard work and wave at us. We wave back, and I still recognize most of them. The smell of fresh-cut grass tickles my nose, conjuring up memories past. Growing up, I used to associate that smell with Brad Summers. The sound of the lawn mower and smell of cut grass usually meant Brad was outside mowing our lawn. Hiding behind my book or a curtain, I would discreetly watch him from the window, wondering if he knew I was there. And that's when we pass it—the Summerses' old house. It looks different now. The house has been painted a dark gray over its original sunny yellow color. The landscaping is more manicured and polished. The lack of toys, bikes, or any indication of family life makes me wonder who lives there now. I almost ask my dad, but I don't feel like talking about Brad, even if somewhat tangentially.

That night we play cards and read in the family room, not unlike many of my other visits. I like that I don't have to fill the time with chatter, but it also makes me realize how quiet my life is and that it isn't too different from my sixty-two-year-old father living alone in a small town in Wisconsin. I don't care to admit how many nights I've spent at home curled up with a book or playing a mindless game on my phone. It's a good thing I came up to visit, because *this* was the wake-up call I needed.

So be it. San Francisco, here I come.

CHAPTER TWELVE

The firm was correct when they said the move wouldn't be that difficult. In one day, movers came and packed up all my belongings in a much more efficient and organized manner than I would've been capable of, detailing all my items inside each box. The relocation agents found me an apartment that's on the ground floor of a Victorian house in a neighborhood called Cow Hollow and secured a suitable tenant to rent my condo. Also, Eric didn't take the news too badly. He said of course he was disappointed, but we both agreed that long-distance relationships never work out. I think he was probably just as relieved as I was for such an easy way to end things. In fact, all of it was so easy that it made me wonder if I had really passed seven years in the same place.

The night before the moving truck is scheduled, I lie in my bed surrounded by all my boxes. A few weeks ago, I had to rationalize moving, but now that it's actually happening, I feel a growing buzz inside me. Maybe I'll have time to write. Maybe I'll fall in love. Furthermore, I haven't even had time to think about "he who shall not be named." So why am I thinking of him now? I haven't mentioned his name since that night at the wine bar with Bridget because I'm still embarrassed to even be thinking about him like some lovestruck teenager. But I cut myself some slack—some habits are hard to break.

I fly out on a Saturday morning with two big suitcases in tow. The firm offered to put me up in a hotel while I waited for my furniture and boxes to arrive, but I'm too eager to move and want to get settled into my apartment and neighborhood before Monday morning. Although I've visited San Francisco several times, the cab ride takes me past neighborhoods I've never seen before, and I am utterly charmed by the rows of colorful Victorian homes dotting the hillsides.

When my cab stops in front of a gorgeous yellow Victorian building with wrought iron gates and flowers blooming around the windowsills, I have to double-check the address because I can't believe my luck. I will have to send a thank-you note to the agent who secured the place. After paying my cab driver, I leave my luggage on the sidewalk and walk up the stairs to the front door. My landlord lives on the top floor of the building and asked me to ring him when I arrived. I'm practically bouncing on the doorstep as I wait.

A fit-looking older gentleman with a full head of white hair and sparkling blue eyes answers the door and smiles.

"You must be Adeline Turner."

"I am," I say.

He reaches out to vigorously shake my hand. "Well, hello and welcome! I'm Henry Goodman. Wait one second while I go get the key."

He returns inside before I can say a word. I look around me while I wait. The building looks great. Check. The landlord seems nice. Check. I am now dying to get into my new digs.

We walk downstairs to a blue door at sidewalk level that leads into the apartment. Mr. Goodman takes me on a tour of the rooms. The place is better than the pictures and flooded with light, with a kitchen, dining area, living room, bedroom, and full bathroom, as well as a little nook area that will work perfectly as a home office. It has a gas fireplace, and off the living room are French doors that lead out onto a small patio overlooking a well-maintained backyard. My new landlord tells me that he and his wife have a gardener who tends to the back garden.

"My wife has a penchant for roses," he says and gives me a wink. My luck! He explains that the patio is mine to do with what I wish, but the yard is their private property. That sounds like the perfect deal to me. This blows the balcony in my condo out of the water. It's all so pretty and quaint, and I can't quite believe it's real. It's the perfect launching pad for my new life.

* * *

My office is also a bit of a surprise. Whereas our Chicago office has hundreds of lawyers and covers several floors, the San Francisco office is much, much smaller, covering maybe half a floor in a skyscraper downtown. But I expected that, knowing that there are roughly only twenty or so attorneys here, doing corporate, intellectual property, and real estate work for local clients.

Feeling overdressed in my black suit as others walk by in what generously might be called business-casual attire (I even spot a pair of flip-flops), I wait for Mark in the reception area.

"Adeline, welcome," Mark says as he walks up to me. He looks genuinely happy to see me, which puts me at ease. "Did you find the office okay?"

"Oh yes. Well, actually my cab driver found it." I shrug and smile.

"You'll get your bearings soon enough. Here, let me give you the tour."

I follow him past the lobby desk, and we mostly walk around in a circle. The tour takes all of ten minutes, the most important features being the bathroom and kitchen area.

"We're planning to expand," Marks tells me. "Right now we're just on this floor, but in the next year or two, we expect to grow and may need new office space."

"That's exciting," I reply, uncertain whether I will be part of that growth.

As Mark shows me my new office, I silently hope that we won't need new space anytime soon because the first thing I notice about it is the expansive view of the bay and hills—a view that I do not want to give up in the near future. The rest of the office is surprisingly traditional. A dark wood desk, shelves, and file cabinets. Maybe because I moved out here for a "high-tech" deal, I guess I was expecting something a little more sleek and modern-looking.

"What do you think?" Mark asks.

"It's great. I can't believe the view."

"Yes, people love this office for that reason. It makes up for the stodgy decor." He grins.

I laugh and hope I wasn't giving anything away with my expression. "It's great. Really. Serious decor for serious work."

Mark laughs and then takes me around to everyone else's offices to officially introduce me. I make a mental note of the two younger associates that Mark has working on Project X. Emma is a second-year associate, petite, with red hair and an infectiously bubbly personality. It's always a nice surprise to meet happy associates because most of them always seem so downtrodden. Then there is Rachel (case in point), a fifth-year associate, medium height, slim and blond, with cold blue eyes that will pierce right through your soul. Okay. I exaggerate. Physically she reminds me a bit of Nora, but behind Rachel's smile and the uneasy look in her eyes, I sense some wariness. I understand that sometimes people can be intimidated by a change in office lineup, but I figure once she gets to know me, her wariness will disappear. Although, when Mark tells me later that Rachel splits her time between work on Project X and her work for Jasmine, a partner in the real estate department, I'm a little relieved.

* * *

Over the course of the first couple weeks, I spend my weekdays at work and my weekends unpacking boxes. Late one Sunday afternoon, as I break down the final empty boxes for recycling, I officially declare myself moved in. My books are lined up on the shelves, all my clothes are now neatly hanging in the closet or folded in drawers, and my personal decor items are dispersed through the apartment. As I survey the cozy space, I take a deep breath and then exhale in gratitude for how well things in my life are going. This calls for a celebratory cup of tea and a catch-up session with my bestie.

"How are things going?" Bridget asks when I call.

"Great! I finished the last of my boxes today. So I finally feel settled in."

"So, what have you been doing?"

"Just working and unpacking. Last week I joined a gym near my office. I haven't needed much of a workout, though, with all this unpacking. Oh, and a couple mornings I've been running by the water."

"BORING!" Bridget sighs. "But what have you been *doing*? Have you tried any restaurants? Have you been to any bars? Hung out in your neighborhood? Museums? Anything?"

I dramatically sigh right back at her. Overall, I think my move has been successful; Bridget apparently has different standards. "Hey, now! I've only been here a couple weeks. I've been moving and working. Give me a minute, okay?"

"So what about the people at work?" she continues, undeterred. "Do you guys hang out?"

"Not really. It's very different. Everyone's nice, but they tend to keep to themselves. Nobody really goes out to lunch together. No after-work drinks. And by six thirty, the office is dead."

"Sounds like they have lives."

"Apparently. Seems like most of them have families."

"Same thing."

"I've gone out to lunch a few times with Mark, and he invited me out to dinner with him and his fiancée, Elena."

"That was a nice gesture."

"Yeah, I thought so. He's definitely tried to make me feel comfortable here, and Elena and I plan on getting together for coffee or something soon."

"You should take her up on it sooner rather than later. When you're the new kid, you need to insert yourself into situations. Otherwise people forget about you."

"Very astute. Thanks for the advice." I smile and miss Bridget's "mothering" nature.

"What's the man situation like?"

"I haven't had a chance to suss out the situation yet." I roll my eyes and sigh. "Geez. *Relax.*"

"Fine," she says good-naturedly, backing down. "Well, when you're all settled, I'm coming out for a visit."

"I can't wait."

* * *

Although it seems too soon to think about dating, Bridget is right about making friends. I've been too busy navigating my new life to feel lonely yet, but it's time to put myself out there. So, taking Bridget's advice, I email Elena to set up a coffee date. There. Project Girlfriends has begun.

That week at work I also decide to reach out to my office-mates. I know Mark is always up for grabbing a sandwich, but I try with the others. I've invited both Emma and Rachel out to lunch before, and Emma always seems happy with an out-of-office excursion, but Rachel is never free because she often brings her own lunch from home. Or so she says. I mean, it seems a bit odd that she can't forgo her homemade lunch for one meal out, but maybe she's a closet gourmet, or saving money, or shy? I'm still reserving judgment on her since I need her help.

I've kind of been hoping that Jasmine, the only female partner in our office, would reach out to the sisterhood and invite me to lunch, or at least stop by my office and say hello, but perhaps I need to take the first step. Different offices might have different etiquette on these things.

So this morning at nine thirty, I email her.

Subject: Lunch today?
Hi Jasmine,
I was wondering if you're free for lunch today?
Adeline

When eleven thirty rolls around, it's been a couple of hours with no response. I know she's in the office, because I've walked past her door several times today on my way to the kitchen and to Mark's office. Perhaps she's working on a deadline and hasn't seen my email yet. Around noon, I'm hungry and feeling a little anxious. *Should I send a follow-up email?* Hunger clouds my decision-making on this point. At twelve thirty, I decide to walk over to her office, and when I get there, Jasmine is sitting at her computer with her email open.

"Hi, Tracy," I say to her secretary. "Would it be okay if I knocked on Jasmine's door?"

Tracy looks at me oddly and says, "Just go right in."

True, her office is right here, the door is open, and Jasmine probably heard our whole exchange. I don't know why I'm being so weird. I shake it off to go knock on her door.

"Jasmine?"

"Yes." She doesn't turn around and stays with her back to me, reading her email.

I take a few tentative steps into her office. "Um, hey. I was wondering if you were doing anything for lunch today?" I say to the tightly wound, jet-black bun where her face should be.

"No. I'm not."

O-kay. "Well, would you like to grab lunch together?"

She turns around and fixes me with her dark eyes and perfectly arched eyebrows. "Sorry. I can't today," she states succinctly without further explanation.

"Okay." Because what else am I supposed to say?

She looks me over, probably sensing my discomfort. "Perhaps we can grab some coffee another time," she suggests, but her tone is flat.

"Sure, that sounds great. I'll see you later," I say, slowly backing out of her office and then hightailing it back to mine. I wanted to ask if she saw my email, but I figure she's probably too busy and didn't have time to respond. Or maybe she never saw it. Or she simply chose to ignore it and me altogether. I tell myself that it's only lunch, so it's nothing to take too personally. Yet something about it gnaws at me. Or it's my hunger gnawing at me, making me paranoid.

I guess it's just a different office atmosphere. Normally when we had new associates at the Chicago office, I would go out of my way to invite them to lunch or stop by their office to chat and make them feel welcome. But then I tend to be friendly with everyone I work with, even if I'm not always their biggest fan (case in point: Roger). Maybe I shouldn't impose my small-town standard of friendliness on others. Besides, I know what it's like to be swamped.

My stomach growls, and I grab my purse and then head over to the elevators, nearly bumping into Mark in my hurry.

"Someone's in a rush! Going to lunch?"

"Yep. Starving."

"Me too. Do you mind if I join you?"

"Not at all!" I probably say this too enthusiastically. But after being snubbed by Jasmine with her icy manner, it's nice to know that *somebody* wants to have lunch with me.

We agree to walk over to one of the many salad places that surround our office building. After we order, Mark looks up at the cloudless sky and says, "It's a beautiful day. Would you like to eat outside, or do you need to get back to the office?"

"Is that a trick question from the boss?"

He laughs. "It's okay to take a break, you know."

"In that case, yes, I would love to eat outside."

We grab one of the metal tables outside the restaurant and make idle chitchat about the weather and some daily news items. I also decide to ask about Jasmine.

"So what's Jasmine working on right now? I know Rachel's doing some work for her."

"Not much. She's a lateral from Levenfield's LA office." *Oh god, Brad's firm.* The name stabs at my heart. "She moved here with some business, but it seems to have dried up lately. So she's mainly been doing client development work, trying to get something drummed up."

I instantly sympathize. That's a tough position—to be a new partner and not be bringing in the new business they probably hired her for. No wonder she looked so pale. I would be very stressed out too. I understand now why lunch with me wouldn't be high on her priority list at the moment. Plus, I feel like I dodged a bullet. Because if she was sitting across from me, I don't know if I could restrain myself from asking about "my old neighbor Brad," who somewhat recently broke my heart into a million pieces.

"That's tough. Hope she gets something."

"Yeah." Mark eats his salad, not seeming that concerned about Jasmine's situation.

"I emailed Elena about grabbing coffee this week," I say, changing the subject quickly, mostly to prevent myself from saying, *So she's from Brad's firm . . .* and from seeming like I want to engage in office gossip.

"That's great! You two should have fun."

And as proof that my email is working, when we get back to the office there's an email from Elena asking if I'm free tonight to meet up for drinks and suggesting a bar nearby. Drinks sound much more fun than coffee, and I immediately type back a big, fat YES!

* * *

After work, I walk down to the bar, which is hidden away off Market Street. As soon as I open the large glass door and walk in,

I am hit with a wave of homesickness. The lounge atmosphere, with its ambient light and music playing, reminds me of bars I frequented in Chicago. The interior is all sleek honey-toned wood, with light leather barstools and rectangular couches and chairs tucked off into corners. It makes me miss being able to call up Bridget and meet her for drinks at a moment's notice. Then I spot Elena, waving at me from her barstool. I smile and walk over.

"Hi!" I give her a little hug before sitting down on the stool next to her.

"Hey there. Is this place okay?"

"This place is great!"

Elena could easily pass as my slightly older, slightly sassier, and definitely more hilarious sister. She is a bit taller and slimmer than I am, with long dark hair and a complexion that evidences her Mediterranean roots. For the next few hours, she and I talk about *everything*. She asks me how my move is going and even offers to help me unpack. She gives me tips on the best hair stylists, facialists, and shopping that she has found in the city. We also talk about work—she's in PR—and how she met Mark. "Online dating. Would you believe it?"

"Nooo . . ." I put down my drink because I need to hear this story in its entirety. "That's funny. I can't picture Mark online. What was his profile like?"

"Well, he selected me. I was going for all these sensitive, artsy types—code for narcissistic. Or your general bad boys who are simply misunderstood and need a good woman."

"Poor guys," I quip.

"Right? Anyway, he emailed me, and it was the most coherent, straightforward email I'd received from anyone. So I checked out his profile and saw that he was handsome, a lawyer, and seemed stable." She ticks off his attributes on her fingers.

"So I thought, 'What the hell? Why don't I do something *crazy* and date someone normal.'" She throws up her hands, grinning.

I laugh. "I'm not entirely sure Mark is normal. He appears to be nice and ego-free. Something very unusual in our field." I nod, encouraging her to continue her story. "So?"

"So, we met at a restaurant. An actual sit-down and not just meet-up-for-a-drink type of thing. He picked the place, not too stuffy, not too hip. Good food, good wine. And he was even better-looking in person, very funny, and charming. It made me wonder why I'd been wasting time on so many losers. Anyway, a year later we moved in together, got engaged, and here we are."

"Wow. You make it sound so easy."

"Only because I haven't told you about the others *before* Mark. That's for another night."

"Trust me. I can probably guess." Although my roster isn't that long, and I've yet to experience online dating.

If only I could meet someone like Mark and have things turn out so easily.

I also learn that Elena is still somewhat new to the city, having been here only three years. "It's longer than you've been here, but believe me, I'm still learning about this place," she admits.

"Then here's to being partners in crime," I say and lift my glass.

When we part for the night, we give each other a heartfelt hug and promise to get together again soon. On my way home in an Uber, I can't help smiling to myself, thinking I may have made my first new friend in San Francisco.

CHAPTER THIRTEEN

*H*anging out with Elena confirms my belief in the importance of girlfriends. Even though Bridget is on my case about testing out the dating scene, I feel that maybe it would be better for me to start courting the ladies. That way when I have that first bad date, I have a drinking buddy to call—though I'm sure Bridget wouldn't mind drinking a bottle of wine over the phone in commiseration.

At the gym the next morning, I make sure to smile at the other women in my spinning class and in the locker room. Some of them smile back (albeit warily), others pretend not to see me, and one actually scowls. I soon realize that it is simply too early in the morning to try to make friends. Also, I have a sneaking suspicion that if I keep grinning maniacally at people, someone might report me to management as the creepy lady in the locker room. Okay, so maybe 7:00 a.m. spin class isn't the ideal place for meeting new friends. And maybe that cup of coffee before class wasn't the best idea, as it might be too much Addie too early in the morning.

I also decide that befriending Jasmine is not in my best interests. Now that I know she worked in Brad's office, I would be dying to ask her questions. And when I see her returning from a trip to Starbucks with her protégé Rachel, I realize that she seems to have forgotten about her offer for coffee. Or, most likely, never meant it at all.

* * *

Despite my best intentions to create a social life, I'm too swamped with work and traveling back and forth between San Francisco and the Peninsula to immediately act on them. Fortunately, Nora emailed me that she's going to be in town on business and will be working out of our San Francisco office for a couple of days.

Though she is mostly tied up in meetings, just seeing Nora around the office, hearing her laughter in the hall, and having her stop by during breaks to gossip about the latest office news back in Chicago does me good. Once her meetings are over, to celebrate, I take Nora out to Boulevard, an iconic Michelin-rated restaurant in the Financial District.

"So how are things going?" Nora asks after we've ordered.

"So far, so good. It's much more low-key here than the Chicago office. I kind of just focus on my work and then go home at the end of the day. Plus, I'm not always in the office all the time. I tend to be off-site directing the due diligence work. So overall it feels less high-pressure, if you know what I mean."

"No annoying Roger coming into your office to see what you're working on and then dumping his less glamorous assignments on you?"

"Yeah. None of that." I laugh at the memory. "But to be fair, he was the one who pulled me onto Project X in the first place.

So I guess . . . without him we wouldn't be dining here in lovely San Francisco."

Nora laughs. "I know! It's classic. And so just!" She can't stop smirking.

"What do you mean?"

"*What do you mean?*" she parrots back. "Uh, hello, Adeline? You totally stole this account from him."

"What?" I'm shocked. "No, I didn't. We worked on it together." I'm also a little insulted because it's not my style to play dirty office politics. "He's still working on it from Chicago."

"Yes, but the client asked *you* to move here. Not Roger. Scott thinks you're the brains in this operation. *Which, you are.* And it's awesome."

I never really thought about it that way.

"Oh, come on. You don't have to be the gracious winner. Let's revel in it. That jerk treated you like his whipping girl, and finally he's got his comeuppance. Now *you're* giving *him* assignments."

Honestly, I didn't think Roger was *that* bad. He's creepy and chauvinistic, yes. But I didn't feel like his whipping girl. I worked with some pretty difficult (okay, sadistic) partners early on at the firm, whereas Roger is just annoying. And I'm not *technically* giving him assignments. Mark has asked me a couple of times to have Roger handle something so I can focus on other stuff. But that's because we're on the same team. Or so I thought.

"Wow. I had no idea. He must hate me." I ponder that for a moment. "I had wondered why he was freezing me out after the conference. *Heck*, during the conference. I thought he was just pissed because I didn't fly up with him as planned."

"He was pissed because the client was totally impressed by you at the meeting and not by 'super-fantastic' Roger." Nora gets a glimmer in her eye. "And I think he may have had some ideas about you guys hooking up romantically . . ."

"Wait, *what*?"

"*Puh-leeze.* You know he had a crush on you in Chicago." Though I suspected it, I don't want to admit the words out loud. Nora rolls her eyes and continues, "Then you blew him off in Los Angeles *and* won his client's admiration."

I cringe. Oh god. Is this the office gossip back in Chicago? If so, Roger probably has a voodoo doll of me in his office. "I kinda wished I didn't know this information," I say, and then take a too-large gulp of wine. I was so caught up in the drama unfolding with Brad and my heartbreak afterward that none of these things registered at the time. I can't share this with Nora, though.

Nora waves her hand, as if to flick away an insect. "Who cares? It's a law firm. Someone is always bitter about someone else. But now that you know, you might want to be careful with him. If you make any mistakes, he'll definitely be the first to point them out. And you're up for partner soon."

"Geez. Thanks for the added pressure. I think we're going to need more wine." I shake my head, still in disbelief at this news.

We're interrupted by our server who brings us our salads.

"So what's the gossip in the San Francisco office?" Nora asks.

"There's not much to tell. It's pretty boring. I guess because it's so small. People seem to just work with who they work with and don't really branch out. No happy hours either."

"That's tragic." She frowns.

"Very." I nod solemnly.

"So who do you work with?"

"Mostly Mark and two younger associates, Emma and Rachel. Emma is sweet. She's a second-year who wants to learn and has a lot of enthusiasm. Rachel is a fifth year. She's a little reserved," I say diplomatically. "But she splits her time between me and Jasmine, a new partner from Levenfield."

Nora's eyes widen when I mention Jasmine. "Oh yeah." She nods, eyes still wide. "I know her."

The way Nora says it, I'm sure there's more.

"How do you know her?"

"I remember when they hired her. It seemed strange since she was a corporate attorney and they hired her in the real estate department. She was friends with another partner in that group who left before you moved. I think they thought she was going to bring up some LA clients, and then it never panned out. The whole thing sounded fishy, though. I heard the same from my Levenfield friends."

"How do you hear all this?" I'm amazed that Nora, in an office several states away, knows more than I do about my colleague who works several feet away from me.

"We all have our strengths. You have the brains and work hard. I'm more of a networker." She gives me a wink. Sitting before the charming, polished Nora Bendtsen, I have no doubt that she'll be a rainmaker when her time comes, and I'm grateful to have her on my "team."

"Anyway, it's a good thing you're not working with her. From what I hear, she's a nightmare. Total backstabber. And your back is already Roger's."

"Great," I say, with no small amount of sarcasm.

Nora then leans in conspiratorially. "Also, my friends over at Levenfield told me she had to leave because she was sleeping with a client. Or was it a colleague?" She wrinkles her brow, trying to remember.

"Really?" I say in disbelief. "I guess we do have office gossip. Maybe this office isn't so boring after all."

"You're just too busy doing your job to notice. Let me be the one to keep you up on the gossip. I love the look on your face when I tell you these things."

"Ha! Not a problem."

"But yeah, if she tries to befriend you, be afraid, my friend. Be very afraid."

"Duly noted."

"That Mark guy seems nice," Nora says, changing the topic.

"Yeah, he is. He's very easy to work with."

"Easy on the eyes too."

"He is a cutie, I will admit." Funny, because I had not thought of that or admitted it before now. "He's engaged, though, and his fiancée is amazing, so simmer down over there."

"I can always appreciate the talent." Nora grins. "Besides, things with Steve are getting serious. What about you? Seeing anyone?"

"I haven't had a chance to date out here yet. I've been too busy with the move and work."

Unlike Bridget, Nora seems satisfied with that answer, and we easily move on to other topics.

After lingering over our wine and then decaf coffees, we realize we've been sitting for almost three hours. It's time to go. I walk her back to her hotel and say goodbye. As we give each other a hug on the sidewalk, her visit combined with my drinks with Elena has intensified my own desire to branch out in San Francisco. I'm reaching my one-month mark here, which doesn't seem like much, but since I already spent several years in Chicago with the same life, I know my tendency to let months, which quickly and quietly turn into years, slide by.

* * *

Somehow one month turns into two months. While I've had the random dinner with Elena and Mark, work heated up, making any possibility of a social life nonexistent. I spend most of my days out of the city and busy overseeing Emma's and Rachel's work. And even though I'd been hoping Rachel would warm up to me, I realized quickly that that was never going to happen. When I tell her I need her help to look at documents at Imogen's offices, she tries to beg off by saying that she's working on a presentation for Jasmine.

Normally in these situations, I would say that the partner's work is more important or I would discuss the issue with Jasmine, but I also took Nora's advice to heart and have stayed as far away from Jasmine as possible. I'm not going to engage in office politics. And honestly, for an associate, billable work is more important and Rachel should know that at her level. So I know now that I'm dealing with a personality issue, and this deal is too important to me to put up with her attitude any longer.

Standing in her office, I find myself saying, "Rachel, part of being an associate is knowing how to manage your time." I cringe inwardly that I am now "that" senior associate. "Business development is important, but more so are our current clients. This is a big deal you're assigned on, and it's closing soon. It's all hands on deck."

Although her face remains placid, she's shooting daggers at me behind her eyes.

I sigh. "When is Jasmine's presentation?"

"As soon as I'm finished with my research. I need to do the research first before she can set up the meeting."

There's not even a presentation yet? Rachel is simply doing research on a potential client before Jasmine has even scheduled a meeting? I know Rachel feels allegiance to Jasmine; maybe she sees her as a mentor or something. Or maybe she hates corporate work and wants to get into real estate law. Now, though, is not the time to figure out her motivations. I don't want to get on her bad side because I need her to work, and I don't want Mark to know that I'm having a hard time managing a younger associate. So I try to remain calm and reasonable.

"Why don't you talk to Jasmine?" I say. "I'm sure she'll understand the situation."

Rachel stares at me for a second, silently challenging me, before saying, "Okay."

"Okay, then. Thank you." I return to my office.

Honestly! I'm glad we're finishing up this thing because I will be more than happy to release Rachel back to Jasmine. Just as I'm thinking this, Jasmine's figure appears in my doorway. "I see you are stealing my associate."

This is a first. I grit my teeth, before saying evenly, "It's just this week. Things are heating up, and I need more of her time." And this is the deal she's assigned on. *Seriously, people, why is this any question?*

"Oh." Her eyes widen briefly. I must not have done a good job of masking my irritation. "No worries. I understand. I was just teasing."

I've been here two months and this is the first time she's even approached me. So how am I supposed to discern that she's joking?

"I can do the research myself." She pauses. "So this deal is closing, huh?"

I'm disinclined to say too much. Maybe I've been poisoned by Nora's gossip, but this is the first time Jasmine has taken an interest in me, and I can't help but be a little suspicious.

"Yup. End of this week."

"Good luck," she says absentmindedly and walks out of my office.

"Thanks."

But she doesn't hear me because she is gone.

From that day forward I have no problems with Rachel and her "workload." Well, hardly any. The first day at Imogen she forgot her laptop, but I put that down to a rookie mistake rather than an act of defiance. Since I was mostly in meetings, I let her borrow mine for the day. After that, she always brought her laptop and handled every assignment from me without a word of complaint. I wondered if Jasmine had talked to her, and my attitude toward Jasmine softened. I was ready to give her the benefit of the doubt. But just in case she is the backstabber Nora heard that she was, I've resolved to give her a wide berth. I can't afford to have anything go wrong with this deal and my impending partnership.

CHAPTER FOURTEEN

Gym, work, sleep, repeat has been my mantra for the month of October until now. This Friday morning at ten o'clock, I sit at a conference table and direct all the key players at Imogen and Moonstruck on where to sign on the flagged pages that I have checked, double-checked, and triple-checked all this week. I'm trying to hide my nerves and elation. This is the first major deal in my career where I've been the point person. I smile to myself, and I can't wait to tell my dad that I was one of the main lawyers involved in the Moonstruck-Imogen deal that he reads about in his *Wall Street Journal*.

That night I attend a celebratory dinner with Mark, Dennis, Scott, Moonstruck's CEO, and Imogen's founder. After the waiter pours us each a glass of champagne, Dennis holds up his glass.

"Congratulations to Scott and Ivan today on the acquisition of Imogen. Moonstruck has always been a leader in animated films, and now with Imogen's technology, I can't wait to see what's next for your company. Here's to great things!"

After we clink glasses all around, Scott raises his glass again and looks at me. "And here's to Adeline, our go-to girl, who I know worked 'round the clock to make this partnership come together quickly and smoothly. Job well done, Adeline."

"Hear, hear," says Mark, winking at me.

As we all clink glasses, I have a big smile on my face and my cheeks flush—*go-to girl?* "Thank you, Scott. It's been an honor to work on this project."

And with this dinner, I know my slot for partnership is secured.

It is also notable, although not regrettable, that Roger spent the day back in the Chicago office, lending his support on the acquisition, but is not here at dinner with us. I think back to the conference in Monterey when Roger tried to make sure I was excluded from the big boys' dinner. I take another sip of my champagne and smile at how karma seems to work some things out.

* * *

When I wake up Saturday morning, I'm about to jump out of bed, thinking that I need to check my email and get into the office. But then I remember that Project X is over. For the first time in several months, I have absolutely no work to do. I should still check my email, just in case, but that's just standard practice, and it can wait. For now, I just want to luxuriate in my bed and enjoy the warmth of the sunlight coming through my window sheers. It's only eight o'clock, but the sun is already out and bright. I roll over and unplug my BlackBerry from its charger. There are a couple of congratulatory emails from Dennis and Mark, thanking everyone for their hard work. I had promised to take out Emma and Rachel for a celebratory lunch next week.

Emma responded heartily yes and thanked me. Nothing from Rachel, not surprisingly.

Even though I have nowhere to be, it's hard to stay in bed with the sun shining. I get up to make myself some coffee and start my Saturday. It's two hours ahead in Wisconsin, and so it seems a perfect time to call my dad.

"Oh, hi, Addie. How are things?" my dad answers.

"Hi, Dad. Things are *great*. The deal was signed yesterday. It's finally over."

"Congratulations! That must be a weight off your shoulders."

"Yes. It's been a lot of work. But both sides seem really happy with everything." I tell him that the client was Moonstruck, and he is suitably impressed, as I knew he would be.

"So what's next?"

"Not sure. Probably some more work for the same client. But for now, I'll just wait and see."

"How are your billables?"

Always the lawyer, my dad. "Thanks to Moonstruck, I'm ahead on hours. So I'm looking forward to a little downtime."

"Well done, honey. You deserve some time off. Enjoy it."

"Thanks. How about you? Anything new?"

"Played a good game of golf this morning. We're having great weather for this late in October. Even saw some deer on the course. But other than that, nothing new here. I'll probably catch a bite with a friend tonight." My dad pauses and suddenly remembers to ask me, "Oh, are you still planning to come home for Thanksgiving?"

"Yes. Unless you'd like to come here?"

"No, just making sure." He pauses again and then says, "Well, I don't have anything else."

"Me neither." Like a lot of our phone conversations, we've run out of topics. Sometimes I wish we could talk about more personal things rather than always talking about my job or surface subjects. Although if we ever delved too much into the personal, I think we'd both pass out unconscious from the shock. "Okay. I'll talk to you later. Bye, Dad."

"Yup, bye." I hear him put down the receiver.

I still have a fresh pot of coffee and no desire to get dressed or go anywhere quite yet, so I call Bridget. Due to the time difference and my late hours recently, it's been hard to touch base with her.

She picks up on the first ring.

"Hey, stranger," she says. "What's up?"

I tell her about the acquisition and the dinner.

"Congrats again, rock star! So, what are you up to today? Are you going to celebrate?"

"We did last night. Tonight I'm lying low." Truth being, I don't have any other options.

"Hmm, that sounds lame."

"Yes, thank you for pointing that out," I say, deciding to turn the conversation to Bridget. "So how are you? What's new?"

"Well," she drawls. "I have a date tonight!"

"Really?!" My ears perk up. "With who?"

"Some guy I met this week," she says airily.

"How did you meet him?"

"Promise not to laugh."

"You know I can't promise that."

"Ha! Okay. Here's the deal." She pauses dramatically. "I met him online."

"Really?" I prepare myself for a good story. "Do tell."

"Okay. So since it's not as much fun these days meeting guys without my favorite wing woman, I signed up on a couple of dating sites and apps."

"No way! So, who is he? Is this your first date?"

"He's the first guy I've agreed to meet in person. There's a lot of freaks on there, so you really have to weed them out. But on Wednesday we met for drinks, which then turned into dinner. Tonight we're going to a movie and then dinner afterward."

"Okay, okay. I need more details. Start from the beginning."

I couldn't believe that she met this guy four days ago and I'm just hearing about it now. I guess that's what two thousand miles will do. His name is Jason, he's an architect, and Bridget sounds crazy about him. And after admitting that she was doing the online dating scene, Bridget conveniently "forgot" to ask me about my own lack of a love life. Which is fine with me.

After hanging up with Bridget and securing yet another promise from her that she'll visit soon, I figure it's time to get on with my day. And who knows? Maybe I'll bump into a handsome stranger at the dry cleaner's and strike up a conversation. Maybe we'll accidentally grab each other's clothes and laugh and go out for a cup of coffee on this sunny morning, which is now moving toward afternoon. I'll never know sitting here in my pajamas.

I make my way to the dry cleaner's, the bank, the drugstore, the grocery store, and so far no handsome-stranger encounters. And is it just me, or do all the handsome strangers out today seem equipped with an equally beautiful woman by their side? Maybe I'm just being sensitive, but my errand running seems fraught with couples rather than singles.

After finishing my errands and downing an energy bar, I go for a run on the Marina Green. Once I get down to the water, there are tons of people out running, walking, and enjoying the weather, and it reminds me of the lakefront in Chicago in the summertime. The views of the water, the hills of Marin, and the Golden Gate Bridge will never get old. After an hour, I realize that I want to have "plans." Somewhere to go, someone to meet.

I'm not *completely* friendless in San Francisco, and I seek out a bench to sit on and text Elena.

> Hi, Elena. What are you up to?

> I'm in the car with Mark. We're in Napa doing some wine tasting and then off to dinner to celebrate your closing. Congratulations, by the way!

Oh. So much for plans tonight. I swallow and force cheeriness into my fingers as I type: Thanks! And, oops, sorry to bother you.

> Oh no bother! What's up?

> Nothing much. I was wondering if you'd be up for catching another movie or hanging out tonight, but it sounds like you're otherwise engaged.

> What about tomorrow night?

My heart does a leap. Tomorrow night works.

> Yay! After seeing Bridget Jones's Baby, I'm totally "jonesing" for another chick flick, and Mark refuses to go with me.

I laugh and text back: Another chick flick sounds great.

Great! We're parking right now at a winery.
Let's touch base tomorrow?

Sure. Sounds good. Have fun!

I slide the phone into my pocket. Looks like I have a quiet night on my own ahead. That's okay. I have plans for tomorrow, and I can certainly think of something to do tonight. I'm a little tempted to go into the office and clean up the paperwork that has taken over my space in the last couple of months, but even I can admit that that would be pretty lame. Rather than run home, I decide to walk back. In doing so, I pass a wine shop where a knowledgeable salesman helps me select a reasonably priced California cabernet sauvignon. As I watch him wrap up the bottle, I feel a slight ache in my heart. I miss Bridget, who would probably drink most of it. But I remind myself that even if I were in Chicago tonight, Bridget would have other plans.

There *is* someone I can still call to make some plans with, and it would probably please my dad. But calling the woman who abandoned me when I was a child doesn't seem like the best bet to take the edge off my loneliness.

Once I'm home for the evening, I shower and begin prepping vegetables for the lasagna I'm making tonight—my favorite comfort food. There's something soothing about preparing a meal. In high school, I used to cook dinner for my dad and me. Though, granted, that was more about survival—if it was left to my dad, then I would've been raised on fish fingers and overdone spaghetti.

As my dinner cooks, I have a glass of wine and fiddle around on the computer. I check out the dating site Bridget told me about today. I try to look up her profile, but the only way to view it is to sign up for the service, which I'm not in the mood for tonight. However, the site does allow me to peruse a limited number of eligible bachelors in my zip code. *Not bad, not bad.* Maybe there is something to online dating after all. None of the pictures are as good as Brad's photo on his firm's website. Oh yes, I go there too. It's that type of evening. But I remind myself that that is an unfair comparison. The dating-site guys are single. Brad is not. It's something to think about.

I eat my lasagna in front of the TV and flip through the channels, looking for something a little more involved than a sitcom or a reality show that I haven't been following. Playing on Lifetime is *You've Got Mail.* How appropriate. It seems even the universe is pushing me to try online dating. "I'll think about it," I promise the universe and settle into my sofa.

* * *

Sitting on a stool in the front window at Starbucks after a yoga class, I slowly sip my latte and gaze out the window, people watching. The crowd seems a little younger, mostly twenty-somethings. The women are in workout wear and the men are sporting jeans and baseball caps. I make my same observations as yesterday—that a lot of people seem coupled up. For a second I think I recognize the back of a head of hair and strong shoulders. My heart stops. Could it be? Then the man turns in profile, and it's not. I chastise myself. I finally have time to let my mind wander, and it wanders right back to Brad. It's because I'm lonely, I know. I don't have enough work or a boyfriend or friends to distract me. The unstructured hours of this weekend have reawakened the brooder in me.

Around one o'clock, Elena texts, Still on for tonight?

I text back, Yes. And I have to restrain myself from adding a million exclamation points.

> Meet you at 6:15 @ Kabuki Theater on
> Fillmore. Tix on me.

> Thanks! See you there.

I arrive at the theater at 6:10 p.m., and Elena is already inside. I spot her instantly with her long dangling earrings and scarf, looking fashionable even just in jeans. She waves when she sees me.

I wave back. When I reach her, we hug. "Hi! How was wine country?"

"It was great! It was so nice to get away with Mark. He's been so busy with that deal. You must be glad it's over."

"Yeah, it's nice to have some downtime." Although after this weekend, I realize that's a lie. That I don't really know what to do with my downtime. That I feel unmoored.

We chitchat about her trip, and she mentions the names of some wineries I have to visit.

"Yeah, I was thinking about that this weekend," I say. "That I should really take advantage of being out here and learn about California wines."

"Ooh, we should do a girls' weekend in Napa or Sonoma."

"That would be fabulous!" And just like that the self-pity of the weekend washes right off me.

Until we see the movie. I had seen the trailer, which portrayed it as a fun, romantic comedy. Instead, it was a bittersweet pull-out-all-the-tissues affair. At least for me. The story line is about a girl who has a crush on a guy in college, but she doesn't think that he would be interested in her. Years later they meet again, and he is engaged to one of her friends. She discovers that she still carries a torch for him, and finds out that he also had a crush on her back in college. And okay, maybe it's not quite the same thing, but it totally reminded me of Brad. As the episode at Starbucks this morning demonstrated, it doesn't take much for something to remind me of Brad. The timing for such a film couldn't be worse. Is the universe just mocking me now? No, I'm not that special. But maybe, just maybe, I should visit a psychic or someone to see if I'm working out some karmic baggage. Or buy some sage to burn away the ghosts of crushes past.

On our way out of the theater, Elena gushes, "Wasn't that great!"

I strangle out a "yeah."

She turns and looks at me. "Adeline! Are you okay?" She sounds worried.

I can feel my cheeks burning, and I'm sure my face looks like a tomato even with my normally olive complexion. I was trying so hard not to cry in the theater, but the emotions have been building up and I'm pretty sure my head is about to explode right now.

"I'm fine," I lie.

"Are you sure?"

I nod.

"Okay. I disagree, but I'll play along." Elena shakes her head. "I think we should get you a drink. There's a bar across the street, and I could really go for a cocktail and snack."

I'm not in the mood because I'm too scared of what will come out of my mouth if I'm forced to talk. At the same time, I don't want to be rude to my new friend—my only friend in San Francisco so far—and the fiancée of my "boss."

We open the door, and I can smell the warm aroma of Indian spices, but only alcohol sounds good to me. After we find seats at the bar and the bartender serves us our drinks, Elena starts in, "I hate to pry . . ."

"But you're going to," I cut in, but with a smile.

She smiles back, taking a sip of her cocktail. "Yes. What *was* that back there? The movie wasn't exactly a tearjerker. Was it that bad?"

I've calmed down a bit, and I manage a small laugh. "I know, I know. I'm sorry. It was just something with the movie. Maybe I've been a little homesick. Or maybe because I'm not dating anyone in particular, or at all, and it was such a romantic movie . . ." I trail off. "Oh, I don't know. Maybe I'm a little lonely."

"That's all?" She sounds slightly doubtful, but also willing to believe my story. "If it's loneliness, then, please, let me set you up! I've been dying to since you got here. Mark has some great friends."

I laugh. "Thanks, but dating my colleague's friends might not be the best move career-wise." I think of Brad and become sad again. "Actually, I don't think I'm really ready to start dating."

"But you just said you're lonely."

"I don't know what I am."

She levels her eyes with mine. "It's a guy, isn't it?"

"You don't let up, do you?"

"Nope." Sitting back, she shrugs and takes another sip of her drink. "So you might as well tell me because I can sit here and drink cocktails all night. And I'm *way* more annoying when drunk."

"Okay, but only because I don't want you hungover tomorrow cursing my name when you have to get up for work. You're right. It's a guy."

"It always is," she says, dramatically rolling her eyes heavenward. "And?"

"And what?"

"Who's the guy? What's the story?"

This is dangerous territory, since she's Mark's fiancée, and since Mark is my boss and Brad's friend. Proving that she's psychic as well as stubborn, she follows up with, "I know I'm Mark's fiancée, but I would never breathe a word about your life to him. I'm a girl's girl and you're my friend."

"Vice versa," I say. Do I tell? I'm dying to talk about him, and I know I won't be able to sleep tonight for thinking about it. And so, why not?

"It's someone from home," I venture. "We've recently been in touch, and I still have the same feelings for him that I've always had. But he's unavailable at the moment."

"You mean long distance?"

Elena is a bride-to-be, so I'm nervous about admitting the next part. "Unfortunately for me, he's married. Apparently there's a divorce in the works, but who knows? And I feel terrible for even coveting someone's husband, and I've never been in this situation before. It will never happen between us, so I guess that's why I got sad after the movie. It was very romantic and all, but these things just don't always have happy endings."

She seems to take this in stride. "Unfortunately as we get older, things aren't always black and white. How long did you two date?"

I can't quite tell her that we never actually dated. It's too embarrassing. And bad enough that I've even said anything, even though it does make me feel better for the time being. "Not long. But long enough, you know?"

She nods understanding. "Is there any hope?"

"No. I don't know where his divorce stands. Nor do I know if he'd want to have a relationship with me. Plus, he doesn't live here."

"Wow. That is three strikes. Guess he's out. But the good news is that your new fairy godmother, me"—she points to herself—"is here to take care of you. I'm going to work on a short list tonight and compare notes with Mark."

"Oh no," I groan.

"Oh yes. You are way too hot to be crying into your martini glass about some guy. We're getting you a new one. Done." She claps her hands once and brushes them together. I have a feeling I am her new project. This could be great. Or this could be disastrously bad. But there's only one way to find out.

* * *

When I get home, I see that I missed a call from Bridget. I listen to her message.

"Hi, Addie. It's me. Where are you? I have to tell you about my amazing weekend with Jason. I think this is it. *Seriously*, you have to try online dating. Much more efficient than meeting random guys at bars. Try it. And call me."

It's too late to call her in Chicago, so I guess I'll have to get the play-by-play tomorrow. And it's probably time to start winding down and getting ready for the week ahead. I feel a buzz in my belly, similar from the night before my move. I have a feeling that my life is about to take another turn, and I will want to be well rested for it.

CHAPTER FIFTEEN

The next morning I wake up with a new attitude. It's a new day, and it's time to get over myself. This sad and lonely, oh-poor-me thing isn't working; so this morning my life is going to change (or at least my attitude about my life). And on my way to the bus stop, I felt like Mary Tyler frickin' Moore, ready to toss my hat in the air.

I'm in no hurry to rush into the office this morning, so I get off a couple of stops early to pop into Peet's for a latte. While there, I smile at the cashier, barista, and the other patrons. Some smile back; some avoid eye contact. I don't blame them. They are not aware of my new "go girl" attitude. You'd think I would have learned my lesson at 7:00 a.m. spin class already. But nope. And it doesn't stop me from simply smiling at myself.

I'm tempted to fish out my phone and type an email to Elena to see if she has put together the short list she promised last night. But no, that would be too eager. I should at least wait until I get into the office, or until after 10:00 a.m., which for no particular reason seems like a more reasonable hour. I'm also curious to hear about Bridget's date. But again, I will wait to call her until I am settled into my office, with the door closed.

I sip my latte and hum a little on the way to work, happy to be alive and enjoying the brisk, sunny morning. I continue humming in the elevator all the way up to my office, despite some odd looks.

"Good morning," my secretary, Nancy, says as I walk in.

"Good morning."

"How was your weekend?"

"Wonderful! Yours?"

She goes into a ten-minute monologue on how her kids were sick, her husband was no help, she thinks she might be coming down with it, and how they're still in the middle of this kitchen remodeling project and her house is a mess. The dark cloud over Nancy, though, does not penetrate me. If anything, I have yet to see her discuss anything positive and decide that this is just her way of interacting with people. I let her continue to vent, until she finally says, "Oh yeah, and Mark came by looking for you."

"Thanks. Did he say it was important?"

"Nah. He said he'd come back later."

Then Nancy waves her hand away as if to dismiss me, I'm guessing so that she can get on the horn with the contractor she just spent the last ten minutes cursing.

When I turn on my computer, I have about fifteen new emails but I see only one.

> Hi Addie,
>
>   I know we haven't spoken since we ran into each other a few months ago, but I would like to talk to you regarding some real estate work. The sooner we can talk

the better. If I do not hear from you, I will
give you a call at your office this afternoon.
    Best regards,
    Brad

It feels like someone has just tried to knock me out of my
chair. After total radio silence, *now* he wants to talk. About *real
estate*? And if I choose not to respond, *he* will call *me*—what
gives him that right? Plus, "best regards"? *Screw you, Summers.*
What the hell type of email is this? What does he want from
me? Does he want work from me? Does he want to sell me something? He sounds like a telemarketer or some cold call. If his
email didn't show the name of his firm, I would've thought it
was a different Brad Summers.

I need to step away from the computer.

I grab my jacket and purse. "Nancy, I'm heading out to
Starbucks. Do you want anything?"

"Thanks, I'm good." She looks at me strangely, but does not
point out the obvious—that I walked in with a large cup of coffee only five minutes ago. But I just need to walk, and walk
somewhere with purpose.

As I stand in the Starbucks line, I try to steady my nerves.
After I order a tea and sit down to let it brew, I let myself stew
while deciding how, or if, to respond to Brad's email. First, he
slept with me when he shouldn't have. Then he felt guilty about
it, *which he should*, but it still hurt my feelings. Then, he tells me
the entire story of his marriage, a true sob story, and I, pathetic
as I am, feel sorry for the guy. I listened. I empathized. Then,
after sharing these incredibly open and intimate moments, I
never hear from him again. And now after several months of
silence, I get this cold email about some real estate work? I hate
this guy. But I know hate is usually the flipside of love, and so

I am even more angry that he is able to cause any emotional response in me at all, as well as being angry at myself for possibly overreacting.

I call Bridget to get her take on this new development, but get her voicemail.

"Hi, you've reached Bridget Cavanaugh. Please leave a message."

"Hi, Bridge. It's Addie. Glad to hear you had a wonderful date. Can't wait to hear more about it. Call me."

I don't want to leave my troubles on her voicemail. I will have to figure this one out on my own.

I could just wait for him to call me this afternoon, but then I'd be jumping every time the phone rang. Plus, that would just be plain torture. No use waiting around.

The tone of his email was cold and professional. Normally I am always professional, but I don't feel like responding in kind right now. First of all, I don't do real estate work, so I highly doubt he wants to talk to me about that. And second, nothing about our relationship has been professional. I decide to cut to the chase and ask the only question on my mind.

I text Brad: Is your divorce final?

No salutations. No niceties. Just the only question I want to know the answer to.

One minute later my phone buzzes. I pick it up and see a one-word response: No.

Well then. It looks like we have nothing to talk about. I drop my phone into my purse and head back to the office.

My morning cheerfulness has dissipated and has turned into resolve. I am determined to forget about this guy for good.

Back in the office, I email Elena.

> Thank you for the movie and everything last night! And anytime you want to set me up, I'm game.
> Let's hang out again soon!
> Adeline

There. I'm moving on. I'm officially ready to start dating *available* men.

Hopped up on caffeine, I get to work cleaning out the papers in my office that have piled up over the last few weeks. Okay, the last few months. Most of the random files and notes can go in recycling since they all exist on the server. I keep a binder of each of the final drafts of everything relating to Project X, but I decide everything else must go. While I'm in the midst of this organizing frenzy, Mark pops his head in the doorway and surveys the scene with a grin.

"Wow! It looks better already," he comments.

"Thanks. It feels good to get rid of all this." I toss another stack of papers into the bin.

"Yeah, I did the same thing this weekend."

"This weekend? But what about Napa?"

"I came in and did it last night while you were out with Elena."

"How covert." And also kind of funny since I was thinking of doing the same on Saturday. "And a little lame."

Mark laughs. "Yes, well, I wanted to start today with a clean slate. May I?" He points to a stack of papers covering one of my office chairs.

"Oh, let me get those."

"I got it." He moves the precarious pile from the chair to my desk and takes a seat. I sit down behind my desk.

"What's up?" I say.

"Looks like we have some more work from Moonstruck."

"Oh? I know we have some final items to take care of for them."

"Yes. You can take care of that. But this is a new project. Scott had told me that once the acquisition took place, they wanted to build new state-of-the-art facilities here. One that will have better technical abilities and that they can grow into."

"That's exciting."

"Yes, it is. Especially since they'd like us to handle the legal side of things."

"Okay. I've never really been involved in something like that. Isn't this more of a real estate or construction law type of thing?" I ask, quickly adding, "Not that I don't want to work on it. I'm happy to expand my expertise."

"While I've negotiated some real estate deals, I'm not an expert in this area either. I'm sure we can handle it, but we'll need a real estate lawyer on this as well."

"Okay." *Uh-oh. Does this mean I'll be working with Jasmine?* She's been fine to me, meaning she still ignores my existence. I've seen her striking up conversations with Mark, though, offering any help on his projects. Although, to my knowledge, he has not taken her up on it, until now. *Gulp.*

"So we're hiring a new attorney." Mark smiles with a twinkle in his eye.

Whoa! Mark would rather hire someone from the outside than offer it to Jasmine. This must be a blow to her, since she's been looking for work. But if Nora's words are to be believed, I'm happier to take my chances with a stranger.

"Okay. Are we interviewing people? Is there anything you need me to do?" I ask.

"Nope. Scott has already selected him and asked us to bring him on the team. He'll be starting in a couple weeks."

"Oh? Who is it?"

"Don't you want to guess who it is?" Mark stares at me, grinning.

"Guess?" Why does he want me to guess? *Wait. Nooo . . . Oh god. Brad's email. Mark's smile. I don't like where this is going.* "Um, I wouldn't know where to start. Why don't you just tell me?" I try to remain composed.

"Our friend Brad Summers." Mark smiles widely, waiting for my reaction.

HOLY MOTHER OF . . .

My heart is beating fast, and I can feel my palms starting to sweat. I try to utter a casual "Oh?" but it comes out as more of a squeak.

"He's done a lot of real estate work for Moonstruck. Apparently, Scott already approached him about these plans when we were in Monterey. Scott really wants him involved and wants him up here in the Bay Area. I guess Brad was already thinking of leaving his firm, possibly for something with more life-work balance." Mark lowers his voice and continues, "You know, with the divorce and everything." He says this as if we are both good friends and confidants of Brad. I might throw up.

"Right."

"Anyway, it'll be nice having him up here." Mark is still grinning, having no idea of the bomb he just dropped.

Nice for you, *maybe.*

In my effort to change my life, I have instead propelled it right into the waiting arms of disaster.

"In other news," Mark says, changing the subject now that I've lapsed into stunned silence, "Elena is hell-bent on setting you up."

As if this change of conversation could be any more awkward.

"Yes." I laugh nervously. "I gave her my permission. At least I know these guys will be vetted, right?"

"I don't know about that. I have a sorry state of friends. But Elena is just as interested in fixing them up as she is you."

"That's why she's in PR. She's a people person." I smile. "Anyway, I trust her judgment."

"Okay. But remember that I warned you."

Little does he know that the warning was about his friend Mr. Summers.

"Will do. I guess I'd better finish cleaning up this place to make room for the new slew of papers coming this way."

"I'll leave you to it."

How is it that in a few short hours my day has already exploded? I look at the clock and realize it's almost noon, which means I have to put on my happy face because I promised to take Emma and Rachel (who RSVP'd this morning with a grudging "okay") out for a fancy lunch in celebration of closing Project X.

* * *

During lunch, Emma is her usual chatty self, enabling me to get my mind off Brad for a little while. Plus, Rachel is in rare form. She was so dour during the whole project, but now she is happy and smiling—even friendly. There's something smug about her smile, though—as if she can indulge me now that we have put this project behind us. Still, her antics seem like a minor annoyance compared to what I have looming ahead of me.

"Shall we do a champagne toast?" I ask. The champagne is really for me.

Emma's eyes widen. "I would love that."

Rachel seems a bit more reticent. "I don't usually drink in the middle of the day."

"None of us do." I groan inwardly and now regret even suggesting it. "But we worked hard and deserve a little treat. Feel free to order what you like."

"Well, if you two are having champagne, then I'd like to join you."

Why is everything like pulling teeth with her? I'm trying to be nice here. Maybe the afternoon drink will loosen her up. Even Roger was less of a pain than she is.

The glass of champagne helps me get through the next hour. Emma asks about what's next workwise. I tell her that we'll probably still be busy on some of the Project X stuff and that we also have a new big project coming in.

"So don't worry about looking for new work because it's coming," I say.

"I have a lot of assignments with Jasmine that I need to get back to," Rachel says, clearly challenging me.

"That's fine. Why don't you focus on that." *Because we can probably get along without you.*

After lunch, we walk back to the office. This is just a formality. After everything today, I plan to check in and, if no one needs me, check out right away.

As soon as I walk into the office, I ask Nancy if anyone has been looking for me. She says no. Then I go knock on Mark's door.

"Hey, if it's okay with you, I think I'm going to leave early and take care of some errands."

"Go for it. I already double-checked the filings this morning, and everything looked good." Mark sits back in his chair, surveying his immaculate desk. "I might take off soon myself.

I'm thinking of going to the store and surprising Elena with dinner tonight."

"Really? That's impressive."

"Hey, what are you doing tonight? Do you want to have dinner with us?"

"That's really nice of you, but I think it might be more romantic if it's just you two."

"We already had a romantic dinner on Saturday." He shrugs. "The more the merrier."

"Thanks, but I'll take a rain check. Next time." I wave goodbye and head out.

I had planned on going to the gym after work, but taking my own advice that one deserves a treat after all that hard work, I instead head to the nearby Bloomingdale's for some undisciplined shopping.

* * *

In Chicago, I had a wardrobe of non-offensive sweater sets I could rely on. Here, since the San Francisco office dress code is less conservative, I can indulge my inner Bridget and be a bit more colorful. One green peacock-print wrap dress later, I'm down in the shoe department asking myself, *Should I?* while debating between a pair of knee-high boots and a pair of pointy pumps. "Luckily" they do not have the boots in my size, which means that buying the heels was meant to be.

Since I just spent several hundred dollars on one dress and one pair of shoes, it's time to move it along, but not before hitting up the makeup counter. I have to admit I've never really known how to do my own makeup. I have some sense of what works on me, but only because Bridget taught me.

As I admire the various shades of NARS eye shadows, a cheerful girl with *waaay* too much eye makeup approaches me. "Can I help you with something?"

"Yes. I need new makeup."

"What are you looking for?"

I look around the counter and shrug helplessly. "Everything?"

She laughs. "Here, have a seat."

I'm a little nervous, but after thirty minutes in her expert hands, my blue-green eyes are shimmering, my cheekbones are defined, and my lips are glossy. "Wow!" I say when she hands me the mirror. "I look amazing!"

She laughs again. "Yes, you do!"

"Thank you so much!" I gesture to the array of products on the counter. "I'll take it all."

I know it's a cliché, but with my new face and new dress and new shoes, I've momentarily forgotten my impending doom and feel just as optimistic as I did when I woke up this morning.

I even splurge on a cab ride home because in for a penny, in for a pound.

But you know as well as I do: The new dress, the new shoes, the new makeup? It's not all for me. It's because on some petty level I want to look smoking hot when Brad walks through our office doors.

CHAPTER SIXTEEN

Not until I'm through my front door do I feel it's safe to check my phone. Normally, I'd have been checking it every few minutes, but I opted to keep my phone buried in my purse all afternoon. Only after I've carefully hung up my new dress, placed my new shoes in the closet, and laid out my new makeup in the bathroom do I decide to rejoin society.

And there it is. Nestled between missed calls from Bridget and Elena is Brad's voicemail. On a subconscious level, I know I left work to miss his call. Well, okay, on a very conscious level. And I know I turned off my phone to avoid having a mini heart attack while shopping. But now secured in my apartment, on my own terms—meaning sitting on my sofa with a glass of wine—I am ready to listen.

"Hi, Adeline. This is Brad Summers. I'm calling because I've been offered a position at your firm and would like to ask you a couple questions. If you could please give me a call back at this number, I would greatly appreciate it. I look forward to hearing from you. Thank you. Bye."

My heart sinks and I shiver. His voice message is even colder than his email this morning. He sounded like a complete stranger. But what was I expecting? And why does he want to talk to me about this? From what Mark told me, it sounds like he's already accepted and will be starting in a couple of weeks. I try to put a finger on my emotions, but I'm not even sure what they are. Hurt? Insulted? Was I expecting a confession, to hear, *I love you, Addie. I've always loved you. I can't bear to be away from you?* The only thing I'm sure about is that I don't want to call him back.

Instead, I call Bridget.

"Addie!" she sings into the phone. "How are you?"

"Good." But my voice sounds strangled. "How are you?"

"You don't sound good. What's wrong?"

"Ugh, everything."

"Tell me."

"You know what, not right now." She sounded so happy when she answered, and I don't want to burden her with my problems quite yet. "I want to hear about this fantastic date of yours."

"You sure?" She sounds suspicious.

"Positive. Go."

Her voice becomes singsongy again, and I know that, uh-oh, this girl is in deep. I haven't heard Bridget talk about a guy like this since . . . I can't remember when. She tells me how they met at the theater, what he was wearing, how they held hands during the movie, how they barely touched their dinner for all the talking, and then went back to her place where they proceeded to make out like a couple of teenagers.

"He went home a little after one, but it was so hard to let him leave. Around midnight, we kept saying how late it was getting, but neither of us wanted the date to end."

"I'm impressed. That sounds like the most perfect night ever."

"I know. I haven't had a date this good in forever," she says. "And we've been texting each other all day. We're going out again Wednesday."

"That's wonderful! I'm so happy for you!"

"Thank you." She sighs wistfully. "It's about time, isn't it?"

"Mmm . . ." I nod my assent even though she can't see me and pick at the chenille throw on my couch.

"So how about you? What's new? Any prospects?"

Even though I've been dying to talk to her since this morning, I hate to put a damper on the mood.

"Addie? Can you hear me?"

"Oh yes. Sorry." I take a deep breath. This is what friends are for, right? "So, I have some crazy news."

"Yeah?"

"Brad is going to work in my office."

"WHAT?!" she says. I hold the phone away from my ear and bring it back. "*What the . . . ?* How is that possible?"

I tell her about Brad's email, and then how Mark came into my office, all excited to tell me that Brad will be working with us, and recite his voicemail to her. "And it's such a small office, so it's not like I can simply avoid him. Plus, he's coming to work directly with us on the same project."

"I'm so sorry."

"I mean, that's it. I can't even ask for advice because it is what it is. And I know I should call him back, but it's too depressing. We had this intense connection, and now I have to pretend it never happened." I pick more furiously at the throw. "Which I've been trying to do, except now I'll have to deal with him every day."

"You know the answer, don't you?"

"No. What's that?"

"To get over one guy, you need to get under another."

"Ugh." I roll my eyes. "Yes, yes. Well, I'm working on that." I tell her about Elena wanting to set me up.

"That's fine and all, but you can't just wait for Elena. You need to be proactive, and I'm telling you, online dating is the way to go."

"Oh, I don't know. It sounds so time-consuming."

"For the love of god, Addie. Just do it! Sign up and create a profile. Just because you sign up doesn't mean you have to marry these guys. It's simply a different and, in my opinion, better way to meet them." Her voice turns resolute. "In fact, this is your homework tonight—*pick* a dating website or app and sign up. I want a full report in the morning."

"Okay, okay." *Why not?*

"In fact, do it before you call Brad. I mean, you *are* calling him back, right?"

"Yeah. But I think I'll wait till morning. The workday is over, and I don't want to bother him at home." *Delay, delay, delay.*

"Uh-huh," says Bridget, knowing that I'm just stalling. "Good. Then tonight you're free to work on your profile."

I groan. "Right."

After we hang up, even though my heart isn't in it, I take Bridget's advice and sign up for the same site where she met her fantastic date. I enter the bare minimum of information, mostly because I have no idea what to write for my profile. I click over to Bridget's profile, which is bubbly and funny and makes me totally want to date her. I can't write the same for me because it would be lying. Not knowing what else to do, I go for total honesty.

"I'm a 33-year-old corporate attorney. Originally from Wisconsin, I just moved to San Francisco from Chicago. When

I'm not working, I like to work out, read, watch movies, listen to music, and go out to restaurants and bars with friends. Looking forward to exploring my new city."

Ha! To think I once harbored dreams of becoming a writer. This is quite possibly the worst thing I have ever written. Because who doesn't like movies, music, or restaurants? I do not add a photo because I can't bear to bring myself to do that. What if someone I know runs across my picture? I would die. Simply. Die. But this should take the heat off from Bridget. And now that I'm "online," I can peruse the eligible bachelors in my area in more detail. Some of these guys aren't bad. I add a couple to my favorites and decide to revisit them when I am feeling bolder. By ten, I've had enough and go to bed early. Tomorrow is a brand-new day.

* * *

In the morning while my coffee brews, I check my email. Overnight I've gotten some hits on my dating profile. I open up the messages. Most are misspelled. All a little creepy. None from my favorites. I'm disappointed yet relieved at the same time. None of these merit a response.

However, another email, this one from Elena, was sent late last night:

> Subject: Napa?
> What are you doing this weekend? Would you like to go to Napa with me, Mark, and Mark's friend Evan?
> Say yes!
> XOXO
> Elena

I don't even have to think about this one. I type back a one-word response—YES.

Before heading to work, I hit the gym. After spin class, I find myself doing crunches and lunges and stretching. I know as soon as I get into the office I'm going to have to call Brad, and I'm in no hurry. I can't let twenty-four hours go by because that would be rude (as if there's some sort of etiquette for these situations). In the meantime, my procrastination has become a great workout.

When I'm finally at my desk, bracing myself, I see an email from Bridget. Another perfect distraction.

> Subject: Dating site
> What's your screen name?

I type back:

> SFAttorney33. Why?

A minute later my cell phone rings, making me jump out of my chair. Thank god, it's only Bridget.

"Hey," I answer.

"Are you freakin' kidding me?!" she exclaims. I hold the phone away from me.

When she finishes her shriek, I bring the phone back to my ear. "What?"

"Okay. One, that is the worst screen name ever. The worst! Two, your profile is not much better. And three, where's your picture?"

"Sorry. I didn't realize that I was under a deadline to get a profile picture up. And anyway, I don't want to put my picture up. What if people see me?" I cringe.

"Um, yeah. That's the point!" she says, clearly exasperated. "Post a photo before I tag some unflattering ones of you online."

"Fine," I say. "But some of us have to work here."

"Have you called Brad?"

"Not yet. I just got in."

"Uh-huh," she responds, calling me on my charade. "Good luck. Call me later."

"Okay."

I know Bridget will keep her word, so I hurriedly post my work picture from the firm's website onto my profile.

A minute later another email from Bridget pops up.

> You did not just put THAT picture up. You are hopeless. Hopeless!

I laugh and then take advantage of my improved mood to tackle the most important item on my agenda. I take a deep breath and dial the number.

"Hello. Brad Summers's office," answers his secretary. "May I help you?"

"Hello, yes. Is Brad there?"

"Who may I say is calling?"

"Adeline Turner."

"One moment."

My heart is beating a million miles a minute. Before I have time to catch my breath, I hear Brad's voice, low and melodious, and dare I say, slightly nervous.

"Hi, Addie. Thank you for calling me back." He pauses, as though he's not sure what to say next.

I'm not sure either, so I stall with filler. "Yes, um, you wanted to talk to me?"

"Yes. Well, as you know, I do a lot of work with Scott Schulman and Moonstruck. Scott has asked me to move up to the Bay Area to get involved with some real estate work they have there, and so I've been offered a position at Gilchrist in the SF office." He pauses. "Has anyone talked to you about this yet?"

I clear my throat, which suddenly feels dry. "Yes. Mark mentioned it to me yesterday. Moonstruck plans to build new facilities now that they've acquired Imogen, and you'll be joining our team to work on this project," I recite.

"Sure. That's the plan at least, but I really wanted to talk to you first." He pauses and then says warmly, "It's great to hear your voice."

And whose choice was that? I wonder, yet the low vibration of his voice as he says those words makes me want to melt in my chair. I try to regain my composure. "What would you like to talk about?"

He sighs and says, "It's been a hard year." I'm not sure what to say to that, so I remain silent. "I guess I just wanted to check with you whether it would be a problem. You know, me working there?" As if he has to spell it out.

But he created this situation, so I'm not going to make it easy for him. "And why should it be a problem?"

"Well, you know . . ." He pauses. "With what happened."

There is a beat of silence, neither of us willing to name aloud the elephant in the room. The hairs on my neck are starting to bristle. Finally, I say, "Well, if Scott wants you here, and this is a good career opportunity for you, then what does my opinion matter?" Maybe I should be flattered that he's checking with me first, but he's already taken the job, so this seems like a pointless conversation.

"It's not just a career opportunity. It's a life opportunity. I think it's best for me to get out of LA for a while."

"In that case, then congratulations on the new job."

"But your opinion matters. If you don't want me there, then I won't take this job."

Really? "But didn't you already take it?"

"I've been offered it, but I haven't signed the papers or resigned here yet. I was waiting to hear from you, but I can't really stall much longer."

Oh. I feel myself starting to soften, but then stop. Gilchrist is *my* firm, after all, so the least he could do is ask before encroaching on my territory.

"What do you say, Addie?"

Realizing I'm slumped back in my chair, I sit up straight and muster my most professional tone. "Sign the papers."

"You're sure."

"Yes." *No.*

"Okay. I'll do it." He pauses, and then begins again, "I was also hoping I could see you before I start working there. You know? Maybe go to dinner?"

It's one thing to have to deal with him at the office, but dinner? His divorce isn't final, so there's only one response. "How 'bout I'll just see you when you get here."

"Oh. Okay." He sounds surprised.

My hands are starting to shake. I need to get off the phone right away. "I have to go. Good luck with the move."

"Thank you. Um, okay. Bye, Addie."

"Bye." I can't put down the receiver quickly enough. Adrenaline is coursing through my veins. Just five minutes on the phone with Brad has me exploding with so many different emotions—anger, confusion, lust—that I think I might actually internally combust in my Aeron chair. Bridget's advice, no matter how flippant it sounds, is true—I need to find someone else.

The only way I can handle interacting with Brad every day is to be in another relationship.

And although I'm looking forward to meeting Evan this weekend, I don't have time to put all my eggs in that basket. Therefore, I shut my door and get down to serious work on my dating-site profile.

CHAPTER SEVENTEEN

Thank god work is slow right now because I seem to have a new full-time job. Every couple of hours, I open up my email and survey the contenders for my next love interest. Creep. Creepier. Lives with mother. Plays *Dungeons & Dragons* (yep, present tense). Star Trekkie, which might be okay if he didn't use a photo of himself dressed as Spock at a fan convention as his profile picture *and* still live with his mother. Blah. No. Okay. *Wait, what's this?*

"I am a commercial lawyer with aspirations to become a published author. . . . My favorite city is Paris. . . . I love all sports and work out frequently. . . . I love travel, dining, art, architecture, live music, antiques, my neighbor's dog. . . . If stranded on a desert island, I would take my BlackBerry and Proust's *In Search of Lost Time*."

Well then. He'll do! He has sharp, angular features and dark, curly-ish hair, a little unruly compared to the commercial lawyers I know. *Hmm, a rebel, perhaps?* The fact that he would take his BlackBerry with him on a desert island is concerning, as that would be the first thing I would conveniently lose. So he's a workaholic. Or maybe it suggests responsibility. There's only one way to find out. I carefully craft an email back.

After a few bantering emails back and forth, I learn that Adrian's office is very close to mine. He suggests we meet up for happy hour nearby—tonight! Though I'm unsure about the etiquette of online dating, isn't it bad form to suggest a date so quickly? Shouldn't we at least try to seem like we have bustling social lives where we're highly in demand? I wonder whether it's a test. One that I fail when I write back that I am indeed free tonight and to just let me know the time and place.

All morning I'm excited about my drink with Adrian—and too distracted to think (much) about "he who shall not be named." Which is Brad, of course. Oh wait, there's his name in my head again. God, I need a distraction.

Fortunately, I'm dressed well—pencil skirt, blouse, and heels. It's not the greatest date outfit, but it's better than my typical trousers and sweater-set look.

I make a vague attempt to focus on work, until Mark swings by my office at noon. "I'm heading out to lunch. Any interest?" he asks.

Lunch with Mark has become a regular occurrence, and I like the camaraderie after my bumpy start with Jasmine and Rachel.

"Sure!" I practically jump out of my seat due to all the adrenaline coursing through my system.

Mark laughs. "Guess you're hungry?"

I smile in response, not wanting to reveal the reason for my antsiness.

"I was going to grab a salad," he says. "Unless you have any different ideas?"

"Salad sounds great," I agree and grab my purse.

After getting our food, we sit outside in the sunshine and eat. Or Mark eats. I take bites here and there, tapping my foot and looking around at the other lunch-goers. I wonder whether I'll spot Adrian since our offices are so close.

"I thought you were hungry?" Marks says, gesturing toward my salad. "You've hardly eaten a thing."

"Oh yeah." I look down at my barely touched salad. "Guess I'm not that hungry after all." And smile a bit to myself.

"Hmm . . ." Mark narrows his eyes and looks at me critically. "I think I know what's going on here."

"What's that?"

"Someone is excited about their date on Saturday."

I laugh. *If he only knew.* But since my date Saturday is with Mark's friend, it might not be appropriate to mention my upcoming drinks with Adrian tonight. "Oh, puh-leeze." I roll my eyes. "I didn't even realize that Saturday was an official *date*."

Now it's Mark's turn to roll his eyes. "Oh, come on! You know this is Elena's big setup. And since you haven't mentioned it to me yet, I thought that Elena was the only one who was all excited about it." Mark nods slowly, as though he has suddenly realized something of great importance. "I see now that she's not the only one excited."

I give him an exasperated smile. "I'm just in a good mood today. I got a full night's sleep. Work's been good."

"Uh-huh." He smirks. "So is there anything you want to know about Evan? That Elena hasn't filled you in on, of course."

I decide to play along for a bit. "Hey, I'm just excited to go wine tasting. Elena tells me that you and Evan are big wine aficionados."

"We are," he says. "What else did Elena tell you?"

"That you guys met at your rock-climbing gym. That you had a little bromance with each other and have been good friends for the last few years."

Mark laughs. "Did she tell you to wear sandals?"

I tilt my head toward him, confused. "No."

"Then I guess she didn't mention his foot fetish." Mark is trying to say this with a straight face and takes a quick bite of salad to stop from grinning.

"Oh my lord!" I raise my hands up in surrender. "I think we're done here." I crumple up my napkin and throw it into my plastic salad bowl to underscore my point.

But the entire way back to the office, Mark cannot help reciting under his breath, "Adeline and Evan, sitting in a tree . . ." and poking me in the ribs. Have I mentioned that Mark is thirty-five?

* * *

After a quick scan of the bar, I realize that I'm the first to arrive. I anxiously position myself at one of the stools in the middle of the bar so that I'll be visible right when Adrian walks in. Even though I brushed my teeth, fixed my hair, and touched up my makeup at the office, I sneak a quick look at myself in my compact to make sure I'm still presentable after the couple minutes' walk from the office to the bar.

I order a chardonnay in order to have something to do with my hands. At 6:10 p.m., I check my phone and start to get nervous. Even though it's only ten minutes, his lateness makes me wonder whether he is going to show up at all. I look down into my wine glass and offer a silent prayer. It works because I hear someone ask in my ear, "Adeline?"

I turn around and experience a pleasant jolt when I look into a dark set of eyes.

"Yes. You must be Adrian." I hold out my hand, which he shakes. I quickly take in his thick dark hair and bright smile. *Wowza*—he's like a young John Stamos. What a relief!

"It's a pleasure to meet you. Sorry I'm late. Someone came into my office right when I was leaving, and well, you know how it is, I'm sure."

I nod understandingly. "Yes. No worries."

"I see you already got started." He gestures to my drink.

"Oh yes. I just ordered." I hand him the menu.

He doesn't need it. He catches the bartender's attention and asks for a gin and tonic. When it arrives, he clinks his glass with mine, says, *"Yamas,"* and takes a sip.

"Do you want to move to a table? It might be more comfortable." He points to some empty tables in the corner.

"Sure."

Adrian hands his card to the bartender to start a tab, and we walk over to one of the small low wood tables in the corner. While we're walking, I notice that he's not much taller than I am in my heels. His profile said six feet tall, but he's more like five feet ten—which is a minor thing, but does not go unnoticed. The rest of him lives up to his picture, though, so I'm willing to ignore this discrepancy.

I learn that his parents are Greek—that explains his dark good looks and toast. He speaks several languages and is well traveled, and regales me with riveting stories about his latest trip to Morocco. He also tells me about how he remodeled his 1940s house into a contemporary "masterpiece" (his words) and has recently begun collecting art, and he recites the names of his favorite artists. I don't talk much because I'm too enthralled listening to his stories, which feels like vicarious vacations combined with HGTV and a grad school–level art history class.

"Have you been to any of the art museums here?" he asks.

"Not yet." I shake my head regretfully. Truth is, I don't have much interest in art (especially with my mother choosing art over me).

"It's nothing like New York or the museums in Europe, but I'll take you."

I smile and say, "That'd be great. I've only been to the Art Institute in Chicago—"

"Oh, the Art Institute! I was in Chicago last month for a conference, and they had this incredible photography exhibit by Aaron Siskind."

Well, that was a little rude. He seems really excited about the topic, though, so I take a sip of wine and let it go.

Over the next few hours and drinks, he continues to tell me stories about his travels, his work, and his family. I learn that they own a small vineyard that produces Greek-style wines. He also points out that I am holding my glass of chardonnay incorrectly.

"You should hold it by the stem so that the wine doesn't get warm."

Fair enough. But I want to point out that this is my third glass, and right now steadiness trumps any concerns of etiquette. Though we started the evening sitting across from each other, he has moved his chair, slowly but steadily next to mine, and keeps putting his arm around me, or his hand on my knee, or holding my hand. Perhaps we are connecting, or perhaps it's the alcohol, but by ten o'clock, I have to take my leave because I am on the blurry line between slightly buzzed and sloppy.

Adrian pays our tab and walks me outside as we wait for my Uber to arrive.

When it pulls up, Adrian opens the door for me, but before I can get in he says, "I had a wonderful time tonight. I hope we can do this again."

"I would love that." Although right now I would love to simply fall into my bed at home.

And taking that as his cue, he leans in and gives me a light kiss on the lips, gentle enough for my buzzed state but filled with promise for the next.

* * *

In the morning, I wake up with a dull headache. The kind where there was too much white wine involved and not enough food. I force myself out of bed and try to remedy the situation with two big glasses of water and some aspirin.

I slump down on my couch, with my hand on my forehead, to wait patiently for my coffee, which cannot brew quickly enough. My thoughts turn to last night. Adrian was gorgeous. There were no two ways about that. And he was interesting—well read and well traveled—but in the cold, hard light of day and with a dull headache, I have to concede that he seemed a tad conceited. Other than asking whether I've visited the art museums here, Adrian didn't ask me any questions at all, and for most of the date, he barely let me get two words in. In fact, when I tried to contribute to the conversation, he interrupted me with more of his own stories.

He *is* hot, though. And there was that kiss, which was nice, and the likelihood of another date. Maybe it was just nerves on his part? Anyway, due to his hotness, I will give Adrian another chance.

Plus, there is still my "big date" with Evan this weekend, as Mark so maturely keeps reminding me.

* * *

Adrian keeps his word and asks me out to dinner on Saturday. At least he's not a game player, and that is a point in his favor. Although, this time I'm happy to inform him that I already have plans that night and suggest another night. Since he has plans on Friday, we settle for a Sunday night dinner, and learning from experience, I make a mental note to give myself a two-drink limit.

Despite Mark's teasing, Saturday morning I wake up early, excited for the big date. Elena had already prepped me on Evan's stats and interests. Even if we don't hit it off, I'm still happy to hang out with Mark and Elena and spend a day exploring wine country. Since I'm not getting picked up until ten, I go for a quick run outside to burn off any nervous energy, then shower and throw on a casual black sleeveless knee-length dress, sandals, and a blue-and-green paisley wrap for when it gets chilly in the evening.

At five minutes to ten, Elena texts me that they're a block away. Since there's little parking in the area, I grab my purse and wrap and run out the door to meet them outside.

"Hi!" I say, running up to the car.

"Hi!" Elena waves happily at me, while Mark gives me a once-over and greets me with, "Nice sandals."

"Thank you." I give him a look that hopefully conveys, *Shut up*. Elena looks at us oddly, not in on the joke.

Thankfully there is no time to explain, as I settle into the back seat where Evan is sitting. He's wearing jeans and a T-shirt. He has light brown hair cut close, brown eyes, and the look of someone who spends a lot of time outdoors.

"Hi," I say to him and smile. "I'm Adeline." I hold out my hand and he shakes it.

"Hi, Adeline. I'm Evan," he says and smiles back at me. "Nice to meet you."

His smile is boyish and his handshake warm. He seems nice and is attractive, but not in a way that sets off any instant sparks, and so I feel immediately at ease.

The best thing about the day is that it doesn't feel like a date. I enjoy watching Evan and Mark banter, and Elena rolling her eyes at them and scolding, "Mark!"—especially after Mark stares pointedly at my feet for the hundredth time and finally has to admit that he told me Evan had a foot fetish (which I thought was hilarious; and no, Evan doesn't). Also, Elena was right that both guys know a lot about wine, and at each winery, they engage our tasting-room servers with thoughtful questions.

At Cliff Lede Vineyards, Elena and I leave the guys at the bar talking to the server while we take our glasses outside to enjoy the scenery and chat in private. As we wander the grounds, admiring the sea of vines against the breathtaking backdrop of the hills dotted with gnarled oak trees and the intensely blue sky filled with dots of puffy white clouds, Elena leans in and whispers, "So what do you think?"

Making sure the guys are still inside, I reply, "Cute. Definitely cute." I pause thoughtfully. "And nice."

"Nice in a bad way? Or a good way?"

I smile at her. "A good way."

Whereas with Adrian, I spent all night getting to know him—as if I had any choice—with Evan, it's just about friends having fun. I learn about him by watching him interact with Mark and Elena. He asks how I like San Francisco, what I've seen, where I've been, and what I'd like to do in the city. He tells me about Napa's history and explains the process of winemaking and why some grapes thrive in certain areas. He asks about my job and what it's like working with Mark. Evan works in product development at Google, and I also find out that he's a very active guy and likes hiking, kayaking, and rock climbing. I mention that I'd like to go hiking one of these days, and he promises to take me. Which, I guess, could amount to him asking me out on a date. But it's so casual, so natural, that I barely even notice.

Although Evan is good-looking and fit, I don't spend the afternoon wondering what he looks like under his clothes, and our conversation isn't that different from how I talk to Mark. At least with Adrian, there was an immediate physical attraction, if not emotional. But being with Evan is friendly and easy. And more importantly, when I'm buzzed after spending the afternoon wine tasting, he doesn't criticize the way I hold my wine glass during dinner. By the end of the evening, the scores are in: Evan – 1; Adrian – 0.

* * *

Sunday night dinner is a bust. Adrian is still hot but also continues to ply me with stories all about his amazingness, not once coming up for air. I drift in and out, thinking that if we cut dinner short, perhaps I can get to the gym in the morning. After enduring as much of his monologue as I can stand, I use the oldest excuse in the book to forgo coffee and dessert and tell him that I have an early morning meeting. He doesn't need to know it's with a spin bike.

When I give Bridget the Monday morning play-by-play, I tell her, "Honestly, he could've just brought a blow-up doll and sat it across from him."

"They can't all be winners." Bridget laughs. "But this Evan guy sounds pretty good."

"Yeah, I think so."

"You don't sound very excited about him, though."

"Really? 'Cause I liked him. I didn't want to rip his clothes off then and there, but I enjoyed hanging out with him. He's cute and nice. And we were also with Mark and Elena. Maybe it would be different if we were on a date alone? We'll see."

Which is not too far off, since on Sunday Evan texted me asking if I would like to go hiking this coming weekend, and I said yes.

CHAPTER EIGHTEEN

I t's hard to believe that just two weeks ago, I couldn't find enough things to fill up the empty hours, nor is work first and foremost in my mind any longer. *How times have changed!* Right now I'm getting so much action on my online dating profile that I'm beginning to wonder if I used my job in Chicago as an excuse to avoid dating, because in my forget-Brad-Summers frenzy, I'm learning where there's a will, there's a way. Adrian asked me out again, and I told him that while I had had fun getting to know him, I didn't think we were a good match. He suggested we be friends instead, and I agreed (which we all know in dating parlance means we will never hang out again but agree to be polite if we ever randomly bump into each other). I'm also doing double sessions at the gym before and after work, and between the exercise-induced endorphins pumping through me, the huge ego boost from the attention my online profile is getting, and my big date on Saturday, I am feeling fan-freaking-tastic.

So when my office phone rings with a certain LA area code, I barely flinch when I recognize Brad's number.

"Hello. This is Adeline Turner."

"Hi, Addie. It's Brad." He coughs. "Brad Summers." He clarifies, as if I wasn't sure which Brad it could be.

"Oh, hi, Brad. What can I do for you?" I'm thrilled that I'm able to sound so pleasant.

"You sound as if you're in a good mood."

"I am." I twirl the phone cord around my finger and sit back in my chair. "What's up?"

"I'm going to be in town this weekend getting my place settled and was wondering if you're going to be around?" he ventures. "I'd love to ask you some questions about the office and San Francisco. We could do dinner."

I really, really don't want to see him. Plus, he already suggested dinner on our last call, and I turned him down.

"Sorry. This weekend is bad. I'm really busy."

There is a moment of silence on his end, which feels like an eternity. Finally, he says, "I see."

I clench my jaw as my body temperature rises. I need to move this conversation along. "What did you want to ask? Maybe I can take care of your questions right now?" I say, more sharply than intended.

"Well, I was hoping we could meet face to face."

Well, we can't.

Honestly, can't he just talk to Mark? I'm sure he has talked to Mark. So if Brad really wants to ask me about my impressions of the office or whatever it is he wishes to discuss, why won't he just talk to me on the phone, right now?

"I'm sorry, but I'm not available this weekend." I stand firm.

"I understand. Maybe another time."

"Okay. Sounds good. I'll talk to you later."

"Sure. Have a good one."

"You too. Bye."

I don't even hear if he says goodbye because I can't hang up the phone fast enough. He obviously wants to talk about something personal, but I don't want to hear it after all these months of silence and when I'm finally moving on. Until I hear he's divorced, there's nothing personal to talk about.

And that is what I tell Bridget on the phone later that afternoon with my office door closed.

"You know what's best," she says. I can hear Bridget clicking away distractedly on her computer. "If it was me, personally, I would want to know. But I understand wanting to move on."

"I just don't know what his deal is with wanting to talk face to face. If he has something to say, he should just come out with it."

"Maybe the soon-to-be-ex wiretapped his phones or something? Or maybe she's breaking into his email and texts and stuff?"

"Or maybe she has a detective following him and would see us having dinner together anyway. Who knows?" And because I'm already on a rant, I continue working myself up. "Whatever! He's going to be here soon enough. He can talk to me at work. Right?"

"Yeah," agrees Bridget, although not as heartily as I would normally expect. Then she giggles.

"What's so funny?"

"Oh, Jason just sent me a funny email." She reads it aloud to me—and it's only funny if you are truly in love with a person.

"Hey, now?" I feel a little petulant. "Aren't girlfriends supposed to give each other one hundred percent attention when we're talking about our guy troubles?"

"Yes, yes, you're right. Sorry," she says, even as I suspect the tapping I hear is Bridget responding to Jason.

I can't blame her, though. She's so happy these days. And she has been patiently listening to my woes concerning Mr. Summers all this time, so I forgive her.

"Oh, go on then. Tell me more about Jason," I say, smiling now and happy to hear my friend so in love, and hoping for the same for me.

* * *

Come Saturday morning, I'm anxiously waiting at home for Evan to pick me up. I'm sporting all-new hiking gear—I'm sure you can spot the trend here—but I wanted to look the part. I'm wearing brand-new trail running shoes, olive-green hiking pants, and a long-sleeve brown T-shirt that has some yoga-like, tribal design on the front (and I'm pretty sure had the word *goddess* on my receipt), all topped off with an orange North Face fleece, because it might get windy and I want to be spotted easily if I fall off a cliff somewhere. I'm hoping Evan won't guess that I've never been hiking before. Of course, my gear is all very new and clean . . . Uh-oh, maybe he'll think I'm trying too hard.

Even though my feelings toward him are still more platonic than romantic, I can't stop my mind from spinning. What if we hit it off? What if we don't? Either way, it's going to affect my relationship with Mark. Maybe this wasn't one of my more brilliant plans. I try to remain optimistic as I nibble nervously on an energy bar.

Evan pulls up in a cute Mini Cooper. For some reason, I thought he would be more the SUV type, and I say as much when I hop in.

He laughs. "I can see that. But who wants to park that in this city?"

"True," I comment as I take him in. He's still good-looking, still boyish, still outdoorsy cute. Objectively, he's attractive—and yet I'm not really attracted to him. But the fact that I'm not totally smitten helps takes the nervous edge off, and we chat comfortably as we cross the Golden Gate Bridge to the Marin Headlands.

Within the first ten minutes of hiking, I think I'm going to die. We're climbing straight uphill, and I swear this trail could kick the stair-climber's butt in the gym any day. So maybe it is obvious that this is my first hike.

Evan encourages me on. "Don't worry. It'll flatten out soon."

I can barely acknowledge his words because I'm still trying to catch my breath, and I can feel that my face is a big red, puffy mess. Evan strolls a few paces ahead. I doubt he has even broken a sweat. I now understand why he is in such great shape. When we reach the peak of this climb, Evan turns around and holds out his hand for me. I gladly grab it, and he helps me up the last few steps. And you know what? It was worth it. We can see the ocean, the hills, and the city shimmering in the distance.

"It's so beautiful!" I say, my eyes fixed on the view, my hand still encased in his.

"Isn't it? This is why I love living here."

"I understand." I watch a large hawk swoop into a valley. It's so quiet and peaceful that it's hard to believe we're just outside the city.

"Hey." Evan turns to me and moves his hand to my waist. I turn to look at him, and I see the look. The look that says he is going to kiss me. And I have to admit there is a slight stirring in me. I smile to let him know it's okay, and he leans down and places a sweet kiss on my lips. He pulls back and grins. "I guess I should've bought you dinner first, but it just seemed like the right moment."

"I'm glad you did."

And because he's so close and I'm still staring at his mouth, this time I lean in to kiss him, and as our lips press together more firmly, it does something electric to my pulse. After this second kiss, Evan pulls me in for a hug, and I'm acutely aware of the heat emanating from his body.

But just as I'm thinking this, Evan suddenly pulls back and says, "Now that *that's* out of the way, we can enjoy the rest of the hike."

I laugh, and hand in hand we walk along the top of the ridge, gazing out at the ocean. I haven't felt comfortable around a guy in a long time. Also, hiking provides many opportunities for chivalry, as he puts his arm around my waist to steer me closer to the path and away from sliding trails. We hold hands while walking along the dusty paths and stop several times to admire the view.

After three hours, we end up back by the beach where we parked the car. Neither of us seems quite ready for the afternoon to end, though. Since it's cold and windy down at the beach, Evan suggests that we warm up with some coffee, and we drive into nearby Sausalito, which is lined with quaint shops and strolling tourists, whom we soon join. Evan knows of a café with outdoor seating, so I let him lead the way, and I snag a table outside while he orders our coffees. I treat myself to a cappuccino. Evan goes for a full-on hot chocolate with whipped cream, which I find endearing.

Sitting on the patio, I engage in my favorite activity, people watching, until I suddenly realize that maybe I'm being rude—and that maybe I'm also being watched.

Sure enough, when I look at Evan, he's grinning at me.

"What?" I say, smiling back.

"Nothing."

"Well, it must be something for you to be smiling like that."

He shrugs. "Maybe I'm just having a lot of fun today."

"Me too." I smile and sip my cappuccino. "So what are you doing tonight?" *Argh!* The second I say it, I want to take it back. Now he'll ask me the same, and I'll have to admit I'm a bit of a loser who has nothing going on this evening.

"Is that an invitation?" Evan asks with a hint of a raised eyebrow.

Or that. I'm a terrible flirt. Not as in, *I love to flirt, please stop me.* But as in, *I'm terrible at flirting, so please, for everyone's sake, stop me.*

"Just making conversation." I hope I'm not about to start blushing.

"I'm going to a party tonight." *Oh.* Now I really don't want him to ask me what I'm doing. "What about you?" And there it is.

"Um, nothing as exciting as a party. In fact, I'm kinda doing nothing at all. I wasn't sure how I'd feel after hiking, so I thought I'd better plan to lie low." *Yes, good cover.* And now the distraction. "So what's the party?" Oh dear, did that sound like I was fishing for an invite?

"It's nothing really. I was going to watch the game with a couple buddies tonight."

I have no idea what the "game" is, but I nod as if I understand.

"That sounds like fun."

"Yeah," he says, looking at me intently. "So what are you going to do at home tonight?"

"I don't know. I figured I'd watch a movie. Maybe order takeout. Nothing too exciting."

"That sounds nice, actually." He drums his fingers on his cup.

Is he going to invite me to watch the game? Or is this my cue to be coy and invite him to a party at my house? I'm too caffeinated, though, to pull that off at the moment. Or ever, really.

We sit in uneasy silence. Finally, just to break it up, I say, "Shall we go?"

Evan looks a little surprised, but says, "Sure."

Once we're in the car, he asks, "So what are you planning to order tonight?"

"Oh." I pick imaginary lint off my jacket, trying to think of my imaginary plans. "I'm not sure. Maybe Thai?"

"You know, I'm a good chef," he says, his tone implying it's more of a question than a statement.

"I did not know that. And that is good information to know."

"I know you planned on staying in, and I don't want to intrude," he says, keeping his eyes on the road and avoiding mine, "but what if I made you dinner tonight?"

I am surprised. Delighted. Delightfully surprised.

"But what about the game tonight?"

"Oh, that's just an excuse to hang out with the guys, and I see them all the time."

A mariachi band seems to be playing full force inside me, and I'm struggling to sit still.

"If you want to. But you don't have to. I mean, of course, I'd love it if you wanted to come over and hang out tonight. I obviously don't have anything big planned." Fine. I've given up trying to look cool.

"Then it's a date." He turns to me and smiles.

"I guess so." I smile back. "So what are we having tonight?"

"What do you like?"

"Everything," I say.

Evan laughs. "How 'bout this? Why don't we hit Whole Foods before I drop you off, and then we can shop for dinner together." He reaches over and squeezes my knee affectionately, sending a wave of the good shivers through me.

"Sounds like a plan." I grin.

At the store, we divide and conquer. Evan sends me out to select cheese, olives, and bread, while he heads to the produce and meat departments. I feel like those couples I see in my neighborhood on weekend mornings running errands together. It's as if we're a team. And grocery shopping with Evan is a lot more fun than by myself.

When we get to my place, Evan tries to help me bring in the groceries.

"No, no, no. You'll have to double-park. Let me get it." I pop out of the car and pull the groceries out of the trunk. I come back to the passenger window, bags in hand. "Shall we say seven? Or should we do earlier to give you enough time to cook?"

"How about six thirty? A little extra time to navigate a new kitchen."

"Of course. See you then!" I wave him off, and when he's out of sight, I rush inside because there's a lot of work to be done.

I hurry putting away the groceries: arugula, butternut squash, onions, brussels sprouts, cranberries, Himalayan sea salt . . . Hmm, I can't wait to see what we're having. But there's no time to sit here admiring the produce; I need to shower and straighten up my place before Evan arrives.

In the shower I exfoliate, do a face mask, extra-condition my hair, and then slather on lots of moisturizer. I finish by spritzing on what I hope is a light but inviting perfume. I take extra care perfecting my makeup for a sexy yet casual look and select a pair of my softest and most flattering jeans, a V-neck T-shirt, and a loose cashmere cardigan. I accessorize with a simple silver chain necklace and silver rings. As I race around my apartment tidying up, I feel a small buzz of excitement in my stomach. Suddenly, I feel that this is the "big date" Mark kept joking about. The trip to Napa was mere child's play. This might be the beginning of a real relationship. *Finally!*

I light some candles in the living room and just in time because the doorbell rings. I give myself a final look in the hall mirror and tell myself, *It's showtime,* before opening the door.

Evan is there smiling, with not one but two bottles of wine. A white and a red.

"I wasn't sure what your preference was, so I thought better safe than sorry."

He looks handsome in jeans and a crewneck sweater with a T-shirt peeking out. And he's actually wearing real shoes, as in leather and lace-up, whereas I've only seen him in sneakers thus far. He cleans up well. As he leans in to give me a kiss hello, I catch a whiff of a fresh-out-of-the-shower scent mixed with subtle cologne, and I swoon a little on the inside.

"Here, let me take those." I reach for the wine bottles so that he can take off his jacket. "And I will lead you to the kitchen," I say mock-ceremoniously. "And to the wine glasses."

In the kitchen, I set the bottles on the counter and reach for two wine glasses. I do not have special white or red ones and feel a little self-conscious, knowing that Evan takes his wine seriously. I'm still a little sensitive after my experience with Adrian pointing out my wine faux pas.

Evan doesn't bat an eye, though. Instead, he surveys the kitchen space and nods appraisingly. "Very good," he says, in a way that for some reason makes me laugh. "Now let's open one of these bad boys."

"I'm already on it," I say, digging through my drawer, looking for the bottle opener. I hand it to Evan.

"White? Red?" he asks.

"Hmm . . . let's start with the white." It's a California chardonnay from one of the area's more famous wineries.

"Let's 'start,' you say." Evan grins as he opens the bottle and pours it into the waiting glasses. "I like that attitude."

I would like to smile coyly, but instead what comes out is a hearty laugh. Evan hands me my glass and we toast.

"To a delicious dinner and good company," Evan says.

"Hear, hear," I say as we clink glasses.

After the first delightful sip, I give Evan a tour of the kitchen. He then gets to work organizing the groceries and preheating the oven. While he begins chopping the vegetables with enviable skill, I set out the olives and cheese on a platter and slice up some of the crusty bread.

"Is there anything else I can do?" I ask.

"Nope. Just keep me company." He grins and gives me a wink.

I settle onto one of the stools by the counter to watch him work his magic and answer any questions he has.

Besides, the kitchen is really too small for two cooks. While he cooks, we chat idly and nibble on cheese and olives. I also read off various movie titles and their descriptions from Netflix. Surprisingly, we both agree on a romantic comedy. I'm relieved that I'm not going to have to pretend to be up for a suspense thriller. Something lighthearted is more my speed.

* * *

Dinner looks amazing. Evan prepared a salad with mixed greens and a homemade dressing—"My secret recipe," Evan whispers theatrically, making me laugh—and a perfectly cooked chicken with lemon and herbs and sweet roasted vegetables. By the time dinner is ready, I notice with a slight buzz that we have finished the chardonnay.

I hold up the empty bottle. "How did that happen?"

Evan shrugs. "Cooking makes me thirsty." Although I suspect that my nerves may have had something to do with it.

"Red with dinner?" he asks.

"I guess so." I pull two new wine glasses from the cupboard. I also get out plates and utensils and set the table.

Evan first serves us salad and then gets up to serve our main course and refill our wine glasses. The food is warm and healthy, as is my company. He even loads my dishwasher, claiming, "It's my mess, so I should clean it up."

The cynic in me says that perhaps he's done this all before and he has this courtship ritual down to a science. But it's a small voice and one that is easily drowned out by the wine and the cozy feeling in my belly. Therefore, when the plates are cleared, it only seems natural to snuggle up on the couch with my feet tucked under me and my head leaning against Evan's shoulder, while he wraps his arm around my shoulders, and we settle in for the movie.

"Thank you for dinner."

"You're welcome," Evan says, kissing my forehead.

In my contented state, I somehow doze off and miss the end of the movie. When the credits start rolling, I wake up, startled. "What?" I pull back and look at Evan and then the screen. "Did I fall asleep?"

Evan laughs at my disoriented state. "You sure did. Sorry. I probably should've woken you, but you seemed really tired."

I shake my head in disbelief. "That never happens. It must've been the hike. How much did I miss?"

"Just the ending."

"Huh. Well, I guess I'll have to watch that tomorrow." I peer at him. "How did you know I was so tired?"

Laughter hiding behind his eyes, he says, "I assumed from the snoring."

I clap my hand over my mouth and feel my cheeks flush. "You're kidding! I don't snore."

"If you say so," says Evan, trying not to laugh. I playfully hit him with a throw pillow.

"Hey, come here," he says, suddenly serious, and pulls me in for a kiss that means business.

I return the kiss with equal fervor. His hands begin to move under my sweater and mine reciprocate. When he asks, "Which way is the bedroom?" I point down the hallway, and he picks me up and carries me to bed.

CHAPTER NINETEEN

When I wake up in the morning, the first thing I notice is that I'm naked. The next thing I notice is that my brain and mouth are fuzzy from too much wine the night before. The last thing I notice is that I am alone. I look at the pillow next to me and see an Evan-sized head imprint and the sheets on his side tucked up with care. My stomach sinks. The last time I woke up alone after a night of sex, it didn't bode well. And this does not bode well either. Not at all. My eyes scan the room, but there is no evidence of Evan. I listen carefully, but there are no sounds from the bathroom, or the kitchen, or anywhere in the apartment. All I hear are the birds outside chirping, which somehow makes me more depressed.

I pull the covers over my head. *Stupid, stupid, stupid.* The only other time I've had sex on the first date was with Brad, and look how that turned out. Have I learned nothing? And Evan sneaking out in the middle of the night? That's another first and new low for my love life. Even though I drank my fair share of wine, I remember the entire night clearly—this is no "did we or didn't we" situation. And it was good. At least I thought so. Maybe he thought otherwise and couldn't wait to get out of here? Or maybe he's a cad? I can't believe I fell for his culinary moves. How many other women has he tried this out on?

And, ugh, he's Mark's friend. Is he going to tell Mark everything? How am I going to show my face at work on Monday? Why do I do such stupid things? Am I that desperate? So far this year I've slept with a married man and now my boss's friend.

With a groan I throw off the covers and go to the bathroom to brush my teeth and wash off the last remnants of makeup from the night before. Coffee. I need coffee. I grab my robe from the back of the bathroom door, wrapping it tightly around my shamed self, and head to the kitchen.

There on the counter is a note.

> Good morning, sleepyhead. Went out to get coffee and breakfast.
>   - Evan

Oh! I look around and spy the clock; it's only a little after eight. I wonder what time he left. More importantly, I wonder if I have time to shower. But that question is answered when I hear the front door opening. Quickly I try to smooth down my hair, which is a futile exercise because it is tangled Medusa-like in every direction. I feel my face getting hot as I remember the cause of its tangled state.

When Evan sees me, his face lights up.

"You're up," he says. Even with his clothes slightly rumpled, he looks good in that way that only guys can pull off. He places a pink box and a bag of fresh-ground coffee on my counter.

"Good morning," I say, wondering what's in the box. A girl could get used to freshly baked pastries in the morning.

With his hands now free, he gives me a hug and a kiss on the lips. "How are you feeling this morning?"

"Very good." *And relieved.* I melt into the embrace. "You?"

"Good," he murmurs into my hair. "Hope I didn't wake you when I left. I took your keys off the counter to let myself back in." He pulls back and throws the keys onto the counter.

"Not at all. Don't be silly." I make a sweeping gesture with my arm toward the coffee and box. "I don't have any cause for complaint."

I walk over to the coffee maker and grab the pot. While I stand at the sink and fill the pot with water, I nod toward the box. "What's in there?"

"Croissants." He walks over to me with the box, opens it, and puts it under my nose. "Regular and chocolate."

I inhale the sweet buttery smell. "Wow! You really know how to spoil a girl."

"All part of the master plan," he says, walking away with the box. And already familiar with my kitchen, he goes into the cupboard for two plates.

I shake my head. Minutes ago, I was bemoaning the state of my love life with the bedcovers over my head, and now I feel like I'm in a play, enacting a scene of domestic bliss. While I prepare the coffee, Evan sets our croissants on the table.

The croissants are delicious. And though I enjoy every bite, I'm kind of wondering whether this is going to be an all-day thing with Evan. I like him, but we could probably use our space today. Luckily, I don't have to wonder long.

"What are you up to today?" he asks, refilling my coffee cup.

"Just catching up on errands. Maybe a little bit of work. You?"

"I'm supposed to meet a friend at my rock-climbing gym." He tears into his second croissant. "We're meeting at eleven, so I should probably head home soon to take a shower and change."

Mystery solved.

After a couple more kisses and a promise to call me later, Evan is on his way. The second he is out the door, I pick up my phone and press Bridget's number.

"Hey, Addie," Bridget answers.

"Hey, you." I can hear music and background noise on her end. "Where are you? What's that sound?"

"Just at Nordstrom returning a pair of boots and, of course, buying two more pairs."

"Of course!" God, how I miss Bridget.

"So what's up?"

"Nothing much," I say coyly. "Except that I had sex last night."

"SHUT UP!" I can tell that I now have Bridget's full attention. "Hold on, I need to sit down. But I mean, who, what, where, when, *how*?"

"Let's see, the *who* would be Evan."

"The Napa guy you were fixed up with?"

"Yes. I'm not sure what the *what* would be, but the *where* was in my apartment. The *when* we've already covered. And the *how*?" I smirk to myself. "Well, Bridge, I don't think I need to explain that to you."

"Oh my god, girl, just give me the details!"

I fill her in on all the glorious details of the day and evening that followed.

"You know I'm dying over here," Bridget interrupts my story. "You never sleep with a guy on the first date." Then, remembering, she says, "Well, except for . . . well, you know."

"Yeah, well, I guess the universe is finally throwing me a bone." And knowing I just set Bridget up for a crude joke, I preemptively admonish her, "Don't say it, okay?"

"Okay, okay." She laughs. "But really, the first date? *Adeline Turner*, I'm surprised!"

"Oh, stop. We already went out on a double date with Mark and Elena, then the hike was our second date, and since he dropped me off and came over later, I'm counting this as our third date."

"However you want to rationalize it," she says gaily. "But really, spill the *real* details. How was it?"

"It was great."

"How great? As great as you-know-who great?"

I hate that she brings that up. "Different, but great," I say affirmatively. At least I think it was great, considering it was only my second sexual encounter this year.

"Okay. So now what? Are you a couple?"

"Obviously too soon to tell, but I think we may be the beginning of one."

"How do you feel about that?" Something a shrink would ask.

"I feel good." Actually, I feel more than good. Last night, I finally turned a corner. Perhaps that's not the *most* romantic thing to be feeling, but it's definitely hopeful.

* * *

Maybe it's my night with Evan, or maybe it's the sunny weather and fresh air, but I feel like a happy little bubble floating in and out of the shops in my neighborhood on this Sunday afternoon. After I talked to Bridget and checked my work email, I had too much energy to sit inside. So I put my hair into a messy bun, threw on some jeans and a sweater, and headed out.

I walk into a couple of clothing boutiques to browse, but don't bother trying anything on, and I go into some home decor stores, but spare any big purchases and instead limit myself to some scented candles. With candles in tow, I spy a bookstore with shelves of books outside on the sidewalk. They have a variety of fiction, history, and biographies. I'm ashamed to admit I haven't been reading a lot these days, or working on my own writing, like I had planned. So I start perusing the books, picking up those that have intriguing covers and titles, and reading the back cover and a couple early pages of each. It is when I'm deep into a story about a husband looking for his long-lost wife that I hear my name.

"Addie?"

My breath catches in my throat, and the sounds of street chatter and traffic are drowned out by the loud thumping of my heart. *No. It can't be.* I turn around.

"Brad?" *Pop* goes my bubble.

Brad is giving me that smile that looks like sunshine, as he tilts his head to the side. "I thought you were tied up this weekend." He doesn't say this in an accusatory way, so I can't even act defensive.

"Yes, I had some downtime between things and thought I'd check out this store." I don't see this man for eighteen years, and I run into him twice in one year—and that's before we've even started working together? He is wearing a navy crewneck sweater, dark jeans, and a day's worth of stubble, and *damn*, he looks good.

"Yeah, I'm pretty excited there's a bookstore so close to my new place."

"You live around here?" *So close to me?!* It's bad enough I'll have to see him in the office on a daily basis, but in my neighborhood as well?

Just when I thought things were looking up, I'm back where I started. Well played, universe, well played.

A young girl with strawberry-blond hair and large blue eyes interrupts us. "Daddy, can I get this one?"

Brad takes a look at the book. "Sure, honey." He puts his arm around the girl's shoulder. "Ivy, I'd like you to meet someone. This is my friend Addie. She used to go to school with me when I was growing up in Wisconsin."

"Hi, Ivy." I put on my most pleasant, child-friendly smile. "It's a pleasure to meet you."

Ivy looks at me shyly but smiles. "Hi . . ." She trails off and leans into her father more closely.

"Do you want to look at more books?" Brad asks her. She nods her head vigorously. "Okay, why don't you go back to where you got this one, and I'll follow you in a minute."

"Okay!" Ivy doesn't need to be told twice and rushes back to the children's section.

"She's shy with strangers," he explains to me.

"Your daughter is beautiful. And very sweet."

"Thank you. She's part of the reason I took this job. So I'll have more time to spend with her."

"Oh," I say, surprised. "That's nice."

I look around us, my stomach churning. If Ivy is here, does that mean Kathryn is too? What about the house in Malibu? Mark said that Brad's move to the Bay Area was due partly to his divorce. So, what's up with that? I want to ask a million questions right now, and I know that if I would simply accept his invitation to dinner, I could ask them all. But it just doesn't feel right. So instead I ask, "Are you excited, then, about the move?"

He lets out a big sigh. "Yes. I'm ready to be out of LA."

Ivy, who was only gone for a minute, is back. "Daddy, Daddy, are we going?"

"Do you have everything you need?" he asks her. *Oh my, what a loaded question,* I think. As a child of divorce, I feel for

Ivy, but she seems to have two parents who want her, so maybe she will be okay.

"Yes," she says softly.

"Okay, then. Let me finish talking to my friend, and we'll go pay for your book."

"Okay." Ivy then turns and stares quietly at me, her obstacle to leaving.

"It was nice running into you," I say to Brad. "And nice to meet you, Ivy." She smiles shyly again and then looks down at her feet. "Good luck with the move," I say back to Brad.

"Thanks. I guess I'll see you around."

"Yep."

Brad looks at me a bit longer than is necessary, but then he finally disappears into the store with his daughter.

With a shaky hand, I put back the book that I was holding and hightail it away from the store.

Suddenly, I don't want to be outside anymore or around anyone. All I want to do is go home and hide on my sofa under the throw, which is exactly what I do. But not before closing my drapes to block out the cheerful, mocking sun. This is a pity party for one, thank you very much.

Standing across from Brad, I felt a physical pull. A pang perhaps. How can this be, after sex last night with Evan? What I told Bridget was true, it was different. Was it better than with Brad? Well, how can one compare years of romantic fantasy leading up to one night of consummation to last night, which turned out to be an unexpected, pleasant surprise? Plus, I've slept with each of them only once. Hardly a record to compare.

And if anything, Evan is going to call tonight. Brad just sends me cryptic emails wanting to meet for dinner to discuss his new job. Suddenly, I feel like I'm living a déjà vu with Eric both pre- and post-Brad. Eric was a great guy, and I totally messed that up by mooning over someone unavailable. I'm *not* going to let that happen again with Evan. *Screw Brad Summers.* Plus, he ruined my plan of some Sunday night reading. I guess it's time to look for a new hobby. I turn on the TV and scroll through to a cooking show. *Hmm . . . this looks interesting. Maybe I'll learn something and can return the favor to Evan by making dinner for him one night?*

But the mindless television shows cannot stop my mind from working. My new relationship isn't strong enough yet to obliterate all my feelings about Brad. Oh well. So I'm not there yet. But maybe in another week I will be.

Or at least this is the lie I need to tell myself in order to not pack up and move back to Chicago.

CHAPTER TWENTY

'M COMING TO SAN FRANCISCO!!! screams Bridget's Monday morning email.

I'm at work sipping my coffee and deciding on my plan of attack for the day when her message pops up in my box. I immediately reply, No way! When?

Bridget writes that she'll be flying in to meet with clients on Friday and asks if would I mind if she extended her stay until Sunday night. Would I mind? Is she kidding? I'm ecstatic and start asking her what she wants to do and see. To which she responds, I don't care. I'm just excited to see you.

The only hiccup is that Evan and I have plans to go out to dinner on Saturday night. On the phone last night he joked that maybe he should take me out on a "real" date, one where we actually get dressed up and go out. So I email him, letting him know that my best friend is unexpectedly coming to town and asking if we can move dinner to another night.

Evan responds promptly, No problem. What about Wednesday?

Perfect, because it gives me Thursday night to get ready for Bridget's arrival. He also writes that he would love to meet her and suggests that we all go out to dinner with Mark and Elena so that she can meet my friends. I hadn't thought of that. It's a sweet gesture, though it also feels a little forward that he wants to meet my best friend from home so soon. But Bridget was the one pushing me to be more social, *and* her visit coincides with when Brad will start working here. If there was ever a time I needed a distraction, this is it.

So I reply, Sounds great!

Even though I want to start surfing the web to think up ideas of where to take Bridget, I really need to focus on work at the moment. I've started doing more work on Moonstruck's new building project and have been doing real estate research on areas I'm unfamiliar with. I need to be on top of my game, because I don't just want to impress Brad with a new dress; I want to impress him at work. Not that it matters. Because I sort of have a boyfriend. But there's nothing wrong with wanting to be prepared and impress a new partner. Right?

I'm so focused that when I hear a knock on my door, I jump a mile.

"Oh, sorry. I didn't mean to scare you," says Mark, although he looks rather amused.

"No. Sorry I was just . . ." I shake my head. "I don't know. Just working." I gesture to the chair across from my desk. "What's up?"

Mark takes a seat and leans into the back of the chair. "So I hear we're going out to dinner on Saturday."

"Um, yes. It was Evan's idea. But if you have other plans, it's no big deal."

"Elena and I were going to take Brad out for dinner that night, sort of as a welcome-to-San-Francisco thing. I thought we could bring him along."

I feel my palms beginning to sweat and try to keep my face neutral while I attempt to form a response. I think what comes out is a *sure, why not*, although I'm having an out-of-body experience right now, so I can't totally be sure. I mean, why not, indeed?

Somehow I get my wits about me to ask the burning question, "So, has his divorce gone through yet?"

"Oh, that." Mark waves his hand dismissively. "Who knows when that will end? But she's living in Malibu now, I guess in some house that Brad bought her." He shakes his head. "I can't believe he bought her a house. It's crazy, but it's probably for Ivy's sake."

So, if Ivy is living in Malibu with Kathryn, does that not bode well for Brad's child-custody rights? I wonder if Mark knows. But it's not my business.

I love Mark's openness. I can tell he wants to discuss it more with me, but I seem to have the information I need. Brad is still married, and who knows when he'll be divorced. That's all I needed to know. Brad is not available to me.

"These things are tricky," I say noncommittally and shuffle some papers on my desk.

"Yes, especially in his case."

I nod but do not add anything. Sensing that this line of conversation is a dead end, Mark changes the subject.

"So what about you?"

"What about me?"

"You and Evan." He leans forward now, resting his arms on my desk, settling in for a story.

Ooh, that! "It's good. It's early days and we're having fun."

"So it's not serious?" He tilts his head with a half smile. "Inquiring minds want to know."

I roll my eyes at him good-naturedly, but I feel a little exasperated. "I didn't say that. We've only hung out twice and are having dinner this week. And come on, we just met." I stop and narrow my eyes at Mark. "Why are you asking? Did he tell you something?"

"I don't know if I can repeat it at work," he says, lowering his voice and giving me a serious look.

Oh my god. Evan must have told Mark we had sex. I rapidly think of how to respond while trying to ignore the flush creeping up my neck. But the next thing I know, Mark is laughing and saying, "I'm kidding, Adeline. But wow! You should've seen the look on your face."

Phew! So I'm not going to die of an embarrassment-induced stroke, but still. "Okay, okay, enough of this nonsense. Some of us have work to do, you know."

"Yeah, you should get to that."

"Just get out of here, okay?" I say, smiling.

"You don't want to talk about your hike and dinner on Saturday?" He grins with a playful twinkle in his eyes.

Uh-oh. He knows. But maybe he doesn't know all of it? Anyway, I don't want to find out. "I plead the fifth, okay? Please, I'm very busy right now and don't have time for girl talk."

"Okay, okay." Mark gets up and leaves my office, chuckling at my obvious discomfort.

Honestly, what is with that guy and his nosiness? But I still smile to myself.

* * *

"Are you serious?" Bridget says, a little too loudly.

I'm already at home, somehow having managed to suppress the urge to call her during the day at work.

"Evan *and* Brad? *Brad* is going to be there?"

"And I haven't even told you yet what happened Sunday afternoon."

"What?" she breathes into the phone.

"I bumped into Brad at a bookstore."

"Shut. Up."

"Yep. And he was with his daughter." I describe the encounter in detail, which, though brief, had seemed to last an eternity.

The first question Bridget asks is, "How did he look?"

I can't lie. "Gorgeous."

"Better-looking than Evan?"

I sigh. I wish she would stop with these comparisons. "They're different."

"Hmm . . . I just don't understand why you won't have dinner with him. Aren't you curious about what he has to say?"

I chew on the inside of my cheek and then say, "Of course I am, but I'm annoyed at the way he's going about it. Why can't he just tell me on the phone what exactly it is he wants to talk about? Hiding it under this 'work' cloak is shady. And I don't want to go to dinner with a married man and not know what it's about. Call me a prude, but I don't want to put myself through that again. Plus, seeing him with his daughter, I couldn't help but think about my parents' divorce."

"Yeah," says Bridget, quietly understanding where I'm coming from. "But maybe he wants to tell you his divorce is almost settled?"

"Actually, I got some info on that today. Mark told me that the divorce isn't final, and in his words, 'Who knows when that will end?'"

"Interesting."

"And I can't date him anyway now because I'm with Evan," I say, trying to convince myself it's true.

"Oh! I didn't realize you were serious." Although something in her voice tells me she doesn't believe me. "In that case, I can't wait to meet Evan on Saturday." But I know she is infinitely more interested in meeting Brad and seeing what all the fuss is about.

* * *

Evan and I have dinner reservations at eight o'clock Wednesday night. This gives me time to go home first and do some general primping. The last couple of days we've been texting each other back and forth and talking on the phone before bed. It's refreshing. Evan doesn't play games. He's straightforward. He wants to talk to me, so he talks to me. Part of me is a bit nervous because I feel like we're moving in fast-forward, and there's the added pressure of having friends in common. But I like him. I do. And maybe I could relax and like him even more if I could get a certain Mr. Summers out of my head. I already threw Eric away because of Brad, and I'm not going to let that happen again.

* * *

The restaurant has a buzzing bar scene, but since we have reservations, we go straight to our table. Tonight Evan is wearing dark jeans with a button-down shirt and jacket. The perfect mix of casual and dressy. I have not yet perfected my "California cool" wardrobe and feel a little too dressed up in a black dress and heels, but since Evan let out a whistle when he picked me up, I put the thought out of my mind.

Once we're seated, Evan tells me about the restaurant, the chef, and what items he recommends on the menu. I knew he was a wine enthusiast, but I'm now realizing that he is something of a foodie as well.

This gives me a great conversation opener. "You really seem to know your food and wine . . ."

"Yes, I started learning more about wines since moving here from Washington," he says, setting down his menu. "Also, my mom used to have her own vegetable garden and was a great cook; so I was spoiled by always eating freshly grown and home-made food. She taught me most of what I know, but I've also taken some cooking classes in the area."

During dinner Evan tells me about his childhood and his brothers. He also tells me about his move to California, his work and what he likes and dislikes about it, his friends, and what he does on the weekends. He tells me where he likes to vacation, which is mostly either a beach vacation for scuba diving or Asia, and recounts stories of his various trips.

There's no lull in our conversation because Evan easily fills up the evening with his stories, and for a fleeting second, Adrian pops into my mind. But whereas Adrian was more interested in himself than me, Evan is just enthusiastic about everything.

Over dessert, which Evan insists that I order, he takes both my hands in his and looks at me seriously in a way that, quite frankly, makes me a little nervous. Worried we've been moving too fast, I'm relieved when he doesn't drop to one knee, but simply says, "I'm having a lot of fun with you, Adeline. And I don't know if you're seeing anyone else, but I would like to just be seeing you."

"Are you asking me to be your girlfriend?" I give him an innocent look, teasing him a little at the same time.

"Yes, I am." Evan smiles confidently, sure of my answer. Why wouldn't he be sure of my answer? I've already been vetted by his friends. I'm still fairly new to town. He already got the milk for free. If anything, we've already been acting like a couple.

"I would like that." I smile warmly at him. I would. I really, truly would.

"Good." He reaches over our dessert plates and gives me a kiss.

Inwardly, I breathe a sigh of relief. It's official! I have a boyfriend. Mission accomplished.

* * *

Friday morning, I skip the gym to instead race around my apartment making sure everything is perfect for Bridget's arrival. I've stocked up on wine, fruit, snacks, and fresh flowers and set out various soaps and lotions in the bathroom. Since she'll probably get here before me, I arrange a little plate of teas and leave a mug out and write a note explaining how to work the remote. She should be all set.

When I get home from work, I notice that Bridget has made herself at home. The tea is untouched, but I spy the wine opener sitting on the counter next to an open bottle of sauvignon blanc. For the first time since I moved to San Francisco, I feel like I'm home.

I drop my computer bag and purse on the floor. "Bridget!"

"Addie!" Bridget sets down her full wine glass and rushes toward me.

"It's so great to see you! I'm so happy you're here!" I give her a big hug, then pull back and look at my friend. Other than wearing her hair a little longer and a little darker blond, she looks the same. Bridget must've been sizing me up as well.

"You look amazing!" she says.

"So do you!"

It's been three months since we've hung out in person, and obviously we're only capable of punctuating our sentences with exclamation points.

"Here, let me get you a glass of wine," Bridget says, turning to the cabinet and pulling out another glass as if she's been here a million times before.

"I can't believe you're here." I shake my head. "How was your meeting?"

"It was fine. They liked our presentation, and I'm sure we got the job." Bridget pours me a glass.

I sit on one of the barstools and kick off my shoes while she hands me my glass, and I raise it up.

"Here's to your visit!"

"Here's to an awesome weekend!" Bridget clinks my glass. We move over to the couch so we can catch up more comfortably.

I had planned on taking Bridget to a nearby wine bar that's known for its tapas-style small plates. But in the midst of talking about work, Jason, and Evan, we end up sitting on my couch the whole night catching up, laughing, and being transported back to my living room in Chicago. We polish off the olives, crackers, and cheese that I bought yesterday, and I promise her a proper meal in the morning.

"Oh, I don't care. I'm just excited to see you." She reaches over and gives my arm an affectionate squeeze. When our eyelids start drooping, we reluctantly decide it's time for bed. I let her take my bed while I sleep on the sofa. Knowing my best friend is in the other room, I sleep better than I have in ages.

* * *

In the morning, as promised, I take Bridget to brunch in my neighborhood and then on an urban hike down to the Marina

Green and through the Presidio to show her the water and the Golden Gate Bridge.

Bridget is huffing and puffing, though. "This is great and all, but some of us aren't in as great shape as you are." She stops for the hundredth time and looks around hopefully. "So are there any cabs around here?"

"Not really. They don't tend to come down this way." I look at Bridget's horrified face and take pity on her. I remember how hard I found the hills when I first moved here, but have now quite literally worked my way up them. Unfortunately, we're not near a good pickup point for an Uber either, so I say, "I'm sorry. I guess I underestimated how long a walk it is. We can head back now."

We spend the rest of the afternoon doing the exercise Bridget prefers—shopping. After looking at a couple of stores, we find a small wrought-iron table and two chairs that Bridget declares would look "adorable" on my small patio. I agree and hand over my credit card.

"Now what you need are some plants."

"But I have the garden."

"Yes, but wouldn't it be nice to have some cute little pots and flowers of your own?"

I guess it would, and off we head, browsing our way to the nursery. In one store, I buy a small picture frame and make a mental note to print out the photo of Bridget and me with the Golden Gate Bridge in the background that I took during our walk.

When we're exhausted from shopping, we stop at a café and order some coffees, a latte for Bridget and a small nonfat cappuccino for me.

"Ahh . . . a little pick-me-up before dinner," Bridget says after taking her first sip. "Are you nervous?"

With the excitement of Bridget being here this weekend, I had managed to mostly forget about dinner tonight and its cast of characters.

"Oh yeah," I groan, looking into my cup. "Maybe we should cancel?" Even though I know it's not an option, it's nice to pretend it's possible.

"Are you kidding?" Bridget's eyes are shining. "True, I know it's going to be pure torture for you. But *I* can't wait to finally meet these people."

Maybe it won't be *pure torture*. At least I'm now officially in a relationship, which should make seeing Brad a lot easier. Again, it's nice to pretend it's possible.

"What are we wearing?" she asks.

"I'm not sure yet."

"Don't worry. We'll make sure you look smokin' hot." Bridget winks at me, and I know I'm in good hands.

* * *

Evan texts, offering to drive us to the restaurant. "That's thoughtful," Bridget says approvingly.

"He's a good one." I smile and text him back our thanks.

Bridget and I had originally planned to get there early and have a drink of liquid courage at the bar rather than walk into the minefield unprepared. But arriving with Evan is even better. Armed with my best friend and new boyfriend, I can face the night. Bridget does, however, recommend one glass of wine at home before the big event.

When Evan picks us up, he comments on how beautiful we both look and says how happy he is to meet Bridget. He is his super-friendly, polite self, and I can't wait to hear Bridget's verdict later tonight. When we're getting out of the car, Evan leans over and whispers in my ear, "You look stunning," and I beam at him.

Bridget went through my closet, as only she can, and pulled out a green dress I haven't worn in years and paired it with some strappy heels, and then raided my jewelry box for a pair of sparkling chandelier earrings that, again, I wouldn't ever have thought would go with this dress. She twisted a couple of strands of my hair back and pinned them, leaving a few tendrils around my face but still showing off my earrings—or as she said, "Your beautiful cheekbones and neck," which she highlighted with some of her powder. "You really must buy this stuff," she said while lightly dusting it on my cheeks. What can I say? The woman is an artist. And if she wants to use me as her canvas, I won't complain.

But as soon as we step into the restaurant, my stomach is in knots. I scan the lobby and bar and see Mark and Elena sitting there. Mark is in a navy crewneck sweater with dark jeans, while Elena is in her boho-stylish glory with a colorful, flowy peasant blouse and statement earrings. They notice us as well and wave us over.

After a round of introductions and greetings, Mark says, "I'll let the hostess know we're all here."

"But"—*leave it to me*—"what about Brad?"

"Oh yeah. He can't make it. He has his daughter this weekend." And—unable to help himself—he continues, "I mean, geez. I don't know why Kathryn wants custody. She'll certainly take any opportunity to pawn the kid off on someone else for the weekend."

Elena puts a hand on his arm. "Mark, I don't think they're interested in your friend's marital issues."

Bridget gives me a look, and I make sure to look away so as not to betray anything. *Oh, Elena, if you only knew how wrong you are.*

"Right," Mark says. "Sorry. I can't help myself sometimes." Remembering his duties, he says, "I'll be back."

Bridget's eyes are sparkling and she's grinning—the drama has already started and she is ready for the evening.

The knot of stress in my stomach dissolves, and I almost collapse into a puddle of relief in the middle of the bar. But then—in some sick, twisted way—I'm slightly disappointed because I look fantastic and have a super-nice boyfriend on my arm. But I shouldn't look a gift horse in the mouth. Plus, I remind myself, I should look fantastic for Evan, not Brad. I give myself a good mental chastising as the hostess leads us to our table.

When we're seated, Elena and Bridget are in conversation and sit next to each other, while I'm sandwiched between Evan and Mark. As Mark puts his napkin on his lap, while still looking down, he says, "You look nice tonight."

"Thanks, you too." I feel a slight flush, wondering if Mark's compliment is innocent, or if he guesses my ulterior motives. I avoid looking at him by quickly opening my menu and feigning rapt attention to the selections.

The restaurant is a popular Asian fusion place that's known for its killer cocktails. Since I feel like I'm still recovering from last night's wine, I nurse mine slowly and indulge in conversation instead.

I appreciate that everyone includes Bridget. Even though Bridget can make conversation with a brick in a wall, it's still nice to see my new friends making the effort.

"So when is the wedding?" Bridget asks Elena.

"Oh, we haven't gotten that far yet." Elena laughs and waves her hand dismissively.

"Oh! Did you just get engaged?"

"We've been engaged for a little over a year," Mark answers, looking intently at Elena.

Elena cuts in, "We agreed on a long engagement. Right now, with work and our families living in different places, I don't have time to plan a big wedding."

"I offered to do a smaller one or a destination wedding, but Elena wants to do the big affair and do it right." He picks up his cocktail and takes a long drink.

"That's nice," Bridget says, which I know is her code for *I don't believe you, but I'll let it drop.*

The rest of the evening Bridget keeps giving me knowing looks. I wish she would stop because I'm finding it distracting; *plus* it's driving me crazy wondering what she's thinking and that I won't find out until we get back to my place tonight.

CHAPTER TWENTY-ONE

s soon as we're through my front door and Evan has driven off, Bridget launches into her opinions.

"Well, *that* was an interesting evening," she says, throwing her purse on the counter and turning around to look at me.

"Really?" I thought it was a fun time, but not really all that interesting. Once the Brad equation was taken out, I thought the explosion potential was gone.

I shake off my jacket and hang it up by the front door. "What was so interesting about it?"

"Mark and Elena, for one thing."

"Be careful," I warn. "Mark is technically my boss, and these are my friends. So don't say anything bad that I won't be able to unhear. Besides, I thought everyone was really nice."

"They were all great. I'm just talking about the group dynamics at the table."

"Okay. But before we talk about Mark and Elena, I want to know what you think about Evan." I plop down on the couch, sit back, cross my legs, and await Bridget's verdict.

She sits opposite me in the armchair and says, "More importantly, what do *you* think of Evan?"

"I think he's perfect. Good job, smart, funny, a gentleman. Honestly? I haven't been able to identify a single flaw yet."

"I can hear the passion in your voice," she says flatly.

I throw one of my sofa pillows at her. "Oh, come on. He's great, right? He's cute. He has a nice body . . ."

"Those are all accurate statistics."

I sigh. "Did you come all this way to mock my life?" Although I would like her approval, because what girl doesn't want her friends to like her boyfriend? "He's great. So unless he admitted some deep, dark secret life to you that I'm unaware of, I don't know what you can say about him that's bad."

"So you like him," she says, eyeing me closely.

"Yes."

"Well then, that's all that matters."

Okay. I was hoping she'd gush about him, but clearly she has something else on her mind she wants to talk about.

"*Fine.* Now you can talk about Mark and Elena. But be nice."

"Okay, okay," she says, throwing her hands up, as if to ward me off. "I liked them too. But if I'm allowed to say so, that Elena is a piece of work."

"What do you mean?"

"What I mean is—they are so *not* getting married."

"*What?* Yes, they are."

Bridget cocks her head at me. "They've been engaged over a year and still haven't set a wedding date."

"True," I say, feeling slightly disloyal dissecting my new friend's relationship with my oldest friend. "But she said she wants to do a big wedding, and they haven't had time to plan it."

"Yeah, she hasn't had time to plan it because she *doesn't want it to happen*."

My mind whirs. Bridget has always been the more astute when it comes to discerning others' motives, but I still feel like I need to be on Team Elena here. Plus, it's hard to imagine someone dragging their feet to marry Mark. "Maybe they're just not in a hurry. Maybe they don't want kids? Not everything has to be on a traditional timeline."

She leans forward in her chair. "I don't want to say anything bad . . ."

I put my hand up in the universal sign for *stop*. "Then don't. I kinda don't want to know, if that's okay."

Bridget looks at me thoughtfully. "Okay," she surrenders. She changes her focus and says, "Mark is great."

"Yeah, I agree."

"He obviously thinks you're great too."

"You think? 'Cause I hope so. We've been working together a lot, and I'm a little worried because we're working on a new project where I'm not as familiar on stuff. That's where Brad is coming in." I raise my eyes heavenward and sigh. "So I've been trying to bring myself up to speed on a lot of issues before the project really gets underway."

"Yes, I think Mark really values your work. But I also meant that he *in general* thinks you're great." She grins.

I narrow my eyes at her, wondering where she's going with this. "Yeah," I say carefully. "He's been really good about making me feel at home here. And, also, since I'm up for partner soon, I need him in my corner." I give her a pointed look.

Bridget does a little shrug, and then swipes her thumb and forefinger across her lips as if she's zipping them.

"So you had fun tonight?" I ask.

"Definitely." She nods slowly. "It was very interesting."

Somehow I don't like that she keeps saying that.

* * *

Sunday night I borrow Evan's car to take Bridget to the airport. As I'm dropping her off at the terminal, I say, "Are you sure you can't just stay?"

"Aww . . . I wish I could. But work Monday morning."

"Fine. Then is there room in that suitcase for me?"

Bridget looks at her carry-on. "Afraid not."

"Okay. In that case, I'll try to get down to Chicago for a night when I'm home for Thanksgiving."

"You'd better."

We give each other one last hug, and she is off through the sliding glass doors, disappearing into the airport.

When I return the car to Evan, he gives me a ride home. Even though he asks to stay the night, I explain that I need to clean up after Bridget's visit and that I have a big day tomorrow I need to prepare for. He seems to understand—more points in his favor—and we agree to hang out another night. Having Bridget here stopped me from worrying about Brad, but tonight I want to be alone.

Once in bed, I mentally prep myself for tomorrow morning. Worrying about Brad's arrival for the last couple of weeks or so has actually taken some of the bite out of it. I've resigned myself to the fact that I will see him daily and am just going to have to be a professional about it all.

* * *

Rather than dragging my feet to face what is only going to be an unpleasant day, I get into the office before nine. Mark emailed me last night and arranged for us to take Brad out to lunch at noon. Remembering my first day, I'm sure Brad's will be filled with administrative logistics, so other than lunch, I hopefully won't run into him much.

Since it's a slow morning, I check the email account that I set up for the dating site. Even though I'm dating Evan now, I haven't gotten around to canceling my account yet. There are some new messages in my inbox. I should probably figure out how to block my profile to take myself off the market. I log in and out of curiosity check out some of the guys who emailed me. Just looking, not buying. Curious how they found me, I change my search to "man seeking woman" to see how my profile stacks up against the competition. What can I say? It's a slow morning, and I need a diversion. *Hmm . . .* Clicking through the women's photos, they're much better-looking prospects than their male counterparts. I choose from my age group and scroll through the profiles. Suddenly, one profile jumps out, causing me to knock over my coffee—because there on my computer screen is a photo of Elena.

Obviously this must be old, from before she met Mark. Or, then again, as the screen displays for me, "active within 24 hours." I'm sorely tempted to respond and investigate, but she doesn't know I'm on this thing. And besides, I'm dating her friend, so it's probably not a good look that I'm active too. I *could* casually email her, *Ha ha! See you're checking out your old profile too!* But I also think about what Bridget said about Elena and Mark's engagement. *Ugh.* I hate when someone plants a seed like that. Anyway, before I can do any due diligence, I have to get my wits about me. What would I say to her?

"Knock, knock."

I'm startled out of my thoughts by Mark and Brad standing in my doorway. Brad in the flesh is always a shock to the system. His hair looks like it's just been trimmed, his strong jawline freshly shaved, and he's wearing a dark gray suit that's perfectly tailored. I swallow nervously.

"Sorry." Mark laughs. "Didn't mean to scare you." He turns to Brad. "This happens a lot actually. Adeline is pure focus."

"I'm sure she is," Brad says and smiles warmly.

I need to say hello. I need to stand up and shake his hand. But my computer monitor is angled kitty-corner to the doorway, and if they take one step closer into my office, they will get a full-on view of Elena's dating profile maximized on my screen.

"Oh, hi! Sorry. Let me just finish something here." I discreetly click the tab to exit the website, but nothing happens. I do it again. *Oh god. Why is my computer frozen?* I then look at the coffee that spilled on my desk. *Did it get on the mouse?*

"Looks like you had an accident in here," Mark says.

"Um . . ." I tear my eyes away from the screen and try to hide the panic in my voice. "Um, yes, I knocked over my coffee." *Way to state the obvious, Addie.*

Sigh. This is *sooo* not how I wanted my first Brad encounter to go today.

"Do you need some paper towels?" Mark seems to be laughing at me.

"Yes. In fact, I was just on my way to the kitchen." I force myself to stand up. "Welcome," I say to Brad. "Hope you are off to a good start?"

Brad looks at me, his hazel eyes focused on mine, assessing my obvious discomfort. "I am. Thank you. It's a nice setup here."

Normally I would shake his hand, but I don't want them coming any closer to my desk. Nor do I want to leave my computer monitor.

"Not to be rude, but I should really take care of this." I gesture to the mess. "I'll see you at lunch?"

"Yes," says Mark. "Noon at One Market."

Brad gives me a small wave and says, "I look forward to talking more with you at lunch."

I nod.

So, that was awkward as hell, but right now not of much importance because I need to get this website off my screen. No way am I leaving it unattended to go to the kitchen. I take a bunch of tissues and wipe off my desk and keyboard, taking care with the mouse. Finally, miracle of miracles, I'm able to sign off of the site.

Phew! I sit back in my chair. So much for my new dress, my new shoes, my being prepared for the day. I had planned to be calm, cool, and collected; instead, I was a flustered mess. Granted, for reasons that actually had nothing to do with Brad, but still.

Strike one. Hopefully I can recover during lunch.

* * *

During lunch, I find that I'm more nervous about meeting Mark's gaze than Brad's. It could be nothing. But really, he and Elena *have* been engaged for a year now. They've been together over two years. I let Mark direct most of the conversation, much of which stays on neutral territory. "How do you like San Francisco so far?" Or work. "Why don't we meet at ten o'clock tomorrow to discuss Moonstruck?"

Until Mark comments to Brad, "Such a small world running into you at the conference, and with Adeline of all people." Mark looks at me and puts on his most charming smile.

Before I can say anything, I accidentally inhale a walnut that I'm chewing from my salad. After a nervous second of wondering if anyone is going to have to perform the Heimlich maneuver on me, I'm saved from responding.

"Yes, well, Addie and I go way back," Brad says.

"Addie?" Mark raises an eyebrow at me.

"Most of my family and friends back home still call me that," I explain.

"I like it," Mark says. "Do you prefer it to Adeline?"

"I never really thought about it before," I say. "I guess I went with Adeline when I started working to sound more professional."

I try to keep the edge out of my voice as I bristle inwardly. Granted, Brad has known me as Addie far longer than as Adeline, but still it denotes a certain intimacy that I'm not sure I like. It's a small matter, but enough that it puts my defenses on alert.

"My full name is Markus, but I'd feel a bit grandiose if people called me that. Like, who's that guy?"

"It would be better than Markie, I suspect." I grin at him.

"True. Just don't say that to my mother." He smiles back and then asks, "So how long have you guys known each other?"

Brad looks at me, maybe wondering whether I want to field the question. But I am again too busy stuffing salad into my mouth.

"All through school, until my family moved when I was sixteen."

"I bet you have some good stories." Mark grins. He's as bad as Nora and Bridget sometimes.

"I don't know about that. Brad was a year ahead of me in school. You know how that is when you're a kid. You might as well live in different countries," I say, hoping to put an end to this line of conversation.

"But you stayed in touch, obviously. You were good enough friends to come to the conference together." Mark looks back and forth between us.

"Sure," Brad says. His eyes meet mine briefly in silent communication. "We kept in touch, especially when we were both in law school."

I nod slightly, complicit.

This is a flat-out lie, but it seems to shut Mark up for the time being. I can see in Mark's eyes that there's a question flickering there, but thankfully he doesn't ask. Or maybe it's because I jump in and say, "So you two know each other from law school? I think that you guys would have much better stories to tell at that age."

"Considering that we met in the law school library, that should give you a sense of how exciting our stories are." Mark does a fake yawn.

As they launch into reminiscences about their UCLA days, I catch my breath. The focus is off me, the banter and conversation are light again, and lunch isn't as bad as I thought it would be. I also learn that Mark is originally from Minnesota. I try my best to stay engaged, but every so often my mind goes back to Elena.

* * *

After lunch, Evan texts asking to come over tonight, but I defer him for another night. I have a secret too big that I'm worried about blurting out. It could be nothing, but because I don't know that for sure, it keeps growing bigger and bigger inside of me. The only person I can tell is Bridget, but I'm waiting until I get home to call her.

Deep in my thoughts, I jump when I hear a knock at my office door around four o'clock. I look up and see that it's Brad. "Oh, sorry. I didn't mean to disturb you," he says.

"Not at all. Come in," I say, gesturing to the chairs across from my desk as my stomach sinks. This is the new normal, so I need to get used to it. "How's it going?"

"Good." Brad takes a seat. "It's a much smaller office than my old one, which is sorta nice. I've pretty much finished my paperwork and don't have much to do until tomorrow morning."

"Mmm . . ." I nod, feeling a little tongue-tied.

"How are you doing?"

"Oh, fine. Not too crazy busy." I nervously straighten some papers on my desk. Brad's presence seems to fill the room, and there's no avoiding him. "But I guess things are going to heat up now that you're here."

Did I really just use that choice of words? I can feel my cheeks starting to burn. I'm about to try to recover, but Brad says smoothly, "Yeah, I'm feeling the pressure."

Are we talking in innuendos here? But he follows it up. "Scott wants me to work on the new building, and I'm sure it will all be straightforward. But you know, new job, new people, having to prove yourself all over again."

"I understand. But I don't think you have to worry about that here. Everyone knows you. The client loves you. You're here because everyone wants you here."

Really, Addie? Do you want him here?

Brad clears his throat. "I was hoping to talk to you about some things. Any chance you could grab a drink after work tonight?" He pauses. "That is, if you're not too busy."

Used to my rebuffs by now, he probably does just want to talk to make sure everything is cool with us, and it probably would be in my best interest to make sure the air is cleared.

But I just can't do it.

"Um, actually tonight isn't good. I have plans."

Brad nods, seeming to expect this answer. "With your boyfriend?" he asks.

What the . . . ?

Perhaps registering the look on my face, Brad says, "Sorry. Mark told me you're dating one of his friends."

Oh, Mark. The man has no filter. Though I suppose it's not a secret.

"Well, Mark is a busybody," I say, and I can't help but smile.

"Yeah, he's a talker. That's for sure." Brad smiles back at me.

The tension is broken. A little.

"Rain check?" I say.

"Sure." But I don't think he believes me. He gets up. "Okay, I'll let you get back to work."

Once he's out the door, I look at the time. One more hour and I can leave.

* * *

Pick up, pick up, pick up, I think as Bridget's phone rings. I haven't even been home a minute.

She answers, "Hey—"

I barely let her get out her greeting. "Are you busy? Is this a good time?"

"Yes, yes. I'm at home. What's going on?" She sounds concerned. "How was the big day?"

"Oh, it was fine. I'll get to that later."

Instead I tell her all about finding Elena's profile on the website.

"You know, I was on there too. So it could be nothing. But why would she have an account after two years?"

Bridget responds, "I'm not surprised."

"What do you mean?"

"Do you really want to know what I think? Or do you want me to be nice?"

"I really want to know what you think . . ." I groan. "But be nice about it."

"Okay. I don't know if you noticed, but during dinner the other night, she was totally checking out guys at the restaurant."

"I don't really remember. And anyway, checking people out isn't a crime."

"When you're sitting next to your fiancé? And did you see her face when I asked about the wedding? There was a split second of horror. I don't know why. From what I can tell, Mark is awesome. I'd be running to the nearest justice of the peace to lock that down."

"You think? Elena and I never really talk about Mark. And frankly, since I work with him, I don't really want to know about their love life."

"You seem to be taking a big interest in it now," she says pointedly.

"It's awkward. You know? I'm friends with Elena, and she set me up with Evan."

"Evan is Mark's friend, though. I don't think that has anything to do with Elena."

Not to make it all about me, but I felt like I was becoming part of a cozy little family out here. But so far most families I know, including my own, have some sort of dysfunction. Elena is my friend and I want to stay friends with her, but I can't stay friends with someone who is possibly cheating on another one of my friends. I don't want Mark to get hurt. I feel like I need to get to the bottom of it.

"So what would you do?" I ask Bridget.

"I wouldn't do anything. It's their thing to sort out. You don't want to get in the middle of that."

"Even if Elena is cheating?" My voice goes up at the end, unsure.

"What are you going to do? Ask her? She won't tell you the truth. And if she did, what are you going to do with it?"

"You're right. Maybe I should ask Evan his opinion?"

"*Nooo* . . ." Bridget's voice goes into warning mode. "Don't even go there."

I sigh. "I just feel uncomfortable with this."

"They're going to implode at some point, and you want to be far, far away when it happens."

Bridget's right. I know she's right.

"So, let's talk about something else. Like how was your first day with Brad?"

"It was fine. Actually, no. It was awkward as hell," I say, and go on to fill her in on the coffee-Mark-Brad-frozen-computer incident.

"Oh my god!" Bridget starts laughing, whether from horror or at the ridiculousness of it all, and I can't help but join her.

I tell her about lunch and Brad's lie to cover up our attending the conference together. Then I tell her about him coming into my office and my faux pas. She is still laughing, but reassures me, "I'm sure he didn't notice."

"So the reason he came in was because he wanted to go out for a drink tonight."

"And?"

"I'm sitting here talking to you, aren't I?"

"I can understand why you don't want to go, but it could help clear the air or something. He keeps asking, so maybe there's something he really wants to talk about. Maybe just do lunch?"

"Yeah, I know. But when I look at him, I can't stop seeing that night. And I'm sorry, but I'm still so attracted to him."

"So you're worried you'll jump him?" she says with amusement.

"Ha ha," I deadpan. "*No.* But I don't want to be sitting there wanting to jump him when I can't."

"'Cause you have a boyfriend?"

"And Brad has a wife."

"That he's divorcing."

"It's all so complicated now. I wish I could just rewind that night and leave it at dinner."

"Hmm . . . the sex was that good, huh?"

"Oh, shut up." And because I feel I've been dominating the conversation, I turn it to Bridget and her favorite topic these days: Jason.

As she's filling me in on the latest developments, I realize that although I like Evan, I can't gush about him the same way Bridget does about Jason. But it's different, and I like that it's drama-free. So far at least.

When I hang up with Bridget, my thoughts turn back to Elena. I know Bridget's advice is spot-on. If I get involved and tell Mark, he'll hate me. And maybe this is just a passing phase for Elena. Plus, I don't have any proof that she is actually dating anyone, only that her profile is on the site and that she's checked it recently. I, too, can relate to the curiosity as well as the ego boost from seeing how many people have checked out my profile. Maybe she was doing the same?

Even though Bridget advised me not to, I still consider just asking Elena about it. I could tell her that I dabbled in online dating before Evan and, how funny, I ran into her old profile.

Or I could do what my fingers seem to be doing right now—logging on to the website to find her profile. Active within the last hour! *What is going on?* I briefly consider creating a new profile and posing as a possible suitor, until I remember a little thing called ethics. I log out of the site and have a restless night.

CHAPTER TWENTY-TWO

When I wake up the next morning, the first thing I reach for is my laptop. I do not get up to go to the bathroom. I do not brush my teeth. I do not drink a glass of water. I do not pass go. I'm too curious to see if Elena has been on the site.

Nothing. This is a positive sign, and I breathe a sigh of relief. I will be able to look Mark in the eye during our morning meeting, which is good because I'm still working on meeting Brad's. I can't keep my eyes glued to the conference table the entire time.

I hit the gym before work, going to my favorite spinning class to get an endorphin rush, which I'll need today. Our meeting isn't until ten, and I get into the office a little after nine. Just enough time to grab a cup of coffee and collect my thoughts.

When I reach the kitchen, I hear voices and realize I'm not the first one here. Standing by the coffee machine is Brad, dressed in business casual today, a white button-down shirt with the sleeves rolled up his forearms and pressed navy pants. Jasmine hovers nearby pouring hot water into a mug. Brad seems to be waiting for the coffee machine to brew, while Jasmine seems to be making pleasant small talk, something she's never bothered to do with me, and suddenly my adrenaline spikes as if I just caught them in flagrante rather than simply caffeinating at the office. I stay very still, trying to get my nerves under control before making my presence known.

"It will be nice to have another real estate partner around here." She smiles at Brad in a sickly sweet way, and my stomach turns. "What do you think so far?"

My law firm survival instincts kick in, and I want to warn Brad, *Danger, danger!* but remain quiet while he answers her seemingly innocuous question.

"It's only been twenty-four hours, but you know, I think it's a great place to build a practice."

"Oh," she says, lightly touching his arm. "Looks like your coffee is ready."

Oh my god, get your hands off him! I want to hurl myself at Jasmine. *He is not yours! He's mine!* Then I remember that he's not mine either. *But he's definitely not yours, Jasmine, so hands off,* I try to telepathically transmit to her. In my mind, her Snow White features morph into Cruella de Vil's.

I feel the hairs on my arm stand on end, while Brad turns his attention to the machine. "So it is. Thank you."

I loudly clear my throat to make my presence known and notice a look of contempt pass over Cruella's face. She does not say anything right away—apparently, I'm not even worthy of a hello.

Brad, however, turns around and says, "Oh, hi, Addie. Ready for the meeting?"

I really wish he wouldn't use my nickname at work. Jasmine appears to be sizing up the situation—or just sizing me up.

"I will be once I have some coffee in me," I say.

"Here. Take mine. I just brewed it. Extra dark, if that's okay? I can make another cup."

"Oh, that's not necessary. I can wait."

"Are you sure?" Brad is holding his cup out to me.

"Um, okay. Thanks, extra dark is fine." He hands me the cup, and I take a sip. Let's face it, he could hand me anything and I'd probably take it.

I remember we're not alone. "Oh, I'm sorry, Jasmine. Are you also waiting for the coffee machine?" I say. *Because Brad gave me his cup and did not offer anything to you. Ha!*

"No, I only drink green tea. I was just getting some hot water and chatting with Brad." She turns her attention back to him. "So what will you be working on?"

I am ignored. But there's no way I'm leaving. I want to hear this conversation, so I walk over to the refrigerator for some milk.

"I'll be working with Addie and Mark on some real estate deals for Moonstruck."

Jasmine turns to me. "But you're not a real estate attorney." She crinkles her nose. "That's so strange that they would have you working on that."

This woman, who has barely spoken three words to me since I've been here, is *now* suddenly taking an interest in my qualifications? *Um, sorry.*

"Not really. They're my client, and I worked on the Moonstruck and Imogen deal. The whole reason I moved here was because their chief counsel requested that I work more closely with them." *That's right, Jasmine—I actually have clients that want me.* "What about you? What are you working on these days?" Knowing full well that the answer is nothing, I almost add, *Still slow?* but I don't have the same taste for bitchiness and office politics, I guess.

"I've got some balls in the air right now," she says coolly, dipping her tea bag carefully into her mug of hot water. She turns her attention back to Brad. "We should talk. Maybe we can get together for lunch?"

Brad, ever the innocent, says, "That sounds great. Today might not work. Depends on our meeting. But sure, let's talk later."

"Okay. It's nice seeing you again. Welcome to the firm."

And with that, Cruella (née Jasmine) walks out and says nothing to me.

I want to wave wildly, *Bye!!!* But I refrain.

"That was a warm welcome," I say sarcastically to Brad.

"Huh?" Brad doesn't pick up on my sarcasm.

I'm about to tell him how she's pretty much ignored me since day one and warn him about her. But then I remember that they're from the same firm, and so maybe he's already aware of her true colors. And if not, he'll pick up on them soon enough.

"Nothing." I shake my head. "I guess I'll see you in a few."

"Yup. See you soon," he says, his head slightly tilted, as if he's still confused by my "warm welcome" comment.

It's still hard to be alone in the same room with him, and it's going to be even harder conducting business together. I return to my office and close the door. I sit down in my chair, lean back, and close my eyes. "You can do this," I tell myself. The shock of seeing Brad every day will wear off, and I will no longer think he's a jerk. In fact, I really need to try not to think of him at all.

What I'm thinking about right now is Elena. Even though I promised myself I wouldn't check it during work, I can't help but log on to the dating site. After all, my door is closed.

I sign in and click over to Elena's profile. *Currently active!* *Oh, Elena. Why?*

But I don't have time to trouble over it, since I need to hustle to my meeting.

Sitting in the conference room with Mark and Brad, I can't look either of them in the eye. Instead, I focus on scribbling notes alternated with looking thoughtfully at some point above their heads while we discuss what we need to do to get started on this building project.

I don't have much to add, since it's really more of Mark and Brad's show, which gives me an excuse to decline their lunch invitation.

"I really want to get moving on this task list," I explain.

I know I should go to lunch with them, but I think my excuse is valid. To make it seem even more so, I head straight from the meeting to our paralegal's office to discuss pulling all the related real estate documents and creating a database for them. There are also some research questions that can be delegated to the younger associates. Though I'd like to work exclusively with Emma, I know Rachel is interested in real estate and that she's never going to get any *real* experience with Jasmine. And in the end, she did pull her weight on Project X. So I divide up the assignments between them and plan to talk to them after lunch. In the meantime, I have my own business to attend to if I want to get out at a reasonable hour.

* * *

After work, I rush home to get ready for Evan's arrival at seven. He texted during the day wanting to meet up tonight. I suggested his place, but he said he actually prefers mine, which turned into some teasing texts about whether he's afraid I'll find the bodies in his loft, since I still haven't been. But he's finishing up a renovation project and is waiting for the dust to literally settle before inviting me over for the big reveal.

When the doorbell rings and I open the door, there's Evan with a bag full of groceries in one hand and a bottle of wine in the other. I had offered to pick up dinner or at least a bottle of wine, but he had insisted both on making dinner and selecting the wine.

"This is so wrong. You've already made me dinner," I say as I take the wine from him to put it in the refrigerator to chill. "At least let me help this time."

Evan gives me a little kiss on the cheek and squeezes me with his free arm. "All right. You can be my sous-chef." He puts the grocery bag on the counter and hands me a bag of wild mushrooms.

"*Ooh.* What are these for?"

"I'm making a mushroom risotto and an arugula salad."

"Mmm . . . sounds delicious."

"You can be in charge of prepping the mushrooms."

"Okay. What would you like me to do?"

"Wash and slice them."

"Sure." I carry the mushrooms over to the sink, grab a strainer, and deposit them into it. I turn on the water and am about to place the strainer full of mushrooms under the faucet when Evan comes up behind me and shuts off the water.

"What are you doing?" Evan asks—dare I say, a bit dramatically.

"I'm going to wash the mushrooms."

"Nooo . . ." He shakes his head at me. "You don't wash mushrooms in water."

"You don't?"

"No. The proper way to clean mushrooms is to first brush the dirt off like this." He takes a paper towel and shows me. "Then, after you've brushed off the dirt, take a damp cloth and rub them like this." He dampens a new paper towel and demonstrates.

"Oh," I say. "I've always rinsed them under water."

"Mushrooms are very absorbent and soak up water, which makes them mushy and affects their taste."

"You learn something new every day." I watch him for a few more seconds and offer, "Here, I can take over."

"That's okay. I got it. Why don't you empty the rest of the groceries?"

I do as I'm told and line up the ingredients on the counter. I see some onions and garlic. I would offer to chop them, but I have a feeling that I may have been banned from vegetable duty. Plus, I carefully applied mascara tonight and am not fond of the raccoon-eye look. So instead I offer to pull out pots and anything else he needs.

Halfway through cooking, Evan asks me to stir the risotto. "When the rice absorbs all the liquid, add another half cup to it, and so on," Evan says as he stirs the broth into the rice. "And don't stop stirring."

"Got it." I take over the wooden spoon and stir while Evan prepares the salad and attends to the mushrooms sautéing in another pan.

We chat idly about our days. Evan talks about some technical issues they're having at work. Though I don't fully understand the details, I listen and ask questions. I sip wine and stir, enjoying the repetitive motion. Evan comes over to check on the warming mushrooms and looks into my pot.

"What happened?" He takes over the spoon and looks worried. "Have you been stirring? You're putting too much liquid in."

"I just added another half cup. It's fine. It hasn't absorbed yet."

As he continues to stir, his brow furrows. I have a feeling I'm about to be taken off risotto duty as well. I take another sip of wine. I've made risotto before and know it will be fine. But I can also see that Evan is pretty hard-core about his food—and a *little* bit of a control freak in the kitchen. Frankly, it's kind of a turnoff. But since he's so easygoing about everything else, I guess I can overlook this. We all have our "things."

The rice is absorbing the broth, as I knew it would, and he looks relieved.

"Are you sure you don't want me to take over again? I don't mind stirring," I say.

"Sure. Here you go." He cautiously hands me the spoon.

"You really take your cooking seriously," I say and give him a little hip check while I stir to let him know I'm teasing.

"Sorry. I just like things done the right way," he says sheepishly, perhaps realizing that he'd overreacted.

When it's time to eat, everything is so delicious that I decide maybe there's a method to Evan's madness in the kitchen. So I brush the incident out of my mind, focusing instead on the meal and my new boyfriend.

CHAPTER TWENTY-THREE

In the morning, Evan uses my bathroom first, since he needs to leave earlier than I do for work. It gives me a chance to check the dating website and Elena's profile as I sip my coffee at the kitchen table. *Active within 24 hours.* Sigh. I click off. I need to stop with this obsession, but I don't know how to ease my mind on this matter.

Evan interrupts my thoughts, coming up behind my chair and placing a kiss on top of my head. "Shower's all yours, babe." He has taken to calling me "babe." I've tried "sweetie," "honey," and "love" on him, but none sounds quite natural yet. But it's early days, and I'm sure the right one will come along.

"Thanks, sweetie." *No. Not "sweetie."* I will keep trying. I get up from the table to say goodbye.

"I probably won't see you tonight. I have a meeting late in the day," he says, slinging his backpack strap over his shoulder.

"That's okay." I wasn't expecting to see him tonight anyway.

"But we'll plan something fun for the weekend." He encircles my waist with his hands.

"Sure."

We kiss and Evan heads out the door, then I take over my bathroom and think about Elena's profile and wonder how many more secrets I can handle before my brain explodes.

* * *

"Oh, sorry!" I've literally bumped into Brad in the hallway as I'm returning from the copy room. It feels like the hundredth time that I've run into him today.

"No worries."

We do an awkward dance of trying to let the other person go by, but each time we do, we end up moving to the same side. Finally, Brad steps aside and makes a gesture with his arm to let me pass. "Ladies first."

"Thank you." I scurry back to my office.

Since Brad's been here, I run into him all the time. In order for him to get to the kitchen, he has to pass my office. Which is apparently several times a day. And every time he walks by, he glances through my doorway. And every time, it's as if I have a sixth sense and I look up or see him from the corner of my eye. Sure, I could close my door, but our office has an open-door policy, and so I only rarely close it. But every time he passes by and our eyes make contact, I feel a stab of pain in my heart. By late that afternoon, I close my door halfway. Now if only I could close my heart halfway.

* * *

Since I'm miraculously finished with work at six thirty and I'm on my own tonight, I treat myself by exploring a new neighborhood and head over to North Beach, hoping to find a café where I can have a light meal and read. As I'm walking by a promising café, I stop to peer in the window. Seated alone at a table for two is Elena. I try to wave, but she is looking at the front door and doesn't see me. I decide to pop in and say hello.

When I walk through the front door, I'm smiling, but my smile freezes when I see her eyes go wide in fright. Not exactly the reaction I expected, yet I continue my uncomfortable walk over to her table.

"Hey, fancy meeting you here," I say, trying to sound cheerful though feeling confused.

"Oh, hey, Adeline," she says, her voice oddly high-pitched. "What are you doing here?"

She doesn't stand up, and I'm awkwardly hovering over the table, unsure whether to pull out a chair. "I was just looking for a good place to read and maybe get something to eat. What are you doing?"

Elena's eyes flit back to the front door. "I, uh . . . I'm just getting some coffee."

She takes a large gulp from her cup. My heart starts to pound. "Is everything okay?" I ask, wishing I had just stayed outside.

"Yes, of course. Like I said, I'm just having coffee. I was supposed to meet an old colleague, but she didn't show."

Yeah, right, I think. Her response is a *tad* too defensive for being stood up by a work friend.

"Oh, sorry to hear that. Do you mind if I join you?" I say, feigning innocence.

She hesitates, as she shifts her gaze quickly to the front door again and then to me. "Actually, I'm supposed to meet Mark tonight for something, so I should probably head out. I don't want to be late." She stands up. "See you later."

"Oh, okay . . ." But before I can say goodbye, she's already fled.

Everything in my being right now tells me that Elena was meeting a date.

* * *

In the office the next morning, I can't help myself—and there staring at me from my computer screen is Elena "currently active" on the dating site. I sit back in my chair, sip my coffee, and ponder the screen. Though I want to believe her, between her activity on the site, her hasty exit last night, and Bridget's observations, the circumstantial evidence against her adds up: Elena is cheating on Mark. And because I'm upset for Mark, it also confirms where my loyalty lies.

I shake my head and log off. There's nothing I can do about it, so I might as well buckle down to work. But right when I'm about to get started, there's a knock at my door, and I look up to see Brad in my doorway.

"Do you have a minute?" he asks.

"Of course. Come in." Hopefully this really will take only a minute because I still hate being in the same room with him.

"I need to review all the agreements that were signed in the Imogen acquisition. Is that something you can get for me?"

"Yes," I respond, thankful that his question is work related. "John, our paralegal, put together a database of all the final documents related to the acquisition. I can have him pull those for you."

"Okay. Or I guess I can ask him?"

"It's okay. I got it. Is there anything else I can do?"

"Just that." But Brad lingers a bit. "Also, I was wondering if you're free for lunch today?"

Oh god. I'm not ready. I'm just not ready to sit one-on-one casually eating a salad across from Brad. I can't think of anything more uncomfortable. I know I should do it, but I also hope Brad understands why I can't.

"I wish I could, but I have to run some errands this afternoon. Can we do it another time?"

"What about tomorrow?"

Damn it. Can't you give a girl some breathing space?

"Um, I'm not sure about tomorrow. Can I get back to you?"

Unexpectedly, Brad gives me an exasperated look. "Fine. I'm not going to beg you to have lunch with me." The words come out sounding defensive.

"I'm . . . I'm sorry, I just . . ." I let the words trail. "It's just a weird week," I say, hoping he can infer my meaning.

"Yeah. Okay," he says brusquely.

Then he's gone. If things were awkward before, I have a feeling it's going to get worse if I keep refusing his overtures. But it would be humiliating now to say that I don't really have to run any errands. So I guess we'll be going to lunch tomorrow. At least I have twenty-four hours to prepare for it.

When I'm ready to head out for lunch, surprise, surprise, I bump into Brad at the elevator.

"Running your errands now?" he asks with a slight eyebrow raise.

My face flushes, but I try to cover myself. "Yes, I have to go to the mall. Hopefully it's not too busy."

He nods, but I can't tell whether he believes me. The elevator doors open, and I step in. Brad stays behind.

"Aren't you coming?" I say.

"No, I'm waiting for Jae. She had to run back to her office for something."

"Oh?" *Jae?*

Oh! Jasmine! But it's too late to ask further questions. The doors close. I try to calm down and tell myself that I'm overreacting. But I saw the way she touched his arm and flirted with him that morning in the kitchen. Didn't they already go to lunch this week? I try to decipher whether I'm feeling jealous, worried for Brad's sake, or worried for my own if she wheedles her way into working with Brad.

That afternoon I get a call from Nora, who wants to talk about some work I've done that's similar to something she's working on. After we talk business, she asks, "So how are things going over there?"

"Things are fine."

"How's the new guy working out?"

"He just started on Monday, but it seems to be going well." I know Nora is going to try to dig further, and since I'm bursting with anxiety on various levels, I decide to uncork the pressure valve some. "There is one weird thing."

"What's that?" I can tell by her voice that she's all ears.

"Jasmine's been trying to cozy up to him."

I give her the details about seeing them in the kitchen, how friendly she was, and them having lunch together.

"You need to break that up," she says, validating my fears. Although, little does she know, not all of them. "Remember what I told you? She's hungry for clients and is going to try to get onto your project. And, while I don't know all the details, according to my Levenfield friends, she's not to be trusted. I would keep her away."

"I know." Even without Nora's warning, the thought of working with Jasmine forms a leaden ball of dread in my stomach. "If Brad didn't work with her at Levenfield, then I would think Mark would've given him the lowdown on her already."

"If not, then you need to get buddy-buddy with him before she does." *Oh, if she only knew.* "Aren't you guys friends from college or something like that?"

"We grew up down the street from each other."

"There you go. He's the new guy, so what you need to do is become the hospitality committee, yourself. *You* need to take him out to lunch, introduce him around, keep him too busy for her to be in the picture."

When did life get so complicated? Why can't things just be black and white and simply self-evident? Lately I feel as if I've been swimming in murky waters. And now, according to Nora, I'm going to have to start swimming with the sharks.

Though I faulted Jasmine for not being friendly to me when I first arrived, I haven't exactly extended an olive branch to Brad since he's been here. If he were anyone else, I would have gone out for drinks by now. I would have taken him to lunch. I would have stopped by his office to ask how things were going. Frankly, I wasn't being very professional, because the fifteen-year-old girl in me got hurt. I have to stop thinking about drinks with Brad as *drinks with Brad*.

Fueled with new determination after Nora's call, I walk over to Brad's office. Luckily, he is there and alone. From the doorway, I open with, "Did you get those documents yet?"

"Yes, John gave them to me. Thank you."

"Oh, good." I enter his office, and he gives me a curious look. "So, um, I was wondering if you were busy tonight?" Good lord, it sounds like I'm about to ask him on a date.

"Why?" he says.

"Well, I wanted to see if you could grab a quick drink after work. Sorry I've been really busy lately. But I'm free tonight." I shrug, hoping to look apologetic.

His face doesn't give away any emotion. "Sure. I can do tonight."

"Okay. Great." My palms are sweating, and I resist the urge to wipe them on my skirt. "What time can you leave?"

"It's the first week." He smiles. "I think I can leave by five or so."

"Okay. I'll give you a call at five, and we'll see where we are."

"That sounds good," Brad says carefully, still smiling, as if he's trying not to scare me away.

"Okay, then." I turn toward the door. "I should get back to work."

And I'm out of there in a flash.

When I'm back in the safety of my office, my pulse is racing. But before I have a chance to calm down, Mark appears at my door with a wide grin. My guilty conscience makes my heart beat even faster, if possible.

"Hey, Adeline. What's up?"

If he only knew. "Nothing much. Just delving into Emma's research. What can I do for you?"

"Nothing. I just came by to say hi."

"Oh." I'm feeling awkward. "Did Elena tell you I said hi last night?"

Mark looks at me weirdly. "No," he says, and cocks his head to the side. "Did you go out with Elena last night?"

"Um, no. We ran into each other at a coffee place. She said she was on her way to see you." *Stop now. Why am I saying this? Am I trying to put Mark on alert?*

"Huh," he says. "She didn't come home till late last night."

"Oh." I let out a nervous laugh. "Well, maybe she didn't feel like hanging out with me and used you as a convenient excuse."

He shakes his head. "Nope. She was working late."

"Oh? Maybe I was confused, then. I asked her if she wanted to join me for coffee, but she said she was on her way out. I guess I just assumed she was meeting you or something." *Now I'm covering for her?* "Anyway, what's new with you?" I change the topic.

He enters my office and closes the door. If he thinks there's anything weird about my explanation, he keeps it to himself as he sits down across from me.

"Actually, there is something I wanted to talk to you about." My stomach drops as he continues, "Jasmine approached me about working on the Moonstruck project."

Oh thank god. He wants to talk about Jasmine, *not* Elena. Though Jasmine isn't exactly a pleasant topic, at least I'm prepared for it after my call with Nora.

"Okay," I say, waiting for him to continue.

"Between you and me, I wasn't a fan of her joining this office. She had just made partner in corporate at Levenfield, yet she quit to join the real estate department here. She didn't bring any new business with her, and then had a falling-out with the attorney who hired her here. The whole thing just felt off." He gives me a knowing look. I nod in understanding (or think I understand). "But she's a real estate attorney, so it would make sense for her to join us if we needed help."

"*Do* we need help?" I venture.

"You and I know their business goals and have a good relationship with Scott. Brad is in the same position and is an experienced real estate attorney. With our knowledge and relationship with the client and Brad's expertise, there's no reason we should need her help." He looks at me meaningfully, and continues, "But she needs work and might convince the higher-ups she should join our team. So we need to make sure we're on top of everything."

I nod again. "Got it. I've been doing a lot of research in my downtime, so I don't think there's anything to worry about. I'll make sure of it."

"Thanks, Adeline." Then he grins. "Or do you go by Addie now?"

I shake my head in mock surrender. "Whatever you prefer, I guess."

Mark looks at me with a smile that says, *I know everything.* Or maybe it's just my paranoia interpreting it as such. I look down at my desk and fiddle around with a pen. "Is that all?"

"Are you dismissing me?" he jokes.

"I guess so. My boss just told me I need to buckle down." I grin at him.

"Ha ha! I see." He gets up from the chair. "In that case, I guess I'll see you later, *Ad-die.*"

When I hear his footsteps fade out in the hallway, I get up and close the door. Brad, Elena, Jasmine . . . My mind is swirling. But, as if I needed Mark to remind me, my top priority right now is work. I need to keep Jasmine off this project, and therefore, I need to make sure I'm giving it all my attention. That means treating Brad like a professional colleague and crossing this Elena quandary off my list. I promptly cancel my online dating profile minutes after Mark leaves my office. Managing my own romantic relationships is stressful enough; I can't worry about his as well.

CHAPTER TWENTY-FOUR

*A*s the clock ticks closer to five, my focus starts to wane. Around a quarter to, I head to the washroom to touch up my makeup and tame a few stray hairs that have broken loose from my low ponytail. It's as if they want to escape as badly as I do right now. But I take a deep breath, telling myself in the mirror that this is for my career. Perhaps I can drill Brad on what more I can be doing on the Moonstruck project?

Back in my office, I sit and wait for "the call." Then I remember that I'm supposed to call him. I let it go until 5:01 p.m. before picking up my phone. Brad answers right away.

"Hi, Addie."

"Um, hi. So I'm just checking if you're still free for drinks tonight."

"Of course." I hear him moving things around on his desk. "Let me just clean up here, and I'll swing by your office in a few minutes. Okay?"

"Sounds good." I mean anything but. When we hang up, I shut down my computer and try to steady my nerves by making a list of things to work on tomorrow morning, but I'm really just killing time. I check myself in my compact again and then quickly stash it back in my purse. I don't want Brad to think I'm primping for him, because I'm not. Although a voice in my head tells me I'm a liar. *Shut up,* I think. Maybe Bridget is right— maybe it is time for that shrink.

I don't have much time to linger on that thought because Brad is at my door, somehow looking more handsome than ever in a dark wool overcoat.

"Ready to go?" he asks.

"Sure." I grab my purse and jacket a little too hastily, losing my balance on my swivel chair in the process. I try to recover. "Wow, I haven't even had a drink yet and I'm already tipsy." I laugh. Old nervous Addie rearing her ugly head.

Brad politely chuckles, but it only makes me feel more awkward. "Where should we go?" he asks.

"There's a wine bar a few blocks away off Market. They serve beer too," I add lamely. "Or if you prefer something stronger, there are tons of cocktail places nearby."

"The wine bar sounds great."

We leave my office and walk to the elevator. Brad pushes the button. He taps his foot and keeps his eyes on the lights that indicate which floor the elevator is on. I wonder if he's as nervous as I am. Luckily, the elevator arrives swiftly. And because it's full with people from higher floors, mercifully we are not forced into conversation.

Once outside, I lead the way. Other than commenting on San Francisco's mercurial weather and noting how much cooler it is outside now than it was this afternoon, we don't say much.

When we reach the bar, Brad holds the door open for me, and we make our way downstairs into the lounge area. This is the same place I met Elena and later Adrian. So I'm starting to think of it as *my* bar, and I know exactly where to sit depending on what level of intimacy we want: for the least, the bar; for the most, the sofas; and for something in the middle, the tables.

"Shall we grab one of the tables?" I suggest, already heading that way.

"What about one of the couches? Those look comfortable." He points toward a low couch with a small table in front of it.

Drat. "Um, sure."

He waits until I'm seated and then sits down next to me. While I am perched on the very tip of the sofa looking at the menu on the table, Brad has relaxed into it with his back against the seat, his legs spread, hands on his knees, and head back.

"This feels incredible." He lets out a pleasurable sigh.

Not sure how to respond, I say, "Would you like to see the drinks list?"

"Sure."

I expect him to sit up, but he continues leaning back. I cautiously hand him the menu.

A server soon appears, and Brad finally leans forward. I order a glass of chardonnay, while Brad orders a local brew on tap. As soon as the server leaves, Brad reclines back into the sofa, while I remain teetering on the edge.

"So how are things going?" I ask.

Brad closes his eyes for a second and then sits up and shrugs. "Things are what they are right now. Kathryn is being a pain in the ass, but I didn't expect otherwise."

"Um, no. Sorry. I meant with work and the move?"

"Oh! Sorry. I guess when people ask me how things are, I assume they mean the divorce."

But I don't mean the divorce, no matter how curious I am. This is hard enough as it is, and I'm determined to stay on neutral ground. The less we can talk about relationships, the better.

Thankfully, our server interrupts with our drinks, and I'm glad for the pause to remind myself why I'm here—be professionally cordial with Brad and keep Jasmine away from him and Moonstruck.

When she leaves, I hold up my wine glass to Brad's beer and say, "Well, welcome to San Francisco."

"Thanks. Here's to a less complicated life." Brad touches his glass to mine.

We each take a sip of our respective drinks, and then Brad relaxes back again into the sofa. "You'll have to excuse me, but I'm loving this couch right now."

Honestly? Are we ever going to talk about work tonight? And knowing our history, is he trying to get me to relax back with him?

From my perched position, I ask, "What's so great about it?"

"It's comfortable."

"Aren't most?"

"Not the one I have at home."

"Well, why don't you buy a new one?"

He laughs. "I did. In fact, I bought all new everything. Since I didn't have much time off of work, I just ordered a bunch of furniture online."

I laugh, mostly at my own ridiculousness for thinking that he was suggesting I snuggle up next to him. When did I get such a big head?

"Oh no! That's terrible," I say, still laughing.

"What's terrible is that couch. It must've taken extra effort to create something so uncomfortable. I don't know how they managed it."

"Well, now that you're settled, I guess you have time to do some sofa testing."

"I might just try to smuggle this one back home. Think they'd notice?" He gives me a conspiratorial look.

"Hey, don't count on me to aid and abet in this crime." I feel myself relaxing a little more and am no longer perched straight-backed over the table.

"Guess I'm on my own, then." He runs his hand propri-etarily over the cushion.

"Other than the sofa situation, how do you like your place?"

"It's fine. Considering I've been living out of suitcases for months, *thanks to Kathryn*, anything is an upgrade."

God, must everything go back to her? But he is a man going through a hard time. I watched my own father go through a divorce, so I know how it colors everything, but I'm still deter-mined to keep the conversation away from Brad's romantic issues.

"What's it like?"

"It's nice. It's in one of those old apartment buildings in Pacific Heights. I looked at some newer places and the Financial District, but I don't think Ivy would like it there as much. This way she can see the Golden Gate Bridge and the water."

Okay. Even though I didn't want to discuss our personal lives, his eyes light up when he mentions his daughter, and it's obvious that he would find any excuse to talk about her.

"How does she like it?"

"She likes it a lot. I let her pick out all her furniture and stuff for her bedroom and bathroom. Pink as far as the eye can see." He makes an expansive sweep gesture with his arm.

I laugh. "Is she moving out here too?"

"That hasn't been worked out yet. I would love for her to be with me full time, and hopefully, that will be the case. But for now, her grandparents are nearby in Los Angeles, and Ivy adores them. So even if we split custody, I tell myself that it wouldn't be the worst thing if she had to live mainly in LA." Brad pauses. "Although, I'd miss her." He looks into his beer. "A lot."

Okay, that was a fail. So much for trying to find a pleasant personal topic to talk about. I guess it's time to get back to the reason we're here.

"So, you wanted to talk to me about work?" I say.

"What?" Brad looks at me.

"You've been wanting to meet for drinks or dinner because you wanted to talk about work stuff," I press.

"Um, yeah." He looks back down at his beer.

"So, what would you like to talk about?"

Brad rubs his thumb on his glass again, still looking at it. "I guess I was concerned about taking the job because I thought it would be weird for us to work together."

"I told you it wouldn't be weird."

He gives me a skeptical look. "Are you sure about that? Because it sure feels weird."

I give a small laugh and come clean. "Okay, yeah. Truthfully? It's weird. But it is what it is, you know." The wine seems to give me some liquid courage. "I mean, it would be weirder if you were some guy I dated and we broke up. But it was one night and one mistake. And despite that mistake, we still seem to like and respect each other, so I think it will be okay."

"I'm sorry, Addie." He winces.

I hold up my hand to stop him and shake my head. "I don't want to talk about it."

Brad nods. "I do like and respect you, so I think it will be okay too. And more importantly, Scott likes us," Brad points out.

"Yes. So even if we couldn't stand each other, I think we'd fake it enough to keep our jobs."

"I see. So are you faking it, then?" Before I can answer this loaded question, he follows it with, "'Cause if so, you need to do a better job."

I playfully roll my eyes at him. "Oh, shut up and finish your drink."

Brad's eyes dance with laughter. In this mood, we order another drink.

* * *

I wake up with a throbbing headache. My teeth and face feel gritty, and I'm still in last night's clothes. *Ugh.* I force myself up and head to the kitchen for a big glass of water or two. It's only seven, and I really, really want to call in sick today. But after Mark just told me yesterday to make sure I'm on top of my game, I don't think it would be appropriate. And even though it's the last thing I feel like doing right now, I decide to go for a run. Maybe some exercise will help.

After a few blocks of some pitiful jogging, I slow down to a brisk walk, letting the crisp, cool morning air wake me up. Once I have some oxygen flowing again to the brain, I review the events of last night.

I remember us ordering a second drink. Brad asked me how I liked things at Gilchrist, and we chatted briefly about Moonstruck. As I suspected, though, we spoke very little about work. We were able to laugh about the conference and how crazy it is how everything turned out with us all working together. Brad said something thoughtfully about how maybe it was all meant to be, and I said something along the lines of how karma is a bitch. But we also talked some about our school days and memories from when we were young. After the third drink, I remember I moved from tipsy to drunk. I don't remember any food ever being involved, which explains my current condition. I remember Brad also talking wistfully about what would have happened if his family never moved from Wisconsin. Would things in his life be different? He started to get a little morose.

At some point I finally leaned back on the couch and relaxed. I think I leaned against him. And now I remember our hands. Brad holding my hand as we sat side by side. And—*oh god*—I remember him trying to kiss me. Did we? I think I said something about having a boyfriend. I think he asked if it was serious, but I'm not sure how I responded. I most definitely do not think we kissed. I conclude that our biggest transgression was some hand-holding.

But still. I turn the tables. How would I feel if Evan went out with an old girlfriend, or any woman, and spent the evening drinking and holding her hand? I would be jealous and hurt. Well, maybe not jealous, since we haven't been dating that long, but my feelings would definitely be hurt. *What's wrong with me?* I swear, lately I just don't know who I am or what I'm doing anymore. I'm tempted to call Bridget, as she is probably just getting into work now in Chicago. But between Elena, Brad, and work, this might be too much for her to listen to this morning. I'll wait until the weekend to call her.

Instead, I take out my phone and call my true lifeline.

"Hi, Addie!" my dad says, picking up on the first ring. "This is a bit early for you."

"Hi, Dad. Yes, well, I'm just taking a walk before work and thought I'd call. How are you?"

"Good. Have some estate matters to work on today, but otherwise nothing new," he says cheerfully.

"You sound in a good mood."

"Yes, well, things are good. How are you?" But before I can answer, he interrupts himself. "Hey now, you're still coming for Thanksgiving, right?"

"Yes, Dad."

"Because it's next week, you know."

I laugh inwardly. "Yes, I know. I'm flying out after work on Wednesday and flying back on Sunday. I sent you my flight details, remember?"

"Yes. I have them somewhere."

"What time are we going to the club on Thursday?"

My dad clears his throat. "Actually, we're going to eat at home."

Oh? This is strange. We always eat at my dad's golf club where they have a huge Thanksgiving buffet. It is always crowded with families and kids running around, and we don't have to worry about cooking or leftovers—or the fact that it's just the two of us. My dad is an only child, and my mother's family stopped inviting us over, or really contacting us, after my mother left. I assume they had to take my mother's side, whatever that was. Plus, it was probably too uncomfortable and embarrassing any-way for my father to spend the holidays with his ex-wife's family.

"At home? Um, okay . . . but you know I've never made Thanksgiving dinner before, right? I suppose I could try, though."

"Oh no, honey!" My dad is laughing. "I'm not asking you to cook."

"*You're* cooking?" My dad can barely heat up a can of soup. He has many great qualities, but being a chef is not one of them.

"No." My dad coughs and then says formally, "Mrs. Collins offered to come over and make dinner. Since her kids are out of state and are both doing Thanksgiving with their in-laws this year, she's on her own."

"Oh, okay. Why don't we take her to the club with us?"

"I offered, but she says Thanksgiving is something you should have at home. And besides, she loves cooking."

"I see." I'm still a bit dubious. It sounds like he's taking advantage of our neighbor. She is a very sweet woman, and I feel bad that she lost her husband five or six years ago. "In that case, please thank her for me and tell her that I'm happy to help out in the kitchen in any way."

"I will." My dad sounds unusually gleeful, and I assume it must be because he's excited for my visit.

"Thanks. Well, I'm starting to near home now and need to get ready for work."

"Okay, then. See you soon."

"Bye, Dad."

Once inside, I drink another glass of water and pour myself an oversized mug of coffee. I feel a little more awake, but not quite 100 percent. Or 90 percent. Maybe 75 percent. But even that is generous. Oh well. It's Friday. I can sleep in tomorrow. Oh, wait—*it's Friday!* I have dinner plans with Evan tonight. Another stab of pain hits my brain. I would love nothing more than to be able to come home from work tonight and curl up in front of the TV until I fall asleep. But it's too early in the relationship to break a date, so I'm going to have to power through. I wonder if I can hook up some sort of coffee IV to myself for the day? With that thought, I head to the shower and pray for a quiet day.

CHAPTER TWENTY-FIVE

I get to work around nine thirty. My wish for a quiet day looks like it might be granted.

I take care of a couple of administrative tasks, answer Emma's questions regarding zoning ordinances, and respond to some joking complaints from Nora on how she will never forgive me for leaving her alone with Roger. Then, before I dive into some research, I check my personal email. There's an email from Bridget saying we need to catch up this weekend. Check. And an email from Elena that reads:

> Subject: Call me
> Saw you last night at the bar. Call me
> right away!
> E

Well, holy hell. I prop my elbows onto my desk and rest my heavy head into the palms of my hands for support. I close my eyes. *Think, think, think.* I search my brain, but no images or blurry memories of bumping into Elena appear. The two cups of coffee I drank at home still haven't fired up my neurons. Perhaps more caffeine, though, maybe this time in the form of some tea, will help. As God is my witness, I swear I will never drink again.

On my way to the kitchen, I bump into Mark in the hallway. I force myself to smile and appear alert.

"Good morning," I say.

Marks nods at me stiffly in acknowledgment but walks on by. He looked like he has a lot on his mind. Was he with Elena last night? Did I drunkenly run into them and say something stupid? Were Brad and I in a compromising position? Speaking of which, where is Brad today? Did he make it in? Maybe I should email him? But back to Mark. Maybe his countenance had nothing to do with me. I'm just paranoid. We *are* at work. Perhaps he had important business to attend to. After all, that's what I'm supposed to be doing.

I finish making my tea, then hurry back to my office, close the door, and call Elena's cell. It goes to voicemail, and I leave a message. Guess I'm going to have to suffer a little longer. And because I need a little more information on what happened last night, I also email Brad:

Hey – Are you in today?

A few minutes later his response pops up:

No. Not feeling well and am working from home. Is there anything I can help with?

Um, yeah, like what happened last night, and did we run into Mark and Elena?

Since this is my work email, it's better not to say too much. I type back:

I'm sorry to hear that. Hope you feel better.

Not getting the answers I need, I try to turn my attention to work.

Finally, at eleven my phone buzzes.

"Elena! Thanks for calling me back." I get up and close my door, again. For an office with an open-door policy, mine seems to be closed a lot these days. "I got your email. What's going on?"

"Can you meet for lunch?" She sounds worried.

"Um, sure," I say. "But I don't know if I can wait that long. Your email sounded ominous."

She sighs. "Last night Mark and I met some friends for drinks at the Press Club."

Oh god. The bar. "Okay," I say carefully. "I have to be honest. I don't remember running into you." *Please don't say I embarrassed myself.*

"We didn't come over."

Okay?

"And actually, I'm not sure if Mark saw you. But *I* saw you canoodling on one of the sofas with someone who was definitely not Evan." Did she really say the word *canoodling*? "And I didn't want to interrupt." She pauses. "Or say anything to Mark."

"I don't remember 'canoodling' with anyone." I try to sound amused, hiding my panic. "But I did have a drink with an old friend of mine, who now works here."

"Brad Summers," she says matter-of-factly.

"Yes." I forgot that she's met him through Mark. "He wanted to talk about work, and so we went for a drink. And then we started talking about our old neighborhood and stuff. You know how it is when you get deep into conversation with someone."

I'm sure you know, Elena, since you're probably having deep conversations with strangers online every day!

"Mmm . . . How about we meet at noon in front of the Ferry Building," she says. "Cool?"

Not cool, but I say, "I'll see you there."

* * *

I'm the first to arrive at the Ferry Building. It's a sunny afternoon, and I keep my sunglasses on as I scan the sidewalk for Elena. After a few minutes of loitering, I finally see her form waving and walking toward me. She is also wearing sunglasses, so I can't read her eyes.

When she reaches me, we hug, but it feels more awkward than friendly.

"Where should we eat?" I ask, trying to act normal.

"How about the tea place? They have great noodle soups."

"That sounds perfect."

At the restaurant, Elena cannot sit still. She fidgets with the menu and taps her nails on the table. Watching her increases my anxiety. It's not like Elena to hold back. Once we order, I finally say, "So what's up?"

Obviously, I want her to fill me in on whatever it is she saw last night, but I also don't want to admit that there was anything for her to see. Tricky.

Elena hesitates, focusing her gaze on the teapot on the table. "Would you like some?"

I'm not sure I need the caffeine, but nod yes. Once she is done fiddling with the tea, she looks down at her cup, then at me. "So last night . . ."

"Yes. Last night. You said you saw me. You should've come over and said hello."

Elena shakes her head. "Just to be clear, I'm a girl's girl. I'm not one of those women who go and tell their boyfriend everything."

"Except when you want to set them up."

She gives a small smile. "That's different."

"Listen, I feel like there might be a misunderstanding here. Please just come out and tell me what you saw, or think you saw."

She takes a deep breath. "I saw you and Brad sitting next to each other in a dark corner, leaning against each other, holding hands. You looked like you were resting your head on his shoulder. It looked pretty suspicious."

"Did you see anything else?" I ask, more than a little worried, since I don't remember resting my head on his shoulder.

"No. As soon as I saw you guys, I didn't want to bring Mark's attention to it. So I was too busy steering him in a different direction."

I send a little prayer to the universe that Mark didn't see us last night.

"Thank you for not drawing attention to us. I'll admit that sounds like a compromising situation, but it was really no more than two old friends drinking too much and reminiscing about old times." I'm aware of the oddly formal tone of my voice as I present my defense.

"Is that what you would tell Evan?" she asks, and then hastily adds, "I believe you if you say there was nothing happening between you two, but maybe Mark saw you. And if he did, Mark is the type of person who would probably tell his buddy. You know?"

I nod. Mark does seem like a loyal friend. "Well, I haven't talked to Evan yet today, so I guess I'll find out. But I'll just tell him the same thing." I feel a bit sick to my stomach, though.

"Have you seen Mark today?"

"Yes. But I haven't had a chance to talk to him." I leave out his tense passage in the hall.

She leans forward slightly, her eyes focused steadily on mine. "Adeline, I'm your friend. Don't feel you have to hide anything from me."

"I'm not." I mean, at least when it comes to last night's events, I'm not hiding anything. But there's no need to tell her my *real* history with Brad.

She nods, but tries again. "I've seen you with Evan, but I've never seen you look like you did last night with him." She asks the next question tentatively. "Are you in love with Brad?"

My eyes widen. But before I can respond, she continues, "It's okay if you are. Don't feel you have to stay with Evan out of loyalty to me or anything. But I would be careful with Brad."

This is crazy! And why is she telling me to be careful? As much as I want to ask her what she knows about Brad, this is dangerous territory. I've got to nip this in the bud.

"No. I'm not in love with Brad. Sure, back in high school I had the usual teenage crush on him. But we were kids. That was a long time ago."

Elena's face is pale, and I can't figure out why she seems more upset about this than I am.

"So are you in love with Evan?"

I give a small laugh. "We just started dating. I'm not sure we should be saying the *L* word quite yet." Although, I have noticed that lately Evan seems to be peppering his speech with the word ("I love when you . . ." and "I love that about you"), which makes me wonder if it is coming up in the near future.

"Can I tell you something?" she asks, her eyes wide, searching mine.

"Of course."

She shakes her head. "No, I'm sorry. I probably shouldn't."

"What?"

"It's just . . ." She shifts her gaze from me to her teacup.

"Elena, what is it?"

She looks up at me and then quickly says, "I don't know if I'm in love with Mark." She drops her head down again and stares into her lap.

With those words, I realize now what is really going on. This isn't about me and Brad at all. Elena is hoping to find a confidant. Someone who is also unhappy in their relationship and looking outside of it. My heart now goes out to both Mark *and* Elena.

"I love him. But I'm just not *in love* with him," she continues.

"But what about your engagement? When did this happen?"

She shrugs. "I think I've always felt this way. He has all the qualities women look for in a guy, so I *should* be in love with him, and I keep waiting for it. But then I wonder if maybe I don't even *know* what I'm supposed to be feeling."

Bridget was right—*she always is.* "What are you going to do about it?"

"I don't know." She shakes her head sadly. "I keep thinking that I'm being stupid. I don't want to break up with him and later realize he was 'the one.'"

"I understand." Boy, do I understand as Miss Letting-Relationships-Happen-to-Me. "But don't you think by this point you would know? It's not fair to either of you to keep this going. You both deserve to experience true love with someone who loves you as much as you love them."

"I have to break it off," she says, her voice a sad monotone.

Not only am I the last person who should be giving her romantic advice, but I also don't want to be responsible for encouraging her to break my boss's heart. But if she's trying to meet new men, then it has probably been over for a while.

"You have to do what feels right," I say.

"I know." She looks at me. "Can we still be friends? Or would that be too uncomfortable for you?"

"Of course we'll still be friends!"

I lean over to give her a comforting hug, though I'm not sure if it's for Elena or for me.

* * *

Lunch does nothing to relieve the pressure in my head, but there are only four more hours to the workday, and then I will have forty-eight hours to recover. When I get back to the office, I open my email and find a message from Mark.

Please meet me in my office at 2:00 p.m.

It's a strangely formal email. I just have to trust that Elena successfully distracted Mark last night, and so I wonder if it has anything to do with his tense look this morning. I hope there's no major snafu on our project. Also, I don't relish the idea of sitting across from him knowing that he has no idea that his relationship is in peril.

At exactly two o'clock, I'm standing in Mark's doorway.

"Hi. Can I come in?" I ask.

Mark is behind his desk holding a document. "Yes," he says, without his usual smile, and motions for me to enter. "And please close the door."

This sounds serious. I do as I'm told and sit down, my pen hovering above a yellow legal pad.

"What's up?" I ask, poised and ready to take down new assignments or questions to be answered.

Mark hands me the acquisition contract from the Moonstruck-Imogen deal. It is opened to a middle page. "Take a look at that page," says Mark.

I look at it. "The paragraph numbers are off." I scrunch up my forehead. "Why is that?" I flip through the pages, wondering why he's showing me an early draft of this contract.

"Because something is missing. Do you see what?"

Most of this contract is burned in my brain, and I can recite entire paragraphs by memory. "Yes, some of the real estate and intellectual property clauses are missing." I continue going through the pages.

"Why are they missing?" Mark says, his tone giving nothing away, and I'm starting to feel like I'm being cross-examined on the witness stand.

I shake my head, not comprehending. "I don't know. Let's see, what version is this?" I look down at the small numbers on the bottom right-hand corner of the page, stamping the version number, date, and time. "It looks like a late version." I turn through some of the pages and notice that the last two pages are signed and notarized. "Why are these attached to this copy?"

Mark looks at me. "Because this is the final copy that was filed."

"What do you mean?" I have a sinking feeling in my stomach.

"What I mean *is*"—he pauses—"the final contract omitted those real estate and IP provisions."

And my stomach drops.

"That's impossible! How did that happen?"

"That's what I'm asking you," he says evenly.

I look at the time stamp again. I'd have to check my computer, but looking at the date and time, I know this probably is the last version. *But how?*

"Mark, I don't know. I don't understand. I would have to look through my documents files, but it seems like the signature pages were simply stapled to the wrong document."

"It's not a mistake. This is the one that we recorded and filed. Which makes this the final document." Mark sighs. "Adeline, Brad brought this to my attention yesterday, and I did some research. The version before this was the final that Dennis and I signed off on. Then for some reason, the night before the papers were to be signed, these clauses were deleted. The revisions came from your computer." Mark leans forward and continues kindly but sternly, "Now, I understand that mistakes sometimes happen when we're under the pressure of a deadline. This is obviously a mistake and was most likely accidental, but unfortunately, it's still a big deal."

How did this happen? I'd checked and double-checked and triple-checked everything. How could I have deleted this? I wouldn't have made any changes the night before.

"These documents were finalized before we signed," I say as I rack my brain. "We had them in the conference room ready to attach the signature pages so we could record them immediately. I'm so sorry." I shake my head, confused. "I will fix this." Though I don't know how.

"I pulled the previous correct version and am going to refile the proper contract. In the grand scheme of things, I don't think this will ruin our current project, as it was an amicable deal between the parties. But what if it hadn't been?" I swallow as he continues his reprimand. "It could've sunk everything. This is a mistake. A big mistake that could cost us our client relationships in the long run," he emphasizes. "It's sloppy and it makes us look bad. I'm going to have to tell Scott what happened and what we're doing to correct it." Mark sighs, clearly upset.

I nod contritely. *Please don't fire me, please don't fire me.* I find my voice and ask, "When did Brad notice this?"

"Yesterday afternoon. He brought it to my attention late in the day. But not before first bringing it to Jasmine's attention. He asked her why those provisions were deleted."

Jasmine? Why didn't he bring it to *my* attention? Why didn't he tell me last night? I feel a white-hot fury coming on. I know I must've screwed up, but why did Brad go to Jasmine and then Mark? Why was I not involved until now? I'm the one who drafted the damn thing!

Mark continues, "Scott is also Brad's big client, and he can't afford to lose him either. So he suggested bringing Jasmine onto the project. He thinks we should have more real estate attorneys involved from now on to make sure these things don't happen going forward."

Fuck. The day after Mark tells me to step up my game, I may have inadvertently screwed us both.

"I'm so sorry. What can I do to fix this?"

"Nothing right now. I'm taking care of it. But you may have to apologize. Profusely." Mark raises his eyebrow. "We'll see how Scott responds."

"I'm very sorry, Mark." I am sorry to the very core of my being.

"I know." Mark nods, looking serious. "These things happen. But they can't happen again."

"I understand."

I stagger back to my office, my face hot with shame. How could I have made such a colossal mistake? And right when I'm up for partner? I moved out here feeling like some big hotshot rock-star attorney, and now look at me—I'm just a big fat failure. And if there's something I've never failed at before, it's work. Yes, I know making mistakes is how we learn. But I don't even know how this mistake was made, so I'm not sure what lesson to take from it.

And Brad. Right now I hate him with every fiber of my being. Why didn't he talk to me about this? He doesn't have a problem dumping all his emotional baggage on me, but he has a problem bringing a work matter to my attention? Something that could affect my career? Instead he goes to *Jasmine* for an issue on *my* project?

Okay, that. That I can blame myself for. She ingratiated herself with him right away, while I kept my distance. Maybe she gave him the impression that she knew about the acquisition deal. Who knows? All I know is that he didn't feel comfortable coming to me, even though I would've been the right person.

But then I waved the white flag and invited him for a drink, where he had the audacity to hold my hand, but couldn't be bothered to warn me—*By the way, you screwed up big time and are going down tomorrow. Better polish up that resume.*

And he didn't even show up to work today. I assumed he was horribly hungover, which he could be. *Or* maybe he really is the jerk I thought him to be and that I keep pretending he's not. Maybe I am learning a lesson here after all.

CHAPTER TWENTY-SIX

To cap off my miserable day, I have to see Evan tonight. The fact that this only makes me more miserable is probably a bad sign. Since we're still in that early getting-to-know-each-other phase, I feel like I have to put on my game face. I'm not sure I have it in me, though. But with my job going down the tank, I can't let my personal life do the same.

I spend the rest of the afternoon trying to re-create what happened to the contract. I check the document on the server, and sure enough the change came from my computer, as last edited by me, "Adeline Turner." But I don't even remember looking at it that day. I thought I had finished it. Maybe I opened it to check for something and then accidentally deleted those provisions? Our paralegal John was responsible for placing the final documents in the conference room in the morning. He must've printed out this version, and this is what was ultimately attached to the signature pages and recorded. Even so, the contract was my responsibility and, therefore, my mistake.

If my life were a movie, this is when they would cue the sad song. After work I walk to the bus in the rain, having forgotten to grab my "just in case" umbrella by my front door this morning. I manage to squeeze into a seat, where the other person clearly does not want me there.

At my stop, I descend from the bus and walk the couple blocks to my apartment, the rain becoming fiercer since I left the office. When I walk through the front door, I'm mildly disappointed that it is my apartment. What once seemed charming, right now does not feel like home. Even though it's my sofa, my bed, my kitchen table, and my stuff strewn about, the sight of it doesn't bring any comfort, as I imagine having to pack it all up and move it back to my condo in Chicago.

I wish I had time to call Bridget, but I need to get ready before Evan picks me up. Since his renovations are finally completed, we're going to dinner in his neighborhood and to his place afterward. I make an effort and change into a simple jersey dress and a pair of knee-high black boots, accessorized with silver hoop earrings and a cocktail ring. I take some time with my hair and makeup, in the hope that looking better will make me feel better. By the time Evan pulls up, I'm ready for our date.

* * *

Evan lives in an industrial-looking area filled with warehouses, brand-new lofts, and high-rises. There are a lot of hot new restaurants popping up in the neighborhood as well, and he wants to take me to the latest, which has only been open a month. It's a cozy, if minimalist, spot serving Northern California fare. Evan says they are known for their burgers, but I opt for the pumpkin bisque and the polenta dish with exotic mushrooms. I let Evan carry most of the conversation. After telling me about the history of his neighborhood, he then dives into telling me about projects at work. I try to ask intelligent questions and appear engaged, even though my day is still weighing heavily on my mind; and since he doesn't ask me why I seem down, I must be putting on a good show.

After dinner, we walk back to his place. Evan's condo is a loft with concrete dividers and exposed ducts in the middle of the living room. He is excited to show off its remodeled state, and he walks me around the kitchen, explaining what it used to look like and how he changed it to what it is now.

"Here, let me show you a picture of the old one so you can see the difference." While he fiddles with his phone, I look around and note that the place is very tastefully done. There's a leather sofa positioned in front of a flat-screen TV, a desk with a gigantic monitor in one corner, a shelving unit with some books (mostly computer related), a mountain bike, and another city bike leaning against one wall. It's very clean, but also a bit sparse.

"Here we go," he says, having located the photo. I look at it. It seemed fine before, and not like it needed a complete overhaul.

"I see," I say. I would like to say it's much better, but I don't know.

"Yes, it was impossible to cook in before. The counter space was terrible. And look at the placement of the sink, stove, refrigerator . . . Who does that?" He shakes his head in disbelief. "And the appliances were awful. So I had my contractor tear everything out and start from scratch."

"It looks great!"

He begins to point out the details—right down to the dovetailing on the cabinets—and I listen politely because he is so passionate about it. After we finish the kitchen, we move on to the bathroom, also fully remodeled. And a painstaking remodel at that, again told in much painstaking detail. After learning more than I ever wanted to know about faucets and feigning enthusiasm for the latest in Japanese toilets, I'm relieved when it's finally time to sit on his couch and chill.

"Your place is fantastic," I say as we settle in.

"Thank you. I'm so glad you like it."

We sit comfortably on his sofa facing each other. Evan is beaming. He takes my hand and strokes the top of it with his thumb. "I want to tell you something."

There's a dim ringing in my ears, and my mouth goes dry. Every time someone has wanted to talk to me today, it hasn't been good. So I say nothing, which seems to embolden Evan to continue.

"I think I'm falling for you."

Oh. I swallow. So much for chilling on the couch. "I really like you too," I say back.

Evan gets serious and speaks the next words slowly as if to make sure I understand. "No, Adeline. What I mean is, I think I'm falling in love with you." He pauses, waiting for my response.

This should be really good news. But whether it's because I wasn't expecting any serious declarations of love or because I'm still preoccupied by today's events, I'm not feeling how I thought I would feel. This seems too soon, and my analytical mind immediately starts dissecting his words. He didn't say, "I love you." Instead he said, *he thinks.* So maybe he's not sure. And the words *falling in love.* That means he's not quite there yet, but may get there. That is okay. In fact, all this is fine.

So I say back, "I think I'm falling for you too." Because I'm not sure of anything at the moment and those words sound safe.

"I think I love you," he says, upping the ante.

Argh. I don't know yet. I want to tell him that it's too soon, but instead squeak out a nonsensical, "Yeah?"

He then continues, "I love you, Adeline."

Oh god. So we are here now. With his eyes wide and hopeful, Evan is waiting for my reply. But in his eyes, I can also detect his confidence that of course I love him right back—except I don't. I like him well enough, and maybe in a few weeks' time I'll feel "in love." But in my current headspace and with my career on the line, I don't want to ruin what might possibly be the only good thing going on in my life. So I take the path of least resistance and say, "I love you too." Though as soon as I utter those words, I feel some misgivings.

He leans over, taking me in his arms, and gives me a passionate kiss. I go through the motions of reciprocating, but though my mouth is moving, my mind is preoccupied. This man just said he loved me. Why am I not feeling completely and utterly elated? And can't he tell?

We continue kissing, and eventually it numbs away my headache, my day, and everything else, and I'm ready to just be in the moment.

I spend my first night at Evan's, and I can tell he took care, as the sheets smell clean and he has music queued up and some candles around the bed. After he falls asleep, I lie there thinking about how surreal everything feels. How things can change so quickly. My job, which up to now has been my security blanket, I've failed at. Yet my love life, which a few months ago was a disaster (okay, so it's been a disaster for years), now appears to be successful. And maybe I do love Evan? It's not like me to rush headlong into things, so perhaps I was just caught off guard that he seems so sure about us. But we're in our thirties, and there's no point in playing games. Evan is in love with me, so he said it. This is better than Brad any day.

Then it hits me—Brad. Just the thought of his name makes my heart pound, and not in a good way. I don't just feel betrayed; I feel rage. Pure, unadulterated rage. I have to think about how to approach him, because I can't and won't take that behavior lying down. God, I can't wait to talk to Bridget tomorrow.

* * *

The only thing more disorienting than waking up in Evan's bedroom is the sight of Evan himself, propped up on one elbow, eyes fixed on me. "Good morning," he says.

"Good morning," I try to say coherently.

"I love that you're here waking up in my bed."

"Me too." What else can I possibly say?

He lies down next to me and brushes the hair out of my eyes. "What do you want to do today?" he asks.

Oh. I wasn't planning on spending the day together. "Um, well, I have some errands I need to run."

"I can help you. I can drive you around."

"Oh, okay," I say hesitantly, because I still want time to myself today to think about things at work. "I also have some work stuff I need to take care of."

"But it's Saturday!"

"Yes. Well, I had a pretty rough Friday. So I need to do some work today to make up for it."

"Oh? Is Mark working you too hard?" He peers at me and, in a mock-macho threatening voice, says, "Do you want me to talk to him?"

I laugh. "No. It's fine. I can't talk about it until I've had some coffee."

"I thought we could go out for coffee this morning. There's a great place in my neighborhood. They have this Turkish-style coffee you have to try. It's super strong."

"Okay. That sounds good," I say, but I'm already mentally planning to head home right after that.

I had packed a small tote bag with some toiletries and comfy clothes to change into so that I wouldn't have to do the walk of shame or some form of it this morning. I take a quick shower in his meticulously researched, high-tech bathroom. I must admit that the water pressure and the waterfall showerhead amount to what really must be my best shower experience to date.

We walk hand in hand to the coffeehouse, and Evan orders for us while I sit at a sidewalk table.

When Evan appears, he says, "I ordered a Turkish coffee for you."

It smells strong and heady and is exactly what I need. "This is delicious. Thank you. How do you find all these places, anyway?"

"I like to seek out the best." He smiles.

"I see. So I should be particularly flattered, then, that I am your girlfriend." I give his hand a playful tap with mine. He catches it and holds it in his.

"You are the best. You're beautiful, smart, talented." He gazes into my eyes.

"Hmm . . ." I tilt my head to the side. "You know, flattery will get you everywhere."

"Are you sure you have to work today?"

"Yes." I sigh, remembering. "I messed something up, and I need to figure out a way to fix it, or if not fix it, just be a star associate this month."

"What happened?"

I'm not sure I want to go into the details, since Evan is Mark's friend. But he is my boyfriend and he has declared his love for me. Isn't this the type of stuff boyfriends should listen to?

I groan. "I accidentally deleted some key provisions in a document before it was signed by a client."

"How did you do that?"

"That's the thing—I don't even remember doing it. I honestly don't know how it happened. The document was finalized a couple days earlier. I must've opened it, and I don't know." I shrug helplessly.

"Huh. So how do you fix it?"

"We redo the signature pages and refile the corrected document. Mark was really nice about it, but I feel awful."

"So, sounds like an easy fix. Why do you have to work today?"

"To make up my hours from yesterday. And to work extra hard so they won't fire me."

"They won't *fire* you." He draws out the word *fire* in a tone that suggests I might be being overly dramatic.

I raise an eyebrow at him. "I was moved out here specifically to work on this deal, and then I messed up."

"It was an accident." He doesn't seem to understand the gravity of the situation, or if not the gravity, then how horrible I feel about it all. "And anyway, so what if they fire you? You'll get a new job." He takes a casual sip of his coffee.

I look at him incredulously and my pride kicks in. "I've worked at the same firm my entire career and I'm up for partner. If I get fired, one, it's really hard to get hired at a big firm in the first place, and two"—I put up my second finger—"even if I interview somewhere else, at this stage in my career they'll assume I was passed over for partner."

"So you want to make partner?" He now looks at me more seriously.

"Yes." Okay, maybe it's not something that is a deep burning desire, but I've worked really, really hard up to this point, ignoring my personal life along the way. So if there's been any clear goal in my life the last seven years, it's been to make partner at Gilchrist & Jenkins.

"What about when you have kids?"

I almost spit out my coffee. "I, uh, I don't think that's something I need to worry about in my immediate future. I'm on the pill, you know."

He laughs. "No, really. I'm talking about when you're a mother. Wouldn't you want to be there for your kids?"

"Why wouldn't I be there?" I had never thought of this question before.

"'Cause you'd be at work."

"Would you quit your job if you had kids?"

"Probably not. But it's different." He shrugs.

I shift in my seat at this window into Evan's parenting views. But while this conversation is eye-opening, just like the *I love yous*, it's too soon in the relationship (and too early in the morning) to discuss it.

"Honestly, I don't know. I've never really thought about it. If it became a problem, then maybe I would seek a different type of law job. But right now, that's neither here nor there." I wave my hand. "I'll cross that bridge when I come to it."

"Interesting." He rubs his chin with his hand.

"What?"

"I don't know. I guess I didn't peg you as so career-driven."

"What are you talking about?"

"You're all about work."

The back of my neck bristles. Considering that this is the first time I've brought up my work troubles, this seems an unfair assessment.

"I'm trying *not* to make it all about work. So maybe we should talk about something else?" I suggest as lightly as possible, hoping to end this line of conversation.

"To be continued," Evan says, smiling at me and holding my hand.

But I'm not so sure.

* * *

The second Evan drops me off at home, I call Bridget.

"Hey, stranger," she answers.

"Hey, yourself." I collapse on the sofa, so happy to hear her voice. "What's up?"

What's up, apparently, seems to be Jason. She tells me how they have been spending almost every night together.

"Is he there now?" I ask.

"No. He left this morning. We're meeting up later." Bridget sighs happily. "I don't know, Addie. I think he may be the one."

"Really?" Although I already suspected as much.

"Yes. We said 'I love you' for the first time this week."

"And?"

"And it was great. It was so natural. We were just sitting on the couch, eating some takeout, or more like feeding each other some takeout and joking around, and then Jason just blurted out, 'I love you' and I laughed and said, 'I love you too,' and, well, we're in love!" She sounds happier than I've heard her in a very long time.

"I'm so happy for you!" And then I don't mean to turn the conversation to myself, but it seems on point. "And that's so weird because Evan told me he loved me last night."

"No way! And?"

I shrug and play with the fabric on my shirt. "And it was a little awkward."

"Uh-oh. What happened?"

I give her the details and then explain, "I had such a crazy week and horrible day yesterday that I didn't have it in me to turn him down or add to the list of horribles."

"What happened this week?"

"*A lot.* In fact, I would cancel all your weekend plans to hear all this."

I fill her in briefly about drinks with Brad and then tell her that Elena saw us together and invited me to lunch. And then I tell her what happened that afternoon with the contract and my being reprimanded by Mark.

"So, wait, why did Brad tell Mark and not you?" she asks.

"I don't know. Maybe because he and Mark are partners, and Mark's been the partner on this deal over here?"

"But you were together Thursday night. Why wouldn't he mention it?"

"That's the million-dollar question."

"Maybe he didn't know the extent of your involvement? Maybe it wasn't intentional?"

"Maybe he's a psychopath?" I offer. I mean, *come on.* He kept saying he wanted to "talk about work," but instead he just used drinks as an excuse to tell me more sob stories about his life. "Honestly? That moment in Mark's office, when I realized Brad spent the entire evening drinking with me, and yet failed to warn me that my career was about to go down the tubes, I was over him."

"Wow, just like that! You're over him?"

"Yes." Except that now I hate him with more passion than I've ever thought possible. "First he betrays me by sleeping with me and failing to mention his wife. Then he betrays me at work by failing to mention the contract. Game over."

"And so what about Evan? Are you in love?"

"I might be." But I might not be. The more time I spend with Evan, the more I notice little things. For one, I rarely speak on our dates, and he doesn't ask me questions. Today was probably the first time he's asked "real" questions about me, and they assumed something of my personality that doesn't exist. Second, he always decides what we're going to do and is always showing me things, but he doesn't seem to be interested in what I might like; he just shows me what he likes. And I know it's wonderful to have a boyfriend who is so proactive, planning all our activities, cooking for me, choosing wine for us . . . but I feel like he doesn't know me, because how could he? It's as if he's in love with the *idea* of me as his girlfriend more than the real me. And because I was desperate to forget about Brad, I've been more than happy to play along.

I don't say any of this to Bridget, because I'm not ready to admit all this out loud yet.

"*O-kay,*" Bridget says, and my guess is she has already figured out everything I'm just realizing—hence her lukewarm attitude toward Evan since her visit. "To be discussed over drinks. You're coming down to Chicago Thanksgiving weekend still, right?"

"Of course! I can't wait to see you!"

"I know! Chicago isn't the same without you."

"Yeah, well, considering how much I screwed up, I may be back for good."

"See, there's a positive in all this."

"Shut up," I say fondly.

"I miss you."

"I miss you too. See you soon."

CHAPTER TWENTY-SEVEN

Immediately after Bridget and I hang up, my phone rings again. Seeing Elena's name on the screen, I answer it.

"Hi, Elena." I sink back into my sofa.

"Adeline," she says, sounding totally distraught. "C . . . c . . . can I come over?"

I sit back up on alert. "Oh my god, what's wrong?"

"I . . . I'm . . ." Her voice is small, and I can hear her sniffling on the phone.

"Where are you?"

"I'm . . . outside your door."

"You're outside my door?" I jump off the sofa and run to the front door where I find a slack-shouldered, red-eyed Elena.

"I broke up with Mark," she says with a wavering voice.

"You what?" I'm not sure that I heard her correctly.

"I broke up with Mark," she repeats more clearly and then starts to cry.

"Oh my gosh. Come here." I give her a big hug and usher her into my apartment. "I'm so sorry." I'm also surprised that she came here and not to a closer friend's place. "Okay, first things first," I say. "Pick your poison: tea or something stronger?"

"Tea sounds good. Thanks." Elena gives a little laugh, or maybe it's a sniffle.

"Okay. While I get the tea ready, make yourself at home on the couch." I point in the direction of my living room.

She nods and follows my orders.

As I fill the teapot, I can't help but wonder if there's a full moon or something this week. I'm also wondering how Mark is doing and if he's as distraught as Elena right now.

Elena's voice from the other room interrupts my thoughts. "I'm sorry to barge over like this, but I just didn't know where to go."

"Puh-leeze. That's what friends are for." The water starts to boil. "I'll be out in a sec."

I pour out two cups of chamomile tea and carry them over to the sofa.

"Careful, it's hot," I say as I place one cup in front of Elena. "Okay. What happened?"

Elena shakes her head disconsolately. "I'm sorry to interrupt your afternoon, but I couldn't stay in the condo. I had to talk to someone, and I can't talk to my other friends. They won't understand." She stares into her teacup. "In fact, they'll be shocked."

"Let's not worry about how your friends will take the breakup news. Let's talk about you."

She sighs. "Yesterday, when we were talking at lunch, that was the first time I admitted out loud to someone my true feelings for Mark. I still love him, but I don't want to marry him."

I nod, remembering her words yesterday. "You love him, but you're not 'in love' with him."

She shakes her head again. "It's crazy. And I'm sorry to dump this on you. I hope this isn't weird for you?" She gives me a look trying to gauge my reaction.

"Stop right there. I'm a girl's girl," I say, eliciting a small smile from her, "and you are my friend, okay?"

"Okay. But Mark is your friend too. He thinks very highly of you."

Not after this week, I think to myself. But I refrain from talking about my problems. "For the love of god, woman, just tell me what happened."

"Last night in bed, Mark brought up picking a date for the wedding. I said I was too tired to talk about it and asked if we could discuss it in the morning. After talking to you yesterday, I was up all night thinking about him and me. I mean, he's absolutely perfect on paper, but I've been waiting for the spark, and it's never happened. I feel more and more like we're just going through the motions, and we both deserve more than that. When he broached the subject again this morning, I cracked and said, 'We need to talk.'"

I gasp. "The worst words in relationship history."

She nods in agreement. "I said I wasn't ready to be married. And Mark—in that way he has—asked, 'Not ready to be married ever, or not married to me?' I think he knew what was up. I think he's known for a long time and has been trying to give me my space to figure it out. Which of course makes him the most perfect guy ever, but still not the perfect guy for me."

"How did he take it?"

"Pretty stoically. I think he knew that by bringing up the wedding stuff, he was sealing the coffin on our future." She shrugs sadly. "We talked for a couple hours. I told him honestly how I felt. He didn't say much. Just listened. I told him that he deserved better than me. To make it worse, he actually kissed my forehead and said that I deserved better as well." She sits back. "So then I left. And I came here and called you."

I reach out and squeeze her hand. "How are you feeling?"

"Sad. But also relieved. It's like this big boulder I've been walking around with is suddenly gone."

Her mention of boulders makes me think of rocks, and I steal a glance at her hand. "You still have the ring?"

She lifts up her hand and sadly admires it. "Yes. I took it off and tried giving it back, but he wouldn't take it."

"Really?"

"Really. It makes me feel incredibly guilty." She searches my face. "I'm not making a huge mistake, am I?"

"No. And besides, when it comes to your feelings, you don't need anyone's approval." I am channeling my inner Bridget, and I think this is what she would say. Because what I would say is that she is crazy to break up with Mark. But at the same time, I wouldn't want Mark with someone who didn't love him 100 percent.

Elena forces a smile. "So what about you? What Saturday afternoon plans do you have that I'm interrupting?"

"A whole lot of nothing," I say. "Evan just dropped me off late this morning, and I was planning to do some work this afternoon."

Elena leans her head back and rolls her eyes. "What is it with you lawyers?"

"It is called the billable hour," I inform her, in all mock seriousness. "But work can wait. I have nothing pressing going on. My day is yours." I spread my arms out to indicate that my schedule is wide open.

"Well, I clearly have nothing going on today, since my relationship is over."

"So what are you going to do? I mean, what's your"—I pause, realizing the delicacy of this—"living situation?"

"Oh god. We talked about it this morning. It's Mark's condo and I moved in. He's being great and he said I could stay for as long as it takes me to find a new place. So I guess my afternoon plan should be to look for a new 'living situation.'" She does the air quotes, smiling and making fun of me. She then drops her head in her hands. "Ugh. I can't believe this is happening."

I set down my cup and reach over and squeeze her shoulder. "Hey. It was the brave thing to do. You'll be okay."

It *was* the brave thing to do, and I admire her for it. I think back to how many relationships I've stepped into that weren't right or didn't have that "spark" Elena is searching for and how much time I wasted because I didn't have the guts to break up with someone. And while Evan and I are still new, our conversation this morning and my revelations while I was on the phone with Bridget niggle at me.

I offer to take Elena out to distract her, but she says she really needs to begin apartment hunting, and so I lend her my laptop and desk to get started. I also invite her to stay over tonight, if going home is too much right now, and she accepts. Since I have some Saturday errands to run, I leave her alone for a while.

* * *

While I'm at the grocery store, my phone rings. It's Evan.

"Hey, babe," he greets me.

"Hi, sweetie." Okay, I'm still working on it. "What's up?"

"So I know we talked about getting together tonight, but would you mind if I bailed?"

I don't distinctly remember us talking about it, but I guess it was assumed. "No problem. Why? What's up?"

"Bad news. Mark and Elena split."

"I heard."

"How did you hear?"

"Elena told me."

"Wow. Bad news travels fast. Mark just told me they broke up this morning. So I offered to take the poor guy out. Distract him. Drink too much, watch too much sports, or something."

"I think that's the right thing to do." Maybe I should say something about hanging out with Elena tonight, but I feel a little guilty, somehow complicit in all this, since she confided in me yesterday. So I just say, "I'll be fine tonight."

"You sure? 'Cause I could come over a little later . . . *later*?"

"Is this a premeditated booty call?" I ask.

He laughs. "You got me. I don't know if we'll be out late tonight anyway. But okay. I can see you tomorrow."

"Sounds good."

"I love you."

"Okay. I love you too. Bye," I say distractedly as I try to juggle my basket and phone and select some ice cream in the freezer aisle.

Does it sound good? Although I know it's a new relationship and we're exclusive, I guess I didn't think we would plan all our "unplanned" hours together. But I don't have time to analyze it, as I have a houseguest at the moment.

I spend the rest of the afternoon working on my work laptop while Elena uses my home laptop to scour Craigslist.

"Do I want to be a roommate at age thirty-five?" she calls out from the kitchen.

"No, Elena. You do not want roommates at thirty-five."

"I didn't think so. Thanks."

In the evening, we hang out on the couch drinking wine and eating delivered pizza (Elena only picks at hers, favoring the wine over food, which is understandable). We talk about men and are able to laugh. She keeps asking, "Is this going to make things weird between us?"

Little does she know that things were already weird when I was stalking her on the dating website. But in my good-friend role of the evening, I say, "Of course not."

And if anything, this distracts me from what is looming on Monday morning.

* * *

In the morning, over coffee at my local Starbucks while watching the passersby, Elena says, "I don't think I can face Mark today." She's wearing a pair of borrowed yoga pants and a T-shirt.

"I understand. I don't want to face him tomorrow."

She turns to me and frowns. "I'm so sorry I've put you in a bad position."

"Oh no! That's not it." I hadn't planned to share my work troubles, but now feel I should explain. "I screwed something up at work. Big-time. Mark had to have a talk with me on Friday." I look into my coffee cup. "It was bad."

"What did you do?"

I tell her about the contract.

"Is that malpractice?" she asks.

Oh god. It probably is, but even I hadn't uttered those words yet. Now I'm even more worried. "Well, it was stupid. Hopefully, it's not super detrimental and can be fixed. But it's *not* good."

"I'm sorry." Now it's her turn to squeeze my shoulder in sympathy.

"Thanks. So I guess you can call off the apartment hunt because you can have mine when they fire me and ship me back to Chicago."

"Oh, please. Mark wouldn't fire you." She waves her hand as if dismissing the thought.

"Well, the client might. But I guess I'll just have to wait and see . . ." I trail off. And then I bring up what's weighing on my mind about the whole thing. "What's really bugging me is how it got brought to Mark's attention in the first place."

"What do you mean? Isn't he supposed to notice these things?"

"Yes. But he also has to be able to trust his underlings." I point to myself. "He signed off on the final. Then somehow I accidentally changed it at the last minute, *even though I don't remember doing so*. And here's the weird thing . . . Brad is working for the same client and is helping with the real estate stuff. He's the one who noticed the mistake on Thursday. He first went to another attorney, Jasmine, and asked her about it, and then he went to Mark. But he never mentioned it to me even though we went out for drinks that same night."

"Maybe he didn't know you were involved?"

"He does. And I'm sure Jasmine readily pointed out that it was my mistake."

"That's weird. But he's also a weird guy." She scrunches up her nose and makes a face. "Mark has told me how he's going through a complicated divorce with this woman he met in law school, which I'm sure you know about."

"Yes, I've heard the story."

But *really*, people have bad relationships all the time and get caught up with the wrong people. This is not an excuse for bad behavior.

"But I feel like something about that story doesn't quite add up," Elena says. "I've met the guy, and he's charming and all, but something is definitely off there. And it can't simply be blamed on having a crazy wife. You know? Sometimes crazy attracts crazy." She twirls her finger by her forehead, the universal sign for crazy.

"Good point." She is right. I still don't quite understand why it was so hard to break up with this girl early on—like, *before* she got pregnant? Because how much can you blame another person for a situation created by your own choices?

"Well, it doesn't sound like he's too clean in all this," Elena says, giving me a meaningful look.

Uh-oh. I feel the heat rising to my cheeks. Does she know? Does she assume? Does she think I'm having an affair with him? She definitely thought the worst on Thursday. Oh god. Does Mark think there's something between Brad and me? I clear my throat and ask ever so innocently, "What do you mean?"

"You guys work together, so I probably shouldn't say. Also, I don't know if it's true. But just picking up on things Mark has said, it sounds like Brad was cheating."

"Really?" My stomach sinks.

"I don't know for sure." She looks at my horror-struck face. "And we probably shouldn't talk about it. I don't want to spread gossip."

Please, it's not gossip if it's just us, I'm thinking. But I don't want to seem too interested. So I just sip my coffee, nod, and change the subject back to my dilemma. "I just don't understand how it happened. Everything was final, and then the night before the closing, I must've opened up the document and accidentally hit Delete or something."

"Did you go back to work after the movie?" She tilts her head, seeming confused.

"Movie?" I frown.

"Yeah, remember? *Bridget Jones's Baby*? You said you needed to clear your head before the big day."

Oh my god. That's right! In my hungover state on Friday, I totally forgot that I went to the movies with Elena the night before the closing. The time stamp on the document said 7:50

p.m., but I was in a theater with no access to my computer at that time.

"No, I didn't go back to work . . . ," I say slowly.

"Then how did you make those changes?"

"I *didn't* make any changes."

Elena looks at me, and then her eyes suddenly widen. "Do you think someone sabotaged you?"

"I don't know. The time stamp on the document shows that the changes came from my computer, but there's no way I could've edited it."

"So someone used your computer?" Elena has livened up considerably at the possibility of corporate intrigue.

"But my computer is password protected, and the only people who know my password are my secretary, the tech guys . . ." I scrunch up my forehead and think. Then it hits me—Rachel logging on to my computer at Imogen because she forgot hers that day. "And Rachel."

"Who is Rachel?"

"Another lawyer there. She wouldn't do anything, though." *Would she?* I don't want to be too paranoid.

"Well, I can tell you that in PR people are always trying to steal each other's clients. I'd think it would be even worse in a law firm."

"Sure. But she's just an associate. She's not interested in my clients. She's not even interested in working for me. She just wants to work for Jasmine." I take a sip of my coffee, which is now cold, just like this trail I'm on.

"And who is Jasmine?"

Adrenaline suddenly surges through me. "Someone who wants to steal my client."

What am I going to do?

CHAPTER TWENTY-EIGHT

I feel slightly sick as I walk into the conference room Monday morning for our ten o'clock team meeting. The first person to greet me when I enter is Jasmine.

"Good morning, Adeline." She smiles, looking bright, chipper, and a bit smug.

"Good morning." *Cruella,* I mentally add. I nod at her and greet the rest of the group sitting around the table. Jasmine is sitting next to Brad on one side of the table. Rachel is next to Jasmine, her eyes down and focused on her BlackBerry. Brad is turned away from me and is busy looking out the window, yet tapping his pen on the table, appearing to be deep in thought. Or at least feigning so. Emma is across from Jasmine. I sit next to Emma, even though it means sitting across from Brad.

"Did you have a good weekend, Adeline?" asks Emma, completely oblivious to the tension in the room.

I smile at her. "I did. Thank you. How about you?"

"It was great. My boyfriend and I went hiking in Point Reyes," she offers enthusiastically. "It was beautiful weather."

"That sounds like fun. Did you just go up for the day?" I focus all my energy on Emma, ignoring the others in the room.

She is about to tell me, but is interrupted by Mark walking in and greeting us. "Good morning, everyone."

Even though I know I should be more worried about my own hide, I can't help but look at Mark and wonder how he's doing. I try to detect any signs of heartbreak. He does look a little strained, but only if one looks very closely. Otherwise, he simply looks like a partner about to run a team meeting.

"Okay, let's get started. As you can see, we're increasing the team to work on this project." I'm expecting him to introduce or welcome Jasmine, but instead he continues, "This weekend I made a list of items we need to take care of."

Mark begins rattling off some assignments. "Adeline, I'd like you to put together some letters to the zoning board. Emma, why don't you work with Adeline on that and do any research she needs."

"And, Adeline, be very thorough. We can't afford to leave anything out," Jasmine says to me. I want to reach across the table and smack her.

"I trust Adeline will be thorough," Mark says curtly and continues on with his list, not letting Cruella get in another word.

When he's finished, he turns and asks Brad, "Is there anything you think I'm missing?"

"Nope, that's the list we went over."

Brad doesn't once look at me the entire meeting.

"Okay, team," Mark says, looking around the table and picking up his legal pad. "I think this should keep us busy this week. Keep me posted if there are any issues or if you have any questions."

The meeting was mercifully short and to the point. But on the way out the door, Jasmine says, just loudly enough for everyone to hear, "If you need any help, Adeline, please let me know."

From anyone else I would consider this a gracious offer. From Jasmine, not so much. Although I politely respond, "Thank you," what I'm really thinking is, *Hell will have to freeze over before I ask for your help.*

I follow Mark down the hall to his office. Before he goes in, I say nervously, "Mark, can I talk to you?"

He turns around, surprised. Then a resigned look crosses his face. "This isn't about Elena, is it?"

"No."

"Okay, I have a conference call for the partners' meeting in Chicago right now. Can we talk after?"

Crap.

"Of course. Maybe we can grab lunch?" I realize this is a rather ballsy move since in Mark's eyes I have screwed up royally and should be lying low—hiding in my office, working hard, and trying not to get fired.

Rightfully so, Mark looks at me curiously. "We're taking the call in the conference room and lunch will be provided. In fact, I should probably get over there. We'll talk later."

"Okay." Though I want to add that it is very important, I don't want to give prying ears any indication of the subject matter.

I spend a nail-biting morning and afternoon in my office. I'm tempted several times to walk by the conference room to check if the meeting is over, but I can't stomach the prospect of seeing Brad and Jasmine. Though I could just ask Mark's secretary to tell me when the meeting is over, I don't want to give anyone an alert. *Patience.*

Around three o'clock, while I'm drafting a letter, my office phone rings. I see Nora's number and answer on speakerphone. "Hi, Nora," I say as I continue typing.

"*What the hell* is going on there?" she practically shouts.

I turn away from the computer and pick up the handset, taking her off speakerphone. "What are you talking about?"

"What is this about you screwing up the Project X deal?"

"What?"

"That you messed up the acquisition contract. That can't be true."

I feel the heat rising to my cheeks. "Hold on." I get up and close my door to make sure there are no eavesdroppers, intentional or not. "Okay, tell me what you heard and from who."

"I just got back from the partners' meeting where we were discussing who to make partner this year. Obviously, you know your name is on the list."

"Yes." I gulp.

"So when we get to your name, everyone is on board with it. Then all of a sudden, Roger speaks up and says that although he's always thought you were a great associate, when you were finally tested with a big project, and for one of our major clients, you dropped the ball. He pulled out the acquisitions contract and showed everyone that you deleted important provisions in it the night before the closing."

I take a sharp intake of breath. "Oh god. Are you serious?"

"Very. Then he said because of this he doesn't think you're ready for partnership or should even remain at the firm."

The blood that was heating up my face now drains.

"*Nooo . . . ,*" I say.

"Yes," Nora says sharply. "But don't worry. No one is talking of firing you."

"Except Roger."

"He doesn't count. Usually," she says a little ominously. "You have enough goodwill that I don't think that would happen. *But* there was some serious consideration of passing you over for partner. Nothing was decided. So I had to call you right away and find out what's going on."

I take a deep breath. "That's what I'm trying to figure out too." I tell her how I was at the movies at the time of the edit and of my suspicions regarding Jasmine, who has been trying to get on this project, and her crony Rachel, who knows my computer password.

Nora listens and then says, "You need to set the record straight. *Immediately.*"

"I know. This morning I told Mark that I need to talk to him, but he was already on his way to the meeting." I sigh. "But I have no proof it was Jasmine, and I don't want to come across as a delusional paranoid. I'm already on thin ice here."

"You should be paranoid. If you're an attorney in Biglaw and you're *not* paranoid, then you're doing it wrong." I roll my eyes because (sad, but true) she's right. Nora continues, "Just tell Mark you weren't at your computer at the time and that you have an alibi. As far as you know, the only people who have your password are Rachel, your secretary, and the tech people. It's for him to investigate."

"That's my plan. And to do it as calmly as possible," I say. "But how does Roger know?"

"He was on the team, so I guess Mark had to say something."

"Yeah," I say sadly, now having confirmed that my black mark extends from San Francisco all the way to Chicago. "I can't believe any of this is happening. It's been a smooth ride the last seven years and then this, right before I make partner."

"That's usually when it occurs. Lawyers are sharks."

She's not telling me anything I don't already know. It's just unfortunate when the sharks are circling around you.

As soon as I hang up with Nora, I hustle down to Mark's office. He's not there, and his computer is off. I walk over to his secretary's desk and ask, "Is Mark still in a meeting?"

"No, the meeting ended a little while ago. He had an appointment, so he left early for the day."

Oh no! He didn't even remember that I wanted to talk to him. This is not good. Not good at all.

"Is everything all right, Adeline?" She must have registered the panicked look on my face.

I try to regain my composure. "Um, yes. I just wanted to ask him something, but I'll send him an email. Thanks, Sheri."

I walk back to my office and try to calm myself down. It's okay. He'll be in tomorrow, and I will just email him again and say I need to talk to him. Considering that there's a possibility my computer may have been hacked, my paranoia will not let me divulge the details over email.

Luckily when I return to my office, there's an email from Mark.

> Adeline – Our meeting ran late and I had to leave early today. Can we talk tomorrow? Or is this an urgent matter?

A wave of relief that he didn't forget about me runs through me, but I'm still too nervous to tip my hand over email. While it *is* an urgent matter for me, I write:

> It can wait until tomorrow, but it is very important that I speak to you. Can you meet for coffee before work?

His response comes back a minute later.

I'm pretty tied up in the morning. Let's have lunch.

I'll take it.

But the next twenty or so hours are going to be dreadful.

I say as much to Evan that night when he comes over.

"I thought it was fixable," Evan says as he pours me a glass of wine.

"Sure, but right now I still have a black mark on me."

He shrugs. "If it doesn't work out, you can always go someplace else."

"But I don't want a new job. I want to keep this one and make partner." I narrow my eyes at him. He's said this before, and I've already told him why it matters to me. Is this his idea of being supportive?

Exasperated, Evan says, "Well, babe, I don't know what you want me to say."

I'm not sure what I want him to say either, so I drop it. And I really wish he'd stop calling me "babe."

* * *

I meet Mark at the elevators at noon.

"Where should we go?" Mark asks. "The usual?"

Our usual is too popular with others in our office, so I suggest something farther afield.

"It's a nice day. How about the Ferry Building? There's a good noodle place there." Yes, it happens to be the same place Elena suggested, but it's the only far enough but reasonable-sounding option that comes to mind.

"Oh." Mark gives me a suspicious look, or at least a look that my paranoia interprets as such. "I have a lot of work today, so I was hoping for something quicker."

"They're superfast. Plus, I really want to talk to you about something away from the office."

"Okay," he says, but he doesn't look thrilled.

I keep up a fast pace on our walk down Market Street, and when seated, I select my order quickly, trying not to waste too much of his time. Once we've ordered, Mark gets down to business. "So what's on your mind, *A-de-line?*" he says in a rhyming manner, his tone lighter away from the office.

Okay, maybe this won't be so bad. Maybe he is in a good mood.

I take a deep breath. "I wanted to talk about the acquisitions contract for Project X."

The pleasant curiosity in his eyes changes into a cloudy dullness, clearly registering that he does not want to talk about the contract. "It's okay, Adeline. What's done is done. These things happen. We all screw up at some point—"

I cut him off. "I understand these things happen, but I didn't do it. I didn't make that change."

I now have his full attention. "What do you mean?"

"Mark, the contract was ready to go. I sent you the final version Monday, and you and Dennis signed off on it Wednesday." I produce the email where he said it was good to go. "I never opened the document after that. Nobody did until the edit was made. But I wasn't in my office at that time, and I didn't have my laptop. I was at the movies with Elena at 7:50 p.m. that night when the change was made." I show him the text exchange between Elena and me and the email receipt for our tickets that she bought online. I feel uncomfortable that his ex is my alibi, but so it goes.

Mark takes my phone from me, reading the exchange and the date. "Does anyone have permission to use your computer?"

"I shut down my computer every night. The only people I know who have my password are my secretary, presumably the tech guys, and"—I say this part nervously—"Rachel."

"Why does Rachel have your password?"

"The first time I brought her out to review documents at Imogen she forgot to bring her laptop. I let her use mine and told her the password."

"You didn't change it after she used it?" I know he is only information-gathering, and there is no hint of judgment in his eyes or tone, but I still feel its weight.

Embarrassed, I shake my head. "No. I didn't." I now realize how stupid this was on my part.

We're interrupted when our soup arrives and Mark hands my phone and the emails back to me. Once the server is gone, he says, "Do you have reason to suspect Rachel made the changes?"

I'm careful because even though she's my prime suspect, my career is on the line. If I falsely accuse my colleagues, this could all turn out worse for me.

"I don't know. But I suspect there's been a security breach, and thought I should bring it to your attention."

Mark focuses his eyes on mine and says seriously, "Yes, you're right to bring this to my attention. Thank you. I will look into it. In the meantime, it's best for you not to mention this to anyone until we know something more. Got it?"

"Got it."

CHAPTER TWENTY-NINE

When my plane lands in Milwaukee, I finally feel like I can breathe again. The long lines, delays, and general Thanksgiving travel aggravations are preferable to being in the office the last couple of days. I haven't talked to Mark since our lunch, and I've been dying to know if he's learned anything. Brad was mercifully out of the office Tuesday and Wednesday (probably with the so-called ex-wife and his daughter). And oddly, Jasmine seems to have taken a sudden interest in me, asking how my assignments are going. As if I'm going to offer her any information that can possibly be used to screw me over later.

My dad is waiting for me curbside. "Addie, honey!" Though he's bundled in his winter gear, his cheeks ruddy from the cold, he looks the same since the last time I saw him. He gives me a big hug.

"Hi, Dad," I say, enveloped in his puffy winter coat, the knot in my stomach finally loosened. "It's so good to be home."

The air outside is crisp and dry. Fall is turning into winter. My favorite season. Although I offered to rent a car, my dad insisted on picking me up, and it feels good to relax back into the leather seat and watch the familiar flat landscape during the two-hour drive home. Though it's eleven p.m. here, I'm still on West Coast time and wide awake.

My dad is in a good mood and fills the conversation with the goings-on at his club. He asks me questions about work. I haven't told him yet about my mess-up. Not now. I'd rather tell him in the morning and get his advice. If there's any to give.

"Deborah is coming over at noon to put the turkey in the oven," my dad says.

Deborah? Oh, that's right, Mrs. Collins. "Cool. I can help her out." In fact, I'm looking forward to it—especially since Evan seems to find me too inept to help him in the kitchen.

* * *

In the morning, as I wake up in my old room and my old bed, everything seems so far away—San Francisco, work, Brad, all of it. For a second, I think that maybe I'm just waking up from a bad dream. *I wish.*

The time change works against me, and I wake up pretty late, but I still have time to get in a quick run. There's no snow or ice, but I can see my breath when I head outside. As I loop around the neighborhood, some houses are sleepy still, and others have many cars in front of them already, probably hosting Thanksgiving. Then, even though I knew it was coming, there looming in front of me is the Summerses' old house.

I slow down my pace. I remember as a young girl walking by slowly, hoping to catch a glimpse of Brad. It feels so long ago. And it was. In fact, it was a whole other life. The Brad Summers I know now is a complicated man; complicated by character or circumstances, I'm still not sure. The old Brad was just a boy. A boy I didn't even really know that well. Just someone I stared at from afar. He was simply a daydream. One I was able to keep going since he moved away. The dream was much better than reality, and I pick up my pace again, not looking back at the house.

When I get home, my dad immediately pops his head into the hallway and says, "I still have the coffee on, but you better get in the shower." He has a sparkle in his eyes but a tone that says if I don't hurry up on that shower, he'll push me in himself.

"Okay, okay." I laugh. It's eleven, and he's right.

After showering, I throw on jeans and a turtleneck sweater. Since we're going to be at home and I'll be in the kitchen, I'm assuming it's going to be a casual affair. When the doorbell rings, I hear my dad, who has been sitting in his office, shout, "I'll get it!"

I start making my way downstairs, and am halfway down to see my dad open the door and Mrs. Collins standing there holding a big turkey.

"Oh, Deborah, let me get that." My dad grabs the pan. "I could've carried it over."

"It's okay, love," she says brightly.

They lean in and kiss.

On the lips!

Hello?!

I freeze.

"Hello, Addie," Mrs. Collins says sweetly.

I try to regain my composure. "Hi, Mrs. Collins. It's so nice to see you."

"Oh, please, dear. Call me Deborah."

O-kay.

Other than my mother, I have never seen my dad in a relationship. Though we never talk about this stuff, how could he not have told me? Or how was I so blind that I didn't guess? Maybe I should've made the connection earlier when he first told me she would be joining us. For all I know my dad may have had other relationships before this, but I guess the sheltered child in me thinks of him as a contented bachelor. *Oh my god! What if all these years he's been getting it on with all the widows and divorcées in our neighborhood?*

I try to get these disturbing images out of my head as I help Mrs. Collins (sorry, *Deborah*) with the food items in her trunk.

"Oh my gosh, is this all for us?" I say as we carry the second load of groceries in.

"Leftovers are the best part, my dear." She smiles.

Deborah ushers my dad out of the kitchen and into the family room. That's good, I guess. I don't know if I could handle also learning that my dad is now a gourmet chef. I see not everything has changed.

Once all the groceries are out of the bags, I ask, "What can I help you with?"

"The hardest part is peeling the potatoes. My hands aren't as strong as they used to be."

"I'm on it," I say and begin searching for the peeler. Once I locate it, I set to work rinsing the potatoes.

"What all are we having?"

"Let's see. We have some squash soup to start, then salad, turkey, stuffing, gravy, mashed potatoes, candied sweet potatoes, green bean casserole, and cranberry sauce." She ticks the items off, looking around the kitchen as if to make sure she has everything. "Then homemade pumpkin and pecan pies for dessert."

"That's so much!"

She laughs. "I guess I haven't learned how to cook a small Thanksgiving meal. And besides, this will give you two something to live off of for a few days."

"Thank you, again." I smile.

As my task is on the potatoes, I focus on that while she assembles the green bean casserole and other dishes while the turkey cooks. She sets out some cheeses, salami, crackers, and grapes for us to nibble on. My dad keeps wandering into the kitchen for some more appetizers.

"How are my two chefs?" he asks.

This one is a little disconcerted, I want to say. Instead, I just raise my eyebrows at him.

I see him hug Mrs. Collins from behind and hear her giggle. "Oh, Tom."

Oh, Tom, indeed! I want to ask Deborah how long they've been dating, but then I also don't want to hurt her feelings by giving away that my father hasn't mentioned anything. I figure it's best to play it cool and corner my dad later. So I ask about her kids, and that conversation takes us through the whole, surreal afternoon.

At dinner my dad gives thanks and the toast. "And to Deborah for this amazing feast before us."

She smiles and waves her hand like it was nothing. And it is amazing. In fact, I don't remember the last time I've had a stay-at-home Thanksgiving dinner like this.

"Everything is delicious," I tell her.

"Thank you, dear." She dabs a napkin to her lips. "So tell me, how do you like living in California?"

I talk a little about it, the weather and the sights and how different it is from the Midwest.

"And how is your mother doing?" Deborah asks.

My hand holding my fork freezes for a moment. I steal a glance at my dad, but he is focused on his food and purposely not looking at me.

I put my fork down and reach for my wine glass. "I wouldn't know," I say, and then take a good swig of my wine.

"Oh, have you not had a chance to visit her yet?" The careful lilt at the end of her question suggests she knows full well I hadn't planned to visit.

"Nope. I've been busy with work." *And considering that she's been too busy the last twenty-one years to visit me, I'm not exactly going to go to great lengths to find time in my schedule.* I feel a sudden heaviness in my stomach that's not from the turkey. It was a given that my mother would come up during this visit, but why is it coming from my dad's new girlfriend?

Trying to think of a way to change the subject, I turn to my dad. "Hey, Dad, you'll never guess who just started at our firm."

"Hmm?" he mumbles with his mouth full of turkey and still avoiding my eyes.

"Brad Summers." I can't believe my changing the topic to Brad would be a welcome relief, but here we are.

For a second it doesn't compute. So I add, "Remember the Summerses? They lived down the street."

Deborah chimes in, "Of course! They moved away ages ago."

My dad, who is now finished chewing, laughs and says, "You're kidding? Is Brad a lawyer now?"

"Yep. He does real estate law," I say faux casually. "He was practicing at a firm in LA and just joined us a couple weeks ago."

"What a small world," Deborah comments.

"I can't believe he went to law school." My dad shakes his head. "I would've thought he'd play sports or something athletic. He didn't strike me as the sharpest tool in the shed."

"He seemed like a nice enough boy," Deborah interjects.

"Sure, sure," my dad says, nodding. "So? Are you working with him?"

"Yes. We're working on the same project."

"How's that going?" My dad is all ears now that the talk is work.

Although I had planned to ask his advice about the contract issue, I realize that he would probably become overly worried about the status of my partnership. So I keep mum.

"It's good."

"Well, tell him I said hello and that my lawn misses him."

"Ha ha! Will do." Although, I won't. Because if I can help it, I am never speaking to Brad again.

Before driving home at the end of the evening, Deborah gives me a hug at the front door and says, "I hope you enjoy the rest of your stay."

"Thank you again for dinner," I say, returning her hug.

While we hug, she whispers in my ear, "And dear, I know I'm butting in here, but please try to call your mother. It would mean a lot to your father."

My spine stiffens as she says this. "I'll see what I can do," I say evenly, although I have no intention of doing so.

When my dad comes back inside from escorting his girl-friend to her car, I raise an eyebrow and say, "Deborah seems nice."

"She was always nice." And he smiles, still not giving any-thing away.

"So how long have you been seeing her?"

"I see her all the time. You used to see her all the time too when you lived here." His eyes twinkle merrily.

"Oh come on, Dad," I say, rolling my eyes at him and slap my hand on the kitchen counter in good-hearted frustration. "You could've mentioned it to me."

My dad shrugs. "I know. But I didn't feel like doing it on the phone. We started going out to dinner more often and becoming friendlier the last few months. It seemed this was the best way to have you two get to know each other better." He smiles at me, and that is as much information as I'm going to get.

I'm happy to see him so happy, even if his new girlfriend is a busybody.

* * *

The next morning I have breakfast with my dad, take Winston for a walk, and then take my car (which I had left here before moving) to drive down to Chicago. I'm sleeping over at Bridget's tonight and will drive back up to Wisconsin on Saturday morning to spend the rest of the weekend with my dad.

Bridget and I have plans to go out to dinner with Jason. Though I'd love to have Bridget all to myself, I'm also dying to meet him. Also, Bridget has promised me that he's going to hang out with his guy friends after dinner so we can have some uninterrupted girl time—which we will probably spend talking about Jason.

During our dinner, I realize that Bridget is right: he really is the one for her. He's medium height, with a slim build, dark hair to Bridget's blond, and wears equally stylish glasses. They finish each other's sentences, look at each other with love and adoration and respect, and most importantly, they don't make me feel like a third wheel.

As promised, after dinner Jason leaves us in front of the restaurant. "I've been told to make myself scarce the rest of the evening," he informs me with a good-natured wink. "You two have fun!" He catches a cab, and we are left on our own.

"Should we go back to my place?" asks Bridget.

The liveliness of the streets and people out and about makes me want to stay out longer. "Hmm . . . what about that wine bar over on Delaware?" I suggest.

"Let's do it!" Bridget says, raising her arm up for a cab. One appears instantly, and we slide in, ready for a night on the town. It's been too long.

The wine bar is packed, but somehow we manage to get two stools by the main bar as a couple is leaving. We quickly order two red wines and get down to the business at hand.

"Sooo . . . what do you think of Jason?" Bridget asks, her eyes bright and shiny and clearly in love.

"I love him! You guys are perfect and will have beautiful babies."

Her smile widens, and she playfully hits me on the arm.

"And I'd better be maid of honor. Not that annoying cousin of yours." I jokingly narrow my eyes at her.

"Okay, okay. I'll let you two duke it out when the time comes." She laughs. "And I'm *sooo* glad you like him."

"What's not to like? Handsome, funny, nice to your friends, and clearly enamored of you."

"Yes. Things are going really well. We're practically living together, and I can see it moving into a more permanent situation not too far down the road." Her gaze turns dreamy; she's probably picking out her wedding dress as we speak.

"I'm so happy for you." I seem to be surrounded by happy couples this weekend. All of whom are clearly much happier than I am with Evan.

"How about you? What's going on? How's Evan?"

"Evan's fine." I shrug, since that's all I have to say on the matter. "Things have been pretty crazy this last week at work."

But Bridget isn't ready to move on to work talk yet. "'Evan's fine'? That's not an answer. What's up? I thought you guys were in love."

It's Bridget. I'm not going to lie. "We're saying 'I love you,' that's true. But I don't know. I'm not sure we're really there yet."

"Then why did you say it?"

"Argh. That whole day had been such a disaster that, honestly, I just said it after he said it because it seemed easiest in the moment."

Bridget eyes me critically, but before she can say anything, I continue, "Actually, Evan is the least of my problems."

With that, I launch into all my work drama of late.

After telling her more about the contract, Brad, Jasmine, and my partnership on the line, I sigh and say, "And all this is especially awkward because Elena is my only alibi witness, and now she's Mark's ex."

Bridget puts up her hand. "Wait, what? Mark and Elena broke up?"

"Yes, but they're still living together until she gets a new place."

"When did they break up?"

"Last weekend. So now my only female friend in San Francisco is my boss's ex." I put my elbows on the bar and rest my head on my hands. "*Ugh.* Honestly, ever since I moved, nothing seems right."

"What do you mean?" She leans forward and crosses her arms on the bar.

"Well, this mess-up at work. The awkwardness of having Jasmine openly dis me and Rachel not liking me. And then Brad, who I slept with thinking he was the long-lost love of my life, is married and now works with me and is screwing me over. Then my one and only female friend in San Francisco just broke off her engagement with my boss, and I'm dating one of his good friends that his ex set me up with, but I'm not even sure I want to date his friend anymore." I can feel the alcohol fueling my rant. "I don't know. It seemed so perfect in the beginning because we could be this foursome, but now I'm just stuck with Evan."

"You were dating him to be part of a foursome?" Bridget looks amused.

"It's a valid lifestyle choice," I say defensively, taking a sip of my wine.

"I think if you want to stop dating Evan, nobody will care."

"What about Evan?"

"Okay. He might care. But *still*. Don't continue dating someone out of people pleasing."

"Hmm . . ." She's right, but that's a different conversation.

"So back to Mark," she says. "Now that he's free, why don't you date him?"

I almost choke on my wine. "Excuse me? It's bad enough that I've already slept with one colleague."

She waves her hand dismissively and says, "That doesn't count. You didn't work together yet."

"Okay, so if it's not a bad thing for me to start dating my boss, what about the fact that I'm already dating his friend?"

"Details, details," she says casually and shrugs.

I laugh, relieved to make light of everything back in San Francisco. "I've missed you, B." I reach across my barstool to give her a hug.

CHAPTER THIRTY

ack in the office on Monday morning, after too short of a trip home and before our team meeting, I receive a firm-wide email reminding us of office security policies and that we should make sure to lock our computers and change our passwords often. This is the first news I've heard since my lunch with Mark. I called Nora on Tuesday last week to give her the recap of what I told Mark. She promised to keep her ears and eyes open, but I haven't heard anything further from her. The security reminder makes me feel even worse, as it implies that I did screw up after all because I didn't change my password. I walk to the meeting with a heavy heart.

For someone who doesn't want to be here, I'm the first to arrive. I take a seat next to the head of the table so that I won't have to make eye contact with anyone. Unfortunately, the next person to arrive is Brad, who takes a seat directly across from me.

"Good morning," he says, his tone flat and unreadable.

"Good morning." I keep my eyes glued to my BlackBerry, pretending to be immersed in checking email.

These are the first two words Brad has spoken to me since we went out for drinks. He should be ashamed that he threw me under the bus, and I don't know that I can be civil with him. I feel betrayed on both a personal and professional level. But Mark told me to keep quiet for now, so unfortunately, I can't give Brad a piece of my mind.

The rest of the team files in, and Mark appears shortly after them. After exchanging some pleasantries as everyone sits down, Mark starts the meeting.

"First things first, I assume you've all seen the email regarding office security this morning."

We nod.

"Good. Please take this reminder seriously. It was sent out because we've had a security breach in our own office."

Jasmine gasps. "Oh no! That's terrible. What happened?"

I inwardly roll my eyes. It's an Oscar-worthy performance. I glance surreptitiously over at Rachel, who is sitting sullenly in her seat, eyes cast downward. All I can think is, *Guilty, guilty, guilty.*

"One of our computers was compromised, and an important document was altered."

Jasmine is still looking concerned. "Recently? How did that happen?"

Mark glances over at me as if to ask permission. Eyes wide, I nod, silently begging him to clear my name.

Mark takes a breath and says, "The acquisitions contract for the Moonstruck-Imogen deal was edited from Adeline's computer, but not by her. She was out and had her computer locked for the night."

Jasmine looks at me, feigning surprise. "How did that happen, Adeline?"

Are you kidding me? She knows exactly how it happened. It's all I can do to look at her and try to keep my voice steady as I say, "I don't know." Though there's probably a burning look of accusation behind my eyes.

Mark continues, "We're investigating with the technical team to figure out what happened."

"That's good," Jasmine says, still looking concerned.

"So as a reminder, if you haven't already, please review the policy in order to keep our documents and our clients' documents safe." Then he turns to our current project and asks each of us about the status of our various assignments.

After the meeting, as we're exiting the conference room, Mark says to me, "Adeline, can I talk to you?"

"Of course." I follow him to his office, where he closes the door. Finally, hopefully, there is some news.

Once we sit down, he says, "I want to give you an update on the hacking incident. First, I looked at everyone's time sheets and cab receipts, and the only person here that evening was the paralegal. He doesn't remember seeing anyone else in the office at that time. I also talked to Rachel and your secretary, and they know nothing. So I reported it to the management committee, and we have the technical team here and in Chicago looking into it. As soon as I hear anything more, I'll let you know."

And because I can't help myself, I blurt out, "What about partnership? I'm up for partner this year. Will this affect my chances?"

Mark leans back in his chair and runs his hands through his hair. It's enough of a pause to make me sweat. "It doesn't appear that you've done anything wrong. You've done a great job with this client, and you really proved yourself this last year with Project X. I'm strongly supporting making you partner, but obviously, there's never any guarantee."

I nod. "Thank you."

I want to tell him that I know what Roger said about me at the partners' meeting, but I can't risk exposing my spy, Nora. I'll just have to wait until I hear further news from her.

After leaving Mark's office, I head to the kitchen for some coffee. I didn't sleep well last night and need the extra caffeine boost. Of course, there is Jasmine making herself a cup of tea.

"Hi, Adeline."

I nod to acknowledge her, but don't say anything.

"That's awful about your computer."

"Yeah." *Stop talking to me.* I turn my back on her to grab a mug from the cupboard.

"How did something like that happen? Are you sure you locked your computer?" she presses.

I spin around and look at her. "Yes. I am sure," I say a little too pointedly.

"Well, sometimes when we're working late, we forget things." She calmly stirs her tea.

"But I wasn't working late. I wasn't even here."

She shrugs and continues stirring. Her gesture makes my blood boil. I know Mark said that no one else was in the office, but I don't trust this woman. I've always prided myself on staying out of work politics, but I can't put up with this shit any longer.

"Be careful, Jasmine," I say ominously.

She looks up and stops stirring. Narrowing her eyes, she parrots back, "'Be careful'?"

"I *know*, okay. Let's just say, I know. Others know too. So I would be very careful if I were you."

Her eyes widen suddenly for a split second before she can regain her cool. "You know what?"

Now it's my turn to shrug. And with that I pour my coffee and walk back to my office.

It's petty, but it's a small victory. How dare she try to make me think this hacking incident is my fault? She's been trying to get on this project since I arrived, and it's obvious she's the one behind all this. Jasmine's days are limited, I'm sure.

An hour later, I receive an email from Brad that simply says, Lunch? in the subject line. No text in the rest of the email. Maybe this is keeping with his not talking to me. *Hell, no*—I do not want to go to lunch with him. I debate whether to reply as such or just ignore him. As I sit back in my chair contemplating what this strange email might mean, I wonder whether he knows something about the contract. Maybe he wants to apologize for the fact that he brought it to Cruella's attention and not mine? Maybe he's been feeling guilty about it? Maybe I have it all wrong? If anything's clear, it's that I can't afford to have any more enemies at work than I already do right now.

So I type back: What time?

He immediately responds: Noon. I'll come by your office.

My mind swirls with anxiety while my eyes watch the clock. What is he going to say to me? How should I play it?

At 12:03 p.m., Brad is at my door with his jacket on. "Ready?" he asks.

"Yes." *As ready as I can be.* I grab my purse. For now my anger has been tempered by my curiosity.

We walk to the elevator where Mark is standing.

"Hey, guys. Going to lunch?" Mark says, looking at Brad and then me. I've worked with him long enough now to detect the suspicious look and tone of his voice.

"Yes," I say. I feel like the polite, normal thing to do would be to ask him whether he'd like to join us. But Brad is less likely to apologize if Mark is there and is noticeably silent too.

The doors open, and now avoiding eye contact, the three of us enter the elevator. Why, oh why, must everything be so tense here? I thought a smaller office would be friendlier. Instead, it's been the most awkward period of my life. Even high school was a million times better than this.

Outside we part ways with Mark and decide to walk to the salad place nearby.

Once we've got our salads in hand, we head to an empty table outside. When we're seated, Brad comments, "This weather's been great lately, hasn't it?"

I am not ready to touch my salad or comment on the weather. Instead, I attack.

"Why didn't you bring the acquisitions contract to my attention?" I say, my eyes boring into his.

"Sorry?"

"When you noticed the missing provisions, why didn't you ask me about it?"

"I didn't know to ask you." He looks at me with wide eyes, not even a blink.

"But you knew I worked on it."

"Addie," he says calmly. "I had just started that week. I was reviewing the document, saw something missing that was real estate related, and so the first person I asked was Jasmine, because she's a real estate attorney."

"But Jasmine didn't work on Project X."

"Yes, that's what I found out. So she told me to point it out to Mark immediately, and that's what I did."

"But you knew I worked on it. You must've known I was in charge of it." I struggle to keep my voice steady.

"I knew you were the associate on the project, yes. But I didn't know it was your mistake."

I'm furious right now and am trying to rein it in. "But it *wasn't* my mistake."

"Yes, we know that now." He takes a big bite of his salad and regards me calmly as he chews.

What an ass. "So you thought it was my mistake, and then we went out for drinks and you didn't mention it at all?"

He finishes chewing and says, "Hey, you invited me out for a drink."

"Right. Because I felt bad that I hadn't had time to go to lunch with you." *Okay, because I was busy avoiding you.* "So why didn't you say anything?"

"Maybe if we'd gone to lunch, I would've asked you." Brad now looks like he's getting agitated. "For all I know, you wanted to go out for drinks to talk about it, and then you didn't bring it up. So if you wanted to talk about it, you didn't."

"Because I didn't know yet!" I'm exasperated. "Mark told me the next day. The day you didn't even bother coming into work."

"I was sick." This time he doesn't bother trying to meet my eyes. *Bullshit,* I think. *Bullshit, bullshit, bullshit.* So much for expecting an explanation or apology. I look at him and wonder how I ever found him attractive. He's infuriating. And not in an I-love-him-and-therefore-I-hate-him way. Just an I-hate-him way.

"So why did you ask me to lunch today?" I ask.

"Because we're friends, and we haven't talked in a while. I wanted to see how you're doing." He bites into his salad as if the conversation of the last few minutes never happened. "How's life?" He chews his food and looks at me earnestly.

Oh my god. I see we are going to play this game. Or is he playing a game? Is it possible that he really is this clueless? I doubt it, so I just give up. He's not worth the energy. "Life is great," I say flatly. "Other than having my computer hacked and a massive mistake blamed on me, everything is fantastic." I give him a sarcastic smile.

"Oh, come on. Don't worry about that. Everyone knows now that it wasn't you," he says. "Do you know what they're doing to investigate?"

"Nope. I'm out of the loop on that."

He nods and then changes the subject. "So there's been a new development in my divorce."

"Oh?" Such a random change of topic—one I don't care to know more about. He starts telling me how Kathryn is trying to take all his money and using Ivy as a bargaining tool. I half listen, unable to bring myself to care. I poke at my salad, counting down the minutes until our lunch is over.

When I see he is finished with his salad, I interrupt his sob story and say, "Are you ready to go?"

"But you didn't eat all your food."

"I'm done," I say. Because I am. I'm done with Brad Summers. "Let's go."

I am walking so fast, I'm practically running back to the office to escape Brad's company. The scales have fallen from my eyes, and I feel like such a fool. I had built him up in my daydreams, but the Brad of my fantasies doesn't exist. In reality, Brad Summers is nothing but a narcissistic drama queen. I wonder if he even wants this divorce to happen or just likes to have something to pull out to make people feel sorry for him. All I know is that I was a fool once and won't be again.

* * *

"Hey, babe. I'm ten minutes away," says Evan, calling from his car.

"Okay. See you soon."

It's the first time we've seen each other since before Thanksgiving. I've just walked in the door from work. Since I got home late last night from Wisconsin, I haven't had time to clean or do laundry. But I figure we must be at that point in our relationship where I can be relaxed, right? Frankly, I'm too tired to put in the effort tonight. I kick off my shoes and head to the kitchen to pour myself a glass of wine.

For dinner, we planned on ordering sushi, which Evan does before he leaves the office, *since he knows the best places, after all.* When he finally arrives we sit on my sofa. He's got some beer I've never heard of before, and I'm nursing my sauvignon blanc.

He leans over, gives me a quick kiss, and then leans back on the armrest. "It's good to see you, babe." He takes a swig of beer. "How was your Thanksgiving?"

"It was nice. We ate at home, and then the next day I drove down to Chicago to see Bridget."

He looks confused for a second. "I thought you were from Wisconsin."

"Yes, I am. I went to Wisconsin to see my dad, and then I visited Bridget in Chicago."

"Uh-huh."

Rather than elaborate further on my trip, I ask politely, "How was yours?"

"Oh my god, what a disaster!" He launches into the minute details—describing everything from his flight to his parents' house to everything they did and discussed and his sister's family and, I swear, for an hour he barely comes up for air.

And okay. I asked. He's telling me. It's an entertaining story. I respond appropriately and ask some questions—which isn't really necessary because he will tell me everything anyway. But I have stories too. Like that my dad has a girlfriend, an old neighbor, and what a shock that was. How she told me to visit my mother, and what gall that was. How great it was to hang out with Bridget and finally meet her boyfriend. Although it may be my fault for not telling my stories to Evan, I've also come to the conclusion that he has no interest in hearing them. In fact, he doesn't even know that my mother lives right over in Berkeley. And ever since the last fiasco over coffee, I no longer share with him what is going on at work. The truth is, he just wants to have an audience for his own voice, and I've let myself be that audience for a while now. It's Adrian, my internet date, all over again, and I don't know why it took me so long to realize this.

When he makes a move, I apologize and say I'm still tired from my flight and the time change, and suggest that maybe, this one time, we just fall asleep.

With Evan asleep next to me, I think about how much I wanted to be in a relationship. How I didn't want to feel lonely in a new city. But somehow I'm feeling much lonelier than I ever did when I was single. But he loves me. And he is good-looking. And he is smart and funny and has a good job. I think back to what Elena said about Mark, *perfect on paper.* I squeeze my eyes shut as if to shut out the truth about this relationship that I can no longer ignore.

CHAPTER THIRTY-ONE

*T*urn right onto . . . ," instructs the robotic woman who inhabits my GPS. I do as I'm told. As soon as I'm out of the city, the clouds disappear and the sun appears. I would prefer a cloudy day, though, to mark the momentous occasion.

The Tuesday night after Thanksgiving, I talked to my dad on the phone and he asked again, "Have you called your mother yet?"

"No."

"Honey, I know it's hard, but it's time. I know you don't understand why exactly she left, but she was the one who wanted to tell you." He has been on my case even more since my visit.

"So why hasn't she told me? She's had the time." Twenty-one years, to be exact.

"Addie." He sighed. "Just call her, okay?"

My dad sounded tired. I didn't want to call her, and I don't understand why I'm the one he's exasperated with. But I don't want to upset my father anymore, and for Deborah to butt her nose in, this must be very important to him. Also, I have to admit that seeing him so happy in a new relationship has me ruminating anew about why my mother left us.

And frankly, it is time.

I'm thirty-three and have not had a single decent relationship in my adult life. Either I build someone up in my head in the case of Brad, sabotage an obvious choice like Eric, or rush into a relationship blindly to avoid uncomfortable emotions, as is my current situation with Evan. Why am I so bad at love? Do I lack the emotional capacity to ever find true love? And could this all be related to my relationship or lack of relationship with my mother? It's time to find out.

Forcing down years of emotions of abandonment and rage, on Wednesday I dialed the number for Camille Dos Santos. While it rang, I contemplated what would be worse: having her pick up or getting her voicemail. I decided voicemail, because then I would have to wait for her to call me back, and I've already waited years.

"Hello?" a soft female voice answered.

I found the courage to say, "Hello, may I please speak to Camille Dos Santos?"

"This is she."

"Hi, Camille. This is Adeline." And just to be clear, I added, "Your daughter." I couldn't quite bring myself to call her "Mom."

There was a pause on the other end.

"Adeline," she said slowly. "Hello. How are you?"

How am I? Well, I'm just swell, I thought. Before I could think of an actual response, she added, "I'm sorry. That was probably a stupid thing to say."

It was. But at least it was maybe clear now where I got my constant self-editing gene.

"It's okay. I'm fine." I summoned up all my courage and told her that I'd like to meet her. But I didn't want to meet her. Well, I did. But you know. I reverted to the explanations of a petty child. "Dad wanted me to call you."

"I see," she said carefully, perhaps trying not to make another faux pas. "He told me that you moved to a firm out here. He says you're doing well and you're a star attorney. Congratulations."

My chest momentarily expands at the news that my dad described me as a "star attorney" but then quickly tightens at also learning that he had filled her in on my life. *Et tu, Dad?* She knew what had been happening in my life, and I didn't know anything about hers, except where she lived.

"Yes. So I'm calling to see if you would like to meet."

"I would like nothing more."

Today, Saturday, is our arranged date. I thought about meeting at a restaurant for breakfast or coffee or dinner, but the thought of seeing my mother in a public place makes me nervous. What if I didn't recognize her? Instead, we decided that I would go over to her house. So now here I am in a rental car, my stomach in knots, my hands clenched on the steering wheel, on my way to see my mother, whom I haven't seen since I was twelve. I have absolutely no idea what to say to her because the only question I want to ask is, *Why did you leave?* But I don't know if I can handle the answer.

However, the events of late have shifted my perspective. My realizations about Brad's character, and that I was merely holding on to a childhood crush, have given me a certain knowledge. The knowledge that sometimes my emotions blind me to the reality of things. So with this new knowledge, I try to keep an open mind about meeting my mother.

My GPS tells me that the address is on the right, and I pull up in front of a picturesque, brown-shingled craftsman with a charming garden in front. The neat row of hedges and flowers contained behind stacked stone walls aren't that different from my dad's front yard, and I can't help but wonder if my dad simply kept her landscaping or if she re-created it here to remind her of us.

Swallowing down the rising lump in my throat, I force myself out of the car and walk up the brick pathway to the house. After taking a deep breath, I press the doorbell. The door opens, and standing in front of me is an older version of myself. My mother's hair, streaked with gray, is what mine would be like without my barrage of hair products and salon visits to tame my unruly tresses. I see my own eyes staring back at me but framed by soft wrinkles. We're the same height, and her curves, the same as mine, have softened with age and are less defined. If I were feeling generous, I would describe them as motherly. She's wearing linen slacks and a loose sweater with a colorful beaded necklace.

We regard each other for a moment. My throat suddenly feels dry, and I feel rooted to the spot. When I was younger, I had dreams of confronting my mother, but now, standing here, I'm at a complete loss for words.

"Adeline," she says, opening the door wider, her voice trembling slightly on my name. "Please come in."

"Thank you," I manage to say as I will my feet to walk into the house.

I wasn't sure what to expect. It's cozy, but also a bit modern with Eames chairs and furniture I would describe as midcentury. A mix of canvases, sketches, and sculptures fill the room. Some are large and abstract, some just pencil drawings of figures. Maybe I'm supposed to say something nice about her house, but I'm not sure of the etiquette in this situation.

"Here, please take a seat anywhere in the living room. I just put the kettle on for tea. I also bought some scones and muffins if you're hungry."

I'm not, but again, I say, "Thank you."

I can hear the kettle whistling in the kitchen. "Let me just get that," she says, leaving me alone in the room. I sit down in one of the armchairs and look around. Scattered among the artwork are photographs that appear to be from various trips and with friends. I look at one in particular of my mother smiling into the camera with another woman, their arms looped around each other's shoulders and a pyramid in the background. As I'm trying to determine my mother's age in the photo, a ball of fur and nails jumps into my lap.

"Oh my god!" The cat jumps off me as quickly as it jumped on.

My mother comes running out of the kitchen. "Artemis! Shoo! Get out of here." And the cat goes running back to wherever it came from. "I'm so sorry, Addie. He's Barbara's cat, and he can be such a beast."

"It's fine." I smooth down my sweater and composure after the attack. I don't know who Barbara is, but her cat is a menace.

My mother goes back into the kitchen and then comes out carrying a tray with a teapot, teacups, and a plate of the aforementioned pastries.

After the niceties of asking me how I would like my tea, she sits down on the sofa, perched on the edge of her seat. I note that I'm also sitting on the edge of my seat. *So now what?*

My mother makes the first attempt. "How do you like San Francisco?"

"It's fine. I work a lot, so I haven't had a chance to see much of it." *This is ridiculous. Is this how we're going to start?* I set down my cup of tea on the end table. "So Dad really wanted me to get in touch with you."

"Yes, how is your father?" she says nervously.

"He's fine." I want to cut to the chase, but I'm not sure what I want the outcome to be. Do I want her back in my life? Do I want her to feel sorry that she's not in my life? Do I want to tell her off? Do I want to hear her story? We're interrupted by a woman flying through the front door.

"It's just me. I forgot my music sheets . . ." She stops when she notices me and turns to my mother. "Oh. Oh! I'm so sorry. I didn't realize you had company." She looks back at me. "Sorry, I'm Barbara. Never mind me. I'm on my way out. Ciao!" And she is back through the door and outside.

I now see where the cat gets it from. Barbara's intrusion, though, seems to calm my nerves and get me out of my head. "Is that your friend?"

"Yes," my mother says. "She's my friend." Barbara's appearance, however, has made my mother's hands shakier. As she reaches for her tea, she almost spills it in the process.

Sitting here in this strange house in Berkeley with my mother, I feel detached—as if I am part of a scene in a movie or play rather than my real life. I try to begin.

"So . . ." I'm about to say "Mom," but it doesn't seem appropriate quite yet. I take a deep breath. "I don't know what you know, but after you left, Dad never exactly told me what happened. Something about how you were unhappy and couldn't pursue your art in Wisconsin. But he's never told me anything else, and I didn't want to upset him by asking questions." The hurt is rising, but I don't want to sound accusatory. "So what have you been doing? What is it that you do? Do you still paint?" I pause because this is all sounding like idle chitchat. "It sounds like Dad has kept you filled in on my life, so it's only fair that I know about yours. And why you left, of course." There, I said it.

She looks into her teacup and then puts it on the table. "Yes. I asked your father not to tell you. It was something I felt that only I could explain." She pauses.

It's been twenty-one years. This better be good.

"Well, you know how I've always loved painting. Now I'm an art teacher, and I also paint on my own time and have had some gallery showings."

Um, you couldn't paint in our hometown? This is the explanation?

She takes a deep breath. "Addie, listen, I loved your father. I still love your father. But I wasn't in love with him." This seems to be the theme lately. "I couldn't be in love with him."

"You left because you weren't in love with Dad? What about me? What about your daughter?" *Didn't you love me?* I start to feel tears stinging the back of my eyes. But I won't cry.

"I loved you more than anything in the world. I still love you, Adeline, but I didn't know what the right thing to do was. It was a different time."

"A time when mothers left their daughters?" I say sarcastically. I'm surprised that I'm taking the tone of a bratty teenager, but she missed those years, so it's time for her to catch up.

She continues nervously. "I fell in love with someone else. But even then I didn't know it was love. I always suspected, but I was confused."

My mother had an affair. That was the scandal. But I'm so hurt and angry on my dad's behalf that I don't know if I can listen.

"Your father was hurt, but he understood. I think he too suspected. The only answer for us was to get a divorce." She pauses and looks down at her hands folded on her lap, then raises her head to look me straight in the eyes. "We only have one life, and I couldn't live a lie. It was also unfair to your father. And I couldn't live in that town anymore. I had to get away. But I was torn because—you have to believe me, Adeline—you were the one true love of my life. But I was also ashamed and scared, and it made more sense for your father to raise you."

"You didn't fight for me?" I say in a small voice. My mother wanted to be with her lover. She says she loved me, but she was willing to sever our relationship just so she could be in love.

"There was no fight. Your father and I discussed at length the best options for you, whether to share custody or have you be raised in a stable home."

"You abandoned your daughter for your lover?"

"That's not it."

"What is it, then? So where is this great lover now?" I say, unable to hide the hurt and anger in my voice.

Her eyes move from my face and rest on the picture next to me. I scrunch up my forehead and look at her, waiting for the answer. Then she nods and points to the photo. I don't understand. I turn and pick up the photo with the pyramid that I was admiring before. I look at the picture of my mom and her friend, and then look back to my mother.

I shake my head, not comprehending and trying to sort out someone in the crowd behind them.

Then my mother says quietly, "Barbara."

"This is Barbara?" I ask, linking the woman who just came bustling into the house with this younger version in the photo.

Then it hits me. *Barbara!* I start to say, "Barbara is . . ."

"My wife."

Oh!

Of all the scenarios I had imagined, this one had never crossed my mind. But all the scenarios I had imagined were worse, so much worse. And now I understand. Sort of. Or I'm trying to.

"You could have told me. Dad could have told me. *Why didn't anyone tell me?*" I start to raise my voice, which is becoming tinged with hysteria. "Somebody should have told me!"

I feel the tears start to sting again and try with all my might not to cry. So many years lost without my mother, *for what?*

My mother comes swiftly to my side, sitting on the arm of my chair. "Oh, Addie, sweetheart. I'm so sorry. It's my fault. I told your father not to tell you. I was scared. I thought you were too young then." She takes my hand, squeezing it gently. "When you got older, I tried to reach out, but you wanted nothing to do with me, which was understandable." It's true. In high school and college, I threw away her letters unopened. "The more time that passed, the harder it became to reach out again, because I was so scared of what you'd think of me for leaving. Looking back, I know it sounds like a flimsy excuse. But I had to move away because I didn't want you to be teased or ostracized. At the time, it seemed that the most generous thing to do was to disappear. And then you were an adult, and I felt I had no right to reach out to you or force myself into your life." She pauses to take a shaky breath. "I think about you every day, and it kills me that I wasn't there to see you grow up." She is starting to cry. "Your father sent me photos and always told me what you were doing. I missed so much. I've spent all these years missing you and wondering if I did the right thing."

She puts her arms around me, and I feel her tears in my hair. "I'm so sorry, Addie. Can you ever forgive me?"

The way she holds me, it's as if she never wants to let go. I believe her—that she thought she was doing the right thing at the time. So I nod and she squeezes me even tighter.

I've never been very good with too much emotion. So thankfully, the rest of the morning we manage to keep our feelings in check as we ask each other questions, trying to learn as much as possible about each other. Hours later when it's time for me to leave, she hands me a canvas wrapped in brown paper. "I wanted to give this to you. You probably don't remember it, but it's a painting I did that hung in your nursery. I should've left it at the house, but it reminded me of such a happy time, and I wanted to keep that memory. I want to give it back to you . . . maybe for one day when you have a daughter?" she says this last part carefully.

I take the painting and hug my mom. And when we say goodbye, it is with a promise to meet again soon and try to make up for those lost years.

* * *

When I get back to my apartment, I unwrap the painting. It is a pastel watercolor of a small dark-haired girl standing in front of a castle, holding a balloon with various animals surrounding her. In the right-hand corner, it says "Adeline's Kingdom" with a date and my mom's initials.

I turn the painting over to examine the back and see written in pencil:

> *Sweet Adeline,*
> *My Adeline,*
> *At night, dear heart,*
> *For you I pine.*
> *In all my dreams,*
> *Your fair face beams.*
> *You're the flower of my heart, Sweet Adeline.*

I recognize the words to a song that my parents used to sing me to sleep. I had forgotten that long-ago memory, as it was buried by other not-so-pleasant memories growing up.

All the tears I was holding back today rush out of me, and I curl up into a ball on the sofa next to the painting. I cry for what feels like forever. I did not know what to expect today, but it certainly wasn't this. I didn't expect all my anger to dissipate. If anything, I'm angry for other reasons. My mother was brave in being true to herself, recognizing that she had only one life to live and so she lived it. But she was also very scared. Her fears were based in a more hostile society back then. But she was also scared what her own daughter would think, and because of that she missed out on having a relationship with her only child.

I've always blamed my fear of getting too emotionally attached on my upbringing or thinking that I have my father's more stoic, reserved stock. But maybe I'm more like my mother in that I'm afraid to reach out to others because I'm afraid to get hurt. To be rejected by those I love.

I can't say whether what my mom did was the right thing—though I can believe that she thought it was. But she was right in one respect—we do have only one life, and we have to make decisions on how to live that life. So far I've been letting life happen to me. *This stops now!*

I sit up. I'm going to make partner this year. I am also going to break up with Evan. And I'm going to start writing a new novel—an older, wiser, more truthful book—because I suddenly see that I've had it all wrong before.

CHAPTER THIRTY-TWO

Tonight is the night I will break up with Evan.

We already had plans to go out to dinner at an Italian pizzeria and wine bar in the Mission this Sunday night. This morning I was pretty exhausted after yesterday and tried to beg off.

Oh, come on, Adeline. I haven't seen you all weekend, he texted.

True, I had a girls' night with Elena on Friday, and yesterday I told Evan I was visiting a relative in Berkeley. But his insistence irked me, and since I'm ready to break up with him, I decided dinner tonight is the time to do it. Emboldened by my mom's story of her much more difficult breakup with my dad, I don't want to waste one more minute on this relationship.

But when I meet Evan at the restaurant, he has different ideas.

"I hope you don't mind, but I invited Mark to join us. Elena's been packing all day, and he doesn't want to be in the way," he says.

I respond, "No problem." Because what else am I going to say in the circumstances? So it looks like Evan gets a free pass tonight, and instead of the cozy foursome I imagined when we first started dating, I am now part of an awkward threesome.

Since Evan already put our name in, we squeeze in at the crowded bar for a predinner drink.

When Mark finds us, he says, "Thanks for letting me crash your date tonight."

"Sure thing," Evan says as he slaps Mark heartily hello on the back.

I can't seem to discern any signs of heartbreak in Mark's eyes, and so I can't help but ask him, "How are you holding up since the breakup?"

"As well as I can," he says. "It was a long time coming. I saw the signs, but I guess I was lazy about it."

"Yeah. I know how that can be," I say, avoiding looking at Evan.

"It's for the best," Mark says. "We're still friends. Though, you know, it might take a while to put this behind us."

"Don't worry, man. We're going to set you up." Evan pats Mark's shoulder. "Do you have any single friends, Adeline?"

Mark laughs and puts up his hands as if he's physically trying to stop us. "Whoa, slow down. It's only been a few weeks, and I'm still living with my ex-girlfriend. Let's give it some time."

"Yes, give the man some time," I say, probably a little too harshly to Evan. But Mark is one in a million—he deserves someone special, not some quickie rebound relationship.

"Whatever. A new lady is exactly what you need," Evan presses. "You're a big-shot lawyer. Women will be breaking down the door."

Mark laughs again and shakes his head at Evan's comment. He winks at me and then says to Evan, "Listen, I'll let you know when I'm ready. And right now, I'm not."

"Sounds good," I say. "Elena's great, but the next person, she'll be the one."

"Thanks, Addie."

"Anytime." I smile at him.

The hostess comes by and seats us at a dark wooden table that has two chairs on one side and a booth on the other. I take a seat inside the booth, and Evan slides in next to me. Mark sits across from me on the outside of the table.

Once we've ordered, Mark says, "This place is great. So, Addie, has Evan been taking you on a culinary tour of the city?"

I laugh. "Yes. That is, when he's not cooking me gourmet meals." Evan squeezes my knee under the table.

"We haven't really had a chance to catch up with everything going on. Would you say you're an official Californian now?" Mark asks.

"I'm still settling in," I say noncommittally. "It doesn't feel a hundred percent like home yet, but the weather beats the Midwest, so I'm not complaining."

"Yeah, that's what brought me out to California," Mark says. "I remember when I first moved here and how green everything was in January, whereas in Minnesota I'd be shoveling six feet of snow off the driveway."

I laugh. "I hear that. But in Chicago, I'd be shoveling it off my car."

"I was born and raised in the Pacific Northwest," Evan says, taking a swig of some Italian-style cocktail the bartender specially mixed for him. "Sorry, guys, but there's no place like the West Coast. You and your cold winters. Not for me." He shudders. "We're making a Californian out of this one." He puts his arm around me and hugs me close. I smile, but feel a little suffocated from such overt PDA in front of Mark.

But I'm also just feeling a little suffocated and hot in this place. I nurse my drink, which burns my throat. I take a back seat in the conversation as the guys share stories about camping trips they've taken in the area, clearly enjoying my horror at some of them. Evan sometimes falls into "buddy" mode by singling out potential new girlfriends for Mark at the bar. "What about her?" To which Mark always shakes his head no and smiles, catching my eye.

After our first dishes arrive, Evan addresses Mark. "Hey, I've been wanting to ask you a legal question."

"Sure."

"So you know how I've been thinking of starting my own business," he says. This is news to me. "Anyway, let's say I wanted to start a new company, like, I don't know"—he waves his hands around as if looking for a thought—"next week or something. What steps should I be taking?"

"Well, the first step would be to hire a lawyer." Mark winks at me.

"Funny," he says to Mark.

"What type of business?" I ask.

"I have this software idea," he says, still looking at Mark. "I think it could be big, so I'm trying to keep it on the down low."

Ah! Okay, this is why he hasn't mentioned it to me before.

"That's smart," I say and understand why he wouldn't want to share his idea in a crowded restaurant. "The first legal step would be determining what type of company you want to be and whether to incorporate it. Figure out any IP issues. Whether you need investors . . ."

"Uh-huh," he says, not looking at me. "So what can you tell me, Mark?"

"I think Adeline is already telling you." Mark nods in my direction.

Evan looks at me. "Thanks, babe, but I want to get a real attorney's opinion." He then turns back to Mark. "So what do I need to know?"

Shock? Horror? Maybe even amusement on some level? Did I just hear him correctly?

I look at Mark and lean forward with my elbow on the table and my chin in my hand. "Yes, Mark, as a *real* attorney, what can you tell Evan?" My question comes out more bemused than annoyed.

While Evan could at least acknowledge that I'm a "real" attorney, at this point, nothing he says about my career surprises me. This relationship is officially over in my book; it's just a matter of informing him.

Mark, however, appears insulted on my behalf. "Evan, you do know that Addie is an attorney. An attorney who works with me at my firm. Who handles big software deals and specializes in corporate law. An attorney who just worked with one of our biggest clients on a deal that made the papers. An attorney who is going to make partner this year. If you're looking for the real deal, she's sitting right next to you."

Evan looks surprised and turns to me. I raise an eyebrow at him and hold out my hand. "Hi, I'm Adeline Turner, corporate attorney. Nice to meet you."

Evan quickly says, "I'm sorry, babe. I know you're an attorney, but I've just known Mark for so long. And you never talk about what you do, so I had no idea." He puts his arm around me and gives me a squeeze. "I didn't mean to insult you."

"No worries," I say and then look at Mark. "It's true. I try not to bring the office home with me, so Evan here didn't know I was quite so accomplished." I say this last part self-deprecatingly, though, and don't say what I'm really thinking: when I did try to discuss my work with him, he was dismissive.

Maybe I should be insulted by Evan's ignorance, but right now I'm just so relieved to hear Mark praise me despite all the craziness of late.

"Now you know," Mark says to Evan.

"Yep, now I know." And with that, he stops asking questions.

When our mains arrive, nothing tastes quite right, and the wine continues to irritate my throat. Plus, exhaustion seems to take over my body, and I'm having a hard time keeping up with the conversation. When we take care of the bill, Evan asks us, "Where to next?"

I look at him and say, "I don't think I can go anywhere else."

"You can't be tired. It's only eight."

True, but my head is fuzzy and swimming. "Yes, but I'm not feeling so hot." I put my hand to my forehead.

Evan feels my forehead too and frowns. "You're burning up. We should get you home," he says.

"I can make it home." I look at Mark and then Evan, not wanting to ruin their night even though I'm feeling dizzy. "If you guys want to stay out, I can take an Uber. It's no big deal."

"No, no," Mark says, shaking his head firmly. "Evan should really get you home, and you should get some rest." He looks at me with sympathetic eyes.

I think I say, "See you tomorrow," but I'm not totally sure.

* * *

I wake up Monday morning in my own bed alone. Evan came in with me long enough to make sure I took some aspirin and got into bed, but once my head hit the pillow, he was out of there. It was for the best. The only thing I was going to do was sleep.

It wasn't just the emotional weekend that wiped me out—it was the flu.

I email work to say I'm out sick. Other than getting up for some water, I am useless and I go straight back to bed. When I wake up later in the afternoon still feeling terrible, I know I'm not going to make it in to work tomorrow either. I email my secretary and Mark to let them know.

Two minutes after sending the email, my BlackBerry buzzes. It's Mark.

> Sorry to hear you're sick. Let me know if you need anything.

That was nice of him. I email back, Thanks.

It buzzes again. Feel better soon.

Another thanks would be repetitive. Besides, I can barely see the tiny letters on the screen. Within minutes I'm back down for the count.

I do not wake up again until early Tuesday morning when the sun starts peeking through my shades. I'm feeling a bit better. Enough to drag myself out of bed and make a cup of tea with honey. The tea gives me the energy to take a shower and put on a clean pair of pajamas because I'm not going anywhere today.

After spending the entire day in bed yesterday, I'm ready to graduate to the couch. I make some buttered toast and carry it over to the coffee table with another cup of tea. With a blanket wrapped around me, I channel surf through some news and reality shows until I fall asleep and then wake up in the afternoon. When I check my BlackBerry, I see an email from Nora: Call me. I should do that, but it sounds draining right now. And then an email from Mark:

I have some news. How are you feeling
today?

I write back to him:

Better. Thank you. What is the news?

A few minutes later, I read his reply:

Glad to hear it. This news is best told in
person. Can I stop by tonight?

This is unusual, and I wonder what the news is. I'm feeling
better, but not great, and type back:

If you're willing to risk it, then sure.
Otherwise, I will probably be in the office
tomorrow morning.

Mark responds:

I can risk it. Will email you before leaving
the office.

Evan has sent a text asking how I feel today. I note that he
does not offer to come over. Somehow I'm not surprised that he's
quite the germaphobe—though I did look and feel like death
Sunday night, so I can't really blame him.

Around six, Mark emails that he's leaving work and asks if
it is still okay if he stops by. Yes, I email back. I force myself off
the couch, out of my pajamas and into a more respectable outfit

of jeans and a T-shirt, and clean up the random tissues around the place.

When I answer the doorbell, there is Mark holding up a white paper bag. "Chicken soup?" he says.

"Oh my gosh, thank you." I take the bag. "Come in, come in." I let him through the front door. He looks around, taking in my place. For a second, I get self-conscious that he's seeing me with no makeup and my hair a mess, but then, I did call in sick, so it's best to look the part.

"Can I get you anything?" I say.

"Oh, Addie, no. Don't worry about that. You just sit down. You look terrible, you know."

"Yes." I give a small, pathetic laugh and sink down into one of my kitchen chairs. "I do know."

The smell of the soup is making my stomach rumble. I take it as a good sign. "Not to be rude, but do you mind if I eat this right now?" I ask. "I haven't had anything but toast today."

"That's why I brought it. Here, I'll heat it up for you."

"Okay. Thanks."

Although Mark has never been in my kitchen, he instinctually seems to know which cabinets house both my pots and bowls, and sets out one of each. I stay put in the chair, pulling my knees to my chin, hugging them.

"How much do you want?" he asks.

"All of it."

I watch him pour the entire contents into a pot on the stove. I know I only have a short time span where I'll be able to have a coherent conversation, so I ask, "So what's up? What did you want to talk about?"

Mark looks at me with a mysterious sparkle in his eyes. "Dun, dun, duuunnn . . ." He turns back to the pot. "I have some news on the hacking."

This perks me up. "No way! *Finally.* What's the news?"

"Patience, patience. Let me finish heating up the soup."

Knowing Mark loves a dramatic story, I know there's no use arguing with him.

Once the soup is ready, he brings a bowl to the table. It smells so good, and in my eagerness to eat real food, I burn my tongue on the first taste.

"Careful!" warns Mark.

I put my spoon down. "So while this cools, tell me. What happened?"

"Okay." Mark pulls out the other kitchen chair and sits across from me. "So we had our tech people in our office working with the guys in the Chicago office to figure it out on the servers. It turns out that the changes didn't come from your computer at all."

What? "Then why was my name on it?"

"Someone edited it the night before in the Chicago office. And with the assistance of one of the tech guys there, they were able to put your name on it."

"But that makes no sense." I had this pinned on Cruella and Rachel. "Who would do that? *Why* would someone do that?"

"Someone who knew the details of the deal and when the papers were to be signed. Someone who might be jealous and felt you were undeserving of the credit you were receiving on this project." He has a small grin as he drums his fingertips on the table.

"I still don't understand."

"You don't?" Mark raises his eyebrows. "You don't think there's anyone who might be jealous of the role you had in this deal?"

I shake my head.

"*Really?* No one who brought you on and then tried to cut you out?" he says carefully.

I'm starting to have an inkling, but I'll be damned if I say the name and am wrong. So I shake my head again.

"Roger Hamilton," Mark says, his eyes twinkling as he relays this discovery. "Or should I say Roger Hamilton, *the third*."

Yes, I've always thought Roger Hamilton III was a bit obnoxious, but I'm too flummoxed to even make a snarky comment about it.

"But *why*?" I remember how he was rude to me at Scott's house after the initial meeting, and how he made sure to exclude me from the big boys' dinner at the conference. I just chalked that up to his usual jerkiness. But to flat out engage in probable malpractice in an effort to sabotage me? That's extreme.

"Because, Adeline, he's had it in for you ever since that first meeting in LA," he says in his best Perry Mason impression. "He dumped some of his grunt work on the project on you, and you did such a good job with it that the rest of the team wanted you on the deal. He's been angling for this client forever, and then at the presentation you blew Scott away and Roger's ego was bruised. Since then, he's been waiting, hoping, for you to screw up. And when you weren't screwing up, he decided to take matters into his own hands."

"How did you find all this out?"

"You can thank Gilchrist's tech team. When they started looking into a possible hacking, one of the Chicago tech guys came forward and said that Roger had asked him to help him out that night. Roger had told him that he was making changes for you on a big deal and needed your name on the edits because you were too tied up. Obviously he thought it was a weird request, but he was able to do it on the server. Roger probably assumed you were working late that night before the deal and knew the document was finalized earlier in the week. He probably didn't count on you remembering."

I straighten up, my head high, and say mock-pretentiously, "And that is why I'm a superstar and he's not."

Mark grins. "That's right." He then gestures toward my bowl. "How's the soup?"

Oh! "Delicious." I take a quick spoonful, as I had forgotten it while I was busy devouring Mark's story instead. "So what happens to Roger?"

"He's been given three months to find a new position."

Of course I would've preferred that he'd been fired on the spot and reported to the Attorney Registration and Disciplinary Committee. But I also know that this is usual protocol, if not quite as satisfying or dramatic.

"I have to say, that was not at all the story I was expecting."

"You expected it to be Jasmine?"

I nod.

"Me too."

"Well, I guess it's a relief that it wasn't Jasmine. I know she wheedled her way onto this new project, but it's weirder to have someone hate you when you've never done anything to them. At least with Roger, sad as it is, it's understandable."

Mark rolls his eyes. "I wouldn't say it's understandable, but I get what you're saying." He pauses. "There's actually some other news that I probably shouldn't share with you."

"Oh?" I raise my eyebrows.

The old twinkle in his eye when he's about to share a good story is back. "Okay, if I tell you, you can't tell anyone." He gives me a warning look but is obviously eager to spill the beans.

"I swear." I raise my right hand as if I'm under oath.

This is the Mark I love. He knows how to tell a story.

"So with the investigation, we reviewed some security footage in the office last week. Just to see who was coming and going in an effort to shed some light on what might've happened with your computer." He pauses. "We didn't see anything regarding the computers, but the cameras did pick up some extracurricular activity happening in the office." He pauses tantalizingly.

I'm all ears. "What?"

"I think it's best to show you." Mark takes his laptop from his bag and sets it on the table. I'm beyond curious. When the computer is ready, Mark clicks on a video on his desktop. "You're not going to believe this. And remember, you can't tell anyone," he warns.

"Promise."

Mark is right. I don't believe it. There in the copier room is Jasmine propped up on the supply cabinet and Brad kissing her while his hands ride up her skirt.

"No!" *Oh my god.* I'm horrified on so many levels, none of which I can show or tell Mark.

"Oh yes." Mark nods his head in an exaggerated fashion and stops the video. "Sure, okay, I know Brad isn't a saint." I keep my mouth firmly shut. "And I'm sure the reason this divorce is lingering on is because both of them are to blame. While Kathryn's no prize, Brad complicates matters by seeking out affairs to escape what's going on at home. If he just kept it in his pants, this divorce could be over with. But she's got the goods on him . . ." Mark shakes his head. "I think he means well, but he's just . . ." He looks at me searchingly. "He's just . . ."

"Kind of an idiot?" I offer.

Mark laughs. "Yeah, that's what I'm trying to say. The guy obviously has terrible judgment when it comes to people. The first person he trusted in the office was Jasmine, and look how that turned out." He points dramatically to the computer.

I laugh. "Yeah. But she came on pretty strong when he started. I witnessed it with my own eyes in the kitchen one day."

"I know. I even tried to warn him about her, but he's got this stubborn streak. He does a great job for Scott, though, and that's all we care about."

"I guess." I kind of wish I could rewind and erase the images of Jasmine and Brad from my mind. Brad is not the only person with bad judgment. What ever happened to that sweet kid who invited me to play HORSE when he learned my mom left? Is that kid still in there, under the layers of Brad's complicated life?

"And once the cameras caught them, guess who had the fun task of telling them to take it outside?" Mark shakes his head and points to himself. "This guy."

"No!" I cringe. "How uncomfortable. What did they say?"

"As little as possible. We were all pretty embarrassed."

"How awful." I nod, dying on the inside to ask more questions but knowing I can't without giving myself away. I silently chastise myself again for falling for Brad's earlier stories. *Brad was, is, and forever will be a cad.*

"Yes. It was stressing me out," Mark admits. "But I'm just relieved now that that task is over. Between the Moonstruck contract and breaking off my engagement, I couldn't handle one more thing."

"I can imagine. So how are things with Elena?"

"Sad, but fine," he says, pausing. "Can I be honest without you telling Elena?"

"Of course." Though I hope it's nothing too terrible.

"Mostly, I'm just relieved." He looks at me, his eyes apologetic. "Sure, when we got engaged we were totally in love. But as time passed, it became clear that we probably weren't the best suited for each other. Dare I use the word *soul mate?*"

"You may," I say mock-seriously.

"She's beautiful and outgoing, but we just didn't have a lot in common. I was willing to overlook it. But after a while, something needs to hold you together, and we didn't have that. But what was I going to do? I gave her a ring. I asked her to marry me. I couldn't quite say that I wasn't sure anymore." He spreads his hands out to the side, gesturing helplessly. "So I did the opposite. After a year of being engaged, I started pressing her for a date. She wasn't exactly rushing to get us to the altar either, so I wanted to see where her head was. Turns out it was right where mine was too." He brings his hands together and folds them in his lap. "I guess we did have something in common after all."

"I'm sorry. Still, it must be hard." Also, when I had first met them both, I had pegged them as the perfect couple, the gold standard to achieve. But again, like so many others, their story wasn't what it first appeared.

"It's sad. But it would've been sadder for us to stay together any longer," he says.

"I know how it is, though. Sometimes you just get comfortable."

"On that note, how are things with Evan?"

"They're fine." He narrows his eyes, and I start to crumble a bit. "Okay. If I can be honest too, Evan's a great guy and all, but I don't know. We're still getting to know each other."

"It's been several weeks." He looks confused.

I laugh. "Okay, I know. But I feel weird talking about him. Especially to his friend."

"Enough said." Mark starts packing up his computer. "I should probably leave you to your rest."

"Thanks for the soup."

"Anytime." We hold eye contact for a beat.

He doesn't ask if I'll be in the office tomorrow, but I am feeling immensely better already.

CHAPTER THIRTY-THREE

It's New Year's Eve, and I am at a crowded bar surrounded by strangers in San Francisco. I had wanted to spend it in Chicago this year with Bridget, but it was her first New Year's with Jason, and I didn't want to crash it.

Evan is not at my side. As soon as I recovered from the flu, we met for coffee and I broke up with him. I explained how that over our last few conversations, I felt we were looking for different things in a relationship (in my case, *respect*). He looked at me sadly before saying, "I kinda figured this was coming." He admitted that right before we met he had just gotten out of a long-term relationship, and that he probably came on too strong. "You're great, Addie, but I'm ready to settle down and have kids, and want someone looking to *lean back* rather than *in*, you know?" I did know, and I was grateful for the easy out.

We had both been guilty of being in love with having a relationship rather than with each other. Though I'm still lonely in San Francisco, it's better than being in a relationship and pretending not to be lonely.

So I'm here with Mark, who is also dateless. Neither of us is interested in dating anyone at the moment, and so we promised to be each other's gatekeepers tonight. Because, let's face it, sitting on the sofa at home alone would've been too sad.

"Here's to making partner!" Mark raises his champagne glass and then clinks it with mine.

"Thanks again!" I laugh because I've lost count how many times he's made that toast since I found out right before Christmas.

So much has happened this past year. Some good and some bad. My life definitely saw more excitement than in the past several years combined. According to Bridget, I "got a life." But what does that mean? Am I any happier for it?

I slept with a married man against my morals, lost my innocent childhood crush, was sabotaged at work, had some nonstarter relationships, made a couple of new friends (but in the case of Elena, already seemed to be drifting apart), and moved to a new city only to find it a bit cold, personally. And even though making partner means I've been "successful," over this past year I've learned I can no longer find sole fulfillment or a hiding place in my job. Frankly, it's all a little empty.

As is my champagne glass. "Do you need another?" asks Mark.

"Please." It takes a good ten minutes to get the bartender's attention, but we finally do.

Once we have our fresh glasses, Mark clinks his against mine and then bends down toward my ear. "So what do you think of this scene?" he asks, gesturing to the drunk revelers in our midst.

"There's definitely some good people watching," I remark.

He tilts his head, subtly pointing out one couple. "Now there's a short story I could write about right there," he says in a low voice.

"*If* you wrote short stories." I laugh.

"I do write short stories." He straightens up and puts his hand on his heart.

"Seriously?" It's so hard to tell with him sometimes.

"Yup. Isn't every lawyer a wannabe author?" If he only knew. "You're kidding. What are they about?"

"Everything. Usual, common-day occurrences that take on more meaning. I guess I'm interested in the inner workings of the mind." He grins.

"Are you for real?"

"Yes. In fact, I've published some of them."

"Wait, published? Not just written and hidden away on your computer?" Needless to say, I'm deeply impressed. Who knew Mark had a secret life? "So where can I read these stories?"

"Oh I don't know, the *New Yorker*, the *Atlantic*, and some other publications."

"Holy shit, Mark!" And you know I rarely swear. At least not out loud. "You're a bona fide author! That's crazy!" I grab his arm, also marveling at what appears to be a muscular bicep hiding under his jacket, and shake my head.

Just then someone bumps into me, and I stumble trying to save my glass, while Mark puts his hands on my waist, trying to steady me. *Hmm. Mark's hands are strong too.*

"You okay?" he asks, and I nod. His hands linger a moment longer before he drops them.

I quickly readjust myself and notice I'm now pressed against Mark under his shoulder and can feel his chest, which feels quite chiseled, against my side. To recombobulate myself, I say, "How do you find time to write?"

"I've been doing it ever since I was a kid. I majored in English in college and really focused on creative writing. Plus, I write short stories, which are much more doable than, say, a novel."

"Would you ever want to give up your job and write full time? I mean, if you've been published in the *New Yorker* and such, then surely you can land a book deal."

"Well, okay, only one story was published in the *New Yorker*. I got lucky. As for writing full time?" He shakes his head. "No. For me, being around people, doing my job, those are the things that give me inspiration. The idea of sitting alone in a room for years writing doesn't appeal to me." It's probably why he's such a good storyteller in person too. It all makes sense.

"I've always harbored the fantasy of becoming a writer. I wrote in high school and college, but I don't know. It didn't seem the most practical career choice." *Should I tell him the truth? Oh, what the heck.* "Actually, I wrote a novel in college that I tried to get published for a couple years." Okay, several years.

"Congratulations!" He squeezes my arm with his free one. "What's it about?" He leans in a little closer, and I can feel his warmth.

"Well, it was about a mother-daughter relationship. But looking back, it had some problems." I've gone this far; I might as well tell him everything. "My parents divorced when I was twelve, and I recently reconciled with my mother. We've been spending time together, and it's given me a new perspective on things. So I've been thinking that it's time to start something new."

"Good for you! You should take it up again. It's like riding a bicycle. The more you write, the more the ideas come. Trust me." He looks at me seriously. "You never know if you never try. It's better to live a life without regrets." For some reason this makes me think of my mom.

"True." I look up at him and feel a little under the microscope, as if he is looking right into the depths of my soul. I try to cover my nervousness with a small joke. "And now that I have an 'in' in the industry, maybe I'll start that new book. Maybe

I will." I notice that somehow I have downed my champagne, again. For whatever reason I'm nervous, and it's not just the intense look Mark is giving me.

Just then I realize why—*I have the hots for Mark.*

And it's not the champagne. I feel completely and utterly sober. For once, I know what I want. I want this man in my life. This man who makes me laugh. Who says the things I never dare say. Who has my back. Who looks out for me. Who has no doubts about my talent.

And with that he confirms it. "I'm sure you're a great writer. You're the type of person that can succeed at whatever you put your mind to."

I don't care if we work together. Heck, I don't care if I get fired.

"Mark?"

"Hmm?"

"Come here." I crook my finger so he will lean down as if I'm going to whisper in his ear. But as soon as he lowers his head, I take it in both my hands and kiss him on the lips, igniting both a fire in my belly and a longing for him. "Thank you," I say.

He looks shocked. "Um . . . you're welcome?"

"Ha!" I can't stop grinning up at him. Mark was my missing piece. *Mark is my One!*

Over his shock, Mark says, "I feel I should be thanking you." He puts his arms around me and gives me the kiss that makes my knees buckle. So much better than Brad because this isn't a fantasy. *This is for real.*

"Let's get out of here," he whispers.

"Yes."

In the Uber we can barely keep our hands off each other. I wonder how long I've wanted him. Was it when we first started working together? Was it at the conference when he joined me at the bar? Was it when I moved to San Francisco and he invited me to lunch and other outings so I wouldn't feel alone? I can hardly remember because he was so off-limits. But now I'm sure of it: he's been the one for me since the beginning.

And when I wake up in the middle of the night and look around, he is not sitting across the room, his head in his hands, looking like it was his biggest regret. Instead, he's lying next to me, his arms reaching for me and pulling me in closer.

EPILOGUE

2019

Mark and I celebrate New Year's in our new home—a larger condo in my old neighborhood in Chicago.

When we flew back to Chicago, this time for good, I made sure I had a window seat. As I watched the mountains turn into plains and farmland, and saw the city skyline come into view, my heart swelled and I almost started crying. Mark, sensing my emotion, took my hand and squeezed it. I was coming home—to Bridget, my dad, and now my life with Mark.

San Francisco never really clicked for me, but without moving there, I never could have had the life I wanted. It may not look so different on the outside—I live in my old neighborhood and go to work at my old office, but I know it couldn't be more different. I have Mark, who is clearly the one, and he must think so too, since he transferred to our Chicago office to be with me. I have my mother, who just spent Christmas with us and couldn't stop fawning over him. Deborah moved in with my dad and they are planning to marry this spring. I was Bridget's maid of honor and am soon-to-be godmother for her and Jason's firstborn. And each day in the early morning hours, I add more words to my new novel.

It took me some time, but I finally realized that I needed to let go of the stories of the past I had held on to if I ever wanted to create new ones—and a life that I never imagined could make me so happy.

ACKNOWLEDGMENTS

A huge, heartfelt thank-you and, *heck*, a round of applause to everyone here for your support and enthusiasm for this book.

To the rock-star team at Girl Friday Productions: Jasmine Barta, Vanessa Campos, Laura Dailey, Georgie Hockett, Katherine Richards, Rachel Marek, and especially Christina Henry de Tessan, who was one of the first readers of this book, helping me cut it down from a 120,000-word monstrosity to just under a respectable 100,000. It feels right that this book has come full circle and found a home with the Girl Friday Books imprint.

To my beta readers and editors in this book's various stages for providing the feedback to help me whip this story into shape, especially to Charlotte Hayes-Clemons, Annie Tucker, and Chrissy Wolfe.

To the wonderful book bloggers, Bookstagrammers, and readers who took the time to review or post a photo of my book to help spread the word, with special thanks to Melissa Amster of Chick Lit Central (one day we will meet and drink Zhampagne), Suzy Missirlian at @suzysbookshelf (Duran Duran Forever!), and Julie Chan of Beyond the Book with Julie.

To the American Writers Museum and the amazing Chicago Council women Olivia Luk Bedi, Heather Grove, and Kathryn

Homburger Mickelson for the fun Zoom book discussion for my debut, and for immediately suggesting another event for this one. I cannot wait to meet *at* the museum!

To the incredibly talented and supportive group of women writers in my circle: Kari Bovée, Mary Chris Escobar, Cerrissa Kim, Mindy Miller, Kristin Noel Fischer, and The NorCal WFWA group. Our regular Zoom calls on writing kept me sane during a very insane time.

To my book club ladies for another year of lively book discussions, and to Irene Yang for checking that, yes, some lawyers did still use the BlackBerry in 2016.

To my family and friends, who were just as incredibly supportive and enthusiastic about this book as they were about the first. All the phone calls, social media posts, messages, texts, emails, etc. to tell me how much you enjoyed *Charming Falls Apart* kept me going to finish this one so that hopefully we can do a book party in person!

To my parents, Catherine and Richard Terry, for everything. And to my husband, Ray, for everything else.

To the reader who took a chance picking up this book: You made my day!

ABOUT THE AUTHOR

Photo by Sarah Deragon

*A*ngela Terry is an attorney who formerly practiced intellectual property law at large firms in Chicago and San Francisco. She is also a Chicago Marathon legacy finisher and races to raise money for PAWS Chicago—the Midwest's largest no-kill shelter. She resides in San Francisco with her husband and two cats and enjoys throwing novel-themed dinner parties for her women's fiction book club. Her debut novel, *Charming Falls Apart*, is a 2021 Independent Press Award Winner.